PRAISE FOR THERE IS NO FEAR
(BOOK 3 OF THE LANCE CHRONICLES):

"If you're a parent, this will scare you to death. If you're a youth, this will make you want to be a part of the Round Table. If you're neither (or both), you'll still be enthralled and thrilled, in equal measure, by the third book in Michael J. Bowler's Children of the Knight series There Is No Fear."

–J.g. Murphy

"You will just have to read this wonderful book. I will, however, say: fasten your seat belts and keep your hands and arms inside the vehicle at all times while it is in motion; as Michael takes us on another wonderful roller-coaster ride in 'Children of the Knight III: There Is No Fear'."

–Dallas Vinson

"Bowler invites us to walk beside Lance as he awaits trial for a crime he did not commit. Despite the compassionate attitudes of the probation staff at The Compound, California's most secure juvenile facility, Lance's confinement is incredibly trying. Along with Lance, we as readers experience the humiliation of being a minor caged in a secure juvenile facility—the forced separation from his family, the complete lack of privacy, being shackled and mishandled by sheriff's deputies, not to mention the stark fear of an uncertain future where he faces consequences as if he were already an adult."

–author Mia Kerick

PRAISE FOR *RUNNING THROUGH A DARK PLACE*
(BOOK 2 OF THE LANCE CHRONICLES):

"A superbly written tale, this book kept me on the edge of my seat as I lost more than a few hours sleep from needing to know what happened next. How was character XYZ's behavior going to be explained? What exactly was Operation Silent Treatment? A difficult past haunts main characters, a mysterious figure becomes a part of daily life in a way that is difficult to figure out, and a wonderfully rich story unfolds in a way that gives me hope that a spark can move mountains. Can children change the world? Watch them."

–Elnora

"Bowler once again hits the mark in setting his tale among movie stars and media moguls, the rich sequestered in their mansions in the hills, never bumping elbows with the throwaway kids on the star-lined streets. Lance flows between both cultures, at times painfully. He knows where he came from, his jaw will never fail to drop at the ostentation that surrounds him. He'll always miss the trickling water deep within the sewers lulling him to sleep. No matter how far up the social ladder he climbs, he's still acutely aware of being the only brown skinned boy at the party."

–City Girl Who Loves To Read

"Heart. That's what fills the writings of Michael J. Bowler. Love, empathy, a warm embrace of humanity, together equals a special kind of goodness that flows through his pages. To be blunt, if you don't like to feel, then don't read his work. But if you're okay with getting emotional, he has the ability to tug at your heartstrings like no one else can."

–Nicole Langan

MICHAEL J. BOWLER

AND THE CHILDREN SHALL LEAD

THE LANCE CHRONICLES 4

Published by Michael J. Bowler, USA stuntshark2.0@gmail.com

And The Children Shall Lead
(The Lance Chronicles 4)
Second Edition Copyright © 2018 by Michael J. Bowler

Cover Art and Interior Formatting by Streetlight Graphics

Edited by Heather Sowalla, Windy Hills Editing h.sowalla@gmail.com

Print: ISBN: 978-0-9903063-6-8
Mobi: ISBN: 978-0-9903063-7-5
epub: ISBN: 978-0-9903063-8-2

Printed in the United States of America Second Edition
August 2018

This book is dedicated to the Native American youth I've worked with over the years – most, sadly, at juvenile hall. However, when I was student teaching an 11th grade English Literature class, one of my students was a Navajo boy I'll call John who always laughed and smiled and brightened every day, even when the day was stressful. It was his ebullient personality I so vividly recalled when creating the character of Kai, and I've never forgotten his sunny disposition and positive outlook on life. I've also learned a lot over the years from my Lakota godson, Derrick, who lost sight of his Native heritage while growing up on the streets of Seattle and Los Angeles, and then rediscovered it in the most unlikely of places. Now clean and sober, he wants some day to help his people on the Pine Ridge Reservation and be a force for good, rather than bad. Like the Native American boys in my book, he's learned that doing what's right is more fulfilling than doing what's easy. And then there's Marcus, another Navajo youth I knew for many years. A great artist who struggled with his own personal demons, Marcus matured from a reckless boy into a strong, decent man. For all of you who struggle to fit into images you think other people want to see, may you come to understand that you are already what God had in mind when He made you. Be yourself. Be decent. Be awesome. To quote Gandhi, "Be the change you want to see." Hope endures…

WHAT HAS GONE BEFORE…

THE LEGENDARY KING ARTHUR APPEARED in Los Angeles with a mission – to save and empower youth. He started a new Round Table of knights made up exclusively of children and teens. A vision from Merlin led him to Lance, a homeless fourteen-year-old who was destined to lead his Children's Crusade. Arthur trained Lance in swordsmanship and archery, taught the boy discipline and self – control. He came to love Lance beyond measure, and Lance finally found the father he'd longed for growing up as an orphan in "the system."

In turn, Lance taught Arthur the complexities of 21st Century American life. They recruited hundreds of "disposable" youth – gang members looking for something better, homeless kids, gay kids, kids of every race and color – the ones most marginalized by society. And they built New Camelot, a safe haven for every child in need.

But Lance's journey has not been an easy one. His abusive past and resultant fears of what he might become pushed him into dangerous behaviors that put his life at risk and embarrassed New Camelot. As The Boy Who Came Back, Lance was catapulted into worldwide prominence, and the sudden fame threatened to topple him and all he'd accomplished. Only Ricky, the newest member of the Round Table—and Lance's closest friend—could steady him, especially when Lance was inexplicably drawn to an unstable teen named Michael. Michael introduced the boys to a partying lifestyle that neither liked, but personal doubts and fears forced them to experience it more than once. After several failed attempts on Lance's life, a specter from his dark past rose up one night to confront him, and that fateful encounter led to his arrest.

Charged with attempted murder against the man who raped him as a child, Lance was incarcerated in a secure facility with other juveniles being tried in adult court. The Los Angeles district attorney—hoping to make an example out of Lance and prove to Californians that violent children must be sent to prison—pushed the case rapidly through the courts. Lance was bereft at the loss of his family, especially Ricky, with whom he was closest. Likewise, New Camelot was in disarray without Lance, who was the face of the entire movement for juvenile rights. Lance's journey through the juvenile justice system was by turns harsh and affirming, and when the case was finally resolved a few weeks prior to the election, he became even more determined to help every kid in California who was a victim of the system.

Confusion in his personal life led to Lance drinking alcohol as a coping mechanism. His conflicted feelings for Michael, Bridget, and Ricky came to a head when the equally confused Ricky ran away from New Camelot. Devastated, Lance spoke before a huge crowd at the final Get Out the Vote rally, confessing that he'd changed his mind on which way the voters should go on his proposition. When Ricky appeared suddenly on stage, the two boys confessed their true feelings in front of the world.

Following the election, Lance revealed his plans for the next phase of the crusade to better the lives of America's children – amending the U.S. Constitution.

The Lance Chronicles Continue…

THE BEGINNING OF THE END

PROLOGUE

H E SQUEEZED HIS FOREFINGER AGAINST the trigger, the boy's face looming larger than life in his scope, and then he heard, like a bullet shooting from his phone, "Wait!"

Instantly, he eased up on the trigger, and then gently lowered the gun to his lap to snatch up the phone in irritation. "Yes, sir?" he said with more deference than he felt. Personally, that kid who came back creeped him out, and he'd just as soon be done with him.

"I've changed my mind," came the boss's voice over the phone, accompanied by the all-too-familiar chuckle. "Shooting them isn't entertaining enough. I want that little fag boy to suffer first."

He sighed with disappointment. "Yes, sir."

"Bring it in for now, Mr. G.," he heard in his ear. "I've got some planning to do before they start campaigning." Gleeful laughter filled the night. "We're going to have lots of fun before this is over."

The phone went dead.

Sniggering, he looked out across the clear night sky at the two boys who had no idea how close they'd come to dying.

Let the games begin.

He silently gathered up his equipment and slunk off into the night.

CHAPTER ONE
NOW I KNOW WHAT I WAS TRYING TO SAY

ONCE UPON A TIME IN the City of Angels, a boy became whole, and everything changed.

"That's all?" Jenny's face fell into such a state of shock that Arthur instantly encircled her with his strong arms and pulled her in close to his heart. She trembled slightly within his embrace and laid her head up against his chest in despair.

They were relaxing within one of the many lounge areas of New Camelot when Jenny finally asked the question Arthur had desperately hoped she would not: "How much more time do you have with us?"

His answer stunned her into a painful, aching silence. Arthur cradled her head and lovingly stroked her hair while attempting to explain the metaphysics of his stay in this era.

"Alas, Jenny," he said, sighing heavily, "Merlin has told me that my time here *must* end when Lance is fit to rule in my stead." He sounded weary, and his heart felt heavy with loss.

"But how will you know when he's ready?"

"Avalon will know."

Jenny tilted her soft face up and looked at him sadly. "Are you sure?"

She sounded lost and forlorn, and Arthur's heart lurched. "There is no hard-and-fast rule, Jenny," he said by way of reassuring her. "Even Merlin cannot be certain of the precise day and time."

"Do the boys know? Have you told Lance?"

He shook his head. "If I were to say something now, he would think of nothing else and be distracted from the crusade. I will tell him when I must."

Her face fell a moment with resignation. Then she sat up and fixed her light blue eyes on him, almost melting Arthur's heart. "We need to get married right away. I want to spend every possible moment as your wife."

Arthur could not help a slight grin crossing his lips at her spirit and deep, abiding love for him. But still, a shadow of doubt flitted across his soul. "Are you certain, Jenny?"

Her eyes burned with passion and love. "I've never been more certain of anything in my life. I love you, Arthur, and I want us to be a family for as long as we have together."

Arthur let out a breathy little laugh of nervousness, and Jenny gasped.

"That's Lance's laugh," she said with a grin. "That nervous one he has when he's embarrassed."

"Alas, our son is rubbing off on me." His face clouded slightly.

"What?" she asked, sitting up abruptly, brows furrowed.

Arthur's eyes narrowed. "What shall become of our boys, Jenny, now that they have found one another as they have?"

She visibly relaxed, smiling wryly. "They belong together, Arthur, you know that. We all saw it from the beginning. They're going to be amazing. Wait and see."

He frowned. "I cannot help but worry for them in this unforgiving world. In my time, there wasn't any thought given to boys who loved other boys, though I feel certain there must've been such boys. This country seems rather harsh in its treatment of these boys, if Jack and Mark be typical."

She squeezed his arms lovingly. "I wouldn't worry too much about Lance and Ricky, Arthur. They go after what they want and don't back down. Pit those two against the world and I pity the world."

His eyes locked on hers, and he smiled through his close-cropped beard. "I love you, Lady Jenny. You always have the words to soothe my soul, especially when I fret over our boys. You are the most extraordinary woman I have ever known, and I wish nothing more than to be your husband. We shall have our wedding here in the gardens as soon as you can make the arrangements."

Jenny's face brightened like the rising sun. "That's perfect, right on that big outdoor stage. The reception can be out there, too. I don't have much family except Sam, but we'll have all the knights and I'll invite a few friends from Mark Twain and—" She stopped and gazed at Arthur's bemused expression. "What?"

He smiled. "To see you happy makes me happy. Plan whatever you like, but I suggest recruiting Reyna to assist you. She would be devastated not to help plan such an event."

"Oh, I know that. I'm calling her right now and we'll get started."

She kissed him, then leapt to her feet like a love-struck schoolgirl and glided from the lounge.

Lance lay atop his king-sized bed, clad in a basic tank top and workout shorts, propped up against his headboard with Ricky's head in his lap. Both boys held *The Great Gatsby* in their hands, faces scrunched with interest, eyes flitting across the pages as they devoured the final chapter.

Being homeschooled by Jenny, they used every opportunity to move ahead in their studies, and Jenny had assigned them a lot of reading. Everyone knew the Children's Bill of Rights would consume extreme amounts of their time, and eventually entail travel across the country to "sell" the idea of amending the Constitution. For this reason, Jenny wanted the boys, now in the eleventh grade, to be on top of their studies.

These two boys, though unrelated, looked remarkably alike, especially with their long, dark hair, almond shaped eyes, and similar skin tone. Despite being sixteen, neither of them displayed a hint of facial hair. Both felt in their hearts that they were two parts of the same boy—rather than distinct individuals—and their physical similarities seemed to back up that fanciful notion.

Lance finished the last few lines of the book, feeling sad and dejected at the emptiness of it all, those partying people who loved no one and nothing and only lived for the next drink or make-out session. He felt himself burn with shame, thinking back on the reckless and empty partying he'd done this past year, amazed that people hadn't changed since the 1920s. In fact, they may have gotten worse, he mused, given his own achingly painful party experiences. That was a lifestyle he wanted nothing more to do with, and he knew Ricky felt the same way.

His thoughts were interrupted by a soft sigh, and Lance glanced down to see the boy he loved close the book and raise his poignant brown eyes.

"Man, that was a sad book," Ricky whispered, laying the paperback beside him on the bed and meeting Lance's eyes. He obviously saw something lost and sorrowful because he said, "What?"

Lance shivered slightly, even though the room was comfortable and he felt the warmth of Ricky's presence suffusing him. "I was just thinking about Michael."

Ricky's soft features clouded over like a wintry sky preparing for a cloudburst, and he sat up quickly, trying hard not to glower. "I thought we were done with Michael."

Lance set down his book as Ricky pulled in his legs and sat facing him, those gentle eyes reflecting the hurt he plainly felt.

"I'm sorry, Ricky," Lance began haltingly. "This book… well, Michael once told me he was like Jay Gatsby and now I get that."

"How?"

Lance struggled to coalesce his thoughts. He forced himself to breathe deeply a few times. "Michael had no friends, Ricky, just like Gatsby. He was rich and powerful and everyone wanted to party with him, but nobody wanted to know him."

Ricky felt his blood begin to pound. "Maybe 'cause he was an jerkbag?" The jealousy in his voice was unmistakable.

"He was. But he was looking for love, too, just like Gatsby."

Ricky's light brown eyes flared a moment, like twin supernovas. "Yeah, from you."

Lance lowered his gaze, unable to face the rejection he saw in Ricky's eyes.

"Truth or dare, Lance," Ricky said quietly, fists clenched in his lap. "How badly were you crushing on him?"

Lance looked up, feeling like he'd been caught with his hand in the cookie jar. He saw the look in Ricky's eyes, and knew better than to try and hide anything. "Pretty badly for a while. But I didn't get till the end that it was 'cause of Jack, that I could feel Jack and see Jack in Michael's eyes."

Ricky eyed him uncertainly.

"Remember, Ricky, that night I got so drunk and Michael took me back to his room?"

Ricky blew out a heady breath. "I'll never forget it, Lance. I thought I'd lost you."

"Remember how I kept trying to figure out what I was telling him before I passed out?"

Ricky nodded apprehensively.

"Now I know what I was trying to say."

Ricky waited.

"I told Michael I was confused, that there had to be something wrong with me 'cause…." He let out a deep, profound sigh. "Cause sometimes I thought I loved him, and sometimes I thought I loved Bridget, but mostly I thought I was falling in love with… you."

Ricky's slim eyebrows shot up in surprise. "*That's* what you were telling him?"

Lance nodded. "Michael always told me I didn't love him, that deep down I knew who I *really* loved. But I was too scared to admit it, Ricky. That's how everything got so screwed up. I love you so much that when you're with me the whole world just disappears and all I can see is you." He stopped then, because a huge grin had slowly crept across Ricky's face, pulling his dimples in for all they were worth. "What?"

"You said you loved me, fool," Ricky gushed, his breath wavering on his lips like vapor in the cold morning air. "How can I not smile?"

Lance grinned. "I do love you, fool, more than anything."

"Yeah, well, I loved you first, so there."

Lance tossed off a little laugh, and that's when Chris stepped into the room, dressed to work out.

"Okay, big brothers, who's ass am I gonna kick today in the training center?"

Lance's jaw dropped open in surprise.

"Better not let mom hear you talk like that," Ricky admonished.

Chris smiled sweetly. "Don't worry, I can handle mom. So, you guys afraid of me, or what?"

The older boys grinned.

"Bring it on, little man," challenged Lance.

They clambered off the bed and the three boys headed downstairs for their daily sparring session.

After a brief workout, the brothers returned to their rooms to shower and clean up for the day's gathering.

This would be the first gathering since the election. As Lance nervously blow-dried his hair and gazed at his reflection in the large, filigreed bathroom mirror, he wondered how many of his fellow knights might be angry with him. By most accounts—exit polls and surveys—it had been Lance's final revelations about himself and Michael, and his expressed desire that maybe a 'No' vote would be preferable, that had swung the electorate so heavily in that direction. Would the other knights feel Lance had betrayed them? It didn't seem that way at the victory party on Wednesday, but then everyone had not been in attendance.

That party had doubled as both victory and birthday party, since Lance and Ricky had turned sixteen on that day. He involuntarily glanced down at the brand-new Galaxy smartphone his parents had given him. Ricky had received an identical one, since both boys lost their phones in the train crash.

Had it only been two weeks since Michael's sacrifice and death? It seemed like yesterday, and forever ago. The throb in Lance's ankle was a painful reminder of that day.

He stared into the glass, his long thick hair trailing around his shoulders and down his back, and stood as straight as he could, attempting to emulate the royal bearing of his father.

A chuckle startled him, and he looked over to find Ricky leaning against the doorjamb. His breath nearly stopped at the sight, the hand holding the hair dryer slowly dropping to his side as he gaped. Ricky wore a formal, scarlet red tunic, brushed brown leather pants, and knee-high leather boots – the standard attire for gatherings. He wore the circlet Lance had given him for his birthday round his brow to restrain his flowing hair, and his face shown with dancing amusement at Lance's openmouthed reaction.

"Caught you checking yourself out *again*," Ricky said with a laugh as he stepped into the spacious bathroom. "In answer to the question you had on your face when I came in, Lance, yes, you *are* the most beautiful boy in the world."

Lance shoved Ricky playfully. "Fool! I was trying to stand like Dad, you know, all regal and kingly and stuff."

"You can't help but look regal, Lance, no matter what you do." Then Ricky chuckled. "But you better get your fool ass dressed or you'll be regal *and* late."

Lance laughed, set down the hair dryer and hurried past Ricky to grab his green tunic off the bed.

Lance eyed Ricky nervously as they descended the lushly carpeted staircase to the lobby, and his other half flashed him a heart-melting smile of encouragement, which slightly quelled the butterflies flitting frantically around in his stomach. This gathering would mark their first since openly declaring their love for one another and Lance wasn't so naïve as to think that all of his father's knights—especially the newer ones who didn't know them on a personal level—would be as accepting as Reyna or Esteban.

He tossed Ricky a smile of gratitude as they made their way down the corridor leading to the backside of the Throne Room. Arthur, Jenny, Chris and Merlin milled around by the back doors chatting when the boys approached. Jenny stepped away from the group and gave each boy a hug and kiss on the cheek.

"Shall we begin?" Arthur announced.

Lance nodded nervously. Yeah, he could do this.

Merlin, dressed formally in his own tunic and pants, and looking none too happy about it, pulled open the door and stepped through. As had become tradition, each had his or her own place on the dais and followed a certain order. Jenny trailed after Merlin, followed by Chris, as Arthur's number three son. Ricky went in next, with Lance trailing behind, and finally the king, himself.

The room was packed, with Arthur's leadership team filling out the front row, followed by row upon row of chatting, excited, tunic-clad youth of varying ages and ethnicities. Mayor Soto sat in the front row beside Reyna and Esteban, wearing his standard grey suit with a sky blue tie. He grinned when he saw Lance and Ricky enter.

Lance looked out at his fellow knights—his peers—as he and Ricky strode to their seats to the right of Arthur's massive throne. All heads seemed to turn as one and focus on the two boys and Lance felt momentary panic wash over him. Forcing himself to stand as proper as possible, he ignored the "looks" he might have been imagining. The chattering quelled as everyone realized the gathering had begun. Yet even as Arthur emerged from behind his throne to stand majestically before it, Lance knew almost every eye remained on him and Ricky.

Arthur, attired in his formal tunic, pants, elegant red cloak, and jeweled crown, unsheathed Excalibur and held the enormous sword aloft, causing the chandelier lights to sparkle off its shimmering blade in a kaleidoscope of rainbow colors. The assemblage quieted and took their seats, gazing up at the king expectantly.

"My noble knights and ladies, welcome to our first gathering of the next phase of our crusade."

There were cheers and applause from the knights, whose eager and expectant faces excitedly regarded their king and mentor.

"As you all know, we ultimately won our battle for the hearts and minds of Californians, for they chose to return childhood to its rightful owners – you."

There was more applause, but also some scowls and shaking of heads from the older kids, Lance noted with dismay. He snuck a quick look Ricky's way, and Ricky's sly wink instantly calmed him.

"Before we move ahead with the next phase," Arthur went on confidently, "we have an honored guest with us today who wishes to address all of you. I give you the mayor of Los Angeles, Julian Soto."

The mayor rose to his feet amidst thunderous applause from the knights, led vociferously by Lance and Ricky who stood to welcome the man up onto the stage with them. Soto had been publicly supportive of Arthur, Lance, and their proposition, much to the dismay of many in the political arena. The short Latino man with the close-cropped hair and round face greeted Lance and Ricky with a huge grin, before winking at Chris and bowing to Jenny.

The mayor went on to greet Arthur with a bow, and the king stuck out a hand of friendship. They shook warmly and Arthur stepped back away from the microphone, sitting in his throne and motioning the boys to resume their seats.

The mayor grinned out at the applauding youth, obviously gratified by their response. He held up a hand to quell them. "You should be applauding yourselves for pulling off the most significant victory for youth this state has ever seen." He raised his hands and clapped with gusto.

The kids cheered, and stomped their feet.

When they again subsided, the mayor looked out over their eager faces. "The election, however, was the easy part. Now the real work begins, and that's where I need your help. Your prop becomes law on January one, and that means the system and the state can no longer give up on kids, can no longer throw them away into jail or prison and pretend they never existed."

More applause and cheers erupted from the assembled kids, and once more the mayor awaited their attention.

Lance turned his eyes onto the crowd as his fellow knights allowed their cheers to subside. All of them were focused on the man at the microphone. But one set of eyes remained riveted on him – they belonged to a tall, lean African-American kid whose name Lance couldn't recall – a new recruit, another ex-gang member. Marvell, wasn't that his name?

Why is he mad dogging me?

The mayor's voice pulled his attention from the glaring boy.

"The problem of troubled youth in troubled neighborhoods, or even in rich ones, won't be solved by me or the government. It will be solved by you who live in those communities. That's why I'm setting up a task force to brainstorm ideas that can solve, or alleviate, some of these social ills that plague our youth, and I want as many of you as possible to sit on that task force. I want to start next week, organizing meetings with you and community leaders and professionals to put into place real and sound interventions. The City Council and I are committed to making this thing work, and give kids more reasons to reject gangs and drugs than to accept them. But you all are the key. You have the answers – it's just that no one's ever consulted you before. Now I am. How many are willing to help me?"

Almost every hand flew upward.

The mayor grinned. "Outstanding. I'll have a sign-up sheet at the conclusion of the gathering for all who are interested. Just give me a way to contact you and we'll begin setting up the groups next week. Thank you all for showing the world that Los Angeles has the best young people in this country and for being the leaders we adults need to emulate."

More thunderous applause, cheers, and foot stomping followed his remarks as the grinning man turned to Arthur. The king rose and shook his hand again, and then Soto bowed to Lance and Ricky before dropping down the three small steps to the floor and resuming his seat.

Arthur returned to the microphone and looked out at the excited young people before him.

"That brings us to our next step forward. As you are aware, my sons have formulated an audacious plan to amend your United States Constitution to provide stronger protections for youth such as yourselves. I do not pretend to understand the workings of this country, but my sons have been doing their homework and they have consulted with my attorney, Samuel, about how best to proceed. To explain their plan and present their new bill of rights, I give you Prince Lance and Sir Ricky."

The applause, to Lance's great delight, became thunderous in its intensity as the knights rose to their feet, some clapping, others waving their swords and stomping their booted feet. And then the chant arose, "Long live Lance! Long live Lance! Long live Lance!" In the front row, Reyna, Esteban, Justin, Darnell, Techie, Enrique, and Luis chanted the loudest.

Lance basked in the adulation of his peers, his fears washing away like dust under a light spring rain.

The chanting died down, and everyone resumed his or her seat. Everyone except the African-American kid Lance had spotted earlier. He remained standing, glaring around him in amazement.

"Don't it matter to none a you all that them two are queer?"

Ripples of wrath swept through the crowd, and Lance blanched. Reyna turned her head, and if looks could kill, the new kid would've been dead on the spot. Esteban clenched his fists and started to stand, but Lance caught his eye and shook his head.

Lance exchanged a look of resolution with Ricky. It was up to them to handle what would likely be the first of many such challenges all across the country. Together, they strode to the microphone as another boy rose to his feet, Caucasian this time, bulky and surly.

"I agree with Sir Marvell over there," the boy called out. "You guys being faggots is gonna make us all look bad."

Again, nasty, angry looks flew at them from all directions, but a few other knights could be seen nodding their heads in agreement.

A girl's voice called out from in back, "Yeah, well, I think they're cute together." That comment generated a short round of clapping.

Lance noted all of this with an outward calm he didn't feel. He stood as tall, with as much royal bearing as he could muster, and locked eyes on those of the Caucasian boy. He tried to place the name in his memory. Sir William was it? No – Sir James – that was it.

"Sir James," he said calmly, "and Sir Marvell, approach the throne."

The two knights exchanged a glance and then both slid their way out of the row each was seated in and sauntered sullenly forward. They stopped in front of the stage and frowned up at Lance.

"A faggot is a stick of wood," Lance announced matter-of-factly. "Ricky and me are not sticks of wood."

The tall black youth growled, "You know what we be talkin' 'bout."

"You mean this?" Lance asked, his voice strong and steady as he took Ricky's hand in his.

Sir Marvell grimaced. "Everybody's gonna think we're queer, too."

Lance and Ricky looked at each other and unclasped their hands. Lance wanted to make a point, but did not wish to be "in your face" about it.

"You already know, as part of our code here within the Round Table, that labels are not acceptable. Especially faggot. Or queer. Or white boy or cracker or beaner or everybody's favorite, the "N" word. Do you guys want us to use any of those labels to describe you?"

Both of the challengers scowled fiercely, anger darkening their faces. "Hell no, but skin color ain't a choice, man!" Sir James hissed.

"My feelings for Lance aren't a choice, either," Ricky said calmly, but with conviction.

"And mine aren't for Ricky," Lance confirmed, eyeing the two boys with a strong, penetrating gaze. "You have no choice but to be white or black. I have no choice but to be brown. And I have no choice about loving this boy. You can pretend I do if that makes you happy, but this crusade is about sweeping away those useless labels and allowing all of us to be exactly the person God had in mind when He made us."

Ricky nodded in affirmation, and there were hundreds of heads nodding throughout the room, along with some agitated murmuring.

Lance waited for them to settle down and then fixed his intense green eyes on the two dissenters.

"Within the Round Table, Sirs Marvell and James, you always have a choice. You may stay and accept me as your prince and Ricky as your First Knight or you may turn in your swords now and leave us. No hard feelings. Which do you choose?"

Sir Marvell turned his tatted face to gaze at the freckled features of Sir James, and both boys suddenly didn't appear so confident or belligerent.

"Look, Lance, I don't mean no disrespect," the black boy stammered, not nearly as certain of himself as he'd been a moment ago. "It's just, in my neighborhood, everybody seen you guys kiss on TV and it didn't go down so good. They be wanting to know if I kissed you too."

He lowered his eyes shamefully to the floor, and Lance almost grinned, but fought it back.

"You can tell them, Sir Marvell, that if any of them wish to kiss me, they must take a number and stand in line."

Laughter rang throughout the room, and Ricky's eyes bulged with shocked amusement. But Lance's comment had the intended effect, because even Sir Marvell grinned, and Sir James cracked a smile.

"Sorry about, you know, calling you a faggot," Sir James muttered guiltily. "You guys are pretty kick ass."

Lance kept his eyes on the boys. "Your decision, gentlemen?"

Sir Marvell slumped his shoulders and lost the haughty pose he'd assumed. "I'd like to stay and be part of the mayor's project."

Sir James looked ashamed. "Me too."

Lance smiled. "Cool. Resume your seats." He waited until the two boys hurried back to their chairs. Then he scanned the eager faces below. "You are the family I never had, all of you, and I wanna be myself around you guys. So does Ricky. It *shouldn't* be a problem for anyone else either, but we understand how it is in this country. So know that, in front of the public, we will act like we always have – as knights of the table."

He glanced at Ricky, and Ricky leaned in to the microphone. "We also get that it's weird for people, you know, 'cause Lance and me are adopted brothers. It's weird for us, too, let me tell you."

There was laughter, and Reyna flashed a huge grin.

"We will do nothing to embarrass you or the Round Table," Lance assured them, but then he reddened with shame. "Other than what I already did to embarrass you this past year, anyway." There were sniggers and grins from many in the assemblage. "But since you're our family, it's important for you to understand that Ricky and me were soul mates from the second we met, and I think most of you with eyes already knew that. Probably before we did."

More laughter and many head nods drew a shy smile to Lance's face.

"Anyway, I've heard the expression 'doing something gay.' I got no idea what that means, but out there in public, we'll try not to. Okay?"

That generated a laugh, and Ricky elbowed Lance good-naturedly.

Esteban shot to his feet, sword held on high. "Yes, sire!" He looked proudly up at the two boys. "Long live Lance! Long live Ricky!"

The others leapt to their feet as a unit and screamed, "Long live Lance! Long live Ricky!"

Behind the boys, Arthur and Jenny sat with hands clasped, grinning, obviously relieved to have this hurdle jumped and cleared.

Lance and Ricky smiled at one another and watched as the crowd settled down and retook their seats. Then Lance leaned in again to the microphone. "Oh, and by the way, I don't like the word 'gay', either, so don't call us that. Especially me. I'm not emo, but I'm *definitely* not happy all the time."

Laughter rippled through the room as Ricky leaned into the microphone. "Oh, he's emo, all right," sparking another wave of titters.

Lance playfully shoved Ricky with a whispered, "Fool."

Sir James raised his sword high in the air and Lance pointed to him. He stood and awkwardly tilted his head. "What should we call you guys, you know, if somebody asks?"

"They can call me Sir Lance and him Sir Ricky."

There was more laughter and a lot of applause.

Sir James frowned. "That's not, you know, what I meant."

Lance would not be afraid anymore. "You can tell them we're two parts of the same boy."

That response generated a new round of clapping, and Reyna elbowed Esteban beside her, who shot a wink her way.

Sir James digested that answer a moment, then smiled and resumed his seat.

"Now enough about Ricky and me," Lance announced. "We have a country to fix."

He gestured at Sir Techie, who pointed a remote control up at the large fifty-five inch flat screen mounted on the wall above the stage. As the television sprang into animated life, Lance pointed to it. "Ladies and gentlemen of the Round Table, we present the next ten amendments to the U.S. Constitution – the Children's Bill of Rights."

A PowerPoint frame appeared on-screen proclaiming 'The Children's Bill of Rights'.

"We'll go through them all and then go back over each one for questions and comments," Lance went on, and Techie clicked the small black remote in his hand.

The next slide appeared with the title 'Amendment 28' and the text of the amendment:

'Congress shall make no law constraining anyone seventeen
years or younger to the servitude or ownership of their biological

parents, guardians, or any other adult or governmental entity; they shall henceforth from the date of passage of this amendment be considered human beings in their own right and not, in any sense of the word, 'property'; likewise, no government or government-sponsored agency shall remove any child from his/her lawful parents without evidence of actual abuse or serious neglect; poverty, alone, shall not be a determining factor; in the event of removal from the home because of proven abuse or neglect, children have the innate right to return to their parents upon evidence of parental stability, and the right to decide for themselves upon the issue of return; likewise, minor children under eighteen years of age shall not find their freedom of speech infringed within any public venue, including family court, nor their right to peaceably assemble, or to petition the Government or government-controlled entities for redress of grievances, including, but not limited to, bullying behaviors inflicted upon them by school officials or by students within those schools whereby no action was taken by school authorities to eliminate it'.

Lance allowed a few moments for the knights to read the text. He heard murmurs of agreement, and saw heads nodding in the crowd. Apparently they never realized they had been their parent's and/or the government's property all this time. He was certain, however, that almost everyone had been muzzled or suspended at one time or other for saying something at school that a teacher or administrator disagreed with, or for wearing some shirt the school authorities objected to. And many, he knew, had been bullied, both by fellow students and administrators. He gestured for Techie to click on the next slide. 'Amendment 29' came up.

'All persons seventeen and younger may not be labeled in any way, shape or form by any government entity, nor any government employee, or on any government documents; they may not be categorized by race, ethnicity, creed, educational ability, or sexual orientation, nor may any of those factors be used either for or against them in any circumstance or within any institution that receives federal funds'.

Again, Lance allowed for reading and digestion of the amendment, knowing this one might spark some major debate. He heard rustling and saw head nods throughout the room. After all, this amendment merely reflected the Round Table philosophy of everyone being of equal value, with only their accomplishments being important, not physical or perceived differences. He waved at Techie.

And thus the amendments clicked onto the screen one by one, and the assembled knights read them each with care. The other eight went as follows:

30. 'No minor child below age eighteen may be compelled by parent or guardian to undertake any activity (including, but not limited to, sports, hobbies, acting, modeling) that the child did not originate for him or herself, thus prohibiting parents from profiting either monetarily or socially by forcing minor children into avenues not originated nor sought after by the minors themselves; all monies accrued will go into a trust that can only be accessed by the child when said child attains the age of eighteen; likewise, if any minor child is asked to perform any inappropriate or illegal actions (for example, appearing nude) in any venue, said minor does not require an adult to prosecute the employer – he or she may press all necessary charges, and expect justice to be served without regard to the power or prestige of the employer; also, no parent may force a child to undergo psychological treatment for issues related to sexual orientation'.

31. 'All persons seventeen and younger shall receive just compensation for their own labors and said compensation shall not be in the control of their parents or any adult; monies paid to working children shall be under the sole control of said children, and no adult may profit off the labors of any child without the child also receiving just compensation; likewise, monies paid by government agencies to house foster children aged six and older within non-parental homes shall be under the sole control of the minor child and can at no time be used by the custodial adult without the express written permission of the child and the child's impartial advocate'.

32. 'The right of children seventeen and younger to be secure in their persons, homes, papers, and effects against unreasonable searches and seizures, shall not be infringed, and no Warrants shall be issued, but upon probable cause, supported by Oath or affirmation, and describing the place to be searched, and the persons or things to be seized; 'probable cause' is defined as a clear

and present danger of criminality that may bring harm to persons or property (walking down the street with peers does not constitute 'probable cause')'.

33. 'No child below the age of eighteen may be adjudicated in the adult court system no matter the nature of the alleged offense – such adjudication will be considered cruel and unusual punishment; every reasonable attempt must be made to rehabilitate minors and quantifiable results must be presented to a panel upon attainment of the minor's eighteenth birthday (as regards serious offenses) for either release back into the community or further incarceration; said panel to consist of a judge, two lawyers, two psychologists, three adults and five minors between the ages of fifteen and seventeen chosen randomly from the community; if the panel deems the now-adult person unfit for release, further rehabilitation must be given until age twenty-five; if after that time, a separate, similarly constituted panel deems the person unfit for release, only then may said person be sentenced to prison'.

34. 'At no time may law enforcement question minor children below the age of eighteen without both a parent and a lawyer present, and questions must be asked in the preferred language of the child and translation provided to the parent as needed; any statements made by minors to law enforcement without the above stipulation, despite the Mirandizing of said minors, will be considered coerced and inadmissible as evidence, nor can such statements be used to even place said minor under arrest'.

35. 'In all criminal prosecutions, the accused minor child shall enjoy the right to a speedy and public trial by a judge well versed in the psychology of minors, accompanied by input from twelve minor children between the ages of fourteen and seventeen chosen randomly from the community; to be informed of the nature and cause of the accusation; to be confronted with the witnesses against him; to have compulsory process for obtaining witnesses in his favor, and to have the assistance of Counsel for his defense'.

36. Minor children may choose what public school to attend and whether or not they wish to take the traditional approach after middle school or go into a vocational or arts-related educational

venue; neither parents nor government may decide which path the child is to take; said decision rests solely with the minor child himself or herself'.

37. 'Within any institution or organization receiving federal funds, minor children under eighteen may not be penalized in any way as a group for the misbehaviors of one, or a small number of individuals, within that group, nor may any of said minors be singled out for cruel or unusual punishment, including, but not limited to, humiliation, public haranguing, name-calling, or physical abuse'.

After every amendment had been presented, the room buzzed with excitement, and hopeful enthusiasm. Reyna grinned proudly up at Lance, and Esteban flashed him a thumbs up of approval. They'd already seen these in private, but the palpable excitement amongst the entire Round Table meant the boys had hit on areas of need the other kids had perhaps sensed or thought about, but had never put a voice to in such a precise way.

The discussion that followed flew fast and furious, with most of these kids having suffered many of the injustices Lance and Ricky had attempted to cover within those ten amendments. Of special importance was number thirty-four, since most of the kids, especially the now ex-gang members, had been hassled and questioned by cops on numerous occasions, always with disastrous results for them. Those cops knew how to trick kids into saying things that could be used against them, and the kids knew the officers often altered in their reports what was actually said in order to make the kid look worse. Lance had experienced this injustice firsthand last summer. Yes, that one was personal to almost everyone.

When questioned about amendment twenty-nine, Jenny stood and asked to address the assemblage. The boys gladly gave her the floor. She explained how, as a teacher, she'd been required every year to document how many white kids, how many blacks, how many Latinos, how many Asians, how many Pacific Islanders, how many males and how many females she had in each of her classes, and explained that such directives were pointless and discriminatory.

"Every kid in my classes was one of my students and they didn't learn differently because they were of different skin colors," she said with conviction. "They learned differently because each was an individual in his or her own right, just as you all are, and everyone should be known and documented simply by their names. Putting people into little ice cube trays by skin color or race just separates us. Our goal with this crusade is to bring everyone together."

She stepped back from the microphone to thunderous cheers and foot stomping. Since a large number of these kids had Jenny for a teacher every day, they knew well her philosophy and they loved the freedom to be themselves, rather than part of some arbitrary grouping.

Jenny resumed her seat. Arthur smiled warmly and squeezed her hand, and the discussion continued well into the afternoon. Even Mayor Soto weighed in as an adult and a politician, cautioning that these provisions would be a hard sell to the Congress in Washington, but might go over better in Sacramento.

"But I warn you," he went on gravely, directing these last remarks squarely at Lance and Ricky, "as with your proposition, you're asking adults, especially parents, to cede a lot of their power and control over kids, and they won't like that." Then he grinned and turned to the crowd, waving a hand towards Lance. "But if anyone can accomplish it, that would be young Mr. Lincoln here."

Lance reddened at the accolade, Ricky shoved him playfully, and the crowd went wild.

All in all, while these ten amendments, if added to the Constitution, would not make minors into adults, they would give kids governmental and legal protections heretofore denied them under current law, and thus the assembled knights wholeheartedly approved the document, giving Lance and Ricky a thunderous standing ovation once the debate concluded at five o'clock.

As the boys shook hands with each and every knight, and the mayor acquired the names for his task force, Lance felt at peace with himself, especially when Sir Marvell and Sir James enthusiastically shook his hand and proclaimed their plan "Epic."

Yeah, he thought, *this will be epic.*

CHAPTER TWO

DID YOU LIKE MY LITTLE SURPRISE?

THE BILL OF RIGHTS WOULD go online Monday at noon, and accompanying the post would be a request for kids all over the country to provide feedback and suggestions for improvements, especially if some serious issue plagued kids in other states that did not affect Californians. These amendments were designed to aid all American children and Lance hoped to hear from as many as possible.

That Sunday flew by—mostly due to the preparations for Arthur and Jenny's wedding—with Reyna taking charge as event planner and organizer. Pastor Tom had come early, as usual, to do a morning service in the Throne Room. However, Lance and Ricky surprised Arthur and Jenny by asking if they could attend mass at a local Catholic church at eleven.

Arthur was listening to Jenny and Reyna explain wedding details in the library when the boys entered and made their request.

"There's a church close to here, Dad," Lance went on, "and they have an eleven o'clock youth mass for kids our age. I looked it up. Ricky made his first communion when he was little and we really wanna keep going to mass and receiving the body of Christ." He paused and glanced shyly at Ricky before continuing. "It makes me feel closer to God."

Arthur and Jenny exchanged a look. Obviously, Lance's request came as a surprise. "What of Pastor Tom's services?" Arthur asked hesitantly. "He has been most generous with his time."

"Oh, we'll keep going to them, too," Ricky put in quickly.

"It's just, well, he doesn't have the Eucharist," Lance went on, "and I got baptized Catholic." He paused a moment, recalling that morning in juvenile hall when he'd had the water poured over his head, and also received the sacraments of Holy

Communion and Confirmation. "I really felt special when I received the body of Christ at Sylmar. I can't explain it, Dad. It just felt good."

Arthur smiled, and Jenny took his hand lovingly.

"I confess, Lance, I stopped going to mass in college," she said with a wistful sigh. "I'd love to experience it again through your eyes. Mind if we tag along?"

Her grin was all Lance needed. He laughed and pulled her into a big hug. "That'd be great."

So the whole family, Chris included, dressed in appropriate, non-Round Table clothing, and headed off to Immaculate Heart Catholic Church. Naturally, despite an attempt to remain inconspicuous, the most famous family in the world was recognized at once, even though they had slipped into a pew near the back of the large, crowded church. The cavernous, curved ceilings and gigantic crucifix behind the altar were a far cry from the intimate masses Lance had experienced at juvenile hall, but the youth choir was great and he enjoyed how teenagers did the readings and acted as ushers. That part, at least, was like the way Father Mike did things at Sylmar.

When Lance received the Eucharist, he felt the familiar warmth spread through him, touching his very soul. He smiled shyly at Ricky as they both returned to their pew. Jenny also received communion, while Arthur and Chris crossed their arms over their hearts and received a blessing from the priest.

After mass, Arthur and the family were swamped with curious parishioners who wanted to shake a hand or just thank them for attending their church. The teens who'd facilitated the service gazed at Lance in awe and told him he should join their youth group. Lance smiled graciously, and Ricky lovingly elbowed him like he always did when people swarmed around The Boy Who Came Back. Lance told the teens he would be really busy with the new bill of rights, but he would love to attend whenever he had the time.

The pastor introduced himself, seemingly in awe just like his parishioners, and expressed his hope that they would join his parish community.

Arthur smiled warmly as he shook the man's hand. "Thank you, Father."

Chris looked up at the man wearing the green vestments. "Can I do that communion thing like Lance and Ricky?"

The man smiled. "Sure, Chris. We have classes for that."

Chris rolled his eyes. "Oh great, more school."

The pastor laughed and the family returned to Jenny's Prius for the short ride home. Lance held Ricky's hand and basked in the glow of love that surrounded him.

After that, it was all wedding talk for the rest of the day. Reyna and Jenny chose the Saturday after next for the ceremony because Jenny wanted to marry Arthur as soon as possible. All the knights would be invited, wearing their formal regalia as they would for a gathering, as well as the mayor, any city council members who wished to attend, the police chief, and of course Sergeants Ryan and Gibson.

Prior to Jenny and Reyna embarking on their quest for flowers, a photographer, and a wedding dress, Jenny sat with Arthur in the Throne Room to discuss his role in the event. He sat back in his throne, dressed in a casual tunic and pants, listening with amusement as she explained how he needed to purchase wedding bands for them both to wear and how he needed to decide whom he wanted for his best man.

Arthur pulled a confused face. "Best man?"

Jenny took his hand, lightly rubbing the palm with her thumb. "The best man stands by your side and hands you the ring, the one you put on my finger." She blushed. "And you need two groomsmen to stand with him."

Arthur paused to consider her words. "The best man I know, Jenny, is clearly Lance."

"And he would be a perfect choice."

Arthur frowned. "But what of Ricky? Chris wishes to carry up the rings and if Lance is this best man, what should become of my other son? Would he not feel left out?"

Her smile faltered. "Who else could be best man, if not Lance?"

Arthur grinned. "I believe I know the solution, milady, but I must first speak with Lance."

She grudgingly released his hand, heading off to the Computer Lab to make plans with Reyna.

Arthur rose from his throne and left to seek out his son.

The boys once again lay atop Lance's bed, Ricky's head in Lance's lap like it belonged there and should never leave. And if Lance had his way, it never would. They were reading up on the Revolutionary War in preparation for an exam on Tuesday. Jenny had promised them tomorrow off school so they could prepare for the Bill of Rights unveiling, so long as they completed extra work over the weekend.

One hand on his book, Lance's other gently stroked Ricky's thick dark hair as his eyes skimmed over the page. His fingers curled around Ricky's silken mane, absently toying with the strands, not even aware he was doing it.

Ricky was aware, however, and clearly couldn't concentrate on the book in his hands. He lifted his eyes from the page and surreptitiously watched Lance read.

Lance noticed him staring, and couldn't help but grin. "It's hard to concentrate with you looking at me like that."

Ricky eyed him with amusement. "It's hard to concentrate with *you* feeling up my hair."

Lance's mouth dropped open and his fingers instantly ceased their aimless wandering. "Sorry, fool, just love your hair."

Ricky tried to look offended. "Only my hair?"

Lance smiled, and then a cleared throat interrupted them.

The boys looked up to find Arthur framed in the doorway. Even though they weren't doing anything improper, they felt awkward and quickly sat up and separated.

"What's up, Dad?" Lance asked, wondering if it made his dad feel uncomfortable seeing them lounging so close together.

Arthur closed the gap between them, looking uncertain. "I wish to discuss the wedding with you."

Lance immediately felt relief that the uncertain look wasn't about them, and both boys leaned forward attentively.

"Your mother has informed me that I require someone she termed a 'best man' for the wedding, and some groomsmen. Alas, times have changed since I married Guinevere, I've discovered."

"Yeah, just a little," Lance said with a laugh.

Arthur grinned. "Lance, as my first son and heir, you are the logical choice for this best man role. You are clearly the best man I know besides your bro—" He stopped then, looked flustered, and added, "Ricky, here." He paused again, flummoxed.

Lance reached out a hand and placed it on father's arm. "It's okay, Dad. It's weird for us, too."

Ricky nodded sheepishly.

Arthur smiled in acknowledgement, and looked relieved to have that topic over with. "About the wedding. Rather than choose one of you over the other as best man, which would disturb me, I thought perhaps to make you my groomsmen—whatever they are—and ask someone else to be best man."

Lance wasn't hurt, just confused. "Who? My *nino*?"

"No, though Sergeant Ryan is a good man." When he told them whom he thought to ask, both boys grinned.

"That's a great idea, Dad," Lance said, and Ricky agreed.

Relieved that they weren't disappointed, Arthur excused himself and left to join the others in the Computer Lab.

Lance watched him go and then looked at Ricky with wide, soulful eyes.

"C'mon, fool," Ricky challenged, "let's get this stuff read so we can ace that test on Tuesday."

Lance shoved Ricky lovingly. Then they settled back into their favorite positions and resumed reading.

Arthur found Jenny, Reyna and Esteban in the Computer Lab along with Techie and a scattering of other knights surfing the net or responding to comments posted up on their website and Facebook page. He noted with surprise that young Sylvia also stood beside Reyna as the three females stared at one of the screens. Since Lavern's death, the thirteen-year-old had attached herself more strongly to Reyna than ever, and seemed to be visiting New Camelot whenever Reyna was present.

Esteban loitered by Techie, both of them scowling intently at Techie's screen. Arthur approached and greeted them before inquiring what they were studying so keenly.

"Look," Esteban said, pointing to the monitor.

The New Camelot website was open to the media link for people requesting an interview or personal appearance with Lance or Arthur or anything to do with the Round Table. Normally, Reyna handled such details, but since she'd become so absorbed in wedding preparations, Esteban had taken it upon himself—with Techie's assistance—to filter through these.

Arthur squinted at the screen, noting request after request for interviews and photo shoots for Lance and Ricky, all dated this past week. He turned to Esteban inquiringly, the mysteries of the Internet still a befuddlement. "What am I seeing, Sir Este?"

Esteban sighed with distaste. "All these requests, Arthur, to interview Lance and Ricky, are all about 'em being gay."

Arthur blanched with concern, and turned to eye the screen again.

"They all wanna talk to Lance about coming out and how it feels to be a role model for gay people and what he might do to help get more rights for gay people. Stuff like that."

Arthur sighed heavily, a deadweight filling the pit of his stomach. "I see."

Esteban's face clouded with anger, and disgust. "And most of these magazines want Lance and Ricky on their covers—with no shirts on!"

That shocked Arthur. "Why?"

Esteban shook his head with revulsion. "Remember what Lance said about the media, Arthur, how they're voyeurs?"

The king nodded solemnly.

"This is more a that, only worse," Esteban went on, struggling to control his rising tide of ire. "They wanna exploit *mis carnales*, get adults out there all excited and hot over their bodies and sh—! Oh, my bad, I'm sorry, Arthur. This just pisses me off so much!"

He visibly shook with anger and Arthur placed a comforting hand on his shoulder.

"No way these perverts are gonna exploit my boys," Esteban hissed. "No way in hell!"

"Lance and Ricky are blessed to have such a great man as their big brother, Sir Este." Arthur patted his shoulder, causing Esteban to redden slightly. "Needless to say, all such requests shall be refused, but I trust Lance to formulate the proper response."

Esteban agreed, looking flummoxed by the king's praise.

Arthur dropped his hand back to his side and asked if they might step off to a quiet section of the room for a moment. Uncertainly, Esteban trailed after him.

In an unobtrusive corner of the lab, Arthur turned to Esteban. "I, um, I have a request of you, Sir Este," the king began hesitantly. "A favor, if you'll deign to grant it."

Esteban looked into Arthur's penetrating brown eyes. "Anything."

That drew a smile to the king's bearded face. "I have discussed the matter with my sons and they are in complete agreement."

Esteban waited while Arthur paused again, apparently collecting his thoughts.

The king stood proud and tall and gazed into Esteban's eyes. "I would be honored, Sir Esteban, should you consent to stand by my side at the wedding as my best man."

Esteban, widely praised for his stoicism and unflappability, nearly gasped, his face collapsing into astonishment. "Me?"

"Other than my sons, Sir Este, you are the best man I know, the most decent and honorable and loyal, and having you stand beside me shall make my wedding day complete."

Esteban looked like he might cry, his entire body stiffened with coiled emotion. Then he grinned with pride. "I'd be honored, Your Majesty."

They shook, a strong, firm handshake, grinning foolishly, with great love evident between them.

Then Arthur clapped him on the back before they returned to the others. The king sat with Esteban and Techie filtering through the interview requests for Lance and Ricky, preparing them for a blanket response once Lance formulated one. As excited as Arthur felt for his impending marriage, and the Children's Bill of Rights, a sense of foreboding filled his heart at the difficult road he knew Lance and Ricky must traverse as a result of their public declaration of love. It seemed horrendous enough that everyone this past year had wanted to exploit Lance as The Boy Who Came Back, rather than for his accomplishments, but to focus on something so personal, and unimportant to the public at large, as his love for another, left a bitter taste in Arthur's mouth. Yes, in many ways, humanity had gotten worse over the centuries, not better.

After Lance and Ricky finished their studies, they dressed in long pants, tunics and skate shoes, and decided to check out the latest Internet comments, pro and con, over the past couple of days.

On their way down the plush, carpeted main staircase to the lobby, Lance told Ricky he wanted to find Merlin first, so they crossed out of the vast, tiled lobby and sought out the main library.

As expected, they found the middle-aged wizard lounging in his usual easy chair, book in hand, wearing a Motley Crue shirt and listening to what Lance considered God-awful metal music from his phone. When the boys entered, Merlin's elven face broke into a grin and one ear bud was instantly plucked out, where it dangled down the front of the shirt, discordant music drifting out of it.

"Prince Lance and Sir Ricky," he said cheerily in that slight, odd accent he possessed. "To what do I owe the honor?"

Lance looked shyly at the man, who remained seated with the book in his lap.

"I just wanna say thanks, Merlin, for what you said last week," Lance offered, eliciting a knowing grin from the wizard.

"What did he say?" Ricky asked.

"He reminded me that I didn't have to be the way everybody said I should be, that I could be a real boy and still love another real boy like you."

Ricky's eyes widened with surprise.

"I do believe you're putting words into my mouth," Merlin offered in a sly tone. "As I recall, we did not discuss Sir Ricky at all."

Lance smiled. "I know. But we did anyway. Thanks."

Merlin's gray eyes seemed to twinkle and he bowed his head respectfully. "Any time, Your Majesty."

Lance lost his smile at the salutation, suddenly feeling the cold weight of responsibility press down on him.

Ricky's hand finding his brought Lance back to the moment, and they left Merlin to his metal and books and headed off to the Computer Lab.

By the time they entered the lab, it was already five thirty and everyone had left to get ready for dinner, or go home. All but Techie, of course. He often slept over, rather than hop the metro for Long Beach every time. Except when he sat in the New Camelot classroom or at a meal in the dining room, the seventeen-year-old lived in this lab and, quite frankly, Lance didn't know how they'd manage without him.

The boys approached and greeted the Vietnamese knight with the fist bump.

"What's up, guys?" Techie asked, his eyes returning to the screen before him, his fingers, as always, flitting over the keys like skittering beetles.

"Just checking on our gay status," Lance said with a smirk at Ricky, who flashed a mock scowl and shoved him playfully. "You know, where Ricky and me are on the hate meter today."

Since making their feelings known to the world, which in retrospect both boys felt might not have been the best idea, the Internet had been abuzz with nothing else. Of course, the most regularly used headline since the past Monday had become 'The Boy Who Came Back Becomes The Boy Who Came Out'.

Lance had expected some reaction to his announcement, but seriously, there could've been an alien invasion in progress and the main topic of conversation everywhere would still have been 'Sir Lance and Sir Ricky gay with each other'. That expression continuously made both boys chuckle – what the hell did 'gay with each other' mean anyway?

Techie minimized his window and opened a new one. He Googled 'Sir Lance and Sir Ricky gay' and instantly hundreds of hits popped up from every conceivable venue.

"I've been tracking and compiling stats, Lance, and at first lots of people were kind of shocked. But now I'd say the consensus is probably seventy, seventy-five percent still supporting what you're doing and not caring about, well, you know, whatever you guys do in private."

He blushed to his ears, causing Lance and Ricky to exchange a look.

"And just what do you think we do in private, Sir Techie?" Lance asked, a bit more testily than he'd wanted.

Techie shrugged, but didn't raise his eyes from the screen. "None a my business. But people on line, well, they're speculating a lot. You know…"

Lance folded his arms across his chest in annoyance. Ricky placed a hand on his shoulder to calm him. "No, I don't know."

Techie squirmed with extreme discomfort. "It's them saying this, guys, not me."

Lance wanted to know, even though he felt sure he wasn't going to like it.

"They speculate on like, who's on top and who's on the bottom and, oh God, you know, stuff like that!" Techie couldn't continue and lowered his gaze to the keyboard.

Lance looked at Ricky, whose eyes were the size of saucers.

Who's on top?

"Oh, God, Ricky, they all think we're…" Lance stopped, flushing red. "And they're wondering which one is… the girl." His knees felt weak. He'd been Richard's 'girl' for so long…

The color drained from Ricky's face, turning him white as a t-shirt.

"That what you trying to tell us, Techie?" Lance added in a breathless whisper.

The tech genius nodded his head.

"Oh, hell," Ricky exclaimed, plopping down into one of the rolling computer chairs behind him.

Lance lowered himself slowly into another chair.

"I'm sorry, Lance, I'm just telling you what's out there," Techie said apologetically, his face red with embarrassment. "None of us care."

Every muscle in Lance's body felt tight with tension, and a growing rage. "Techie, look at me," he said in a commanding tone that left no room for argument.

Grudgingly, still red to the ears, Techie turned his head and met Lance's fiery green eyes.

"Ricky and me are *not* having sex, Techie," he stated calmly, with conviction. "Period. And we don't plan to for a long time, at least till after we turn eighteen and even then we don't know for sure what we might do."

"And it's nobody's damn business, anyway!" Ricky spat in anger.

Techie looked even more embarrassed, if such a thing were possible. "You don't have to tell me this, guys."

The fire in Lance's eyes intensified. "Yes, we do. We know how nasty those people out there can be. I've always been straight with you, Techie. Do you believe me about this?"

Techie grinned. "Course, I do." Then he added shyly, "And it wouldn't matter to me anyway. You guys are perfect together."

Lance let out a breath of relief, exchanging a look with the still-mortified Ricky. He gripped Ricky's knee and squeezed it gently to calm him, and then pulled his hand back. "What else is going on out there about us?"

Back on safer technological ground, a relieved Techie pulled up the list of gay magazines and activist groups who wanted interviews, appearances or shirtless pictures of the boys, causing both Lance and Ricky to blanch anew with disgust.

"Shirtless pix?" Ricky exclaimed with a shake of his head. "Aren't we still minors?"

Lance grunted. "Doesn't matter. If they can get grown-ups to drool over our hot bods, they might make more money or something."

"Well, you do have a hot bod."

Lance shoved him, causing the chair to roll away several feet and bump into a computer table.

Techie eyed them with amusement. "How do you want to respond to these requests, Lance?"

Lance considered a moment. "Any TV shows want us on?"

Techie scanned the list. "Most of 'em, especially Ellen. Her producer has sent a bunch of messages since Tuesday."

Lance looked at Ricky, and both boys smiled simultaneously.

"Ellen will work, Techie," Lance said. "She's cool. We'll say everything we're ever gonna say about our relationship on her show. The rest can just crib from there. And those groups who wanna exploit us, well, they aren't gonna like what they hear."

The three exchanged a conspiratorial high-five.

"C'mon, guys, it's time for dinner," Lance announced, rising to his feet. "I'm starved."

And so the three boys left the Computer Lab for their nightly trek to the Renaissance Dining Room.

The following morning, the boys rose early, as they normally would for school, showered and dressed in casual t-shirts, jeans and skate shoes. No longer shy around each other, they paraded uninvited into and out of each other's rooms, borrowing this hair dryer or that item of clothing because theirs was in the wash.

After a quick breakfast, they headed to Jenny's classroom to drop off their completed work. Despite Jenny being their soon-to-be adoptive mother, they always turned in schoolwork during school hours so the others would not perceive any advantage or favoritism on the part of Jenny the teacher, as opposed to Jenny the mother.

She thanked them, and they waved to the class before exiting. Darnell and Justin gave them the head nod, and several others threw out a thumbs-up. Lance knew that once school let out at noon, every one of the knights would head to the lab and go online for the reaction to their amendments.

Feeling almost like they were ditching, the boys hurried through the lobby and down another hallway to the Computer Lab. For once, the spacious room with its hundred computers sat silent and empty, with even Techie not taking up residence until nearly noon.

They sat down at their usual stations, logged onto their website, and pulled up the Children's Bill of Rights, intending to check it over before the public unveiling.

Slipping out quickly for some lunch at eleven, the boys were back in their seats by eleven-thirty when Jenny dismissed school for the day and the Computer Lab began filling up with eager, excited children and teens. Chris, of course, made his way straight to Lance and hopped onto his lap.

Like the captain of a starship, Techie sauntered in and resumed his seat beside Lance, firing up his screen and verifying that Lance had everything set up correctly. The media had already been alerted to the noon reveal, and a tweet would go out to the millions of New Camelot followers with a link to the Children's Bill of Rights.

Lance felt nervous, his palms sweaty as the noon hour approached. Chris finally jumped off his lap and planted himself in front of his own computer, allowing Ricky to reach out and take Lance's trembling hand. Their eyes met, and Lance gratefully squeezed back. He noted Techie's eyes fixed on their clasped hands uncertainly, but then the seventeen-year-old smiled.

"Someday I hope I have with a girl what you guys have together," Techie said, a touch of envy evident in his voice.

Lance grinned. "You will."

Ricky nodded in agreement.

At that moment, Reyna and Esteban blew into the lab like twin tornadoes, each having cut out early from their college classes to be part of this historic moment. Esteban was currently taking classes at Los Angeles City College, while Reyna had enrolled in Cal State Northridge.

"Are we ready to roll, people?" Reyna called out by way of announcing her presence.

She swept between the tables to engulf Lance, and then Ricky, in a bone-crushing hug each, acting like she hadn't seen them in forever. Esteban gave them the fist bump.

The time on Lance's phone finally ticked over to twelve o'clock, and he gave Techie the word. The Children's Bill of Rights went live and everyone in the room sat back to await the feedback.

The reaction was instantaneous.

'Likes' inundated their Facebook page almost at once, leading Lance to believe many people weren't even reading the document, but just liking it on general principle.

Almost as fast came the comments on their website – positive, negative, outraged, excited. And with the comments began coming suggestions for revision.

Clearly, the anticipation must've been high with so many people pouncing on the document the very second of its release.

Techie began scrolling the news sites – the world had apparently been put on hold for this story. As the day wore on, the various talking heads weighed in on CNN, Fox, and MSNBC about parents' rights versus government protection of children, and whether or not children should be in charge of their own money, or even if they should have free-speech rights at school – exactly the debates Lance and Ricky hoped their Bill of Rights would generate.

Tomorrow would be a live press conference in front of City Hall that Lance knew would attract all the national and local news outlets. He and Ricky would leap from the hot seat right into the frying pan because the questions would likely be strong and specific now that the amendments were live. Both boys knew the amendments inside and out—they'd written them, after all—and felt prepared for the grilling to come. Still, apprehension eventually prevailed and they slunk out of the lab at three-thirty for a sparring session to work off the nervous energy. Tomorrow, they knew, would be a very long day.

Dinner that night proved a raucous affair, with Reyna, Esteban, Techie, Justin and Darnell and a host of other knights sticking around to celebrate the launch of their next big salvo in the war for America's children.

Despite the jovial atmosphere, Lance knew once again he'd be on the spot tomorrow when he faced the press and public at large to address their proposal.

Oh, well, he thought, *I'll enjoy this moment while I have it.*

And he did just that, laughing and joking and enjoying every moment with his family and the boy he loved, ignoring the nagging sensation that tonight marked the last peaceful moment he'd have for a long time.

Sergeants Ryan and Gibson arrived the following morning with the news that Chief Murphy had once again assigned them to permanent duty as the protectors of Lance,

Ricky, and Arthur whenever they ventured forth into the public arena. With Michael's death, the LAPD had closed the case on the attempts on Lance's life, but the FBI had, as yet, drawn a blank on the person or persons responsible for the attack on Arthur that had killed Lavern and three other children in San Francisco the previous May.

Now, with their even more contentious Bill of Rights before the public, both Murphy and Mayor Soto felt the need for renewed security.

The press conference, scheduled for three-thirty, drew even bigger crowds than all the previous ones. The national media crammed in with the local reporters around a stage set up on Temple Street in front of the towering Los Angeles City Hall. The public, too, came out in force – parents with their children, single adults, and many, many teens, including nearly all of Arthur's thousand-plus knights from across the Los Angeles area.

Unlike previous appearances, Ryan and Gibson escorted Arthur, Jenny, and the boys—all attired in their finest tunics and pants, the males sporting swords sheathed to their belts—through the vast, marbled and columned City Hall lobby. They exited on the Temple Street side and proceeded straight to the enormous staging area, thus avoiding that long, unprotected walk through the gathered throng anxiously awaiting their appearance.

Mayor Soto greeted the family when they stepped up onto the stage and all were welcomed with boisterous applause from the assembled crowd. When he shook Lance's hand, the diminutive mayor smiled wryly. "Well, if it isn't the young Mr. Lincoln."

Lance laughed.

Given the enormity of this new endeavor, the entire city council—led by President Sanders—and LAPD Chief Murphy, were also present, greeting Arthur and the family warmly. Their bill of rights, while enormous in scope, would not directly or indirectly affect them or their political lives as the proposition had done, so the welcome was heartfelt and worry-free.

The mayor stepped to the podium and quieted the multitude, which surrounded him on three sides like the ocean around a peninsula. "Greetings fellow Angelenos," the mayor began, and was instantly interrupted by a tumultuous shout of approval from the ebullient crowd, especially the youth. "We are gathered here today," the mayor went on, his voice booming out over the crowd through enormous speakers set up around the staging area, "to once again set Los Angeles's young Mr. Lincoln,

Sir Lance Pendragon, loose to work his magic, only this time he's going after the whole country. As for me, I'm betting *against* the country."

That drew a tremendous laugh, and lots of whoops from the kids.

"As all of you know, their monumental Children's Bill of Rights went live yesterday and has caused, how shall I put this, a bit of an uproar?"

He grinned as the crowd again laughed, and the kids whooped even louder.

"Before I introduce them, Sir Lance has asked me to inform you that he and Sir Ricky will answer no questions about their personal relationship. They will appear on the Ellen Show next week and that will be the only time they will publicly discuss the matter. So, for those of you with questions about that, I suggest you tune in to the show."

The crowd laughed and the teens cheered wildly, which caused Lance and Ricky to grin. They hadn't expected so much support in that arena from their peers.

Soto grinned. "I give you two young men I personally feel honored to know, Sir Lance and Sir Ricky."

He stepped away from the microphone to thunderous applause from the assembled kids and teens, with more muted support from some of the scowling, wary adults. Lance and Ricky, beaming, shook hands with the mayor and he ushered them forward before resuming his seat beside Sanders.

Nervousness filled his soul and threatened to drown him as Lance shyly eyed Ricky while they approached the podium. He knew Ricky felt the same nauseous waves of anxiety, but he also knew Ricky expected him to do the lion's share of the talking. He was the young Mr. Lincoln, after all.

Lance scanned the crowd, and the reporters. He made eye contact with Helen Schaeffer of *Channel 7 News* in her usual place in front, and waved. Of all in the media, she had been his staunchest supporter from the beginning and had never doubted him, even when he doubted himself. He even spotted Yellow Hair a little ways behind her. He was a tabloid reporter who'd spent much of the past year heckling him. But since last week's rally, the man seemed different, more human and less paparazzi than before. Lance met his eye and gave him the chin nod. Then he cleared his throat, and waited for the crowd to settle.

"Welcome everyone," he began, hoping his voice sounded strong and confident.

The crowd cheered again, giving Lance a moment to steal a glance Ricky's way. His other half wore that look, the one that said, 'You're all that's important in this world,' the one that always filled Lance with peace. And it worked again. He smiled and turned back to the crowd.

"As you all know, Ricky and me put something on the Internet yesterday that, for some reason, people think is a big deal."

That drew major laughs and applause, especially from the youngsters.

Lance spotted Justin, Darnell and Techie down in the crowd, clapping excitedly. What surprised him was that Bridget and Ariel stood with them. His heart caught a moment in his throat as he thought back on the past year and all that had passed between he and Bridget. But she looked happy, and that assuaged some of his guilt.

"Okay, here's the deal," Lance went on when everyone had quieted down. "After I got out of jail in September, Ricky and me got to talking about the Bill of Rights and how we kids didn't have any of them, even when we're being tried as adults, which thanks to the people of California can't be done here anymore."

More applause and whoops arose from the teens.

"Unfortunately, all around the country, kids are still treated as adults without having any protections real adults have. So we thought what kids need is their own Bill of Rights in the Constitution that will protect them, not only from government, but from grown-ups who just want to act like we're property."

He paused for another round of clapping. The kids, he was happy to see, were stoked by this new venture. The trick, as he knew from the prop campaign, was to win over their parents.

"It's funny how people forget that other piece of famous American paper, what was it called?"

He snapped his fingers as though trying to remember.

Ricky leaned into the microphone. "You mean the Declaration of Independence, fool?"

Lance pretended to frown and gave him a playful shove. "I was just about to say that, fool. Stop interrupting."

Everyone laughed, and Soto shook his head in amazement.

Lance turned back to the crowd after a mock mad-dog look at Ricky. "Anyway, as I was saying before this fool interrupted me, yeah the Declaration of Independence. I know it's not the law, but it does say 'we hold these truths to be self-evident, that all men are created equal, that they are all endowed by their creator with certain unalienable rights, that among these are life, liberty and the pursuit of happiness'. Now I know when it was written, men were everything and women not so much. But, it does have that magic word 'all' in it. Aren't us kids part of the 'all' too? It doesn't say 'all adults'. Shouldn't we have constitutional protection against bad people and bad government like you grown-ups do?"

The kids in the crowd shouted, "Damn straight!"

That drew a huge laugh, even from the adults.

Lance grinned, slightly taken aback by their use of his now-famous phrase.

"So, we won't start shopping around the CBOR, as I call it for short, to Congress people and senators till early next year. We want as much feedback as possible, from kids and grown-ups all over the country. The current CBOR is a draft, waiting for you all to weigh in. We know what goes down here in Cali, but not in all the other states. We've gotten lots of responses so far, and ideas for revising, and we're gonna put in anything we feel is needed. But there won't be any more than ten amendments, since we based ours on the originals." He turned to Ricky with a dramatic flair. He knew he was on camera and had learned to play to it. "Did I forget anything?"

Ricky paused as though thinking deep thoughts. "Dunno. Think they might have any questions?"

"Hell, no, fool." Lance turned back to the microphone. "None of you have any questions, do you?"

There was more boisterous laughter and every media hand flew into the air.

Lance turned to Ricky. "Guess you were right."

They high-fived.

As always, Lance pointed to Helen first. "I know you think I'm playing favorites by always picking Lady Helen to go first… and you're right." More laughs drifted up from below. "Lady Helen?"

As usual, Helen grinned up at the boys, clearly happy to be first out of the block.

"Sir Lance, the biggest concern adults seem to have raised about your CBOR, as you called it, is that it undermines, and might even destroy, parental rights over children in this country. How do you respond to that assertion?"

Lance and Ricky exchanged a look, as though deciding who should respond first. Ricky held up his hand to indicate Lance as the one to answer. This was all part of their 'act'.

Lance smiled warmly down at Helen. "Good question, Lady Helen. And I'll answer it with a question – are children property of their parents? Or, like in my case, if parents dump kids like yesterday's trash, are we the government's property?"

"Hell, no!" shouted the hundreds of kids and teens crowding in towards the restraining barriers, causing the LAPD officers to apprehensively move closer to each other.

Lance grinned. "I guess we know where the kids stand on that question."

The crowd laughed and the teens cheered.

"But," Lance went on, serious and sober, "where do *adults* stand on that question? If they think we're property, then they'll be against our CBOR, though I thought the whole 'people are property' thing went out with, you know, the thirteenth amendment? But maybe I didn't understand that part too well in school."

The kids in the crowd looked mystified by Lance's reference, but many in the media gasped. Helen grinned, and Mayor Soto chuckled to himself.

"So, if adults agree in principle that children are not property," Lance continued solemnly, "then we can have a serious talk about our CBOR and how to make it work for everyone."

More reporters thrust their hands into the air. Lance pointed to man wearing a 'Fox News' polo shirt.

"Sir Lance, do you believe it's the parental role to make decisions for their children?"

"No, I don't."

That answer created something of a uproar from the adults, and another cheer from the kids.

"Let me explain," Lance continued and everyone settled down. "I think, and this is from my experience and Ricky's and all the knights in our Round Table who've told us their stories, that it's a parent's job to take care of kids, to make sure we have the things we need, like food, shelter, love, and protection from harm. It's a parent's job to set a good example and teach us how to behave, how to know the difference between right and wrong." Then he smiled in a knowing way. "I bet most of you didn't do your homework and read *Frankenstein* yet, did you?"

That drew a big laugh.

"Didn't think so." Another laugh ensued, and Lance turned serious again. "Having said all that, it's *not* the job of parents to tell us kids what to think or feel 'cause we're our own selves, not little clones of them. That's why some of our amendments deal with that. Maybe I been spoiled this past year and a half since my dad took me in, but he doesn't do those things. Neither does my mom. They *show* us how to be good people, and teach us *how* to think, but don't tell us *what* to think."

Lance glanced at Ricky for that reassuring look, and got it. Grinning, he pointed to a guy wearing a 'CNN' shirt.

"Sir Lance, could your CBOR, if passed by the congress and the states, make it easier for good parents to get caught up in some legal nightmare?"

"You mean like good kids getting arrested for attempted murder and put through hell by the system and the media before finally being released? That kind of 'caught up'?"

The man looked momentarily stunned by Lance's response. "Well, sort of, yes. I mean, most parents probably do a good job. What if their kids get mad about some little thing or other and try to sue under your bill of rights?"

Lance sighed dramatically, again playing to the cameras. "Look, I don't think there's anything in our CBOR that will let a kid sue their parents, but in this country, like Michael taught me, there's always the law of unintended consequences. Good parents who listen to their kids and don't try to make the kids into little clones should have nothing to worry about. But our society doesn't value children as human beings, and we kids have no standing under the law. Just this year, Children's Services tried to take me and Ricky and Chris away from our dad because he kept swords on the premises and those swords 'might fall into the wrong hands'." He snorted derisively. "They didn't even care about what we thought or wanted, and younger kids like Chris aren't even allowed to talk in court unless the judge is super cool like Judge Baker was with us. So yeah, we need the Constitution to guarantee us those unalienable rights." He pointed to another reporter, a lady from CBS.

"Sir Lance, why do you feel parents should not be in control of their children's money?"

Lance and Ricky exchanged a look and Lance waved a hand toward the other boy. Ricky leaned in to the mic. "How about because the parents didn't earn the money, the kids did?"

That answer got a huge swell of support from the teens in the crowd.

"When I was little, everybody thought I was 'such a cute little boy'," Ricky went on, using the air quotation marks to mimic overly hyperbolic adults, "and they kept telling my dad and mom that I should be a model 'cause they could make all kinds of money off a me."

Lance chuckled. "Modeling what, fool, diapers? You could still do that now."

Ricky scowled and shoved Lance away from the microphone. "See what I gotta put up with? Anyway, my birth father thought modeling was for girls and sissies and said no. But most parents don't say no. They put their kids into acting or modeling or whatever so *they* can make money. If a kid wants to do it, fine, but the money earned is his and the parents shouldn't get a dime of it."

"It's like bribing people to pimp their kids out for money," Lance asserted, and then frowned. "That's like foster care too. I'm sure most foster parents are awesome and honest. But not all of 'em. Kids in foster care, older ones, anyway, should be the only ones in charge of their money, not the grown-ups. I never saw a dime of the money those people got for me, so I know what I'm talking about. And our amendment doesn't say kids can have all the money they earned whenever they want it. It's put into a trust under their name that can be accessed by them only when they turn eighteen. That seems fair."

He pointed to another raised hand, this lady wearing an NBC hat.

"Sir Lance, we all know of your experience within the adult court system, and that's one of the main reasons Californians voted to repeal such laws. However, more than half the other states have laws putting children even younger than fourteen into adult court. Your amendment number thirty-three forbids this practice. Are you attempting to trample on states' rights here?"

Lance had expected such a challenge, and was prepared with an answer.

"That's a great question. If these amendments become law, they apply to the country as a whole, just like the first Bill of Rights did. So just like that one forbids cruel and unusual punishment for adults, our amendment thirty-three says that putting kids into adult court is cruel and unusual punishment. I guess at that point, each state will have to figure out how to deal with it. So no, we're not telling any particular state what they can or can't do."

Ricky leaned in. "Does that answer your question?"

The lady thanked him, and there were nods of approval throughout the crowd.

The questions continued in a similar vein, some addressing specific amendments, while others were more general regarding the role of parents if the Children's Bill of Rights became the law of the land. Lance and Ricky answered each deftly, having practiced with Jenny over the past few days. The boys joked around some more and played for the cameras, especially when they'd give each other a shove and call the other "Fool." Even the adults, while wary or hostile at first, warmed to the boys' playfulness and that seemed to relax the overall atmosphere.

By the time the press conference drew to a close, Lance and Ricky had charmed everyone, even those likely to oppose their amendments.

As they followed Arthur down the short steps to ground level, with Lance waving to the people behind the stage, Ricky heard a strange creaking sound and looked up. One of the enormous speakers, set atop a thick, metal tripod, began toppling – right toward Lance.

Instinctively, Ricky grabbed Lance by the shirt and yanked him back, sending both boys tumbling backward up the steps, Lance landing in Ricky's lap. The huge speaker toppled hard to the lower steps, splintering them with an explosive *bang!*

Arthur whirled, leaping away from the crashing sound, eyeing the speaker, the splintered wooden steps, and his stunned sons huddled together just above the damaged area. "Are you all right?" he exclaimed fearfully, even as Jenny and the mayor turned in shock at the commotion.

Lance nodded, his heart thudding wildly in his chest. Ricky's arms were around him, holding on like he never wanted to let go.

"You sure?" Ricky whispered into his ear breathlessly.

Lance turned his head and their eyes met. He felt the chill of death calling for him again. That had been close. *Too* close.

"You have that Final Destination look again, Lance. Still think death wants you back?"

But Lance was too rattled to respond to the joke. Ever since he came back from death the first time, he'd had this unsettling feeling it wasn't over yet, that death wasn't finished with him.

"Maybe," he whispered, afraid his voice would betray the fear within.

Ricky gave him a playful shove. "If death wants you, pretty boy, it'll be over my dead body."

That made Lance grin. "Dumbass."

Then Arthur was there, stretching out a hand to help Lance up and over the fallen speaker. Ricky followed. Most of the crowd in front of the staging area obviously knew the speaker had fallen, but couldn't see the aftermath and milled around uncertainly. Reporters and camera people scrambled to get around the stage for a better view.

The mayor was beside himself, red faced and flustered. "I'm so sorry, Lance, I don't know how that happened. Are you sure you're all right?"

Lance felt his heart slowing, his breathing returning to normal. "Yeah, Mr. Mayor, I'm fine. Dumbass here saved me." He gave Ricky a loving shove.

The mayor looked relieved, and waved over some of the sound people to clean up the mess as the media and their cameras arrived to film the scene.

Lance met Arthur's gaze and saw the fear in his father's eyes. "Really, Dad, I'm good. Let's go home."

Arthur smiled and placed one arm around Lance's shoulders and one around Ricky's, while Jenny led an agitated Chris by the hand. They followed Ryan and Gibson back through City Hall to their cars, ignoring shouted questions from the media pool.

Lance brooded about the close call as he and Ricky sat in the back of Ryan's four-door sedan. The others had gone with Gibson in his beamer.

Ricky nudged him. "Going emo on me again, Lance?"

Lance offered a tiny smile. The phone in his pocket vibrated with an incoming text message. He slipped out the smartphone and thumbed in his password to unlock it. He gasped.

Ricky leaned in at once. "What?"

Lance held up the phone. The text was from number "000-000 – 0000."

"Oh, hell," Ricky whispered breathlessly.

Ryan swiveled his head around halfway. "Everything okay back there, boys?"

"Just a sec, *nino*," Lance replied while he and Ricky read over the series of messages. Lance's blood ran cold in his veins.

'Hello, Lance, it's your old pal Jacky again. Forgot me already? You must have, since you're all hot and heavy with your queer brother. That's the problem with you fag boys, you just go from one guy to the next. Sick! So, did you like my little surprise with the speaker?'

Lance trembled, and Ricky grabbed his arm for support.

'It's only the beginning. I'm going to kill you, Lance, but like any self-respecting cat with a mouse, I'm going to play with you first. You gave up drinking, so vodka won't work anymore. LOL The coaster and the train were fun, but just warm-ups. I had another opportunity to take you out since then, but chose not to because I want to watch you suffer when I kill your disgusting little boyfriend first. Ha! You'll never know if something is an accident or on purpose. It could be as simple as a trash truck plowing through a red light and smashing into your godfather's car on the way home.'

Lance glanced up and frantically looked out his side window at the oncoming traffic, while Ricky searched desperately out his. No trash trucks were in sight. Both boys returned their wide-eyed gazes to the phone.

'Or it could be a piece of falling construction equipment. But don't worry. Before you die, you'll know who I am and why I'm killing you. Oh, and don't think I forgot your old man. San Francisco was just the beginning. So play your politics, little boy. Go ahead and push your childish bill of rights on the American people. They're just stupid enough to pass it. But know that I'll always be there, just like before, toying with you, watching you squirm. And when the time is right, I will have my revenge and crush you like the worthless loser you are. Later, Lancey boy.'

Lance's breath had practically ceased, his heart constricted with terror as he met Ricky's fearful brown eyes. Revenge? For what? He hadn't hurt anyone!

The car suddenly stopped, and both boys jumped with alarm. Ryan whipped his head around and Lance realized they had merely come to a stoplight.

"What is it?" the detective asked.

Hand trembling, Lance handed him the phone, and Ryan scanned it quickly. "Hellfire!"

But then the light turned green and the older man handed back the phone so he could return his eyes to the road.

Lance dropped back against the seatback and expelled a deep breath, lowering the phone heavily into his lap. Ricky grabbed his other hand, intertwined their fingers, and squeezed gently.

"Michael was innocent, *nino*," Lance muttered, almost without breath. "Just like I said."

In the rearview, he saw Ryan nod his head solemnly.

Lance met Ricky's wide, frightened eyes, and gratefully squeezed the other boy's hand. "He was innocent."

Ricky looked abashed and afraid, at the same time.

Michael was innocent, but somebody else wanted them dead, in the worst way.

CHAPTER THREE
DID YOU MEAN WHAT YOU SAID?

"I TOLD YOU GUYS, I DON'T know," Lance repeated for probably the tenth time, his voice exasperated, his nerves frayed. They were all gathered in the expansive hotel library discussing the latest threat Lance received on his phone.

Most of the Round Table leadership team was present – Lance, Ricky, Reyna, Esteban, Justin, Darnell, Techie, and Chris – along with Arthur, Jenny, Merlin, Ryan and Gibson. Surrounded by towering oaken shelves filled with books, they were seated around the room, every one of them feeling tense and uncertain. They'd already spoken with the mayor and police chief via conference call. Both men expressed deep concerns and vowed to give Arthur all the power at their disposal, including reassigning Ryan and Gibson as round-the-clock New Camelot guardians and offering as much police protection as needed whenever anyone ventured forth from the hotel.

Lance looked straight at Sergeant Gibson, who had asked him *again* if he could think of anyone he might've pissed off. "Sergeant, you know me. I don't get in people's faces. There's nobody I can think of who hates me like that." Then he shivered. "'Cept maybe Richard or Mr. D."

Gibson exchanged a look with Ryan.

"Maybe one of those guys hired somebody," Ricky put in with a twinge of hope. If it wasn't either of them, they were sitting ducks for the real maniac.

Gibson considered the idea, turning it over in his mind. "Possible. Of the two, Diosdado is better connected. We'll explore that avenue. And we need to keep your phone for now, Lance. The FBI'll want it."

"Mom and Dad just gave me that phone for my birthday," Lance protested, not wanting to part with it. "'Sides, this guy always gets my new number. Even

Michael couldn't figure out where he was sending from." He glanced at Arthur and Jenny. Their faces were creased with worry. Both, he knew, were in their thirties, but suddenly they looked older than ever. He felt terrible, not so much because of the threats against him, but because this whole business was spoiling their wedding plans. And more than anything, he wanted them to be happy.

Jenny offered a tight, but loving smile. "We'll get you a new phone, honey. Don't worry."

Lance tried for a grateful smile, but knew it probably looked more like a grimace of indigestion. "*Nino*, Sergeant Gibson, I need you guys to do something for me."

Then men appeared taken aback, as though Lance might think there was something they wouldn't do for him.

"Anything," Ryan said.

Lance looked straight at them. "I need you to clear Michael's name."

He heard Ricky suck in a breath beside him, but refused to look.

"Lance," Ryan began hesitantly, eyeing his partner for backup. "We have bigger problems to worry about."

Now Ricky spoke, his voice tight with barely contained jealousy. "Yeah, Lance, Michael's dead, anyway."

Lance flashed him such an angry look that Ricky recoiled. "Exactly. He can't clear his name anymore."

Gibson cleared his throat. "Lance, if we announce that Michael was innocent of those attacks, that might frighten the public because they'll know the real culprit is still at large."

Lance's gaze never wavered. "Sergeant Gibson, I've learned a lot from my Dad these past couple of years and one of the most important things is that a man's good name is all he's got in life. I don't want Michael's reputation to be someone who was just a monster. I want it to be the truth. I owe him that much."

"I agree with my son," Arthur said, casting a look of pride Lance's way.

"Very well, Lance," Gibson said. "I'll tell Chief Murphy and the mayor to make a statement to the press, clear Michael's name."

Lance grinned for the first time since receiving the ominous text. "Thanks." He lost the grin as he turned to meet Ricky's eyes boring into him. His heart lurched at the sad, betrayed look on his face. He felt bad, but knew he'd done the right thing for Michael. He'd work it out with Ricky later, after the meeting ended.

"Okay," Gibson went on, "this is how it's got to be from here on out. This place is on lock-down status. I know those Kabbalogy folks are gonna be pissed, but so be it. No one enters this facility without a complete and thorough background check by us, just like before. No one will leave without armed police escort – either Sergeant Ryan or myself or one of the uniforms the chief will have patrolling the grounds. Justin." He turned to his son.

The tall African-American knight sat up straighter in his chair and focused on his father. "Yeah, Dad?"

"Get as many of the older knights as you can back on 24/7 patrol duty inside this house and grounds. Triple the numbers, if you can. I want every window and door on the ground floor checked at five minute intervals, and the outside gates at three."

"Yes, sir."

Gibson gave his son a grin of approval.

"What about the wedding, Sergeant?" Reyna asked anxiously, sitting on Esteban's lap, the two of them buried within an enormous stuffed chair.

Gibson turned to Arthur and Jenny. "Anybody coming who's not part of the Round Table already?"

"Uh, my friend Karla from school," Jenny said, leaning forward in her chair. "A couple of friends from the gym I used to go to. That's about all." Reyna nudged her. "Oh, and Reyna's parents."

"Father Mike and Pastor Tom," Lance added quickly.

Gibson digested this information. "That's it?"

"Yes," Arthur confirmed.

"As a precaution, we'll double the uniforms for the wedding," Ryan put in. "You should also hire a private security firm for the day, Arthur. I'll get clearance on a few agencies and let you know."

"Thank you, James."

The meeting wrapped up shortly after that, with Ryan, Gibson, and Justin setting off to establish their base of operations within a sector of the Computer Lab, and to begin mobilizing the needed patrols. In addition, Gibson would contact the FBI and have them send over the agents assigned to the San Francisco bombing to retrieve Lance's phone.

Reyna gave Lance and Ricky a hug each, and Esteban placed a thick, meaty hand on each boy's shoulder. "They want you, *carnales*, they gotta go through me." He grinned, and the boys returned it.

After they left, Arthur turned to Merlin, who'd sat attentively during the entire meeting without saying a word. "Any thoughts, old friend? Does your sight offer any answers?"

The ageless wizard sat pensively in his favorite stuffed armchair, clad in a

Metallica tee, with the ever-present ear buds dangling down the front of his shirt. "Alas, Arthur, I see very little ahead." Then he frowned, chewing his bottom lip absently.

"What?"

The wizard frowned. "But I sense deep sadness and loss."

Lance sucked in a breath.

Arthur looked grave. "Nothing more than that?"

Merlin's almost otherworldly features crinkled, and his pale gray eyes glossed over a moment in deep thought, and then he shook his head. "No."

"If you do see something, Merlin, would you tell me?"

Merlin's face went blank and expressionless, his eyes unreadable. "You know the answer to that, Arthur. I am not permitted to interfere, merely to advise as I see fit."

Arthur nodded sadly, flashed a tight smile at Jenny, and then both of them approached the boys.

Lance and Ricky stood to face their parents. Both boys were taller than Jenny, but still felt small and lightweight next to the towering Arthur.

"We will endure, my sons," Arthur said with conviction. "Many a man tried to take me down in the past, and all failed. And no one shall hurt my boys. No one." His eyes burned with anger, and love.

Impulsively, the boys leaned in and hugged him, Lance reaching out to pull Jenny in.

"I know, Dad," Lance said against the man's tunic. "And we got *your* back, too."

Later that night in Lance's room, Ricky lay sprawled out across Lance's bed, head once more atop Lance's lap, as Lance sat propped against his headboard. Both had been trying to study, but found they could not. The weight of the threat against them frayed their nerves, and they finally set down their textbooks and just lay there lost in thought.

Lance toyed with Ricky's thick strands of hair while Ricky held Lance's other hand and played with the long, slender fingers.

"I know you wanna talk about Michael."

Ricky released his hand. "No, I don't. Somebody's out to kill you and all you think about is Michael."

"Do you understand why I want his name cleared?"

Ricky sighed heavily, finally turning his eyes to meet those of Lance above him. "Yes, but..."

Lance frowned. "But what?"

Ricky sat up now, and Lance's lap felt almost lonely. "Am I gonna hafta compete with the ghosts of Michael and Jack for the rest of my life?"

Lance reached out and cupped his face, forcing their eyes to lock. "No. You're the one I love. The only one."

"For now and always?"

"For now and always."

He sealed the promise with a kiss.

The next week passed rapidly. Justin stepped up the patrols as ordered, uniformed LAPD officers patrolled the perimeter of New Camelot, and more protestors massed outside the front gates. Besides the Lance Cultists who believed he was the new messiah, there were also parents' rights groups protesting the CBOR, as well as anti-gay groups protesting Lance and Ricky with signs reading 'Gay Boys Burn in Hell' and 'Queers Can't Be Role Models for Our Kids!'

In addition, plans for the wedding also moved forward. Reyna pulled out all the stops, wanting it to be the biggest event of the decade. Jenny had to restrain the younger woman's excesses, lest the entire hotel be overrun with flowers and the kitchen staff overburdened with extreme demands.

More and more comments and suggestions came into their website and Facebook page about the CBOR, and Lance was especially pleased to get emails from Mark's dad in Washington and Jack's mom in Idaho pledging their support. Lance asked them to head up the creation of "Yes On CBOR" groups in their hometowns and both agreed.

The only big event that week prior to the wedding was the appearance of Lance and Ricky on The Ellen Show. Ellen had arranged to do a live broadcast and to fill the studio audience with teenagers so they could ask questions of the boys. Because the show would be live, word had gone out to every media outlet and billboards popped up throughout Los Angeles advertising the event. Unfortunately for Ryan and Gibson, this meant the taping would be a likely target for the person or persons stalking Lance. Security would have to match that of a presidential visit, if not surpass it.

The show was recorded on Stage 1 of the Warner Brothers Studio back lot in Burbank, and the day of the boys' appearance probably freaked out everyone who worked there. Cops with bomb sniffing dogs arrived to sweep the stage and surrounding areas. The entire soundstage was searched repeatedly from top to bottom, with officers standing guard all day checking on everyone who entered or left. They even recruited the television crewmembers to scour the area, including all rafters above the set for any defective or loose lighting fixture that could be potentially lethal should it fall.

Finally, the studio audience of one hundred fifty chattering, boisterous teens dressed in everything from ties and skirts to skin-tight jeans and muscle shirts filed into the seating area under the watchful eye of Ryan, Gibson and uniformed officers strategically placed at each entrance.

Lance and Ricky stood nervously off in the wings. They were dressed in their finest knightly tunics, pants and boots, with both sporting regal-looking circlets round their brows, long vibrant locks streaming down their backs like twin waterfalls.

They scanned the enormous set spread out before them – beautiful, gleaming reddish wood floor and walls, with plants scattered about and decorations on the walls. There was a table that looked like a slice of tree trunk surrounded by three enormous red chairs. The back wall was a huge flat-screen currently projecting the biggest image Lance had ever seen of himself and Ricky, taken the day they'd kissed in front of the entire world. This shot had them grinning broadly, hands clasped and raised triumphantly into the air. Lance nudged Ricky and pointed to the image. They giggled.

Esteban and Reyna hovered nearby, he with his sword and she with her bow and quiver of arrows. Their eyes scrutinized every crewman, even the camera operators, for any suspicious behavior.

Lance gave Esteban the chin nod as Ellen's assistant approached and told the boys the show would be starting in two minutes. Ellen would enter, do her opening routine, and then introduce them.

"Remember, boys, the show will be live," she admonished, sounding like an elementary school teacher. "There will be a five-second delay, but please no profanity." Then she walked away to speak to one of the camera operators.

Lance and Ricky exchanged a look. Profanity? When had they ever cussed on TV before? Reading his mind, as always, Ricky smirked. "She's probably thinking of when you screamed at them reporters in January."

Lance flushed red with embarrassment. He'd forgotten that less-than-princely moment. Then he grinned. "Yeah, but I'm not hung over this time, so when I do cuss, it'll be on purpose."

Ricky returned the grin and they shoved each other back and forth. Then Ellen's opening music came on and the assistant was back, shushing them. When her back was turned, Ricky stuck out his tongue and Lance had to clap a hand over his mouth to keep from busting up.

Ellen entered through the audience, singing and dancing her way up and down the aisles as the excited teens clapped and whooped. Once on stage, Ellen joked with the kids about them having ditched school for this live taping and how "*I* won't tell your parents if *you* don't." That got a big laugh from the crowd and Ellen mugged for the camera. "Oh, yeah, we're live. They probably already know. I'll let you all sneak out the back door just in case."

Another big laugh.

Lance was impressed. He didn't watch her show, but he'd been on before talking about Proposition 51, and she was good with the crowd, natural and easy-going. That's why he and Ricky agreed to this gig – they felt comfortable with Ellen, as all these other kids obviously did, too.

"And now, ladies and gentlemen and all of you out there in live TV land," Ellen said excitedly, "the moment everyone has anticipated for the past two weeks. I think we all saw the most famous kiss since Rhett Butler kissed Scarlet O'Hara—yes, kids, there *was* one more famous than Bella and Edward."

The audience laughed and clapped.

"So, without further delay, I present Sir Lance and Sir Ricky of King Arthur's Round Table. Let's give it up."

She waved her hands at the crowd and they burst into thunderous applause.

The assistant practically shoved Lance and Ricky forward, embarrassing them even further. Stepping out onto the burnished wood of the stage and into the bright klieg lights shining down on them from above, the boys were caught off guard by the crowd leaping to its collective feet and chanting their names.

"Long live Lance! Long live Ricky! Long live Lance! Long live Ricky!" Over and over they chanted as the applause grew to a frenzied pitch.

The boys waved shyly to the audience as they stepped toward Ellen and the waiting chairs. Normally, Lance didn't feel this nervous in front of a crowd anymore, but these were peers and the topic of conversation would be his personal life. That combination almost froze the breath in his lungs.

Ellen beamed, clapping and pointing at them as the crowd went wild with more applause. She shook each of their hands and invited them to sit. Lance ended up in the seat closest to Ellen, with Ricky on his right.

Ellen looked casual and relaxed in her off-white, corduroy pants suit, sneakers, V neck white shirt, and glittery necklace. "I have to tell you boys, that kiss, oh my God, I almost melted when I saw that."

The boys blushed, and the kids in the audience cheered loudly, prompting Ellen to encourage them.

"Am I right, was that a beautiful kiss or what?"

The audience cheered and whooped some more, and one girl's voice could be heard calling out, "Kiss me, Sir Lance!" causing another round of laughs and cheers.

Lance squirmed with discomfort. This was already embarrassing and they'd barely started!

"So, Sir Lance and Sir Ricky, can I just call you Lance and Ricky, is that okay?" Ellen went on in that ebullient, hyper-kinetic manner she often adopted.

The boys nodded simultaneously, and Ellen grinned. "Cool. Now, you two are a couple, correct?"

"Yes," Lance said.

Ellen made one of those dramatic faces she often did for the camera. "The last time I had you boys here, you were the adopted sons of King Arthur, and now you're, well, what should I call you, boyfriends?"

The boys exchanged a look, and Lance deferred to Ricky. "We like to say we're two parts of the same boy."

The audience went wild, clapping and cheering, and Ellen grinned. "I like that. It's poetic. But tell me, does it feel strange to go from brothers to two parts of the same boy?"

Lance smiled shyly. "To quote myself, Ellen, damn straight." That got another big laugh. "It's awkward," he went on gingerly. "Probably more for the rest of the family and the other knights. Though we found out later, it looks like they all kind of knew we were in love before we did." He blew out that nervous breathy laugh. "I mean, we are one spirit in two boys, but, yeah, it does take some getting used to."

Ellen accepted that answer. "So, would you now call yourselves gay?"

Lance pulled a face. "Me? Hell, no. Am I happy all the time, Ricky?"

Ricky shook his head. "Emo as hell, Ellen, this one."

Lance reached over and shoved the other boy. "Am not. I'm just a little moody."

Ricky grinned at Ellen and winked. "Emo. Trust me."

She laughed.

"What this fool is trying to say, Ellen, is I'm not happy all the time so I can't be gay. You happy all the time, Ricky?"

"With your emo-ass around, hell no!"

That drew another laugh from the crowd and another shove from Lance. Lance wished they could see the face of Ellen's assistant each time they cussed.

Ellen gazed at them with a smile, obviously wondering what they were up to. "After that kiss, though, you don't call yourselves straight, do you?"

Lance instantly rose to his feet and assumed a rigid posture. "Am I straight, Ricky?"

Ricky grinned at him. "Look straight to me, fool."

Lance slapped his arm. "No, fool, stand up and check my posture."

With a heavy sigh, Ricky stood and rolled his eyes. They'd rehearsed this part well.

Lance eyed him. "Okay, do I look crooked or deformed?"

Ricky ran his hand up Lance's rigid back. "Nope, straight as an arrow."

Lance relaxed. "Now you, fool. Stand straight."

As rehearsed, Ricky stood at military attention, his posture perfect. "Am I straight, fool?"

Lance grinned. "Damn straight."

Ricky cracked up, and the audience hooted with laughter and applause.

The boys resumed their seats. Before Ellen could say anything, Lance said, "Have I always been straight with you, Ellen? Told you the truth?"

Ellen pulled a confused face. "As far as I know."

"Thank you," Lance said with dramatic relief. "On the streets growing up we had an expression, *pura paja*, which means pure BS. On the streets that's pretty much all you get. But since I been with my dad, I try to be straight with everyone, and so does Ricky. I mean, I'm not perfect. You saw that this year. But, most of the time I'm straight with people. So to answer your earlier question, yes, we're both straight."

Now Ellen grinned even as the audience laughed and clapped some more. "I get it, Lance. You're playing with words."

"No, Ellen," Ricky said this time. "The country is playing with words. Our mom is an English teacher and she taught us the power of words."

Lance sighed. "I know the word 'gay' is the accepted term these days, but we don't want that label. And we aren't crooked or deformed, and we tell the truth, so it's an insult to say we're not straight."

"And what about 'queer'?" Ricky interrupted before Ellen could speak. "We got invited to something at the state capital next spring called 'Queer Youth Awareness Day'. Can you believe that? Politicians and grown-ups calling us queer? I admit, we're both kinda weird in our own way, but isn't everyone?"

Then Lance leaned in just as Ellen was about to open her mouth. "And what about 'tolerate'? Don't you just love that word, Ellen? Don't know about you, but I tolerate things that are annoying if I have to, but I don't want people *tolerating* me. I'm just like everyone else."

"And then there's 'acceptance'," Ricky said, jumping right in the second Lance finished. "Why should somebody 'accept' me? Aren't I a real person, just like they are? Isn't that putting me down by saying, oh, all right, I'll accept your ass? Hell, no!"

The boys fell breathlessly silent and the crowd went wild.

Ellen grinned broadly. "Now we know why these two are taking over the country."

The audience laughed and clapped some more, a few whistling enthusiastically.

"We'll be right back after these words from our sponsors," Ellen concluded, and clapped along with the audience.

When the camera lights went out, signaling a break in the filming, Ellen stared at the boys, and shook her head. "You guys are good, and I like your approach."

The boys high-fived each other.

There were a few calls from the audience for autographs and one boy called out, "Kiss each other, you guys!" The boys reddened simultaneously, causing Ellen to smile. She let them know she wanted to continue this discussion of words and labels when they resumed, and then she'd open up the floor to questions from the audience. They agreed, and the three chatted amiably while Ellen occasionally mugged for the studio audience.

When the producer's voice came over a loudspeaker saying "Five seconds to air," the boys settled back into their comfy seats as Ellen turned to look right into the camera.

"And we're back live with Sir Lance and Sir Ricky," Ellen began, tossing a smirk in the direction of the boys, "who were just giving us an English language lesson."

The audience laughed.

Ellen turned to the boys. "Okay, you made your point about those words, and now that you put it that way, most of them probably are inappropriate."

More applause and whistles.

"So tell me, then," Ellen went on, "would you call yourselves 'homosexual'?"

Lance and Ricky exchanged a look, and Ricky gestured for Lance to field that one.

"Well, let's see, that means 'likes the same sex'. Yes, I do like other boys, most of 'em, anyway, unless they're jerkbags. But I also like lots of girls, Ellen, like you and Reyna, so I guess I'm heterosexual, too, right?"

Ellen shook her head in amazement. "You two are something else. What are you trying to say here?"

"That these are all labels, Ellen," Lance went on soberly, all trace of banter gone from his voice, "and labels only do one thing – separate us from each other."

"Our mom told us," Ricky said, picking up the thread, "that when she was teaching in the public schools, every year she had to list how many black kids, how many brown, how many white, how many everything and turn that information over to the government. What difference does it make what color we are? Are they gonna start counting how many boys fall in love with boys next?"

Ellen looked mystified. "I didn't know that was done in schools."

"Well, it is," Lance went on almost breathlessly. "And all it does is put us kids into those little ice cube trays people keep in their freezers. Separates us, instead of bringing us together. We're all individuals, but we're more alike than we are different. I first learned that from skating, and then big time in the Round Table. The differences that matter are in our talents and abilities and ideas, not in superficial stuff like skin color or sexual orientation." He finally stopped, running out of breath.

Ricky grinned and shoved him playfully.

"Everybody wants to call us Latino, too," Ricky added, "but we're American, same as you. We were born here and we have more in common with our brothers in the Round Table than we do with kids in Mexico. So, what does the rest matter?"

Ellen threw up her hands. "Well, you've got me. If you don't want to be called Latino or gay or homosexual, what do you want to be called?"

Lance looked her right in the eye. "Human."

Ellen's face fell in shock, and the audience let loose with a thunderous roar of approval.

"Human, it is," Ellen said with a wink and turned to the audience. "How many of you out there would prefer to be called 'human' over the other labels people have for you?"

The "Yes!" from the crowd was deafening.

Ellen turned back to the boys. "Now I know why you have an anti-labeling amendment in your bill of rights."

That drew a chuckle from the boys.

"I understand," Ellen went on, "that you've gotten lots of offers from magazines for interviews and from various gay activist groups wanting you to support their causes. Is that right?"

Lance nodded. "Tons."

"Are you planning to get involved in any of them?"

The boys didn't even glance at one another before blurting simultaneously, "Hell, no!"

Ellen appeared visibly taken aback by their response and mugged again for the camera, a look that said, 'uh oh, I just opened a can of worms, didn't I?' She looked seriously at them. "Why not?"

Lance glanced at Ricky. "Hey, it's your turn, fool. I been doing all the talking."

"Okay, fool," Ricky replied, generating another laugh from the audience. "We're not gonna be anybody's poster boys, Ellen, for gay marriage or Queer Nation or GLA—what is that, fool?"

Lance tossed off a slight smirk. "GLAAD, fool."

"Yeah, that one, too," Ricky went on. "Those are probably all good groups, but see, our goal is to help *every* kid in this country, just like with our campaign here in Cali. We represent kids all over America and we're not gonna let anybody with group-think exploit us to make money or push their agenda, even if that agenda is good. We're not, period."

"Well said, fool," Lance said with a shove.

Ricky shoved him right back.

"I've heard that this show," Ellen went on, playing to the crowd, "is the only place you plan to discuss your relationship. Is that right?"

The audience cheered again.

When they quieted, Lance said, "Yeah, Ellen, 'cause we think you're cool." That got another rousing response from the crowd. "See, these magazines that wanna interview us, they wanna make us poster boys too. They wanna put us in that ice cube tray that's labeled 'gay' and leave us there. And worse, they wanna us posing with no shirts on."

Ellen wiggled her eyebrows. "I bet a lot of us here today would like to see that, wouldn't you?"

The crowd whooped and hollered and cheered.

Lance felt his face grow hot. "You're doing the same thing, Ellen, joking about turning underage boys into sex objects for disgusting adults to drool over and stuff. It's nasty. People call us nasty or sick 'cause we're two boys in love, but those adults, male or female, who wanna have sex with boys our age or get turned on by boys our age, they're the sick ones. Ricky and me've had way too much experience with perverts like that!"

Ricky placed a calming hand on his arm. Lance flicked his gaze over. Ricky gave him the 'look,' and Lance calmed down.

Slightly taken aback by the response, Ellen took that moment to announce another commercial break, and when the cameras shut off she turned apologetically to Lance. "I'm sorry, Lance, I didn't mean anything. It was just a stupid joke."

Lance's thumping heart began slowing. "I know. But selling kids as sex objects to grown-ups isn't a joke, Ellen."

"You're right. I apologize."

She spent the rest of the commercial break prepping the audience to ask questions of the boys, admonishing them to keep the questions clean and not too personal.

Within a few minutes, the producer signaled the resumption of the show, and Ellen looked directly into the camera.

"Before we open up the floor to questions from our studio audience, I wish to apologize publicly to Lance and Ricky for my previous joke. They are correct – any media outlet that markets minors as sex objects is deplorable, and adults who lust after minors need serious help. These boys have had more than their fair share of traumatic experiences in that area, as most of you no doubt know. So please accept my apology."

Lance and Ricky nodded, and the audience clapped loudly.

Ellen turned to the boys. "You guys ready to take on our teen audience?"

Lance grinned. "Bring it on."

"Anybody with a question for our guests?"

Every hand flew into the air, waving frantically.

Ellen pointed to a boy near the front.

The excited teen, with pink hair and several facial piercings, almost squealed with delight. "Are you guys, you know, having sex yet?"

Ricky's face collapsed into shock.

"Of course not," Lance exclaimed, burning with embarrassment.

Ellen held up a hand. "Just a minute, Lance." She turned to the pink-haired boy. "I told you no personal questions like that. It's none of your business."

Recovering from his initial surprise, Lance said, "It's okay, Ellen, I'll answer him." He glanced momentarily to Ricky, who gave him that look again. Suffused with warmth and calm, Lance studied the eager questioner. "How old are you?"

The boy stood, trying to look bigger than his slight frame permitted. "Fifteen."

"Are you a grown-up yet?"

"Almost."

"'Almost' doesn't cut it," Lance said with authority. "We just spent a year here in Cali getting childhood back for kids like us, for everyone under eighteen, and you wanna go pretend you're grown up and have sex? What other adult stuff are you ready for? Paying bills and working full time and raising a family? I've learned the hard way that childhood is the shortest part of our lives and it's over real quick. Ricky and me barely got two years left. We wanna stay kids till we hafta be adults. Does that answer your question?"

The boy looked puzzled. "No. I mean, if you're in love, you're supposed to have sex, right?"

Lance sighed, exchanging a quick glance with Ricky.

"Ricky and me *are* in love. For now and always. And we have our whole lives to explore sex. For now, we're just loving being in love. That's what you should explore too. I know kids our age all wanna jump right into sex, but what good is that without love? I've had plenty of sex without love. Ricky too. And it sucks, let me tell you. Do yourself a favor, kid, find somebody who loves you that you can love back. Learn love first, and save the sex for later. That's my opinion, anyway."

Ricky leaned forward. "Do you wanna know what's the sexiest thing this fool does for me?"

The pink-haired boy nodded expectantly.

Ricky held out his hand to Lance. Smiling lovingly, Lance took it, intertwining their fingers.

"This," Ricky finished, almost breathless with excitement. "I could hold this boy's hand all day, every day. His hand fits perfectly in mine. Try it with someone you love, and maybe you'll understand just how amazing that can be."

The audience roared its approval, and Lance and Ricky released each other's hand to await the next question.

More kids waved their hands and Ellen pointed to a girl with short hair wearing overalls and a t-shirt that said, 'Being Gay isn't a choice, but being a bigot is'.

"Is one of you more feminine than the other?" the girl asked, her voice strong and deep.

Lance and Ricky exchanged a 'wth' look, and Ricky indicated that Lance could take this one.

Looking at the girl and feeling the beginnings of anger, Lance fought for control. "What is it with people wanting one or both of us to be feminine? We been seeing that on the Internet, too. Both of us are boys, okay? We may have long hair, but there's nothing female about either one of us. Back in the day growing up, I'd punch out anybody who called me a girl. And I can still kick anybody's ass who says it now. So can Ricky. But that's not what a real man does. We learned that from our dad. A real man stands up for what's right, not what's easy. A real man has honor and integrity. That's the kind of man I wanna be."

"Me, too," Ricky echoed with passion.

Lance looked out at the expectant teens. "If it makes any of you out there feel better about yourselves to pretend one of us is feminine, go for it. We know who we are. We don't call each other baby or honey or stuff like that. I call him fool and dumbass 'cause that's who he is."

The audience laughed.

"And I call him fool and dumber-ass, 'cause that's who *he* is," Ricky added with a grin.

He and Lance did the fist bump, while Ellen and the audience laughed again.

"So to answer your question," Lance concluded, "Ricky and me are pure boy all the way."

The girl smiled and sat down while the other teens, especially the boys, whooped and cheered.

Ellen signaled to another girl, holding hands with the girl next to her. She leapt to her feet excitedly, yanking her apparent girlfriend up with her.

"I can't believe I'm getting to talk to you guys. Oh, God, this is so exciting." She fanned her face frantically with her hand, like she might faint if she didn't.

Ellen and the boys laughed.

"Okay," the girl went on, "what's your opinion on same sex couples having children?"

Lance and Ricky were momentarily taken aback by the question. They'd discussed this issue prior to the show, but only because they thought Ellen might ask it, not one of the kids. As previously agreed, Lance leaned forward to answer.

"You know what? My opinion on that is the same as it is for every couple, no matter their orientation. I wish people who can't have kids without some kind of Frankenstein-laboratory stuff, would just adopt someone like me." His voice became wistful and quiet, almost introspective. "There are *so* many kids out there whose parents don't want them, but if they're in the system, or the birth mom was a drug addict, or they're not babies or cute-ass little toddlers, nobody else wants 'em, either."

He looked out at the silent girl with as much sincerity as he could muster, while struggling to douse the old pain rising to the surface.

"I would've killed to have been adopted by two ladies or two guys who loved me and wanted me. But all I got was the system, and it sucked." He exchanged a quick look with Ricky. "Someday we're gonna adopt kids like me, older ones nobody else wants. Cause we don't care if the kid looks like us or has our blood in him. That's not important. Love and family are. When I was little and praying every day that someone would adopt me, I used to think people wanted kids so they could do right by their kids, but now I know that's not always true. Sometimes, they just want somebody who looks like them. Over these past two years, we learned from Arthur and Jenny what being good parents means, so yeah, we'll adopt kids someday. No Frankenstein stuff for us. Does that answer your question?"

The girl nodded solemnly, looking like she was about to cry. Her girlfriend grabbed her hand and pulled her down, throwing an arm across her shoulders.

Ellen pointed to yet another boy way in the back. He stood and Lance could just make out glasses and a polo shirt of some kind.

"Are you proud to be gay, or whatever you want to call yourselves?" the boy challenged, sounding haughty despite his mousy appearance.

Again, Ricky deferred to Lance, who shoved him playfully. "Fool, I'm gonna get you for making me do all the talking."

"Gotta catch me first."

That drew a laugh from Ellen and the crowd.

Lance squinted out at the boy in back, attempting to make eye contact, but the stage lights and shadows made that impossible. "I'm proud of what I accomplished here in California with our proposition and how we convinced the adults to give us our childhood back. Ricky is, too, 'cept this fool is too dumbass to talk good on TV."

Another laugh followed and Ricky shoved Lance again.

Ellen looked positively charmed by their antics.

"I'm proud of my skating," Lance went on, "'cause I worked hard and I kick butt on a board. I'm proud of my archery skills and ability with a sword. These are things I worked for, so yeah, they make me feel proud. Am I proud to be in love with this fool?" He shoved Ricky and flashed him a sly grin. "No, 'cause there's nothing to be proud of. I'm blessed that he loves me and that I found this most amazing boy in the world. All joking aside, he's amazing."

He glanced at Ricky and saw him look down in embarrassment.

"But am I proud that inside me I'm meant to love another boy? No, 'cause I didn't choose that. Everybody tells me I have such cool eyes and amazing hair. That's nice, but I'm not proud of those things, either. They're just part of how I was born, same as my being able to fall in love with Ricky. I learned in juvenile hall that I'm exactly what God had in mind when He made me. But I also learned that I'm God's gift to the world, and what I make of myself down here is my gift to God. It's also my gift to other people. I'm a warrior of right and a warrior of light. And I'm proud of myself that I made those choices."

"Me too," Ricky said with a grin toward Lance. "So don't go looking for us in any parades because our goal is to help *all* kids and not put ourselves into ice cube trays. We're done with that. We're the Round Table, and the Round Table is for everyone."

Lance turned to Ellen. "See, once in a while this fool says something useful."

Ricky shoved Lance. "Fool."

The boys laughed and Ellen grinned broadly.

The remainder of the hour flew by with more questions and answers. Once the cameras ceased rolling, Lance and Ricky chatted some more with the audience and signed autographs. Some of the kids expressed interest in joining the Round Table, and Lance passed out Arthur's business card. Ellen hugged both boys and invited them back any time they wanted. She also thanked them for giving her and all of America something to think about, and vowed to support their Children's Bill of Rights. Lance promised to keep in touch on their progress.

Reyna hugged them and Esteban grinned, shaking his head at their performance. Ryan and Gibson were just relieved to have the whole thing over without incident, and quickly led the group out to their cars.

Jenny and Arthur gushed over the boys' performance upon their return home, and after dinner that night Jenny insisted they watch the show on the DVR. She assured them they would be on TV many more times during the course of this political campaign, so they needed to see themselves as others saw them.

The boys joked around and laughed at themselves on the big Throne Room flatscreen, but Jenny didn't need to point out the moment Lance nearly lost his temper. He spotted that right away and realized how close he'd come to making himself and Ricky look bad, promising both parents that he would not allow anyone to rattle him in the future.

The next few days were devoted to wedding preparations. Reyna recruited the boys to move this planter or that flower arrangement. The back gardens were already picture-perfect, but Reyna had wanted the stage area looking more festive, so she ordered a moveable arch made of roses under which Arthur and Jenny would exchange their vows.

Of course, Reyna had also helped pick out the wedding dress with Jenny, and when it arrived that Friday she refused to even allow Lance and Ricky to see it, saying it was bad luck for men to see the gown ahead of time, even men who weren't the groom. Since this was a Round Table wedding, no formal tuxes were ordered – Esteban and the grooms would wear their finest tunics and pants, and Arthur his kingly accoutrements.

The wedding was scheduled for noon the following day. Of the media, only Helen and two cameramen were given clearance to film the proceedings. However, there was such anticipation from the public that Channel 7 agreed to allow other networks and stations to tap into their live feed, which meant every station would be covering the wedding to some extent. The event was likened to the royal weddings of Charles and Diana and William and Kate, and was expected to draw even larger ratings.

Saturday morning dawned early for everyone, and the knights began trickling in around nine, with other invited guests arriving a bit later. Everyone milled about the expansive gardens waiting for the event to begin. The weather was crisp and clear for November with the sun shining and the temperature hovering at 68°. Lance spotted Jenny's teacher friend, Karla, from Mark Twain, all decked out in a long black gown, high-heeled shoes and a hairstyle like something out of a music video.

Of course, Reyna was nowhere to be found because she'd gone up to get Jenny ready. Esteban looked dashing in his striking blue tunic, leather pants and boots, sword strapped to his waist. His hair had even been styled and when Lance laughingly commented on its "road kill" look, Esteban grimaced and assured him it had been "Reyna's idea."

Lance and Ricky both laughed, feeling grateful that Reyna had been so caught up with Jenny and Esteban that she'd never gotten around to "Making them look presentable," as she'd promised. Of course, they'd hidden themselves every time they'd heard her voice, so that also contributed to their 'natural' look for the event.

The boys had seen to dressing up Chris for the occasion, and giving him a small circlet of his own to restrain his flowing blond hair. Reyna had hinted earlier in the week about getting it cut, but Chris had hidden away with Lance and Ricky every time he'd heard her calling. Chris loved his hair and had no intention of cutting it until it dragged on the floor.

As Lance adjusted the circlet, he suddenly realized that Chris had gotten taller, and momentarily felt guilty that he hadn't noticed. "Man, you've grown a lot this year, Chris."

Ricky heartily agreed.

Chris beamed, like he'd known all along this would happen. "I promised Jack I'd be a big, buff football player like him one day, and I will."

As always, the mention of Jack's name caused a lump to form in Lance's throat, and he couldn't reply for a second. But Ricky was there, rock solid and steady with a hand on his arm to soothe him. And it worked. Flicking him a grateful grin, Lance eyed the smiling Chris appraisingly. "I have no doubt, little man."

Ricky handed Chris the coveted ring-bearer's pillow upon which he would carry up their mother and father's rings. The little boy clutched it to his chest as though daring anyone to take it away. Then the three of them descended the grand staircase to the lobby.

Lance was thrilled to find Father Mike chatting with Pastor Tom and hurried over to them. Lance shook Pastor Tom's hand, but fixed his gaze on the taller, white-haired Catholic priest with genuine affection.

"Reverend," Father Mike said, offering that impish grin Lance so loved.

Lance hugged him warmly and then the juvenile hall chaplain greeted Ricky and Chris with the same appellation.

"I'm not a reverend," Chris insisted politely. "I'm the ring-bearer."

Father Mike laughed, and Lance led them out to the back gardens to show them the outdoor stage—brightly decorated with flower stands—and the rose-covered archway for the ceremony. The priest and the minister thanked Lance, and the two boys headed back into the lobby.

Lance stopped suddenly and Ricky plowed right into him.

"Hey, fool watch where you're going," Ricky admonished with a playful shove. Then he gasped.

Standing with Darnell and Tai, the towering Samoan knight, were Bridget and Ariel, dressed to kill in long, frilly dresses, their hair styled as though for prom, chatting animatedly with Justin and Techie.

Lance's mouth dropped open in shock, and he looked at Ricky, whose face revealed an equal amount of surprise. Bridget looked over at that moment, met Lance's eyes, and smiled.

Feeling weak in the knees, Lance gulped and then crossed the crowded lobby to the small group. Everyone fell into an awkward silence.

"Uh, hi," Lance said, and Ricky nodded his hello.

The girls shyly exchanged a look, but seemed unsure of what to say.

Justin cleared his throat self-consciously. "I invited Bridget, Lance."

Techie, looking sharp in his fancy tunic, hair combed and moussed, grinned sheepishly. "And I invited Ariel."

Tall and imposing Justin, who'd not so long ago thought himself a bad ass gangster and drug dealer, suddenly looked small and timid, despite his height advantage over Lance. "We, uh, we didn't think you'd mind."

Lance and Ricky exchanged a quick look, and grinned broadly.

"We don't mind at all," Lance said. "You look great, Bridg."

"You, too."

"And you look good, too, Ariel," Ricky added as the girl bashfully waited for his greeting.

"Thanks," she said quietly, glancing at Techie beside her.

The computer whiz grinned more broadly than Lance had ever seen.

There was a moment of uncomfortable silence until Tai piped up with, "Where's the food, anyway?"

Everyone busted up and the awkwardness ended.

"Have a great time guys," Lance said with a warm smile, and then he and Ricky wandered the lobby, welcoming other attendees. They spotted Reyna's parents and greeted them in passing. Lance noted her father's wary eye squinting at the two of them, looking like he expected them to do 'something gay', but the man said nothing and moved on.

The time was nearly noon, and Arthur had not put in an appearance.

"Think maybe he's nervous?" Ricky asked, eyeing the empty staircase.

"Dad?" Lance scoffed. "Hell, no!"

Just then Esteban appeared at the top of the stairs and descended to join them.

"Where's Dad?" Lance asked.

Esteban shrugged, touching his own moussed and wavy hair absently. "Probably still playing with his hair and crown. Man, Lance, I never seen him so nervous."

Lance and Ricky cracked up.

Everyone milling in the lobby suddenly ceased their chatter, and all heads turned toward the top of the grand staircase. There Arthur stood, looking more kingly and majestic than Lance had ever seen him. He wore a soft purple tunic with ruffles around the collar and sleeves, his finest light brown brushed leather pants, leather boots with a jeweled fringe around the top, thick brocaded scarlet cloak draping his shoulders, and atop his smooth, wavy brown hair sat his formal crown, glittery and adorned with jewels and gold. Excalibur, as always, dangled in its sheath from his sword belt.

Lance stood mesmerized as the man slowly descended the staircase looking like something out of a movie. The expression 'awe-inspiring' took on a whole new meaning. Everyone watched as Arthur approached his sons and best man. He stopped, and grinned nervously.

"How do I look?" His voice, normally strong and confident, sounded almost small and timid.

Lance grinned. "You look amazing, Dad!"

Ricky, Chris and Esteban heartily agreed.

Father Mike approached with a smile. "You look impressive, reverend," he offered, which drew a smile to Arthur's bearded lips. They shook hands and lanky, Ichabod Crane-like Pastor Tom joined them.

"Shall we begin?" the pastor asked, and Arthur agreed.

Once everyone had gathered in the gardens, Father Mike and Pastor Tom stepped through the rose-garlanded arch and stood to one side. Next, Ricky passed through and took up a position to the other side. He was followed by Lance, and then Esteban, who stood closest to the arch. After a moment, Arthur stepped through and bowed to the crowd before moving to Esteban's side. The best man shook the king's hand, and then nodded to the DJ seated off to one side.

The wedding march began playing, and all heads turned toward the huge beveled-glass double doors leading into the hotel.

Lance scanned the massive throng of formally attired knights spread out amongst the ornate topiary and flora of the garden, suddenly realizing that, other than sneaking through here to meet Michael, he'd never spent any time at all in this garden. And it was beautiful.

He watched as Sylvia appeared, dressed in her soft pink tunic, standard pants and boots, bow and quiver of arrows attached to her back. Her hair had been styled, by Reyna, no doubt. Long and dark black, it had been pulled up into an almost tiered look in back with a light dusting of bangs across her forehead. She carried a large basket of roses and tossed them one by one onto the ground along either side of the red carpet that had been laid across the expansive garden.

Chris stepped out onto the carpet, looking princely and proper and cute. Or so Lance thought, nudging Ricky and nodding toward their little brother. Chris's posture was perfect as he held out the fancy lace pillow upon which sat two glittery gold bands, and proceeded up to the stage. Sylvia stepped up and moved to the left. Chris climbed the three small steps and stood beside Esteban.

Lance and Ricky focused their eyes on the double doors just as Reyna stepped through. His sister, always beautiful and striking with her wide smile and high cheekbones, looked more stunning than ever. She wore a sleek-fitting silvery tunic that accentuated her curves, tighter-than-normal brushed leather pants, and the knee-high boots. Her face appeared especially radiant, and her long, resplendent hair was done up in a bun with small sections appearing to fall outward like the streams of a fountain. Her own longbow and quiver hung easily across her back as though permanently attached.

Lance glanced at Esteban and grinned. His big brother's face had nearly collapsed with awe, and Lance understood the feeling.

Reyna slowly worked her way up the aisle and ascended the three steps. She blew a kiss at Esteban and Lance heard him suck in a breath. For a split second he saw the Esteban of old, the gangbanger who'd once tried kicking his ass to impress Reyna, and ended up humiliating himself in the process. Now, standing and gaping openmouthed at Reyna's beauty, Esteban obviously no longer cared what anyone thought.

Lance suddenly heard a collective murmur from the crowd and turned back toward the hotel. He gasped, and heard a similar sound from Ricky beside him. Jenny had entered the garden, one arm linked through Sam's. Sam was dressed in a loud suit and even louder tie, with a Scottish sash draped across his chest from left shoulder to waist.

But Jenny looked breathtaking. She wore a long white dress with a train that had to be six feet long. The bodice was cut in a V, but a modest cut, with the shoulders and long sleeves made of some filigreed see-through material revealing her tanned skin underneath. She wore dangly diamond earrings and a long white veil, the top of which was highlighted by a glittering silver and diamond tiara keeping her long blonde hair from falling onto her luminous face. She carried a bouquet of lily-of-the-valley, and Lance had never seen her look so happy.

He nudged Ricky and they exchanged a look. Amazement blanketed both their faces as they watched their mother slowly move up the aisle to countless cameras snapping her picture. Lance finally spotted Helen, looking dressed to kill, he thought, in her own slinky dress, slightly off to the side. Charlie, her cameraman, he knew, was filming from an upstairs window to cover everything from above, while another camera operator hovered behind the arch to capture the ceremony in close-up.

As Sam led Jenny carefully up the three steps, taking care not to step on her train, she glanced over at the boys and grinned. They grinned right back. Reyna hurried over to lightly lift the rest of the train up the steps and lay it out behind Jenny as Sam led her to Arthur. The blustery Scotsman, all smiles and pomp, took Jenny's hand and extended it to Arthur, who reached out to take it. Sam stepped back and retreated down the steps as Reyna moved in to take Jenny's bouquet from her hand.

Then the couple-to-be turned to the grinning faces of Father Mike and Pastor Tom, both dressed in their traditional white collars and clerical vestments. The music drew to a close and a hush fell over the crowd. There was a gentle breeze that wafted Arthur and Jenny's hair, mixing it together as though urging them to hurry up and make their bond permanent.

"Welcome everyone, to the wedding of the last fifteen centuries," Father Mike began with a grin, and the crowd laughed.

Arthur and Jenny seemed to have eyes only for each other, and appeared to miss the reverend's joke.

"It is my distinct pleasure, along with my colleague of the cloth here, the Reverend Tom, to join these two remarkable people in holy matrimony, a marriage that spans the centuries to bring these two individuals, so made for each other, together at long last."

"Before we have the happy couple repeat the traditional vows of commitment, Arthur and Jenny have written their own commitment promises they wish to exchange at this time," Pastor Tom said with a wide smile stretching the already tight skin of his skeletal face.

Arthur looked into Jenny's soft blue eyes, looking vulnerable and helpless. "My dearest Jenny," he began, his deep voice carried by the lapel mic up and out over the expectant crowd. "I have waited two lifetimes for this moment."

She grinned with delight, and the crowd laughed.

"From the moment I laid eyes upon you, milady, my heart belonged to you as it had to no other woman. I knew then, as I know now, that, to quote our amazing sons, you are the keeper of my heart, for now and always, and I love you more than it may be possible to love."

He smiled then, almost timidly.

Watching from the side, Lance's heart beat wildly to hear his father quote the phrase he and Ricky so often used, and he glanced at his other half beside him. The love reflected back in those soft brown eyes nearly made him faint.

Jenny looked up into Arthur's face, and beamed. "My dearest Arthur, until I met you, I never knew a lady could fall in love watching a man topple off a skateboard."

Laughter drifted through the crowd, and Arthur grinned.

"But fall I did," she went on softly, her voice breathy and excited. "I saw in that moment your love for Lance, your compassion and your goodness and, being the smart, gifted, well-educated, strong woman that I am, I ignored my feelings because I was a fool."

That comment elicited more laugher.

Jenny flashed a radiant smile. "I love you, Arthur, and however much time we have together, I want to spend every moment of it with you."

A sudden chill slithered up Lance's back. What did she mean by that? *However much time we have?*

Father Mike turned to Chris. "The rings, if you please."

Chris proudly held the white cushion out to Esteban who smiled and took both rings in his hand. With a wide grin, he passed one to Arthur and the other to Jenny.

Father Mike looked to Arthur with a twinkle in his eyes. "Do you, Arthur, take Jenny as your lawful wedded wife, to have and to hold, in sickness and in health, for richer, for poorer, to love and to cherish according to God's holy law till death do you part?"

Arthur locked eyes with Jenny. "I do."

"Do you, Jenny," Pastor Tom intoned, "take Arthur as your lawful wedded husband, to have and to hold, in sickness and in health, for richer, for poorer, to love and to cherish according to God's holy law till death do you part?"

She smiled, and her face lit up like sunlight. "I do."

Father Mike nodded to Arthur, who lifted Jenny's left hand and held her gold band between his thumb and forefinger. "With this ring I thee wed, with my body I thee worship, and with all my worldly goods I thee endow, in the name of the Father, and of the Son, and of the Holy Ghost." He slipped the ring onto her finger.

Grinning, Pastor Tom turned to Jenny. She lifted Arthur's left hand and held the other gold band in her right. "With this ring I thee wed, with my body I thee worship, and with all my worldly goods I thee endow, in the name of the Father, and of the Son, and of the Holy Ghost." She slipped the band onto his finger, shaking slightly and giggling.

Father Mike and Pastor Tom exchanged a glance, and then simultaneously said, "We now pronounce you husband and wife."

Father Mike nudged Arthur, who stood as though disbelieving that this moment had finally arrived. "You may kiss the bride, Arthur."

There were chuckles from the crowd.

Arthur bent down to Jenny and their lips met. Both of them looked like they'd been born anew, and reluctantly separated.

"I present to you Mr. and Mrs. Arthur Pendragon," Father Mike announced, as the newlyweds turned to face the throng. The crowd erupted into thunderous applause and foot stomping. Since the majority of onlookers were teens, the reaction was heartfelt and powerful, for they deeply loved both of these adults who had given each and every one of them more than anyone else ever had.

At this point, Esteban reluctantly stepped back and took the microphone from the DJ behind them, and cleared his throat into it. "Uh, there's food gonna be served so why not find a table and sit while the, uh, the bridal party gets pictures taken in one of the other gardens. Okay?"

Justin and Darnell, standing just in front of the stage, saluted smartly and grinned. "Yes, sir!" Then they laughed and fist-bumped, drawing a grin from Esteban to cover his awkwardness.

As the crowd fanned out to the surrounding tables, Esteban turned to find Reyna by his side, grinning with giddy joy. Impulsively, he leaned in and kissed her. Laughing, she took his arm and directed everyone through the arch and off the stage to the spot she'd selected for the official wedding pictures.

The photo session seemed to go on forever, making Chris nearly frantic with boredom and forcing Lance or Ricky to continually chase the boy down and drag him back for "Just one more." The photographer posed the family in every conceivable grouping and position, with even Lance and Ricky fidgeting from the tedium.

Lance noted that Sylvia, looking lovely in her pink tunic that contrasted sharply with her light brown skin, seemed to be eyeing Arthur whenever the photographer changed a setup and the group milled about. It occurred to him that maybe she was thinking about Lavern, since she had been sweet on the boy. Thinking of that awesome kid, murdered by the psycho still stalking him made Lance's blood boil. He had to force calm back into his veins, especially as Chris tried to sneak away again and he had to make a grab for the boy.

At one point, while the photographer was rearranging Jenny's dress just so, Lance whispered into Ricky's ear, "We're gonna elope and skip all this stuff," causing Ricky to look at him in open-mouthed astonishment. Lance leaned in for a quick kiss.

Finally, the photos ended and everyone headed back to the main reception area. The boys, Reyna and Esteban, all sat with Arthur, Jenny, Merlin, Sam, Father Mike and Pastor Tom at a large, and appropriately round, table. The hotel kitchen staff had prepared a full-course dinner, even though it was only lunchtime. There were soups and salads, braised lamb shanks and Yorkshire puddings. There was wine and ale for the adults and all manner of ciders and soft drinks for the youth.

Just prior to eating, Reyna nudged Esteban to remind him about the toast. As always when addressing a group, even just family as right now, Esteban rose timidly and, belying his muscular physique, appeared small and uneasy. He held out a goblet of cider and tapped the glass with his spoon to get everyone's attention. Then he looked straight at Arthur and Jenny. Arthur's bearded face shone with pride and joy.

"I toast this man on his wedding day, this man who made *me* a man," Esteban began, pausing to marshal his emotions. "He took an arrogant, knucklehead kid and showed him what it means to be a man, what it means to be a father. This man *is* my father, and who he's made me, I will pass on to my own sons one day." He raised his glass and everyone at the table did the same. "To Arthur, the greatest man I will ever know, and his amazing bride Jenny. Godspeed on your new life together. "

"Here, here," went around the table as everyone clinked glasses.

Arthur met Esteban's eye as they clinked, grinning with gratitude. Esteban grinned right back.

After eating, Arthur and Jenny wended their way between the various tables, chatting with knights and guests, greeting and thanking each of them for attending. As their sons, Lance, Ricky, and Chris did the same.

After everyone had eaten, Reyna tracked down Lance and Ricky and told them it was time for the first dance. She and Jenny had selected all the music, and Jenny had chosen a particularly romantic ballad for the first dance.

She dragged Esteban by the hand up the steps and onto the stage. The arch had been removed during lunch and the area in front of the stage cleared of the red carpet in preparation for dancing. Reyna took the microphone from the DJ, who'd been playing music throughout the meal, and stepped out front.

"We hope everyone is having a great time," she called out exuberantly.

A loud cheer rose up and filled the gardens like an explosion.

"If I could have the bride and groom come forward – it's time for their first dance as husband and wife." She beamed broadly as Arthur and Jenny made their way through the tables to stop just in front of the stage, Jenny holding her train in one hand. Both grinned happily up at the girl.

Reyna signaled the DJ, and she pulled Esteban off the stage. The soulful and touching "Little Things," a song by One Direction that Jenny loved, poured forth from the speakers. It was a slow song that Arthur and Jenny easily slipped into, his arms around her waist, hers on his shoulders. They moved gracefully, their faces alight with love, seeing nothing but each other.

Lance listened to the lyrics about how it's the little things we cherish most about the one we love, and realized how much it applied to he and Ricky too. After a few moments, Reyna took Esteban in her arms and waltzed him out onto the dance floor, their bodies pressed together as they slowly moved to the achingly heartfelt ballad.

Lance and Ricky exchanged a look, and then Lance smiled, extending his hand. Ricky took it shyly and they joined the others on the dance floor. His hands on Ricky's waist, Ricky's arms wrapped tightly around his neck, their bodies pressed together, Lance eased into the closeness the song inspired with its simple message of love. Lyrics about how one person's hand fits within the other's like it was made just for him swamped his heart with tenderness, and spoke directly to his feelings for this amazing boy in his arms.

They pressed into one another, heart beating against heart, one spirit in two boys, and smiled lovingly as their parents swept past them on the dance floor. In one another's arms, nothing seemed important anymore – not the Children's Bill of

Rights or even the death threats against them. Lance knew he could do everything and survive anything so long as this boy, and all the little things he cherished about him, remained by his side and loved him back.

The dance ended and everyone applauded. Then the DJ segued into some lively dance songs, and more wedding guests joined them on the floor. Lance and Ricky laughed as Arthur tried to keep up with the rock music, flapping his arms and kicking out with his legs. They knew their dad was clowning and that made it all the better. They clowned, too, flopping around and knowing they were both lousy dancers, but laughing with delight nonetheless.

For Lance and Ricky, as well as for Reyna and Esteban, it was the slow dances they treasured. Both couples would simply disappear into their dance partners, becoming a single unit, relishing the love they shared. Sometimes Lance and Ricky had their arms wrapped around each other's necks, their foreheads touching, their eyes lost within the other's. Sometimes they kissed, as sometimes Reyna and Esteban kissed. Girl melted into boy and boy melted into boy, and love reigned supreme.

The remainder of the wedding flew past with more dancing, the cake cutting and, of course, the throwing of the bouquet. To no one's surprise, Reyna, who'd muscled her way to the front, caught Jenny's tossed flowers like a professional football player. That generated lots of backslapping from all of the guys for an embarrassed Esteban.

Ryan and Gibson, while technically on duty, also had fun and relaxed as the day wore on. Lance learned from Justin that his dad had brought his mom as a date, and that maybe they might get back together. The big, intimidating boy looked so childlike when he'd said it that Lance felt emotion clog his throat. Arthur had a gift; there was no doubt about that. He seemed to bring people together, even people who swore they never could be.

While Merlin had sat at the wedding party table, he'd spoken little except to congratulate Arthur and Jenny, and refused to be part of any photos. Mostly, he and Sam chatted about Britain and Scotland. As always, the wizard appeared to feel that remaining as invisible as possible was the best course of action.

All told, the Wedding of the Ages, as the media later dubbed it, was a resounding success, and the happiest day thus far in the lives of Arthur, Jenny, and their boys.

Later that night, after Arthur and Jenny retired to a seventh floor room for an uninterrupted wedding night, Lance and Ricky sat facing each other on Lance's bed, wearing t-shirts and workout shorts, relishing the presence of the other. Ricky traced the lines of Lance's palm with his fingertips, while Lance absently fingered strands of Ricky's hair.

"That song, Ricky, the first one we danced to?"

Ricky smiled.

"That's how I feel about you," both said at the same time. Then they laughed.

"Even that," Lance said with sigh, "how we know each other's thoughts. I love everything about you, Ricky."

"I love everything about you too."

They rested their foreheads against one another, green eyes locked on brown.

"Did you mean what you said, Lance," Ricky whispered, almost without breath. "About eloping?"

"Hell, no."

Ricky frowned and pulled away. "Huh?"

Lance's grin grew so wide it split his face. "When I marry your fool ass, I want the whole world there."

Ricky grinned, lighting up his face with pure joy, and setting Lance's heart aflutter.

"What makes you think I'd ever marry a dumbass like you?" Ricky asked with a tender smirk.

Lance chuckled. "Maybe 'cause you love every little thing about me?"

"Well, there's that."

They kissed.

Arthur and Jenny did not appear until dinnertime on Sunday, which caused the kids, including Reyna and Esteban, to snigger with amusement, especially at how radiant both looked when they finally came downstairs. While they had seemed older during the past few months, especially with all of Lance's personal drama, this night they looked younger and more vibrant than ever. For Lance, seeing the fulfillment of a real relationship based on love and commitment convinced him that his and Ricky's decision to move slowly was the right one.

CHAPTER FOUR
CAN'T YOU GUYS STOP THEM?

THE NEXT FEW DAYS PASSED quickly as the family prepared for Thanksgiving. This would be their second Thanksgiving at New Camelot, but Arthur and Jenny's first as husband and wife. Jenny had already sent in the paperwork to Judge Baker of Children and Family Court to legally adopt the three boys, and the granting of that request was a mere formality, most likely to come within two months.

Jenny also made it a point to buy Lance another Galaxy smartphone to replace the one Ryan had given to the FBI. As of yet, the old one hadn't been returned, and the IT guys who worked for the bureau had been unable to trace the source of the threat.

Justin and Techie had cornered Lance and Ricky at school that Monday morning to rather nervously ask if it was okay for them to ask out Bridget and Ariel, and even invite them over for gatherings and other CBOR events. They'd had so much fun at the wedding that they wanted to see more of the girls.

Lance assured the two awkward knights that dating the girls would be awesome. "They're great girls."

Justin and Techie, so different in background and temperament, fist-bumped with glee.

"But you treat 'em good," Ricky admonished good-naturedly, and the boys laughed.

Due to the massive showing for the wedding, Thanksgiving dinner this year was a more intimate affair, with most of the knights spending it with their families. Besides Arthur's family, there was Sergeant Gibson and Justin, Sergeant Ryan, and Merlin.

As had become tradition the previous year, Arthur asked around the table for each person to acknowledge something he or she was grateful for. Naturally, he was grateful for his new bride and his outstanding boys. Jenny, likewise, thanked God for the gift of Arthur and her new family. Lance and Ricky also gave thanks for their new mom, but mostly for the gift of each other. Reyna and Esteban gave thanks for each other. Only Justin seemed to differ – he gave thanks for the possibility that his mom and dad might get back together. His wish almost made Gibson redden with embarrassment.

Sergeant Ryan hesitated a moment when it was his turn. He eyed Lance and Ricky, who were seated beside an expectant Arthur and Jenny. "As strange as this may sound," he said in his gravelly voice, "I'm thankful for Michael—"

Lance gasped slightly, but Ryan merely gazed at him soberly.

"—because Michael gave me back a gift I hope I never lose, my godson." He lowered his eyes to his wineglass and fiddled with his silverware, clearly flustered by uncomfortable emotions.

Lance's mouth dropped open, and Ricky laughingly reached up to close it.

Arthur grinned. "I second that." He raised his goblet high in the air. "To Sir Michael the Good, Knight Eternal of the Table Round."

Everyone raised their glasses and toasted. "Sir Michael," each one mumbled.

And then the meal began. Lance had sunk within himself at the mention of Michael's name, and Ricky had to prod him to pass the cranberry sauce. "It's Thanksgiving, Lance, no emo stuff today."

That drew a grin to Lance's face and he elbowed Ricky right back before handing him the cranberries.

Everyone was laughing and clowning and enjoying the delicious food prepared by the hotel kitchen staff, when one of the maids entered and announced that someone was at the front door looking for Lance.

Instantly the banter vanished and everyone sat at attention.

Ryan stood, hand already moving to the holster beneath his jacket. "Who is it?" he asked gruffly.

"He wouldn't say, sir," the young Latina offered cautiously. "He's a young man, maybe a boy, and he asked for Sir Lance of the Round Table."

Lance eyed the maid appraisingly. "What does he look like?"

"He appears to be an Indian, sir," the young woman answered with the extreme politeness of all the hotel staff.

"Indian?" Ricky exclaimed, pulling a face.

"Yes, sir," the maid went on. "He's wearing those Indian shoes and carrying a big bow and some arrows."

"Thank you, Maria," Ryan said crisply. "We'll handle it from here."

"An Indian?" Lance repeated, clearly mystified. "A Thanksgiving prank, *nino*?"

"How'd he get past the guard at the front gate?" Justin asked pointedly.

Ryan looked cautious. "Let's find out. Gib, you and me'll open the door and block Lance and Ricky, in case it's a setup."

Gibson stood, and Justin jumped up along with him. "I'm going, too."

They looked to Arthur for confirmation, and the king silently nodded, his hand slipping anxiously into Jenny's.

Lance and Ricky rose to their feet, and Lance shrugged at his parents. "Don't worry, guys, I'm just going to the front door." He flashed his winning smile, and the adults visibly relaxed.

"Eat, Arthur, we got this," Gibson said, and then he and Ryan led the three boys out of the Renaissance Dining Room and down the corridors to the lobby, where they stopped before the double front doors. The beveled glass panels revealed little in the darkness without, despite the porch lights being lit.

Each man drew his service pistol and grabbed onto the handle of one door. Lance and Ricky hovered just behind them, with Justin prepared to tackle them to the floor if necessary.

Gibson whispered, "One, two, three!" And they yanked open both doors, guns aimed straight ahead.

The young man standing outside moved so fast Lance barely caught the movement. He dropped a duffel bag, leapt for the ground, whipped out an arrow, fitted it to his bow, all on one roll. Then he was up on his feet, arrow pulled back taut and wavering between both detectives.

"Is this your Thanksgiving tradition, to kill Indians like the old days?" he said, his voice tight and stilted, but steady.

Lance looked between the two detectives at the young man— boy—really, and sensed the fear the boy wasn't allowing himself to display.

The two detectives exchanged tentative looks, clearly not sure what to do.

Lance stepped between them and put a hand on each shoulder. Ricky and Justin leapt forward to grab him, but Lance announced firmly, "Enough."

Everything stopped. The guns were still aimed at the Indian, and the boy's arrow pointed straight at Lance. Lance saw that the boy was, in fact, wearing moccasins of some sort, along with regular jeans and a t-shirt, covered over with some kind of buckskin jacket. His long black hair trailed down his back to hang just above the crook of his knees. There were feathers tied to sections of his hair with what looked like beads.

Beneath the porch light, Lance met the boy's squinting brown eyes, noted the rigid posture, the stance, the rock steady hands on the bow and arrow.

This guy is fearless, and sincere.

"Put away your guns, *nino*. He's cool."

Ricky slid anxiously up to Lance. "More of your soul whispering, Lance?"

Lance nodded.

"Are you sure?"

Lance nodded again.

Keeping their eyes pinned to the young Indian, the two detectives lowered their weapons.

Lance smiled at the boy. "It's okay. We don't kill Indians on Thanksgiving. We invite them in for dinner."

Ricky sucked in a breath, and even Justin reacted with surprise, but Lance stepped in between Ryan and Gibson to stand before the boy with the arrow, which now pointed straight at his heart. They were about the same height, Lance noted, as he fixed his eyes on those of the other. Without breaking eye contact, he lifted a hand and gently pushed the arrow down and away from him.

"My name's Lance," he said calmly, still meeting the other's suspicious gaze.

The young man lowered his bow arm slowly, but his body retained its rigid posture. "Dakota Cloud Eagle," he said, his voice deep and flat and proud. "Oglala Lakota, formerly of the Pine Ridge Reservation in South Dakota."

"Welcome, Dakota Cloud Eagle. Cool name."

Lance stuck out his hand, but the young man merely noted it without expression. His eyes narrowed.

"Does your Round Table always greet visitors thus? I had heard your brotherhood welcomed all."

Lance felt embarrassed. "I'm sorry about that, man. See, there's somebody who wants to kill my ass so…." He let the rest of the thought trail off with a shrug.

The young Indian straightened up even more, puffing out his chest. "I'm a warrior. I'll protect you."

Ricky stepped forward. "Uh, that's my job."

The boy raised his eyebrows questioningly.

"This is Ricky," Lance offered by way of explanation, "my—" He faltered then, not sure what to say. "Well, I'm sure you already know. Anyway, he's got my back."

Dakota eyed them both with a powerfully discerning gaze, flicking his eyes first to Lance and then to Ricky. He returned his arrow to its quiver and slung the bow over his shoulder before reaching into a multicolored cloth messenger bag hanging across his chest by a shoulder strap. He pulled out an envelope and presented it to Lance. "A letter, from my tribal council, for you."

Lance took the letter, turning it over in his hand. "They couldn't, like, just put a stamp on it? Or send an email?"

Dakota squinted. "I have seen computers, but have hardly used them. And we do not trust the government letter service. I volunteered. It's about your Children's Bill of Rights. And I wish to join your Round Table."

Lance's eyebrows shot up in surprise and he looked at Ricky, who shrugged.

"Lance," he heard Ryan's gruff voice behind him. "Let's not stand out here all night. We're sitting ducks."

"Okay, *nino*." He looked at Dakota, who was studying he and Ricky with a discerning eye.

"You are both native, like me," the Lakota boy announced like it was already a proven fact. "First People."

Lance said, "I don't know nothing about my parents, but I could be."

"Mine come from Mexico," Ricky added with a shrug. "So I guess they could be, like, Mexican Indian or something. They never said."

Dakota continued his steady gaze, studying the faces of both boys. "You have my eyes, and the shape of your faces. You're native."

Lance smiled. "Cool. Listen, um, Dakota, come on in and have dinner and we can talk some more. My *nino* says it's dangerous out here."

Dakota hesitated. "My people do not celebrate Thanksgiving like white people do."

"Yeah, but I'm native, right? And I'm thankful you came all this way to deliver a letter."

Still, the other boy hesitated.

"C'mon, man," Ricky insisted. "It's getting cold, and you're a guy, so you gotta be hungry, right?"

Dakota nodded slowly, and then snatched up the duffel bag and walked between Lance and Ricky past the cautious gazes of Ryan and Gibson. He gave the muscular Justin a squinty look, and then everyone was back inside with the doors locked. As they returned to the dining room, Justin asked Dakota how he got past the guards at the gate.

"I'm an Indian," was the cryptic response, causing Justin to look at his dad with raised eyebrows. Gibson indicated with a "look" that they'd discuss the security breach another time.

Upon entering the Renaissance Room, Lance indicated Dakota's bow and quiver of arrows and the young man slipped them off hesitantly, like they were a part of his body, and set them down on an empty table; his satchel and duffel, as well.

All eyes were fixed on them as Ryan, Gibson, and Justin resumed their seats and Lance and Ricky led Dakota forward to Arthur and Jenny.

"Dad, mom, this is Dakota Cloud Eagle," Lance announced. "He came all the way from South Dakota to give me a letter, and he wants to join us."

Arthur and Jenny both stood.

Lance noted the awe in Dakota's eyes at Arthur's height and physical stature, recalling his initial meeting with the man and how 'wowed' he'd been, too.

Arthur smiled warmly, his eyes convivial. "Welcome to New Camelot, Dakota Cloud Eagle. I am Arthur."

Without obvious expression, but clearly struggling to contain a sense of awe, Dakota said, "I have heard you are a great leader, and I have come here to become one of your knights. I am a fierce warrior and fighter and will serve you well."

"Your kind praise is appreciated, but here we are warriors of right, Dakota, not might." The boy frowned slightly, but Arthur placed a hand on Jenny's shoulder and said, "This is my wife, the Lady Jenny."

She extended a hand and smiled broadly. "Welcome to New Camelot."

This time Dakota reached out and shook her hand. "Among my people, we are of our mother's clan." Inadvertently, he flicked his eyes toward Lance and Ricky beside him and then back at her.

Jenny understood and smiled. "They're adopted."

Dakota nodded, but said nothing.

"Sit, Dakota," Arthur went on, extending a hand toward an empty seat, "and give thanks this day for family and friends."

The boy looked at Lance, who smiled and tilted his head toward the chair next to Chris. "This is our other brother, Chris," he said, as the young Lakota moved to the chair and sat.

Wide blue eyes fixed on Dakota's buckskin jacket, Chris blurted, "Wow, a real Indian!"

Everyone laughed, but Dakota did not change his facial expression, causing Lance to wonder if the kid *ever* smiled.

Lance introduced him to Reyna and the others before more food was passed around. Dakota eyed each person cautiously and then heaped great amounts of everything onto his plate, causing Lance and Ricky to eye one another. Lance could tell Ricky was wondering the same thing–when did this boy eat last?

There passed a few awkward moments while everyone eyed the young Native and his heaping portions of food, but then conversation returned to normal.

Lance and Ricky nudged and elbowed each other playfully, causing Dakota to watch them with curiosity. Between mouthfuls of turkey and stuffing, Lance asked him, "So, Dakota, you said your tribal council was interested in our CBOR?"

Cheeks bulging with mashed potatoes, the teenager squinted curiously at Lance's choice of words.

"Sorry, man, that's what we call the Children's Bill of Rights, so we don't have to say the whole thing every time."

Dakota swallowed his food. "It does not include native children, your bill, and my tribal council would like you to add them in."

Lance frowned. "Why wouldn't native kids be part of our bill? It's for all kids."

Dakota pushed back his flowing hair and eyed Lance peculiarly. "Native children are treated differently by your government. Didn't you know that?"

"How? They're American citizens, right?" Ricky asked as everyone halted their eating to follow the conversation.

Dakota paused a moment, his youthful features scrunched with consideration. "Our tribal lands are like a separate country with its own government. The state and the federal government can't tell us what to do 'less there's a big crime committed." He stopped here a moment and looked down at his food. "Then the FBI has to be called. But they usually don't care about crimes against natives."

"But what about the kids?" Lance asked when Dakota fell into a brooding silence.

Dakota looked up and met his gaze. "They are taken from their families by South Dakota's department of social services and given to white families to raise because your federal government pays the state money to do this. It's in the letter."

Lance could feel himself paling at the boy's words. "That's sick!" he blurted, more angrily than he'd intended, and turned to Arthur and Jenny. "Did you hear that? Just like they tried to do with us!"

"But they failed, son," Arthur reminded him in a calming tone.

His blood pounding, Lance turned back to Dakota. "Can't you guys stop them?"

Dakota shrugged sadly. "The courts allow it to be so. My people have been trying to fix the Indian Child Welfare Act for many years, but...." He let the thought trail off. "It's in the letter."

Lance fumed, pulling the letter from his pocket and starting to open it, but Jenny reached over to lightly touch his hand. He looked at her sharply.

"I know that look, Lance," she said gently. "It's a horrible thing, but we'll work on it tomorrow. Sam can help. For now, enjoy your dinner."

"But Mom," Lance began, but she squeezed his hand and he settled down. Injustice like this truly rankled him, but he understood her meaning. The same children would be away from their homes tomorrow, just as they were tonight, and nothing could be accomplished through anger.

She pulled her hand back and he slid the letter back into his pocket. He turned to face Ricky, who gave him the 'look.' He smiled, and Ricky's eyes danced with joy.

When Lance glanced over at Dakota, he saw the new boy eyeing them strangely before quickly dropping his gaze back to his plate and rather inexpertly shoveling more food into his mouth. He began to wonder if maybe Dakota was the *only* person on earth who didn't know about him and Ricky.

He also noted the odd way the boy held his spoon—he gripped it like one might the handle of a saucepan and used it like a shovel. Odd, he thought, before returning to his own meal.

Just then, the same young maid re-entered the dining room and approached Arthur and Jenny. "Excuse me, King Arthur, but there's another young man at the door looking for Sir Lance."

Chris looked up from his food with a big grin. "Another Indian boy?"

Lance knew he was joking, and smiled. But the smile faltered when Maria replied, "Yes, Sir Chris, I think so."

Lance and Ricky turned to each other with one of their almost patented 'wth' looks, and then Lance turned to Dakota. "What's with you native guys and Thanksgiving?"

The boy's poker face displayed no emotion. "I told you, we don't celebrate it."

Lance sighed. "Okay. I'll go check it out." He turned to Ricky. "Wanna come?"

"Where you go, I go."

Lance smiled and looked across the round table at Ryan, already rising to his feet and fingering his sidearm. "Uh, *nino*, let's just open the door this time."

"Okay, Lance. But *I* open the door."

"No problem," Lance said as he and Ricky stood to follow the detective from the dining room.

Once more crossing the empty lobby, their boots clicking against the marble floor, Lance hurried to catch up with his godfather. "No commando stuff, remember."

Ryan grimaced, but agreed. His right hand slipped to the gun in its holster, but did not draw it, as they stopped before the double doors. Lance and Ricky stood just behind him as the sergeant reached out with his left hand and eased one of the doors open.

Standing outside was a smallish teen boy of indeterminate age. He wore jeans,

Vans, a flamboyantly orange Hollister t-shirt, and denim jacket. A duffel bag slung over his shoulder completed the look. His long, pitch-black hair was woven into two dangling braids, and he wore a multicolored bandana wrapped around his forehead. His eyes, Lance noted, were thinner than his own, or even Ricky's or Dakota's, almost like the eyes of the Asian knights he knew.

Lance stepped around Ryan. "I'm Lance. You're looking for me?"

Almost a polar opposite of Dakota, this boy broke into a grin that spread so far across his face, Lance thought it would break through the skin. His eyes positively danced with laughter. "Of course you are," he gushed, eyeing Ricky, as well. "And you're Ricky. Wow, it's so cool to meet you guys."

Lance and Ricky grinned, and then Ricky asked. "What's your name?"

"Kai Begay," the boy answered, still beaming with delight.

Ricky's smile faltered. "Did you… just call us gay?"

The boy's smile crumpled into a look of apology. "Oh, no, guys, sorry, that's my name. Kai Begay. B-E-G-A-Y."

"That's your name?" Lance asked, not sure he'd heard right.

The boy laughed, an open, infectious laugh. "Everyone says that when I tell them my name. Actually, Begay is a very respected Navajo name going back all through our history. My great-great uncle was a code talker in World War II."

Lance and Ricky visibly relaxed. They'd been reading ahead in their history text and had heard of the Navajo Code Talkers. Their language, Lance recalled, was the only code the Japanese couldn't break.

"Cool," Lance responded, extending his hand. "Nice to meet you, Kai."

Unlike Dakota, this boy shook hands with both of them.

"Lance," he heard Ryan's tight voice behind him. "Let's take this inside, please."

Lance glanced over his shoulder. "Oh, yeah, *nino*." He turned back to the newcomer. "C'mon in."

Once within the lobby with the doors secured, Lance faced the eager new boy with raised eyebrows. "So what brings you to New Camelot on Thanksgiving?"

Still smiling, the boy said, "Oh, we don't celebrate that."

"Yeah," Ricky chimed in. "We just found that out. So what's up?"

Almost breathless with excitement, Kai gushed, "Well, I want to join the Round Table, you know, and become a warrior for right. Oh, and I bring greetings from the tribal council of the Navajo Nation."

He dug into his bag and fished around a moment before extracting a large, sealed envelope, holding it out to Lance.

Lance couldn't help but smile knowingly as he took it. "Let me guess, no email and you don't trust the government."

Kai's broad grin faltered, but only a little. "That's right. How'd you know?"

"Lucky guess," Ricky added, drawing a fit of giggling from Lance, who quickly recovered.

"Inside joke," Lance muttered, bringing giggles out of Ricky.

A huge grin breached Kai's smooth, hairless face. "You guys are good together."

Lance looked straight into those laughing brown eyes for malice or ill intent, but found nothing but openness and not a trace of guile.

"Well, c'mon in, Kai Begay of the Navajo Nation, and have some dinner. I don't know about this fool—" He indicated Ricky with a thumb. "—but I've spent more time at the door than the table and I'm hungry."

Ricky elbowed him. To the amazement of both, and what seemed a sheer impossibility, the newcomer's grin grew even larger. "Thanks, man. I'm hungry, too."

Feeling more relaxed with this one than Dakota, Lance ushered the boy forward. "By the way, Kai," he asked as they started down the long hallway toward the dining room, "how'd you get past the guard out front?"

Kai laughed airily as though the question was foolish. "I'm an Indian, Lance."

Lance eyed Ricky and they snuck a smile between them. Indians, Lance decided, must travel in stealth mode, and he filed away for future research a desire to learn that particular secret.

Upon entering the dining room, Lance indicated the table with Dakota's things for Kai to deposit his duffel bag. As the four of them stepped toward the table, Ryan slipped around to his seat while everyone looked up and eyed the newcomer curiously. Dakota had his head down, still downing food like he hadn't eaten in days, his long hair obscuring his peripheral vision.

As Lance and Ricky led Kai toward Arthur for introductions, Dakota's head popped up like a duck coming up for air, and his eyes narrowed. Kai stopped suddenly, causing Ricky to plow right into him.

"Cloudy Boy," Kai said, all trace of laughter gone. He looked surprised, and yet something in his tone struck Lance as "off."

Dakota squinted at Kai with what looked like distaste. "Laughs A Lot."

As though on cue, Kai laughed, but it was a nervous one, his eyes taking on a lost, wistful look that touched Lance.

"It's been a long time," Kai said, his voice breathy and filled with deep emotion.

Dakota said nothing.

Reyna cleared her throat. "I take it you guys know each other."

"Yes," both newcomers answered at the same time.

Reyna elbowed Esteban. "Oh, great, another pair."

"Another pair of what?" Dakota asked Reyna, his tone laced with suspicion.

"Another pair of boys who think the same things at the same time," she answered. "Like those two over there." She grinned and pointed at Lance and Ricky, who bowed ceremoniously.

Then Lance introduced Kai to Arthur and Jenny.

Kai gushed with enthusiasm and energy. "I want to join the Round Table and become a knight like Lance and Ricky," he said, almost breathlessly.

"You shall be most welcome," Arthur replied with a smile of acceptance.

Dakota grunted into his cider. "He's no warrior, that one. He *draws*." He said that last word almost sneeringly.

Kai's buoyant face flushed red and he looked down at the carpet.

Arthur placed a hand on his shoulder, and he looked back up. "We are warriors of right, Kai, not might, and all talents are welcome."

Kai beamed with gratitude.

Lance watched his father charm this boy, make him feel good about himself with just a few words, and marveled at the ease with which it could be done. Why, he wondered for the umpteenth time, couldn't more people be like Arthur?

Kai sat next to Dakota, which seemed to make the Lakota boy uncomfortable. But clearly Dakota was too proud to admit anything that smacked of weakness.

True to his earlier statement, Kai was hungry, and devoured nearly as much food as Dakota. It almost seemed a race between them to see who could consume the most the fastest.

Reyna was amused by their antics, but made no snide comments.

By the time pumpkin pie came around, everyone was stuffed and content, even the two Indian boys who, they'd learned were both seventeen years old. That revelation concerned Arthur and Jenny after their previous wrangling's with the Department of Children and Family Services.

Jenny looked over at both boys. "Do your parents know you're here, boys?"

The two looked up from their food and, mouths full, nodded.

"We might need to talk to your parents," she added uncertainly. "Just to avoid problems with our own children's services out here."

"My mother sent a note," Kai explained while swallowing some turkey. "It's in the letter."

Jenny eyed Dakota, whose face became even stormier than before. "If you ask my mother, she'll say she has one son, my brother. She has no phone." He resumed eating without awaiting a response.

Kai took a swig of cider and said, "Not many phones on our rez, either, 'cept the pay phone at the general store. 'Sides, we're seventeen." To Dakota, he added, "You do your vision quest yet?"

"Course I did," Dakota grunted in annoyance.

Rather than look insulted, Kai laughed as though it was the response he expected. He turned to Lance and Ricky. "At seventeen, us Indian boys go through our vision quest and become men. In our culture, we're not kids anymore."

"Huh!" Dakota grunted into his goblet.

That drew a curious look from Kai, and Lance exchanged a look with Ricky, who shrugged. These two intrigued him.

Arthur said, "We will consider you men within the Round Table, but out in the city you are not yet legal adults, so we need to be cautious."

The Indian boys nodded, but said nothing as their mouths were full once again.

Lance noted how Kai continually tried to engage Dakota in conversation, but the young Lakota merely offered grunts or nods in response to questions or comments. Finally, Lance thought to ask the question he'd wondered about earlier.

"Say, guys, why don't you Indians like Thanksgiving?" he asked. "I thought, like, you know in 1620, or maybe it was 21, the pilgrims thanked the Indians for helping 'em by throwing a big dinner and they all ate together. Isn't that a good thing?"

Dakota snorted. "It would be if it was true."

"Whadda you mean?" Ricky asked.

Kai saw that Dakota wasn't going to answer and said, "What Cloudy Boy is trying to say is, that version of Thanksgiving was mostly made up by Abraham Lincoln during the Civil War to, you know, mend fences and stuff."

Lance glanced at Jenny, who was listening attentively. "You ever hear this version, Mom?"

"No. Please continue, Kai."

The young Navajo sighed. "Well, there *was* a good harvest in 1621 and the pilgrims *did* have a feast, but they didn't invite the Indians to eat with them. The Indians just showed up with food and so they kind of had to eat together so nobody got pissed off. The real Thanksgiving holiday was started in 1637 by Governor Winthrop of the Massachusetts Bay Colony. It was a big celebration 'cause his people came home after massacring like, seven hundred Pequot men, women and children. They were thankful for the victory over us savages." He fell silent.

No one moved, or scarcely even breathed.

"That's horrible," Reyna whispered, taking Esteban's hand in hers.

Lance and Ricky exchanged an appalled look, and Chris's mouth hung open in shock.

"That's what we been taught, anyway," Kai added solemnly.

"And that's why we don't celebrate Thanksgiving," Dakota said quietly as he turned to fix his brown eyes on Lance.

Lance felt sad and wistful that these boys carried the weight of such history on their shoulders.

Dinner ended shortly thereafter, that story having dropped a subdued mood over the entire table. Reyna and Esteban left to return to their homes, Arthur and Jenny took Chris upstairs to get him ready for bed, while Lance and Ricky led Dakota and Kai up the grand staircase to the second floor to find them rooms.

Not sure why he did so, though maybe, he surmised later, it was because these two had some history together, Lance led them to the only other two rooms on the second floor with an adjoining door between them.

The group entered the room designated for Dakota, while Lance explained the arrangements, and both newcomers stopped and gaped at the opulence of their surroundings. The giant bed, lush carpeting, heavy brocaded drapes and fancy light fixtures clearly flummoxed both of them, much as they had Lance and Ricky upon first moving into New Camelot.

Lance waved his arm toward the door adjoining Kai's room. "Pretty cool, huh? Oh, your room is through there, Kai. Same layout."

Kai just stared, so awed he didn't even laugh. Dakota's face remained deadpan, as always, but his narrowed brown eyes swept over the room and its furnishings, as though fearful something might attack him.

To break the awkwardness, Lance said, "So what is it with you guys and different names? Are you also called Cloudy Boy and Laughs A Lot at home?"

Dakota grunted noncommittally, but Kai grinned. "No, they're nicknames we gave each other. I've known this guy since we were six, and even back then I told my mother I met a Lakota boy with a cloudy face, 'cause, well, it was like a cloudburst waiting to happen. So that's what I called him."

Suddenly shy, he glanced over at Dakota, who stood stiffly, bow and arrows and duffel bag still slung across his back.

Dakota's face did, Lance realized, look like a cloudburst waiting to happen.

The Lakota boy shrugged. "Yeah, well this bonehead never stopped smiling or laughing since he was six. He thinks life is funny or something. So, my six-year-old ass called him Laughs A Lot."

Kai looked sober all of a sudden, as though he wanted to ask something, but instead he sighed. "Life without laughing isn't life, Cloudy Boy. Try it sometime."

Dakota ignored him. Instead, his gaze remained fixed on Lance and Ricky, whose hands brushed lightly against each other. The Lakota's eyes traveled to those hands, and back up to the faces. "You two are brothers?"

That question struck Lance and Ricky as random.

"Well, yeah, I mean Arthur adopted us both. We're not related by blood or nothing," Ricky answered.

Dakota looked over at Kai and studied his silent features a moment, before turning back to Lance and Ricky. "Wínkte," he said, drawing a puzzled look from both boys.

Kai sucked in a breath of surprise. "*Two-Spirit*, Cloudy Boy."

Dakota shrugged, his eyes boring into Lance and Ricky.

"What's winte, or whatever you said?" Lance asked, noting Kai's reaction, and fearing he already knew the answer.

"It means Two-Spirit in Lakota," Kai quickly interjected, but Lance waited for the silent Dakota to respond.

"Homo," Dakota said dispassionately. "It's Lakota for homo." His gaze never faltered, as though challenging Lance to deny it.

Lance heard Ricky gasp lightly, but he maintained eye contact with Dakota. "Here in the Round Table, Dakota, we use '*Sir* Homo'."

Ricky stifled a laugh, and even Kai chuckled. But Dakota didn't even blink, the joke going over his head.

Lance turned to Kai. "You're right. He *is* Cloudy Boy." Then he looked back at the stiff-postured young Indian. "Look, we don't use words like homo in the Round Table, Dakota. By now I thought everybody knew about Ricky and me. It's only been, like, the biggest news story all over the world."

Dakota squinted thoughtfully, obviously turning this information over in his mind.

Kai cleared his throat, drawing their attention toward him. "Natives don't use that word either and he knows it."

Dakota grunted again. "Course *you* don't like it. You're homo, too."

For the first time that night, Kai's face crumpled into shock. "How do you know? I never told you."

Lance and Ricky exchanged a surprised look at this new revelation.

Dakota almost smirked, but Lance couldn't honestly tell if his facial expression shifted or not. "I knew you since six. Think I didn't figure it out?"

Kai blushed, even through his dark, sun-drenched skin. "I would've told you. I wanted to tell you…'cept you weren't at, like, any powwows for the last four years." Then he looked at the carpet beneath his feet.

Dakota flinched ever so slightly, and then regained his aplomb. But he didn't respond.

"What's a powwow?" Ricky asked to break the silence.

"Big native gatherings," Kai replied, pulling his gaze from the floor. "Tribes get together to dance and eat and trade stories. They're awesome. Hopefully you'll get to see one if you travel around for your amendments." His suddenly poignant eyes returned to the brooding Dakota, who maintained a posture like he thought he might be attacked at any moment.

Gazing at the Indians, Lance felt the weight of an entire history between these two that might make or break their success at New Camelot. Much more was being left unsaid than was being said. His soul-whispering talent, as Ricky had dubbed it, was working overtime.

"So, uh, Kai," he said, breaking the awkward silence. "What's this Two-Spirit thing you said?"

Kai pulled his gaze from Dakota's stoic reticence and said, "It's kind of a blanket word the Indian tribes came up with for any of us who're gay or lesbian or trans. Otherwise, every tribe had a different word for it. Like in *Diné*, my language, it's *nádleehé*."

"But why Two-Spirit? I mean, what's that about?" Ricky asked.

"It's like we have two spirits in one body, both male and female."

Lance bristled. "We already covered this on the Ellen show."

Kai and Dakota both looked at them blankly.

"You don't watch television?" Ricky asked incredulously.

Both shook their heads.

Lance sighed. "Look, there's nothing girly about me or Ricky, okay? We're all boy. *Nothing* female." He knew he sounded slightly angry, maybe even petulant, but he was tired of all the 'which one's the girl?' stuff on the Internet.

Kai looked genuinely apologetic. "I'm sorry, man, that's not what it means. It just, well, it covers trans people, too. I mean, I'm not feminine, either." Dakota snorted, and Kai cast a glare in his direction before continuing. "It's just, well, we're boys, but we fall in love with other boys the way girls fall in love with boys. So, Two-Spirit. See?"

Lance knew there was no derision in the other's voice, and read the sincerity in his eyes, so he calmed down. Ricky's hand slipping surreptitiously into his helped.

"Okay, I get it. Better than homo, faggot, and gay, for sure." He looked at Ricky. "What's your fool-ass think?"

Ricky grinned. "I think it sounds kinda cool, but I still think we're one spirit in two boys. Dumbass."

Lance grinned, too. "I guess Two-Spirit is okay within the Round Table, if it has to be brought up at all. But here, none of us are black or brown or native. Here, we're just human."

Kai looked at Dakota. The boy's squinting eyes widened a notch, as comprehension filled them.

Kai seemed to study the other's high cheekbones and thin lips a moment before asking, "So how come?"

"What?" Dakota said, clearly mystified.

"How come you weren't at the powwows?" His open face indicated concern, not nosiness.

Dakota shrugged again, a gesture Lance began to understand stood for many emotions within the boy. "Tribal Council banned me from all tribal functions."

Kai gasped in shock, causing Lance to realize such actions must not be common among Indian tribes.

Dakota crossed the room, slipped off his bags and weapons, and tossed them onto the bed.

"Why?"

Dakota turned to face him and Lance sensed a deep sadness, maybe even guilt, living behind those narrow brown eyes.

Without expression, Dakota replied, "Because I tried to kill my brother. For that, I was disavowed by my mother."

Kai's mouth fell open, but Dakota's stare and sullen silence sent a clear message: this topic is off-limits.

Lance squeezed Ricky's hand tightly. Could this mean the Lakota boy posed a threat to them? Could he be a plant, sent by whoever wanted him dead? But looking deeply into the boy's sorrowful brown eyes, Lance concluded that his initial soul-whisper had been correct. This boy was sincere. Damaged, but sincere.

He cleared his throat. "Uh, shower's that way, Dakota, if you want to clean up. We have lots of tunics and pants and boots. If you need some regular clothes, we're all about the same size, so you can borrow from Ricky and me. We're just across the hall." He saw Kai's eyebrows rise. "In separate rooms," he added quickly. "C'mon, Kai, let's get you settled in."

So they left Dakota standing beside his bed and used the connecting door to enter Kai's nearly identical room. Only the pattern of the bedcovering differed. Once they'd pointed out the bathroom and closet, Lance and Ricky bade Kai a goodnight and headed for Lance's room.

Lance could feel Kai's eyes on his back as he and Ricky crossed the hallway and entered the one room, and felt compelled to turn and say, "There's a connecting door in here, too, from my room to Ricky's."

Kai nodded, his expression for once not laughing or open, but almost cloudy. Like Dakota.

Once in Lance's room, the boys plopped down onto the rumpled, unmade bed and sighed. He wasn't much for making up his bed, and the hotel staff had Thanksgiving off.

Ricky blew out a breath. "Well, that was some weird-ass Thanksgiving, huh?"

Lance smiled slightly, and agreed.

"You thinking what I'm thinking?"

Lance looked over and smiled. "If you're thinking you're a dumbass, then yeah."

Ricky shoved him. Lance shoved right back.

"Do you think Dakota might be a problem?"

Lance reflected again on what he'd seen, and felt, in the Indian's eyes. "No."

"You sure?" Ricky asked hesitantly. "I mean, he tried to kill his own brother."

"We don't know why, Ricky, so let's not judge him, 'kay?"

"'Kay."

They kissed goodnight at the connecting door before both retreated to their individual bathrooms to prepare for bed.

Over the next few days, Lance and Ricky took the Indians under their wings to acclimate them to their new home, and began instruction in the ways of knighthood. Lance was shocked, and dismayed, to learn that Dakota was his equal with the bow and arrow. Even Reyna was stunned when she witnessed their initial competition. Both boys could not only hit a bull's-eye dead center every time, but could split each other's arrow as it stuck out of the target. Lance would fire and split Dakota's arrow. Dakota would haughtily step forward and split Lance's. This went on and on, with a tense Ricky, Reyna, Esteban, Kai, and Chris all in breathless suspense.

Knowing he shouldn't, Lance felt his pride rankle at this usurper, and didn't want to stop until the other boy missed a shot. After a half hour, his shoulders and arms throbbed, while Dakota appeared unruffled by fatigue. Finally, Reyna stepped in and clapped, drawing nervous applause from the others.

"We'll call this a draw, guys," she announced with a big manufactured grin. "Amazing shooting. Even better than me."

Lance looked at Dakota, and Dakota met his gaze. Yes, there was a haughtiness in those eyes that irked Lance, but there was also admiration. Obviously, Dakota had never met his equal, either. Lance extended a hand. "Glad you're on my team, man."

Dakota shook it. Lance noted the firm grip, but there was a slight tremor, too. He saw something familiar in the boy's eyes, something he used to see in his own this past year when stress or deep sadness clawed at his soul, but he couldn't pull the memory from his subconscious. Then they released hands, and the moment vanished.

Kai was adept with the bow and arrow, but nowhere near as impressive as Dakota. However, his drawing skills were astonishing. Just with a pencil and paper, he could create a lifelike image of anyone in short order. Lance suggested he do a wedding portrait of Arthur and Jenny, and they could post it up on the website, and Kai readily agreed.

Sword and shield training was foreign to both boys, though they had battled each other as children with long wooden poles. Dakota, ever in warrior mode, it seemed, took to the hand-to-hand combat with gusto. Kai, not so much. Dakota was the more athletic and muscular of the two, Lance had noted while sizing them both up, but Kai was fleet of foot and had a keen eye for details.

The new boys also settled into the daily routine of school. The mixture of ages within the same classroom echoed their own reservation school experience, except they were encouraged to speak more here than they had been back home.

Over that next week, Lance and Ricky studied both letters sent by the two Tribal Councils. They'd conferred with Sam and Jenny about how changes might be made to the CBOR to include Native children, and then led Dakota and Kai to the Computer Lab on the second Saturday after Thanksgiving to do some revisions. There had been no gathering on Thanksgiving weekend, so at today's meeting both newcomers would be formally introduced, and their requests brought before the entire Round Table.

The Indians stopped and stared in awe upon entering the Computer Lab.

"I've never seen this many computers in my life," Kai exclaimed breathlessly, turning to Dakota. "Have you, Cloudy Boy?"

The other shook his head, his eyes sweeping the room with suspicion.

Lance and Ricky introduced them to Techie, who shook their hands before returning his gaze to the monitor before him.

Lance grinned at the boys. "Techie's our computer whiz. New Camelot would crumble without him."

Techie grinned from beneath his big glasses. "You know it," he said with a laugh. Then he glanced up at Ricky uncertainly.

Ricky smiled. "All's good with Ariel?"

Techie grinned. He nodded, and swung his gaze back to the computer screen.

Lance and Ricky led the boys to some empty computer stations nearby, sitting each of them down before his own machine. Kai logged into his email account for messages, explaining to the boys that there was no Internet access on his reservation except at the high school. Dakota merely stared at his screen like it might bite him.

Both boys had taken to wearing some of Lance and Ricky's shirts. As Lance sported a bit more muscle than Ricky, his shirts fit Dakota better, while Ricky's worked for Kai, though they were a bit baggy on the skinny Indian. In addition, both newcomers had chosen tunics and leather pants and boots to be worn for gatherings and other official functions.

Lance eyed Dakota curiously. The boy obviously had no idea what to do and it clearly made him uncomfortable.

"I'll help Dakota and you help Kai?"

Ricky smiled and stepped over to the terminal beside Kai, while Lance settled in beside Dakota a short distance away.

Dakota sat rigidly upright in the high-backed chair, hands on his lap, eyes fixed uncertainly on the screen before him. Lance dropped his gaze to the hands and noticed a slight trembling of the fingers. "So, I guess you haven't used computers much?"

The boy shook his head, but refused to look over.

"Don't worry," Lance said reassuringly, "I hardly ever used one till I moved in here, either."

He reached for the mouse as Dakota eyed him warily. Lance pulled up the New Camelot website and demonstrated the tabs and drop down menus, especially the section devoted to the Code of Chivalry and requirements for knighthood.

"That's the part you need to study to become a knight," he told the silent boy, whose wide eyes absorbed everything Lance was doing.

He let Dakota take over the mouse and practice navigating his way through the website, including the photo section.

As he was scrolling through pictures, Lance asked, "Did you hear anything about our crusade on the reservation?"

Dakota's fascinated gaze never left the screen. He appeared mesmerized. "Yes. It was in the reservation newspaper. I read every story three times."

That response surprised Lance. There must not be much to do out there, he thought. "Did you, uh, read about my, uh, embarrassing stuff too?"

Dakota looked over and met his eyes. "Yes."

"And you still came here to be one of us?" Lance asked, startled. "Knowing I'm second in command after my father?"

Dakota nodded. "I understand better now after meeting you. Natives can't handle alcohol."

Lance was confused for a moment, but then glanced down at the trembling fingers lightly resting on the mouse. Then he realized what he'd seen in the boy's eyes. "When did *you* start drinking?"

"When I was ten," Dakota answered matter-of-factly. "Alcohol is banned on the rez, but white people sell it to us anyway."

Lance gasped. *Ten?* "I'm sorry, man."

Dakota asked quietly, "Why did you start, Lance of the Round Table?"

Lance burned with shame, knowing it made him look weak to the tough, warrior mentality of the other, but he couldn't help himself. "I was trying to fit in at parties. And I had a crappy childhood, always hating on myself."

Dakota narrowed his eyes, but said nothing.

"You wanna see me when I'm drunk? I'll show you."

Lance took the mouse and minimized the website. Then he opened up a special folder he'd saved. Within were his various speeches, and also his embarrassing videos and pictures.

Dakota watched as Lance played back that part of the press conference where he talked about being raped. Then he played the videos of him making out with Bridget and dancing with Michael. He hated watching them, and grimaced with disgust to see how out-of-control he'd been when under the influence. He froze the image and turned his eyes on the impassive Dakota. "Sure you still wanna follow me?"

Dakota looked from the frozen image of Lance kissing Michael to Lance's questioning expression. There was a moment of silence between them.

"Yes," Dakota replied with vigor. "If you lead half as good as you shoot, you are a great chief."

Lance blew out his breathy little laugh. "Thanks, man."

Dakota studied the image of Lance and Michael kissing. Then he said, in a voice almost too low for Lance to hear over the beehive hum of the computers, "I was drunk when I stabbed him."

Lance studied the boy's profile, so striking did it look with the long black hair framing the high cheekbones, aquiline nose, and pinched mouth. But he said nothing, and waited.

"I was fourteen, my brother thirteen," Dakota went on quietly, his voice trembling with remorse. "We were drinking and playing with knives. I blacked out. When I woke up, I had a knife in my hand. There was blood everywhere, and he was barely alive." He stopped, eyes still fixed on that frozen kiss.

Lance sat stupefied, his whole body coiled and tense.

"He was practically brain-dead from bleeding out. He's a vegetable now. My mother has to do everything for him. And she disavowed me. They all did. I deserve it." He turned then to look right into Lance's eyes. "He was only thirteen and I ended his life." He paused again, as though composing himself. "Now you know why I was kicked out."

Lance wanted to reach out a hand and touch the other boy, but feared an adverse reaction given his negative view of Two-Spirits. *Oh, screw it*, he decided, and placed a hand of comfort on Dakota's rigid shoulder. The boy looked over sharply at the hand, and Lance smiled sadly, with understanding.

"Basic human contact, man. We all need it."

Dakota narrowed his eyes again, but made no attempt to flinch off the hand. "Do you still want to drink sometimes, Lance?"

Lance nodded, removing his hand and lowering it to his lap.

"How do you not?" Dakota asked desperately, his fingers trembling again.

Lance smiled warmly. "I reach out and take Ricky's hand." Just the memory of holding it filled him with peace. "Holding that boy's hand is better than any drug. When he holds my hand, I'm Superman, Dakota. I can do anything."

Dakota digested that information. "I've never been loved by someone like that."

"You're kidding, right? I mean, you're pretty hot and have kick-ass hair and you're all athletic and stuff. You never had a girlfriend?"

Dakota shook his head. "There were some girls on the rez who might have wanted me, before I…" He let the rest of the thought trail off, but Lance understood.

"You're with us now and we're gonna travel the country. You'll find someone like Ricky. A girl, I mean."

Dakota eyed the screen once again. "Maybe."

"Uh," Lance felt compelled to add, "you might try smiling once in a while, though. Girls love it when we smile."

Dakota didn't respond, nor did he attempt a smile.

Lance told him to keep scrolling through the website so he could familiarize himself with the Round Table and its overall goals. In particular, he directed Dakota to the most recent press conference about the CBOR.

"I'm gonna work with Ricky on revising our bill of rights to include native kids."

Dakota's eyes were already roaming pictures on the screen. "Cool."

Lance stood and watched Dakota a moment, but the boy sat transfixed by the power of imagery opening and closing before his eyes. He moved down the line to Kai and Ricky.

He noted that they were sitting close together, his eyes going to their thighs, which were clearly touching. He and Ricky were leaning in to the screen and giggling at something they were watching. As Lance watched, both boys moved a hand for the mouse at the same time and their fingers touched. Startled, Ricky looked over at Kai's face, and spotted Lance standing just beyond.

He yanked his hand back like it was on fire and turned redder than Lance had ever seen him. Kai's gaze quickly returned to the computer screen.

Lance stepped around behind them. "Everything okay here, guys?"

Ricky sat upright in his chair and moved slightly back from Kai. "Uh, yeah, Lance, no problem. Kai's had some practice on computers."

Kai looked sheepishly up at Lance. "Only at school, or when I go into the city, to the library. My rez is small and out there we barely even get many TV stations."

Lance noted that Ricky wouldn't meet his gaze. "Uh, Kai, we're gonna work on amending the bill, so maybe you could help Dakota."

Kai got to his feet quickly. "Sure, Lance. That dope probably never even used a computer before." He hurried away to join Dakota.

Lance looked soberly at Ricky, whose eyes remained downcast. "You guys were looking pretty friendly over here."

Ricky flicked his head up and their eyes met. "He's just fun, Lance, that's all. Dakota's right—he does laugh a lot. I like him."

Lance felt an uncharacteristic surge of jealousy. "You like him." That was all he could get out.

Ricky grinned. "Dumber-ass is jealous."

Lance stiffened. "Am not." He paused, his breath catching in his throat. "But he is good-looking and funny and I get all emo, you said so yourself, and—"

He didn't get any farther because Ricky was on his feet, one hand over Lance's mouth, cutting off his words. "You're the only one I love, Lance, all emo-ass and everything." He lowered his hand.

"For now and always?"

"For now and always."

They gazed breathlessly at each other a moment before suddenly realizing that all activity had ceased. They turned to the silent onlookers, grinned with embarrassment, and then bowed. Everyone laughed and applauded, Kai loudest of all. Dakota, as always, maintained his stoic demeanor and watched them dispassionately.

Secure in their oneness, they sat down to revise the Children's Bill of Rights. Lance slipped both letters from his pocket, the one from the Oglala Lakota and the other from the Navajo Nation.

Their concerns were similar, and shocking to the boys. Both tribes mentioned the rampant taking of Native children from their families into foster care, with those children never returned to their homes or families even if the mother or parents corrected whatever issues social services had originally objected to. As Dakota had told Lance, alcoholism was a huge problem. Mostly it was poverty, but Lance knew they had already mentioned poverty in the CBOR. Thirty-two out of the fifty states abused the Indian Child Welfare Act, which was supposed to protect Native kids from being taken from their homes without recourse.

In South Dakota, they discovered, over seven hundred Native children were taken from their homes every year, and only three per cent of those homes had ever been classified as abusive. As Lance and Ricky knew so well from all their forays into the political arena this past year, it came down to money. According to the information from the Lakota Tribal Council, the federal government's Bureau of Indian Affairs paid the state of South Dakota over seventy thousand dollars for each Native child placed into foster care, and another twelve thousand or so for every one adopted by a white family. Talk about a bribe! Lance's blood boiled every time he read that part, and he felt a fiery determination to help these kids.

Other serious issues amongst Native youth were alcoholism, of course, but also a high suicide rate, and an egregiously high number of children raped every year, boys as well as girls. When Lance had first read that part, it had taken Ricky's hand in his for thirty straight minutes to keep him from flashing back and freaking out.

The rapists of these children were almost exclusively white, and due to a Supreme Court ruling in 1978 called Oliphant v. Suquamish, Natives were not allowed to prosecute non-Natives for any crime, including rape or murder. Sam had already looked up that case and gotten the particulars. It involved a guy named Mark David Oliphant who was a non-Native living on a reservation, which was apparently not uncommon across the country. This guy was constantly getting into fights, beating up both men and women. He even beat up one of the tribal cops who intervened once. He was arrested on battery charges and sent to court.

For some reason, the Supreme Court took up this case and ruled that the Suquamish tribe didn't have the power to even charge Oliphant in their tribal courts because the guy was a white, non-Indian. As Lance and Ricky had listened to Sam explaining the case, both sat staring open-mouthed at their own brown skin and couldn't believe the country still did stuff like that.

Knowing these to be serious and weighty issues, and understanding that Tribal lands fell under a different legal umbrella than the rest of the country, the boys opened their Children's Bill of Rights and considered how best to make the revisions.

"Since native tribes are like, you know, their own little countries," Ricky began soberly, "how can what we put in here affect them?"

Lance considered a moment. They had learned the shocking fact that it wasn't until 1924 that Congress passed a law making all Indians United States citizens. Even the fourteenth amendment hadn't done that because some Indians didn't pay taxes to the federal government. That part hadn't surprised either boy, with money seemingly the only thing that mattered to government. Even after 1924, however, many states didn't know what to do with Indians, and Natives were banned from voting in state elections.

Lance and Ricky were stunned when Sam had explained all of this, and remained stunned now. Because Natives were both citizens of their tribal nations and the United States, and those tribal nations under U.S. law were called "domestic dependent nations," a separate Indian Bill of Rights had been passed by Congress in 1968 guaranteeing Indians the same rights as other citizens under the original Bill of Rights.

1968!

Lance had been shocked yet again that for all the years prior, Natives had no civil rights like other Americans. But that seemed to be their ace in the hole. If they tapped into the Indian Civil Rights Act of 1968, they should be able to include Native children in their CBOR.

So that's where they began as they scanned each amendment they'd written for language that could be changed to reference the ICRA, and the Indian Child Welfare Act. Apparently there was a flaw in that bill which allowed states to place Indian children with non-Indian parents without giving preferential consideration to other Indian homes that would maintain the cultural connection. Lance felt such contempt for these social service agencies that his body tightened with rage at this scandalous behavior.

In reviewing their Amendment Twenty-eight, the boys decided to insert a clause about placing children who *did* need removal because of serious abuse or neglect with another family member or someone of the same Indian tribe. The revised amendment read thus:

28. 'Congress shall make no law constraining anyone seventeen years or younger to the servitude or ownership of their biological parents, guardians, or any other adult or government entity; they shall henceforth from the date of passage of this

amendment be considered human beings in their own right and not, in any sense of the word, 'property'; likewise, the government nor any government – sponsored agency shall remove a child from his/her lawful parents without evidence of actual abuse or serious neglect—poverty, alone, shall not be a determining factor; if removal from the home is a necessity due to serious neglect or abuse, the child will be placed with a stable relative or member of a tribal community, in the case of Native American children, in order to maintain cultural and familial stability; in the event of removal from the home due to proven abuse or neglect, children, including Native Americans, shall have the innate right to return to their parents upon evidence of parental stability and the right to decide for themselves upon the issue of return; these provisions regarding Native children will supersede similar language within the Indian Child Welfare Act; likewise, minor children under eighteen years of age shall not find their freedom of speech infringed within any public venue, including schools and courtrooms, nor their right to peaceably assemble, or to petition the Government or government-controlled entities for redress of grievances, including, but not limited to, bullying behaviors inflicted upon them by school officials or students within those schools whereby no action was taken by school authorities to eliminate it'.

The boys sat back and reviewed what they had added. It looked clear enough, but they'd need to run it by Sam, and hopefully get feedback from the Tribal Councils, before putting it out to the public. As they considered the inability of Natives to prosecute non-Natives, even for so horrific a crime as raping a child, Lance flashed back to his own violation. If he'd reported it, Richard might have been put in prison and never hurt any other kid. But what about Michael? He *had* told his father, and the man had ignored the rape, covered it up, even.

What if children, themselves, could bring charges against adults who raped or assaulted them? If that were the case, and the CBOR became law, then Native children, at least, could bring charges against any rapist, even if that rapist was non-Native. It should invalidate the egregious unfairness of Oliphant v. Suquamish and allow prosecution of child rapists of Indian children. They tinkered with Amendment Thirty-Two, since that one involved giving minors rights against harassment by law enforcement. They played with the wording a bit and ended up revising the amendment in this way:

32. 'The right of children seventeen and under to be secure in their persons, homes, papers, and effects against unreasonable searches and seizures, shall not be violated, and no Warrants shall be issued, but upon probable cause, supported by Oath or affirmation, and describing the place to be searched, and the persons

or things to be seized; 'probable cause' is defined as a clear and present danger of criminality that may bring harm to persons or property (walking down the street with peers does not constitute 'probable cause'); any minor child who is raped or sexually abused, including Native American children raped or abused by non-Natives on or off tribal lands shall have the right to bring charges against the attacker, with or without adult support, and shall have the expectation that an arrest will be made and the case brought to trial, at which time the child may testify against his or her attacker; said testimony may be recorded on video to protect the child from having to directly face his or her assailant in court'.

Again studying what they had written, the boys felt satisfied with the wording. Sam would have to be the final arbiter, and they would alter any phraseology per his recommendations. Sadly, they did not know how their CBOR could address the high alcoholism and suicide rates amongst Native youth, but then, much of that could be due to the removal of children from tribal lands and the unspoken-of sexual abuse. Lance knew all too well how his own horrific childhood experiences had contributed to the drinking he'd done earlier in the year.

The boys sat for a time, side by side, hands clasped between them, relishing the presence of the other. Lance glanced over a moment at Kai and Dakota, who seemed oblivious to anyone but each other. Kai was chattering on about this picture or that one, while Dakota grunted and nodded, but continued moving the mouse around like he was flying a plane.

Ricky looked down at his and Lance's intertwined fingers, and then indicated the computer screen. "You're getting pretty good at this political stuff, Lance. Maybe you should take the mayor's advice and run for president someday."

Lance laughed. "And if I did, you'd be the First Lady. Ha!"

Ricky feigned an angry glower. "Don't even go there, fool."

Lance sat up quickly and raised his free hand, snapping his fingers. "I got it, Ricky! This is how we'd be introduced." He cleared his throat and deepened his voice, trying to replicate a loudspeaker. "Ladies and gentlemen, the President and the First Fool." He busted up as Ricky's eyes went wide.

"I am so going to kick your ass," Ricky said with a shake of his head, but grinning nonetheless.

Still laughing, Lance shoved him. "Yeah, you and what army again?"

Ricky shoved him back and joined in the laughter. But their hands never unclasped. They were one spirit in two boys.

At the gathering that afternoon, Dakota and Kai were introduced to those of the Round Table who hadn't met them in school during the week, and the newcomers were welcomed with a hearty round of applause. They were also something of a curiosity since, other than Lance and Ricky fitting the image, most of these kids had never seen a real Native American before. Lance explained the need to amend the CBOR to include Native American children, and then had Techie project onto the flat – screen the two revised amendments.

Everyone approved of the changes, including Jenny, Arthur, and Merlin. The assemblage was shocked to learn of the abuses heaped upon Indian children because of their murky dual citizenship status. Those who grew up in the inner city finally found out that there were kids worse off than they were. It was sobering for all.

Some knights reported on the mayor's City Hall meetings, and everyone liked what they were seeing. They'd met representatives from Homeboy Industries and other community groups serving the various neighborhoods. All had given the mayor and city council many ideas on how to make life better for kids growing up in those areas, and the mayor hoped to begin implementing these ideas at the start of the new year.

Lance and Ricky noted, without any awkwardness, that Bridget sat beside Justin and Ariel beside Techie at the gathering. The girls, lovely as ever, Bridget outgoing and effusive, Ariel shy and timid, both smiled warmly at the boys before the gathering began, and bade them a pleasant good-bye when it ended.

Lance felt relieved that Bridget didn't hold a grudge against him. But then, she'd told him that night he'd confessed the truth to her that she'd suspected it for a long time, and understood. Yep, Bridget was some girl and he hoped it all worked out for her and Justin.

Knowing he couldn't keep anything from Ricky, later that night as they lay side by side on Lance's bed, Lance revealed Dakota's story.

Ricky, ever in protective mode, worried that Dakota might start drinking and encourage Lance to do the same.

Lance looked over at this boy who held his heart in the palm of his hand, and smiled warmly. "Fool," he said breathlessly. "The only alcohol I need is you. And I'm drunk on you 24/7. So get over it."

Ricky's eyes lit up with delight. "Have I told you lately that you're a dumbass?"

"Practically every hour."

"But have I told you that I love you more than I thought it was possible to love a dumbass?"

Lance laughed, and slipped his hand into the place where it belonged. "I think you just did. Dumbass."

Ricky chuckled, and squeezed the other's hand. As uncertain as the future appeared, it would all be perfect as long as they had each other.

But that was before Christmas, when everything changed.

CHAPTER FIVE

A DANCE TO THE DEATH

THE NEXT FEW WEEKS LEADING into Christmas flew past as more and more people across the country commented on the CBOR. Lance and Ricky had shown their changes to Sam, who fostered the opinion that they were "Soundly written for now, but will no doubt be hotly debated by the politicians whenever the CBOR goes before Congress."

Dakota and Kai settled into the routine of school with the other young knights seeking high school diplomas. Both had been accustomed to having a male teacher on their reservations, and sitting around a large table discussing issues was also new to them. They'd been used to the standard desks of most American schools, but quickly adapted, especially the gregarious Kai.

When not in school, the newcomers spent their time training with the sword and shield or acquiring computer skills under the direction of Sir Techie. They watched every video related to the Round Table, especially Lance's numerous press conferences, and voraciously devoured the Code of Chivalry in preparation for knighthood. Both declared the Code and the general precepts of Arthur's Round Table similar to their own cultural traditions.

Dakota told Lance and Ricky that the Lakota had a phrase— *mitakuye oyasin*— that meant, "We are all related" or "All my relations." They believed that all living things were connected, and all peoples were relations, much like Lance's credo that everyone was simply "human."

Not to be outdone, Kai told the boys how the *Diné* believed there were two classes of beings—the Earth People and the Holy People—and that the Holy People taught the Earth People how to live the right way, in harmony with the earth and all living things on it.

To Lance and Ricky, both traditions sounded similar, and in striking alignment with Arthur's beliefs, and the teachings of the Round Table. The two Indians, while vastly different in temperament and personality, obviously shared a long and ambiguous friendship since early childhood that transcended Dakota's distaste for Two-Spirits, and since Thanksgiving they had become inseparable. Both continuously insisted that Lance and Ricky were of Native blood, too, which intrigued the boys and seemed to forge a quick and strong bond between the four of them, a bond that would be tested before year's end.

Because they were in college, Reyna and Esteban spent less time at New Camelot than they would've liked, especially during the week. On weekends, however, both showed for gatherings and training practice, and assisted the others in responding to comments or questions about the CBOR. They had all talked about the need to travel the country at some point down the line, and Reyna volunteered to organize their route when that time arose.

She happily pointed out to Lance that Mark's father in Washington State and Jack's mother in Idaho had garnered much adult support in their respective areas, and were now reaching out across the country.

Lance thanked them for their help. Both adults were broken at the loss of their kids, but neither shirked his or her responsibility in that loss, and freely shared their culpability with the entire country as an example of why children needed more Constitutional rights – to protect them from weak or ineffectual parents like themselves.

For his part, Esteban kept in regular contact with the former gang members who watched over their neighborhoods, many of whom were now part of the mayor's task force. These knights, spread out over Los Angeles, reported in to Esteban on a regular basis all developments within their respective areas, and he offered advice to suit the situation or need. Very rarely these days did he need to consult Arthur, or Lance, for both trusted him to make the right choices.

Because Reyna was so occupied in the Computer Lab, Sylvia had taken over archery instruction in the Training Centre. She'd taken Chris under her wing, improving his technique and accuracy, something Lance was happy to see. He felt guilty for not spending more time with Chris, and thanked Sylvia one afternoon before heading to the Computer Lab.

Sylvia almost blushed. "Oh, he's a fun kid, Lance. I don't have a little brother of my own."

Suddenly Lance realized he knew little about her background. She'd said her mother didn't pay much attention to whether she was home or not, but had never talked about anyone else. "Do you have any older ones?"

"One. But he's much older and doesn't live around here. I barely know him."

Lance frowned sadly and placed a hand on her shoulder. "Well, you have all of us as your brothers and sisters. Don't forget that."

She beamed and headed off to the Training Centre.

During these weeks, Lance received no more threats. The FBI had drawn a blank on the origin of the last threatening text, though they had not yet given up. The seeming randomness of these threats had them baffled. Ryan and Gibson remained on high alert at all times, but Lance and Ricky—being boys—began to worry less and less about a possible attack, instead focusing their energies on the CBOR, their relationship, and teaching Kai and Dakota the ways of the Round Table.

As it turned out, both Indians were avid horsemen and loved seeing the pictures and videos of Llamrei. They had grown up riding, and considered themselves experts with horses.

Ricky laughed when he heard that. "Oh great, two horse whisperers and one soul whisperer," he said, playfully shoving Lance one day when they were all in the Computer Lab.

Lance shoved him right back. "Yeah, and one fool whisperer."

Both boys laughed, and Kai joined in.

Dakota, as always, remained poker-faced. "You're not like any Two-Spirits I ever saw."

That intrigued Lance. "What do you mean?"

Dakota shrugged. "The way you mess with each other, but you say you love each other."

Ricky grinned. "Oh, that's 'cause we're boys."

"And fools," Lance chimed in.

"That, too," Ricky agreed with a laugh.

Kai looked on in admiration, but Dakota merely stared, his eyes narrowed with bewilderment.

The Indians ached to meet Llamrei and ride her. Despite having his rotation of knights grooming and caring for her, Arthur had been too busy since the wedding to take Llamrei out for exercise, so when Lance approached him the week before Christmas with the idea of he, Ricky, Kai, and Dakota going to the stables, the king at first thought it a good idea. But then the threatening words from Lance's phone came back to him, and he hesitated. True, they'd been attending mass on most Sundays without incident, but this outing sounded more questionable.

He called in Ryan, Gibson, and Justin for their opinions. Needless to say, they were dubious at the notion of taking the boys to such an open venue as the Equestrian Center, especially if it involved riding horses through Griffith Park.

"Talk about a shooting gallery," Gibson remarked soberly.

"How would anyone know we're gonna be there?" Lance asked, glancing at Ricky for support.

"Yeah, Dad," Ricky said to Arthur. "You never told them ahead of time you were gonna visit Llamrei, so we won't either."

"Yeah," Lance chimed in. "We just show up and nobody'll know till after we're gone."

The two detectives exchanged a look. Lance could see their faces and he knew they were recalling in vivid detail the unannounced visit to Manic Mountain last summer that had almost gotten them killed.

Justin ran his hands through his mop of hair thoughtfully as he eyed Lance, a nervous habit he'd adopted since growing it out. "You know, Lance, that everybody who sees you is gonna get right on their phones and text that you guys're there. You're too famous to just wander around, man."

Gibson looked impressed. "Good point, Justin."

Then Lance got an idea. He turned to Kai and Dakota. "Say, you guys got any of your Indian clothes we can wear? If we all dress up as Indians and have our bows and arrows, strangers'll either think we're either native or crazy, but probably won't recognize us."

"I brought some regalia with me," Kai said. "Did you?"

Dakota nodded.

"You got extras for me and Lance?" Ricky asked.

Simultaneously, both answered, "Yes." Kai laughed at their synchronicity, but Dakota looked mortified.

Lance turned to Arthur. "C'mon, Dad, my *nino* and Sergeant Gibson won't let anything happen to us."

"I won't, either," Dakota announced in his deep, powerful voice.

"I'll protect you, too," Kai added, glancing at Dakota, but the Lakota boy grunted dismissively.

Now all eyes were on the king, as he sat in his throne and contemplated the idea. "Should you dress up in this regalia of theirs, Lance, would that not attract *more* attention, rather than less?"

"Probably, but we *will* look different than we usually do, Dad. We can even do this." He yanked the circlet off his head and whipped his long thick hair right into his face where it dangled across his eyes and down his cheeks. "Who's gonna recognize me now, 'specially if I don't say anything. I'll just look like one of Merlin's head-bangers."

Catching the idea, Ricky flung off his own circlet and did the head banger routine, too, making both boys resemble members of a heavy metal band.

Kai laughed, but Dakota looked at them aghast, Lance noticed from behind his hair.

That boy needs to lighten up, he thought as he awaited Arthur's answer.

The king sighed heavily. "I suppose we cannot be prisoners within our own home. Our enemies will win without having done anything. Very well, but never stray from the watchful eye of either sergeant."

Lance whipped his hair back from his face and grinned. He missed Llamrei, too, and wanted to see how the new boys could ride. He himself didn't feel all that confident on a horse and, in fact, had never ridden Llamrei without his dad. Still, he missed her calming presence.

Jenny, however, was not so calm when told of their plans later that day, but the boys assured her they had plenty of protection in the two detectives and the two Indians, and they'd be armed with bows and arrows, anyway.

Lance, who'd never known a mother, and Ricky whose mother abandoned him, loved how she fretted over them, but being boys on the cusp of manhood, they also felt the need to step out and handle things on their own.

So it was settled that the trek to the L.A. Equestrian Center would take place two days before Christmas in the hopes that the riding trails would be less crowded due to holiday shopping and preparations.

Of course, when Chris found out they were going he wouldn't stop pestering Jenny until she allowed him to go, as well. He insisted he could wear a beanie and no one would recognize him. "Lance and Ricky are the ones on TV all the time, not me."

Arthur also felt badly that Chris had not gotten to ride Llamrei for his birthday, as had been planned, and talked Jenny into it.

Lance and Ricky met Dakota and Kai in Dakota's room the night before the visit to decide which regalia each would wear.

Most of the stuff was brightly colored with fringes along the cuffs and even around the ankles, and Lance felt these might call too much attention to them. Dakota produced a breastplate made up of carved wooden dowels made to look like bones, strung together with leather strips and adorned with feathers.

He eyed Lance. "Take off your shirt."

Lance was caught off guard. "Huh?"

Ricky looked sharply over at Dakota, but the Indian remained calm and impassive.

"This is made to be worn with no shirt."

Lance shook his head. "No way, Dakota, I can't ride around in public with no shirt on. Especially in December. It's cold."

Ricky giggled. "C'mon, Lance, try it on anyway."

"You just wanna see me with my shirt off."

"Course I do," Ricky remarked with a laugh. "Now off with it. Show these guys your buffness."

Reddening slightly, but not wanting to appear weak in front of Dakota, Lance slipped off his shirt and dropped it onto the bed.

Ricky heard Kai gasp slightly, but he couldn't pull his eyes from Lance's smooth, defined torso. Dakota eyed the others with amusement, his own gaze sweeping over the obviously embarrassed Lance with admiration. He slipped the breastplate over Lance's head and stepped behind him to tie the leather strip around his neck. Then he stepped back.

Lance felt naked and exposed.

Ricky blew out a breath. "You look kick-ass, Lance. Beautiful as hell."

Kai smiled shyly. "You do."

"You gotta wear that, Lance," Ricky added with an excited laugh.

Lance shook his head vehemently. "Hell, no," he said with an embarrassed chuckle.

"It suits you, Lance," Dakota said, giving him an appraising once over. "But I have shirts, too."

Dakota untied the leather strip, and Lance lifted the breastplate up and over his head, handing it back to him. "I think it'd look better on Ricky. Why not show these guys *your* buffness, huh?"

Ricky suddenly looked mortified. "No way I'm goin' naked, either. We need real clothes."

Kai laughed and it almost seemed like Dakota cracked a smile. Almost.

Lance slipped his shirt back on and they finally settled on long fringed leather pants, and for Lance a red long sleeved shirt Dakota had brought with rectangular strips down each sleeve and down both sides of the front. These strips contained colorful triangular shapes that Dakota said were tribal symbols.

Ricky took one of Kai's long sleeved shirts, white with Southwest patterns of orange and yellow and blue, also in triangular shapes, adorning the front and sleeves. Dakota pulled out a beaded headband made up of red, white, blue and orange beads, with a big colorful wheel in the center of the forehead, and dangling feathers from each temple.

Kai produced something similar, also beaded, but in more muted colors, with a bigger circle in the center and, rather than dangly feathers, his sported long strings of large beads with a circular hoop at the end. The Indians laid out similar clothing for themselves and everything was set for the outing.

Lance and Ricky left Kai and Dakota to return to Lance's room, and plopped onto the bed, as had become their nightly ritual. Lance lay back and Ricky placed his head in his lap. Lance grabbed Ricky's hair and tugged.

"Ow!" Ricky cried out, looking up at Lance with surprise. "What was that for?"

"For making me take my shirt off in front of them," Lance replied with a playful shove at Ricky's shoulder. "Dakota looks like he's pretty built and you embarrassed me."

"Can you blame me for showing off the body I love?"

"Fool."

Ricky reached for Lance's hand. Suddenly, he frowned. "You think Dakota looks built? You checking out other guys, Lance?"

Lance smiled with amusement. "I may be the soul whisperer, but you're the jealousy whisperer."

"Am not," Ricky protested, but then relaxed into a grin. "Well, sometimes. How can I help it when you're, like, the hottest boy in the world?"

Lance blew out a breath. "I only love *you*, fool. What part of 'for now and always' didn't you get?"

That seemed to settle Ricky's fears, and a graceful peace swept over them.

"You sure we're gonna be all right tomorrow?" Ricky asked quietly.

"What could go wrong at a stable?"

Ricky fell silent.

Little did either boy know just how much *could* go wrong at a stable.

Especially when someone wanted you dead.

The following day dawned clear and sunny, but cool—a typical December day in Southern California. The boys all had breakfast in the dining room before returning to their rooms to dress in their Indian clothes. Arthur placed a call to the Equestrian Center and talked with the director explaining that he was sending a delegation to take out Llamrei and some other horses for a ride, but to keep them away from the general public as much as possible. Llamrei, he knew, had become something of a recognizable celebrity in her own right. The director agreed.

After donning their Indian regalia, and with Chris "In disguise," as he kept saying, with an extra-large beanie covering his hair, the boys all descended the stairs to meet Ryan and Gibson in the Throne Room.

Jenny gasped with surprise upon seeing them. "Wow," she said, and Arthur smiled at her reaction. She immediately put the boys together for some photos, using a new Canon DSLR she'd been given as a wedding gift. Then she put all five boys into a shot with Arthur, and lastly asked Gibson to take a family portrait.

Lance rolled his eyes. "C'mon, mom, we're not goin' to the prom or something."

Jenny grinned. "I don't care. I want a family shot with my boys. Oh, and James, you, too."

Ryan looked startled. "Me?"

Lance laughed. "Of course, *nino*. You're my godfather, aren't you?"

Ryan joined them, standing beside Arthur. The three boys stood in front of the adults and Gibson snapped off a few shots.

Then it was into Ryan's sedan for Lance, Ricky, and Chris while Gibson took Dakota and Kai in his beamer.

The Los Angeles Equestrian Center wasn't far from New Camelot, technically in the city of Burbank, right at the northern tip of Griffith Park. At seventy-five acres, it was the largest such venue in Southern California and boasted trail riding, cricket fields, training rings, the Equidome Show Ring for Olympic-style events, and acres of barns and stables, grass and dirt, and lots of large shade trees, all surrounded by two-tiered white fencing.

Lance and Ricky had never been there. It had always been Arthur or his rotating knights that visited Llamrei, or the horse had been driven to New Camelot. Lance was impressed by the sheer immensity of the center as Ryan pulled in through the gigantic, barn-shaped entry and into the parking lot. Gibson's beamer slid into an empty spot beside them and everyone piled out.

Lance saw by their faces that Dakota and Kai had never seen anything like this place, either. As he looked around, Lance spotted several sleek, beautiful horses being put through their paces by trainers. He glanced back at the others, all in their fancy Indian regalia, and grinned. Dakota's hair hung loose down his back as always, restrained by a colorful headpiece, while Kai wore his hair in his usual braids with a traditional headband as adornment. With all four sporting bows and quivers of arrows slung across their backs, they'd absolutely call attention to themselves, but not as Knights of the Round Table.

As had been pre-arranged by Arthur, one of the directors of the center met them in the parking lot. He eyed the boys and their attire with curiosity, but didn't ask questions. Arthur had explained that they were Native American knights who were also expert horsemen, and the director simply led the group past numerous horse stalls in search of Llamrei. The Indian boys could not take their eyes off every horse they passed, and Lance knew they itched interact with each one in turn.

Finally, they saw a white head sticking out of a stall window, long flowing mane flicking lightly from side to side as Llamrei shook her head at some annoyance or other. Lance broke into a huge grin.

"Llamrei!" he called out, and pelted toward the mare. Upon hearing her name, she turned her massive head and whinnied. Lance stopped just in front of her and grinned. He hadn't seen her in such a long while and didn't want to spook her.

"I'm sorry, girl, for not visiting," he apologized quietly as the others joined him. "Can you forgive me?"

Llamrei neighed and stuck her head out further, rubbing her muzzle against his cheek, causing Lance to laugh with delight.

"I guess that's a yes," Ricky said with a grin, reaching out to stroke the silky mane before him.

Kai let out a soft breath of amazement. "She's beautiful."

Dakota stepped forward and held out his hand to the mare.

Llamrei sniffed it and then immediately began rubbing her snout into his palm.

Lance was impressed. "Wow. She likes you."

Dakota grunted, but said nothing more. He placed his hand on her neck and stroked it, softly and with reverence. Llamrei loved it. She turned her head to eye the boy, and Dakota eyed her right back. No words were spoken, but Lance could instantly see a connection.

"I wish to ride her," Dakota said, his deep voice soft and respectful.

"That's why we're here," Lance said, petting Llamrei.

The director had the stable hands saddle Llamrei and another horse for Kai. Lance and Ricky wanted to see what the boys could do, and after they'd demonstrated their aptitude as horsemen, then other mounts would be brought around for Lance, Ricky and Chris to take a trail ride through Griffith Park.

Ryan and Gibson stood on high alert, suspiciously observing anyone who even looked in their direction. As it was morning on a weekday, there weren't many visitors. Dakota eased up onto Llamrei's back as though he belonged there, and Lance could tell the mare was smitten. Ricky had been right—Dakota was some kind of horse whisperer. He deftly directed the mare out of the stable area with barely a command and cantered her out to the nearest training circle. She instinctively knew what he wanted. Lance was deeply impressed.

Kai was almost as proficient with his mare, named Lady, a brown American quarter horse with a short tail and mane, four white socks and a white snout. As with Dakota, the horse instantly slipped into the boy's rhythm and they became a single entity as he trotted her around the open area alongside Dakota.

Lance and Ricky watched Kai and Dakota direct their horses into one of the training circles and execute easy, fluid moves with their mounts.

"Yep," Ricky muttered, "that's horse whispering all right."

He tousled Chris's hair and Lance chuckled as they observed the boys put their horses through a series of trots, gallops, and reverses.

After several minutes, Kai and Dakota happily cantered over to where Lance and Ricky stood with the others. The director began telling them what impressive riders they were when he was suddenly flung backwards with a strangled "Oomph!" and fell sprawling to the ground, dazed.

Everyone spun around to see several golf-cart type vehicles plowing up the road toward them, each carrying two men, one man in each cart with his arm outstretched aiming a long-barreled handgun straight at them. Everything seemed to happen at once. Ryan grabbed Chris and they dropped to the ground as Gibson pulled his gun.

"Lance!" Dakota called out.

Lance spun to see the Indian with his hand outstretched, and instantly understood.

"Ricky, with Kai," he shouted as he stretched out his hand and clasped Dakota's. The Indian pulled as Lance leapt and suddenly he was up and into the saddle behind the other.

"Lance!" he heard Ricky yell even as Kai trotted up to him, hand outstretched.

"Do it, Ricky!" Lance yelled and suddenly Ricky's hand was in Kai's and he was up and into the saddle behind the other boy.

Terrified, Ricky clung tightly to Kai. He glanced at Lance, whose arms encircled Dakota's waist, and then the two Indians dug in their heels and the horses bolted.

Ricky almost lost his balance, but managed to hang on.

Behind him, Lance heard Gibson fire his gun and then they were away from the practice circle and galloping headlong down the road toward an open gate. Lance felt something whiz past his head and knew they were being shot at. He glanced over at Ricky, clinging desperately to Kai as the quarter horse paced Llamrei, and then turned to look over his shoulder.

The three golf carts were chasing them now, leaving Ryan and Gibson scrambling in the distance for some way to pursue. Lance saw Gibson raise his phone as Ryan yanked Chris to his feet and began running sidelong toward some other golf carts parked by the fence.

Their pursuers were gaining, but he couldn't get a clear shot facing forward. Another bullet whizzed past him as Dakota rode Llamrei in a zigzagging pattern.

"Dakota!" he called out against the wind, flinging the dangling feathers away from his eyes. "I'm gonna flip around so I can shoot. When I do, throw the reins over me and tug tight so I don't fall."

"You got it!" he heard, but Dakota's eyes remained forward. By now they were out of the Equestrian Center and galloping onto the light traffic of Riverside Drive, dodging and weaving in between cars and creating a spectacle for so early on a weekday.

"Head into the park!" Kai called out as the roadway took them over the L.A. River, and Dakota yelled, "Right!"

Lance slipped his right leg up and behind Dakota's back carefully, his arms remaining around the other boy's torso. He let out a sigh of relief when he was over and sitting sidesaddle behind the Indian youth. Then, with a desperate grin at Ricky, Lance flung his left leg up and over Llamrei's rear, reaching behind desperately for Dakota's body to hold on to. He overshot the move slightly, and began to slip.

"Lance!" Ricky screamed in horror, but Dakota's right hand let go the reins and flung back to grab Lance's arm, righting him on the horse.

"Thanks, man!" Lance called out, his heart pumping with momentary terror. "Now toss me the reins!"

Dakota flung the long circular rein over his and Lance's head. Lance caught it and tugged, signaling Dakota to pull taut, which he did. Lance felt the tightness of the reins against his midsection, and knew he wouldn't fall. Now he could fight back.

The carts were gaining on them, but being electric vehicles and not street-legal, he figured they couldn't make more than fifteen or twenty miles per hour. Lance slung his bow off his back and reached behind for an arrow, nocking it with ease. The up and down motion of the horse forced him to aim more carefully, but his eye was excellent. He let the arrow fly and it struck the left front tire of the first cart, sending the cart veering off to the side of the road. Cars screeched as it careened into the embankment.

Lance looked over at Ricky, who gazed at him aghast, his own hair and headpiece flapping wildly in the wind, and flashed a thumbs-up. Ricky grinned and slipped off his bow, snatching an arrow and doing his best to load it while not toppling off the bouncing, zigzagging horse. Kai dodged in between cars, just as Dakota did, and suddenly the 101 freeway loomed overhead. Horses and riders flew beneath it and they were into the park, veering sharply left onto Forest Lawn Drive.

Lance was dismayed to see that the other two carts managed to avoid being crushed by the cars and had plowed into the park after them. Suddenly, another cart flew at them from the side. Lance caught sight of it in his peripheral vision, but couldn't take a clean shot.

"Ricky," he shouted. "To your left!"

Ricky's head spun quickly and he saw two men in the cart, heading straight for him on a sideways collision course. One man raised his arm and the gun glinted in the morning sun. Ricky swung his arms up and over Kai's bent head and took aim at the man, letting loose his arrow without hesitation. The arrow struck the man in his upper arm, causing him to cry out and drop the gun, which clattered and skipped along the pavement of the roadway.

"Yes!" Ricky called out, using one hand to desperately grab Kai's arm for stability. By then Lady was past that fork in the road and galloping neck and neck with Llamrei as they headed deeper into the park.

Lance grinned over at him. "Nice shooting."

Ricky grimaced.

Then Lance raised his bow again, strung another arrow and let it fly. It struck the man in the cart behind them full in the chest. The man flinched, but the arrow just bounced off. Lance's breath caught in his throat. What the hell…

He nocked another arrow and fired at the other man, the one raising the gun. The arrow struck, again straight to the chest, but the man barely flinched before raising his gun arm again.

Another arrow flew past Lance and struck the man's hand, drawing spouts of blood and sending the gun flying back into the road.

Lance looked across at Ricky, and called out, "Thanks, fool." And then he understood. "Ricky, they're wearing bulletproof vests or something. Aim for the arms or the head!"

"I think I already figured that out, fool!"

"Hang on, Lance!" Dakota called back, his body-length hair practically blinding Lance as he turned his head. "I'm taking her off the road and it's rocky."

"You, too, Ricky," Kai called out. "Hang on!"

And then both horses were off the paved road and galloping frenetically across the empty grass toward the hilly, rockier terrain dead ahead.

Lance watched as the carts veered off-road in pursuit, but began quickly losing ground as the land became more uneven. He saw one man raise a walkie-talkie to his mouth and knew that couldn't be good.

Trails wound in and among the hills and little valleys, but the Indians felt on safer ground by avoiding these. They were correct, too, because the carts had to veer onto those paths and come at them from obtuse angles, which made shooting a trickier prospect.

That was when Lance heard it. A loud *whup whup whup* in the air above them. A helicopter, easily as large as any police chopper he'd ever seen, rose up over the trees and bore down on them. It sported a nasty-looking machine gun-type weapon attached to one side, but Lance could make out nothing of the pilot.

"Dakota, faster!" he shouted, brushing his and the other boy's hair from his face and nocking another arrow. "Hang on, Ricky!" he called out as the copter veered down and swung around after them. He took aim and fired. The arrow struck the shield protecting the pilot, but bounced off and drifted harmlessly to the ground.

"Oh, hell," Lance mumbled as the machine gun took aim and began firing. Dirt kicked up from the ground behind them as the bullets struck, but Dakota and Kai executed a sideways maneuver that took them down into a slight gulley before sending them up in another direction. The chopper changed course to follow.

Suddenly, they were out of the rough terrain and galloping across a huge expanse of green grass with trees on either side. Lance heard Llamrei's frantic panting, and noted the frothing of Lady alongside. They had to find shelter quickly or they'd all be dead.

The helicopter picked up speed even as Dakota flung the reins side to side in an effort to keep Llamrei weaving back and forth, making her a more difficult target. Kai attempted the same with Lady, but she was smaller than Llamrei and appeared to be tiring. Kai and Ricky fell behind, and to his horror Lance saw the helicopter targeting them. The gun resumed firing. The grass kicked up divots in a line heading straight for Ricky.

"Ricky, look out!" Lance shouted at the top of his lungs, his heart in his throat.

Ricky turned to look just as a bullet struck Lady in the flank and she reared, neighing wildly in pain. Caught by surprise. Ricky toppled off her back as Kai struggled to control the frantic mare.

"Ricky!" Lance screamed as the boy landed hard on the ground and rolled a few times before lying motionless. Without hesitation, Lance tossed the reins up and over his head and leapt from Llamrei's back, landing hard on his feet and crumpling to the grass.

The *whup whup whup* was coming back.

Lance scrambled to his feet as the helicopter circled for another run at Ricky. Lance didn't hesitate. He bolted forward, bow still in hand as Ricky began to stir on the grass twenty-five feet away.

"Ricky!" he called out in terror.

Ricky pushed himself to a sitting position and grinned sheepishly. "I just fell, fool."

Then Lance was there, his arms around this most precious person in the world. "Oh, thank God, I thought you got shot!"

The helicopter noise got louder. Both boys looked up in horror. It was nearly upon them. Lance scrambled to his feet and dragged Ricky up. "You go for that propeller thing in the back," he ordered, "and I'll take out the gun."

Ricky shook his head to clear it, snatched up his fallen bow and arrows and nocked one, as Lance did the same. Both boys took careful aim—Ricky at the rotor in the rear of the chopper, and Lance at the gun barrel itself.

"Now!" Lance ordered, and both arrows flew. Lance's slipped right into the barrel of the gun as it began firing, and the entire unit exploded in a shower of sparks and flying shrapnel. Ricky's arrow connected with the rear rotor and they heard a screeching of metal, as though the chopper cried out in pain.

"We got it!" Ricky shouted gleefully and moved to high-five Lance.

Lance's mouth hung open. "Hell, no!"

Ricky looked and saw the damaged copter spinning out of the sky—right toward them!

"Run!" Lance screamed, and they both sprinted as fast as they could along the grass.

"Where the hell're Kai and Dakota?" Ricky called out breathlessly.

Lance was wondering the same thing when he heard the pounding of hooves against ground. He glanced over his shoulder. The Indians were charging their horses side-by-side right in their direction, the falling helicopter spinning out of the sky straight at them.

"Lance, grab on!" Dakota called out, as Kai yelled the same to Ricky. Then Llamrei was beside Lance and Lady beside Ricky, one hand of each rider extended and grasping. Lance reached out and felt Dakota's rock-solid grip take him and then he was up and onto the horse behind the boy in one fluid motion.

He looked over at Ricky, still pelting along, panting from exertion, his own hand grasping wildly for Kai's. "Grab it, Ricky!"

Kai made a lunge, missed, and then swung his arm out again. This time they connected and Ricky flew up and back, landing heavily in the saddle behind an obviously relieved Kai. Both riders spurred their horses forward with strong kicks just as the chopper crashed heavily to the ground behind them in a rending, grinding, crumpling mass of metal and plastic.

Lance glanced back, certain the thing would burst into flames, but it just rolled one last time and then lay there on the grass like a dead dinosaur.

Hair streaming like a wild animal's, Dakota called out over his shoulder, "Where to now, Lance?"

Lance scanned the terrain ahead, glancing over a moment to make sure Ricky was safe, and then back ahead. He saw a paved road with no carts on it. "Try that road!" he yelled, pointing.

Dakota veered Llamrei in the indicated direction, and Kai followed just behind. As they galloped onto the road, Lance saw the sign—Zoo Drive.

"Hey, I think this leads into the zoo!" he shouted, loud enough for both Dakota and Kai to hear. "Maybe we can hide in there."

Dakota grunted, the sound almost lost in the wind. But they continued forward as Lance slipped his bow over one shoulder and pulled out his phone. He speed-dialed Ryan, praying there was cell service within the park.

In a moment, he heard Ryan's crackling voice in his ear. "Lance, where are you?"

Lance could barely make him out. "On Zoo Drive!" he shouted into the phone. "I think we're headed into the zoo."

"Okay," crackled his godfather as the signal wavered. "I got backup—" And then nothing. The signal cut out.

What was he about to say?

But he didn't have time to contemplate an answer because suddenly, from a side trail, came two more of those stupid carts bearing more guys with guns!

Lance slipped the phone back into his pocket and called out to Ricky. "You take the first one, I'll get the second!"

Ricky nodded.

Both boys whipped up their bows and nocked arrows with lightning speed, just as they'd been trained to do. Turning to shoot back while facing forward was awkward at best, but they twisted their trunks around as far as possible and fired. Ricky's arrow missed, but Lance's struck the rear tire of the second cart and sent it staggering off the road into the dirt.

"Yes!" Lance called out, but there was no time to celebrate as the passenger in the remaining cart had his gun raised and began firing.

Lance and Ricky ducked as Dakota and Kai bobbed and weaved and controlled their mounts like drivers in an auto speedway. Lance poked his head back out to peek forward and his heart leapt. Just ahead *was* the zoo entrance, and three police cruisers blocked the road in front. Cops crouched behind each car aiming their weapons at the pursuing cart, but were obviously unable to get off a shot for fear of hitting horse or riders.

He spotted Ryan and Chris crouching low, Chris with his bow cocked and aimed straight at them. Despite his terror, he grinned at his brother's fearless stance.

"Dakota," he called out, "can you jump her over the cop car?" He knew his dad had that ability, but wasn't sure about the Indian.

"I can do anything with a horse," the boy called back without hesitation. Then he glanced over at Kai. "Did you hear him, Laughs A Lot?"

"I can do anything you can, Cloudy Boy," Kai shouted back.

Oh, great, Lance thought, *this is so not the time to prove something.*

He looked across at Ricky as the horses bounded ever closer to the police cars and mouthed, "I love you, fool."

Ricky mouthed it back.

Then they were airborne and Lance grabbed tightly to Dakota's waist as Llamrei muscled her way high into the air. Lance looked down as the red and blue lights of the cop car passed beneath him, and then the horse landed deftly to the pavement on the other side, jolting Lance forward into Dakota's back and nearly dislodging him. He looked over frantically just as Lady's hooves clattered onto the pavement beside them and Ricky grinned like a fool.

Lance whipped around to see what was happening. His heart nearly stopped as Chris rose to his feet and fired his arrow before any police officers even got off a shot. It struck the incoming cart square in the left front tire, and the vehicle careened off the road into the dirt. The cops were up and running before Lance's breathing even resumed.

Dakota turned to Kai and they let loose with an ear-piercing war whoop, swinging their fists into the air. Lance and Ricky joined the Indians in their whooping, while Chris pelted toward them.

Lance slipped off Llamrei and scooped the boy into his arms. "That was some shooting, little man!"

Chris grinned proudly, his arms tightly wrapped around Lance's neck. "Damn straight."

Lance laughed as Ricky joined them. The boys hugged and held one another as Dakota and Kai trotted over on their exhausted, frothing mounts.

Poor Llamrei, Lance thought. Not exactly the workout she was used to. He set Chris onto the ground and stroked Llamrei's sweaty snout lovingly.

"Thanks, girl," he said before looking up at Dakota and Kai sitting solidly and calmly atop the horses, and shook his head in amazement. "That was some incredible riding, guys."

"That's for sure," Ricky echoed with a nervous laugh. "I thought I was a goner a grip a times."

Kai laughed and grinned at the impassive Dakota. "See, fool, I told you I could ride as good as you."

Dakota grunted, but Lance saw genuine admiration in his eyes.

Kai looked at Lance and heaved a huge sigh. "Man, Lance, if I'd known the Round Table was this exciting, I'd have joined up a long time ago."

Lance chuckled, his wildly beating hearts beginning to draw down. It had been a rush, all right, a rush that almost killed them. Then Ryan and Gibson were there.

"Are you guys okay?" Ryan asked with breathless fear while Gibson hovered nearby, gun still drawn.

"We're fine, *nino*, but I think Lady got shot," Lance said, suddenly recalling the mare rearing so abruptly.

Kai dropped down at the same time Dakota slipped off Llamrei. Both boys examined Lady's flank, while Lance and Ricky joined them. Kai ran his hand over the smooth brown skin, noting a large bruise forming above her left thigh. He squinted in confusion at Dakota, who also leaned in for a closer inspection.

"She's only bruised," he said, clearly surprised, exchanging an uncertain look with Kai.

Ryan ambled over, Chris in tow. "Rubber bullets, Lance."

"Rubber?"

"Yeah. The center director who got hit, same thing. Bruised, but not hurt. We found this nearby." He held up a hard, bullet-shaped chunk of hard rubber, and handed it to Lance.

Lance rolled it around on his hand and tossed it to Ricky. "So he's just messing with us," he said quietly, shaking his head in disgust. "Letting us know he can take us out any time he wants."

"Afraid so," Ryan agreed, his voice heavy with fatigue.

Just then one of the uniforms sprinted up to Gibson. "Sorry, Sergeant, but they got away. Must've had a vehicle stashed."

Gibson cursed under his breath.

Ryan holstered his gun. "C'mon, let's get these boys home."

Somber and thoughtful, Lance and Ricky walked beside Dakota and Kai as they led the two horses back to their stalls. Chris pressed between his brothers and grasped one hand of each like he never wanted to let go. Lance squeezed his hand lovingly, his thoughts on the attack. And *his* response to it, which set him to brooding all the way home.

By the time they got back to New Camelot, video of the boys galloping down Riverside Drive and into the park had already been uploaded to the Internet and had become "Breaking News" on every local station.

Ryan had phoned Arthur and Jenny to let them know everyone was safe, and both adults were relieved, insisting on hearing all of their voices over the phone. Lance assured them they were uninjured and regaled both parents with the heroics of his Native brothers.

When Chris got on the phone he gushed, "I took out this big-ass golf cart with one arrow."

Lance heard Arthur chuckling over the speaker.

By the time they got home, the headline on every TV news broadcast was "Indians Evade Helicopter Attack in Griffith Park," or something similar. Thus far, no one had connected the incident to the Round Table because no one had recognized Lance or Ricky, and the police were keeping mum on the details.

Ryan, in particular, was stunned to get a report that there was no pilot in the downed copter, just a dummy. "The thing was remote controlled," he told Arthur and the rest after ending the call.

Gibson frowned, crinkling his eyes at the same time. "That means whoever this is, he's got bucks. Big bucks."

"Why do you think that?" Ricky asked.

"Because toys like that don't come cheap," the detective replied.

Lance considered a moment. The only really super-rich people he knew were Michael's parents, except he never even met them. Why would they want to kill him? It was true, they were now under investigation since Lance had revealed Michael's secret to the world, but could they be this vengeful? From what Michael had said, the answer was probably yes.

Arthur praised Dakota and Kai effusively and suggested that at the next gathering, after Christmas, "In honor of your heroism, I should like to knight you both into the Table."

Kai grinned wider than Lance thought was humanly possible, and even Dakota's eyes widened a moment in surprise before settling back into their usual narrow state.

"We would be honored to take the vow, King Arthur," Dakota said, his voice deep and stately and very formal. He glanced at Kai, who laughed and nodded excitedly.

Gibson left the Throne Room to phone the FBI in the hopes they might learn something from the crashed copter, or the abandoned golf carts.

Later that night, after the Indian regalia had been put away and all four debriefed on what had happened and ways they could better protect themselves in the future, Dakota and Kai committed themselves to protecting Lance and Ricky from harm. Their declaration pleased Lance in ways he didn't even understand. These boys were virtual strangers, and yet they swore fealty to him and vowed to safeguard his health.

"Lance is the future chief and the chief must be protected above all others," Dakota explained, which both pleased and troubled Lance in equal measure.

Lance, and Ricky, thanked them, and the two returned to Lance's room for their customary alone time. Even Ricky's head resting in its usual spot in his lap didn't lighten the dark mood that had fallen over Lance since their earlier adventure. And he knew why.

As Ricky gently held Lance's hand and played lovingly with the fingers, Lance gazed sightlessly across the room, deep within himself, feeling fear and anxiety.

"It doesn't take a soul whisperer to figure out something's wrong. Cough it up, fool."

Lance pulled his gaze from the roll top desk against the far wall and lowered it to Ricky's inquisitive face snuggled up against his midsection.

Ricky's eyes narrowed with fear. "What's wrong?"

Lance gulped and fought to control his voice. "Today, Ricky," he began breathlessly, "was a trial run."

"I know. The jerkbag was messing with us. So?"

"No, Ricky, it was a trial run for me. A test, and I failed."

Now Ricky sat up and pulled his legs in. "What test?"

"Remember that text, Ricky?" Lance went on, almost too afraid to speak. Ricky nodded. "He promised to kill you first, to make me suffer."

Ricky shrugged. "So?"

Lance locked his wide, fearful eyes onto those of the boy he loved. "So they were after you today, not me," he said, his voice barely a wisp of breath. "When you went down, Ricky, my heart stopped. For real. I couldn't even breathe. I thought you were shot. I froze. If you had been killed, I'd have just knelt there and let them kill me."

Ricky frowned, and then grinned. "I have that effect on people."

Lance's eyes turned stormy. "I'm not messing around, Ricky. I'm s'posed to be in command out there, a chief like Dakota keeps calling me. If I freeze, people could die. That's why he's going after you first, to make me weak. To make me fail."

Ricky placed both hands on Lance's cheeks. "You're never weak, Lance."

"When it comes to you, I am."

Ricky looked lovingly into Lance's haunted eyes. "You're the most kick-ass chief ever and you'd never freeze up, not even for me."

Lance reached up and took Ricky's hands from his face, intertwining their fingers. "But I would, Ricky. That's how much I love you. And that bastard knows it. He'll use you against me."

Ricky's eyes became fiery. "Like hell, he will."

Lance pulled himself together, taking on that commanding look that so reminded everyone who saw it of Arthur. "I won't let him. From this moment forward, I'm assigning Dakota and Kai as your personal bodyguards, along with me. When we're out in public, all of the Round Table will be ordered to protect you first, above all others."

Ricky was aghast, his mouth hanging open in shock. "Lance, you can't give that order. I'm not more important than Dad."

Lance paused only a moment. "Dad has Excalibur. He's safe." Ricky started to open his mouth again, but Lance put a hand up to his lips to quiet him. "Look, you spent the last year protecting me and now it's my turn." Again, Ricky tried to speak, and again Lance's fingers to his lips cut him off. "He's not after me, Ricky, he's after you. He's saving me for last, remember?"

"I can take care of myself, Lance."

"I can take care of you too."

Ricky's eyes flared a moment. "I'm not a helpless little kid."

Lance's breath wavered on his lips, and his heart fluttered with anxiety. "No, you're a bad-ass boy who's the keeper of my heart and soul, and if anything ever happened to you, my life would be over. Don't you see, Ricky? Without you, I'm nothing."

"You'll never be nothing, Lance. And thanks for watching out for me." Then he smirked. "But it doesn't change anything. I can still kick your ass one-on-one."

Lance grinned. "Aren't you getting too old for make-believe?"

Ricky raised his eyebrows tauntingly. "You mean this isn't a fairy tale?"

Lance's grin dropped in shock. "Now *there's* a word we forgot to mention to Ellen."

They both cracked up.

Christmas came and went as another memorable day. The family attended midnight mass, at Lance's insistence, and the Indian boys accompanied them. Everyone proclaimed the service beautiful.

The family made certain to give Kai and Dakota lots of presents to make them feel at home, mostly clothes and shoes, because they hadn't brought much with them from their reservations. They were flummoxed by the goodwill of people they'd barely known a month, and Lance reminded them that the Round Table was a family, and they were now a big part of that family. At Lance's insistence, the newcomers were also given cell phones, so they could all keep in constant contact.

Everyone chuckled on Christmas morning as the two boys turned the phones over and over in their hands, trying to figure out how to turn them on. Lance helped Dakota and Ricky assisted Kai in teaching them the most basic functions, especially calling and texting.

Jenny took lots of photos with her new camera, and the hotel kitchen staff prepared a full course dinner of turkey and ham and numerous side dishes. A good time was had by all.

At the next gathering, Dakota and Kai stepped forward for their knighting into the Table. By now, all of the Round Table had heard of their heroics in protecting Lance and Ricky, and thunderous applause greeted them as they strode forward, swords in hand.

Dakota had chosen a bright red tunic that blended well with the tribal headpiece wrapped around his brow. His straight black hair fell like water down his back, with feathers tied at strategic spots, separating sections out into layers. Dangling from each temple were multicolored beads and hawk feathers, and the beaded circle on his forehead was framed in red. Lance thought he looked larger-than-life, proud and awed at the same time. His demeanor, as usual, remained serious and stoic.

By contrast, Kai sported a bright yellow tunic, more in keeping, Lance thought, with his sunny personality. His hair hung down straight in the back, not as long as Dakota's, or even Lance's, but nearly to his lower back. The front sections of hair on either side of his face were woven into his traditional braids and he, too, sported the same headband he'd worn that day at the stables. The beads were all in yellows and oranges and burnt reds—the colors of the Southwest—and dangling from each temple were long strands of similarly colored beads and tiny feathers. Dakota's polar opposite, Kai grinned from ear to ear as the boys took their places before Arthur.

"In recognition of their fealty to Lance," Arthur announced to the expectant gathering of excited youth, "the Prince will perform the knighting." He stepped back to sit on his throne beside Jenny and Merlin.

Lance exchanged a surprised grin with Ricky and stepped forward. He dropped to one knee before Arthur and bowed his head. Then he stood, and the king handed him Excalibur. Lance took the fabled blade, surprised that it no longer felt heavy in his grasp. When first he'd tried to heft it, soon after Arthur recruited him, he'd barely gotten the sword to waist height. Now he could hold it in one hand and cut the air with ease.

He felt proud, privileged, and grown up as he stepped toward the two Indians before him. Kai grinned like crazy and Dakota elbowed him, causing Lance to smile broadly. He waved them to their knees with a gentle waft of his hand, and the boys complied. Each placed his sword, point downward, into the grooves set within the stage.

Raising Excalibur above them, Lance ordered each to speak the oath of knighthood.

Kai went first, bowing his head. "I thank thee, Heavenly Father, for permitting unto me the use of this sword to repress the wicked and defend the downtrodden. You, who in thy infinite wisdom created the order of chivalry, and who planted goodness within my heart, doth charge thy humble servant here before thee to never use this sword to strike anyone unjustly, but to use this sword only to protect. Grant me, Lord, the strength to be now and for all time, a warrior, not for might, but for right." He looked up at Lance, his brown eyes alive with excitement.

Lance smiled and lightly touched each shoulder with Excalibur's tip. "I hereby proclaim thee Sir Kai, Knight of the Table Round."

Kai leaned forward and kissed the hilt of his sword.

Lance looked down at Dakota, who gazed up at him with wonder in those usually taciturn eyes. Dakota spoke the oath, and Lance knighted him with the touch of Excalibur's point. He wasn't sure, but it seemed that he saw something in those eyes other than the usual stoicism – pride, and something resembling gratitude.

Applause and whoops rose from the assembled knights as the boys stood and hefted their swords overhead in triumph. Kai grinned happily at Dakota, but the

Lakota boy gave him a noncommittal look in return. Then both resumed their seats down in the front row beside Reyna, Esteban and the rest of the leadership team.

Once Lance returned Excalibur to Arthur and resumed his seat, the king stood and continued with the other business of the day. He took reports from those knights working with the mayor, and from the neighborhood patrols that alerted Ryan or Gibson to the first signs of new criminal encroachment. He seemed pleased with the progress Mayor Soto had made toward improving conditions for the youth of Los Angeles. Since January was mere days away, the reforms would soon have to be implemented, and Arthur commanded all those knights on the mayor's task force to personally monitor what was happening within their own neighborhoods.

At this point, he indicated Lance and Ricky. The boys rose and crossed the stage to stand beside their father. Arthur looked soberly out at his troops, and explained about the death threats Lance had received, and how everyone needed to be on guard at all times, especially after what had happened at Griffith Park. As he was instructing them on the essential importance of keeping Lance safe, Lance stepped forward and did something he'd never done before—he interrupted his father during a gathering. "Uh, Dad, can I say something to them?"

Arthur turned to him in surprise, but did not look angry or offended. He immediately gestured to the microphone and stepped back.

Lance gave him a tight smile of thanks and stepped up to the mic. Ricky grabbed his arm and hissed, "Don't do this, Lance!"

Lance looked at him, his green eyes burning with determination. Ricky let go his arm and reluctantly stepped back. Lance gazed out over his peers, his fellow knights, his soldiers in the event of war. And a war had been declared on the Round Table.

"My fellow knights, I have never been one to go against my father's orders, for he is king and rules over me," he announced in a flat, deep voice. "But today I ask you to ignore his last order, and I ask him to take it back."

He glanced over his shoulder at a surprised Arthur as a flurry of buzzing confusion swept over the room. Arthur furrowed his brows questioningly, but said nothing. Lance turned back to the assembled knights. "The threat I got promised to target Ricky first. I'm the one the killer's saving for last. So I want you all to protect Ricky before anyone else. That's my order, unless my father says otherwise."

Ricky bowed his head with shame.

Lance turned his gaze back to Arthur, who met it straight on, man-to-man. Arthur stepped back to the microphone, taking it from Lance's trembling hand. He looked out at the crowd.

"My son's order stands. Wherever we may be, protect Sir Ricky before all others, even me."

There were gasps from the crowd, even from Reyna, and much yammering amongst the others. Lance looked at his father and smiled wanly. When he turned to Ricky, suddenly the large flat-screen TV on the wall turned on, drawing everyone's attention.

A message appeared on-screen: 'Hello Round Table. It's me, the one who's going to destroy you'.

Lance flung his gaze down at Techie in the front row. "Techie, can you——"

'Techie can do nothing' appeared on-screen, now accompanied by a robotic voice reading the text aloud.

Techie, already on his feet, resumed his seat beside Darnell and played with the remote, aiming it at the TV and pressing every button. Nothing happened.

"I hope you fag boys liked my little surprise at the park last week," came the next message read by that creepy, inhuman voice. "I'm just getting started. Oh, and if you think those two Indian bitches can save you, you're dreaming."

Lance glanced a moment at Kai and Dakota. For once Kai wasn't laughing, and Dakota's face looked like a real thundercloud ready to burst.

"But you gave me a good idea, Lancey, with those Final Destination movies. You were right, little boy, death is coming for you, but slowly and only after it takes out the people you love. Oh yeah, King Arthur, don't think I forgot you. You're high on my list, but Lancey is the prize. So go ahead, try and protect your pretty boyfriend, Lance. When I'm done toying with you, he'll die anyway. In the meantime, get used to being messed with. Oh, and don't count on your street trash gangster pals to save you. Right, *Sir* Esteban? You threatened to get me in San Francisco. So bring it on. You think that sword and tunic make you anything more than street trash? You're wrong. Get in my way, and you'll die, too, along with your whore."

There was a pause in the scrolling, and both Lance and Ricky turned to Esteban and Reyna. Esteban boiled with rage, and Reyna gripped his hand tightly, her face livid.

Suddenly the voice resumed, and everyone looked back at the screen. "Ultimately, it's going to be just you and me for the final dance, Lancey boy, a dance to the death. Man-to-man. Or should I say, man to queerboy? Ha! I'm so looking forward to the new year. Aren't you?"

The screen went blank, and suddenly Techie had control over it once more. There was a moment of stunned silence, and then chaos ensued as everyone tried to speak at once. Lance and Ricky turned to Arthur grimly. Jenny's face had gone white as snow, her eyes brimming with tears of terror. Arthur reached out to take her hand, even as his gaze found those of his sons.

He released Jenny's hand reluctantly and stepped forward to the microphone, unsheathing Excalibur and holding the gleaming sword aloft to quell the panic.

Gradually, the knights settled back down, though Lance saw Reyna's enraged expression and Esteban whispering soothing words to calm her.

"Sir Techie," Arthur began, forcing a calm into his voice he clearly didn't feel. "Do you have any idea how this person got into our system?"

The boy looked shell-shocked. "I put up firewalls, Arthur. I thought we were impregnable."

Arthur looked solemn. "The moment we adjourn, please review your fail safes for any flaws. I'll have Sergeant Gibson send his computer expert to look over our system. In the meantime, my noble knights, you have all heard the threat. Lance's previous order stands—protect Sir Ricky first, since he will likely be the primary target. Lance?"

He looked over at the boys and raised his eyebrows questioningly.

His heart thumping with fear, Lance forced air into his lungs. Arthur handed him the microphone.

Lance cleared his throat. "It looks like we're at war, guys, a war we didn't want." He paused. "I honestly have no idea who this could be or why he wants me dead. You all know me—I don't piss people off. But this guy sounds pissed." He tried for a smile and there were a few chuckles from the crowd. "Just so you know, we're not giving up. We have a bill of rights to get passed, and I'm not quitting till we do."

There were cheers and applause, which emboldened Lance.

"Over the next few months, Ricky and me'll be shopping the CBOR around to congress people, and if that means we gotta travel, then we gotta travel. No one is gonna stop us. I understand if any of you want to stay away from Ricky and me, 'cause you'll be safer that way. No worries. We got Kai and Dakota as backup, and I don't care what Mr. Text Message said, those guys kick ass!"

He grinned at Kai and Dakota while the surrounding knights applauded, whooped, and hollered. Kai smiled and elbowed Dakota, but the other boy remained somber.

Lance offered the best version of his winning, confident smile he could muster. "The new year looks to be exciting, so I say to mister little bitch out there who hides behind text messages – bring… it… on!"

The room erupted with stomping and whooping and applause. Even Reyna joined in, leaping to her feet and pounding her hands together.

Lance exchanged a look with Ricky, and saw nothing but love and devotion. Chris ran over and grabbed their hands as Arthur and Jenny stepped forward. Lance looked into his father's eyes and saw a mix of wonder, trepidation, and immense pride. He grinned, and Arthur smiled.

Merlin sat thoughtfully in his chair, eyeing the king and his family, his expression unreadable.

Yes, Lance knew in his heart, the New Year would be fraught with danger and uncertainty. But as long as he could protect Ricky, the two of them together would, for now and always, be unstoppable.

WE, THE YOUNG PEOPLE

CHAPTER SIX
I'D PROBABLY KILL MYSELF

J ANUARY BLEW INTO LOS ANGELES with a vengeance, wet, cold, and windy. As a rule, January and February were the months for rainy, inclement weather in L.A.—when it rained at all—and the gloomy, overcast days made the sky look, to Lance and Ricky, like Dakota's standard facial expression – sour and angry.

Being restricted to the hotel, however, allowed the boys to step up their physical training, especially improving their prowess with the bow and arrow. Sylvia continued coaching new recruits, and assisted Chris in improving his technique, but the four Native Knights—as Reyna had taken to calling them—trained as a unit. At Lance's instigation, they practiced scenarios, whereby one or more of them had been attacked or disabled and required rescue.

These scenarios often involved guerrilla tactics outside in the massive back gardens whenever the weather permitted, and Lance found Kai and Dakota to be especially adept under these conditions, and fearless if he or Ricky "fell" in one of their scenarios. Lance now understood how the Indians managed to sneak past security on Thanksgiving – they moved like ghosts, silent and swift, and could sneak up on Lance or Ricky before either knew the other was there. Of course, none of them knew how or when the next attack would come, but at least their reflexes would be top-notch when it did.

The FBI sent over two agents who looked like the Men in Black from those movies, right down one being Caucasian and the other African-American, with both sporting dark sunglasses, to investigate the latest threat. The LAPD IT guy who'd cracked Michael's digital trail came up blank at New Camelot, and the FBI promised to send one of their guys to do a check on the system.

The two agents, Black and White, as Lance and Ricky nicknamed them, smirked at the two boys as though just being together in one room meant they were doing something dirty. Jeez! They weren't even holding hands! Lance was miffed, but Ricky gave him the 'look,' and Lance's temper cooled.

Black and White questioned the boys at length, and also asked Arthur a number of questions. Lance mentioned Michael's parents as possible suspects, and was told they were already under investigation, as were Richard and Mr. D. and everyone else Lance and Arthur had come into contact with since their crusade began. Many of these people had already been under surveillance since the San Francisco bombing, but thus far none had acted in any way that would suggest they were guilty.

The remote controlled helicopter had not revealed any useful information—no prints, no place of origin, no record of purchase. Same with the electric golf carts used to chase the boys.

Everything came up blank. Black and White told Lance to call them if he thought of anything else, and handed him business cards, eyeing Ricky with amusement.

"You, too, boyfriend," White added as they left through the front door.

Lance opened his mouth to say something, but Ricky clapped a hand over it. "Not worth it, boyfriend," he said with a chuckle.

Lance eyed him. "Is that what I am? Your boyfriend?"

Ricky grinned. "Damn straight."

They both laughed.

Mayor Soto, knee-deep in his massive project to implement Proposition 51 and provide alternatives for needy kids, also communicated with some of his colleagues in higher office, both at the state capital and at the federal level, regarding the CBOR. He suggested Lance contact as many representatives in California as possible, and then move on to other states, to gauge their feelings about his amendments. Many in the media had already dubbed the CBOR 'Lance's Folly', and dismissed it as a 'Childish proposal that would go nowhere'.

Over the phone, Soto explained to Lance, "You have to convince two-thirds of both houses of Congress in Washington to back your bill of rights, and that'll take some heavy political stumping just to get someone to bring it to the floor for a vote." To that end, he sent over the email addresses of every U.S. representative and all one hundred senators, as well as their phone numbers. "You'll need every one of your young Mr. Lincoln skills to pull this off," the mayor added with a chuckle.

When the call ended, Lance sat back in his chair in the library, eyeing Ricky, perched atop his lap, and his new friends sitting directly across from them. The sheer weight of what he was attempting finally dawned on Lance, and almost engulfed him. He'd researched the amendment process, and knew it would be daunting. The

Congress these days was so divided ideologically that he didn't even have a clue which side might consider his CBOR.

Those on the right might balk because they'd say it would undermine the family unit and take power away from parents, something he'd already seen online many times since the CBOR went live. The ones on the left might not like it because the CBOR put more rights into the hands of individuals—in this case, children—and took it away from government and government agencies, like Children's Services, which wielded a great deal of power. So he decided it would be best to target people in the middle. Then, if the others didn't come around, Lance thought wryly, he'd bet money their own kids could convince them.

Ricky tilted his head quizzically, his soft brown eyes almost making Lance melt beneath their gaze. "What, Lance? You're not gonna emo-out on us, are you?"

Lance let out his breathy laugh. "No, and I do *not* emo-out, do I guys?" That last was directed at Kai and Dakota.

"Lance," Kai said with a flick of his thumb toward Dakota beside him, "when it comes to emo-ing out, you can't compete with the champ here."

Dakota glowered at Kai. "I am not emo," the Lakota youth announced formally. "I just do not find life funny as you do, Sir Laughs A Lot."

Lance chuckled, as he did every time he heard that. Unable to give up their childhood names for each other, Kai also called Dakota Sir Cloudy Boy. Feeling vindicated, Lance smirked at Ricky. "See, fool, I'm not emo. Now c'mon, you heard the mayor, we got work to do."

He playfully shoved Ricky off his lap onto the floor, and Ricky's expression of surprise was so comical, even Dakota chuckled.

January was the month Jenny's adoption of the boys became final, a cause for celebration, but it was also the month former mayor Villagrana's trial on corruption and conspiracy to commit murder charges began, a source of trepidation for Lance. Villagrana's attorney contacted Lance through Sam, and Lance agreed to testify about what Mr. R. had said when he'd held him and Jack hostage.

Lance hadn't seen the former mayor for almost a year, he realized, as he paced back and forth in the hall outside a courtroom in the Criminal Courts Building one morning near the end of January. As always, Ricky, Dakota, and Kai joined him, as well as Sergeant Ryan, Justin and Darnell. The tall boy with the basketball player frame and fancy cornrows had become Justin's number one go-to guy, and usually accompanied the New Camelot Security Chief whenever he was needed.

Having seen within Villagrana's eyes the previous year a man repentant of his sins, Lance didn't mind telling what little he knew about the former mayor's relationship with R. But just thinking back to his abduction brought to his mind, front and center, images of Jack, the boy who'd sacrificed his life so that *he* could live.

Just then, the doors opened and the bailiff called him inside.

Stepping into that Superior Courtroom also brought back horrific memories of his own incarceration, and he had to quash the panic threatening to overwhelm him.

He walked up the center aisle, dressed in a fancy tunic and pants, every inch King Arthur's son, ignoring the whispers of surprise from the gallery. Obviously, he was a witness no one expected. After being sworn in, he sat in the little box beside the judge's bench and proceeded to answer the defense attorney's questions.

All he knew for certain was what Mr. R. had said in the limo that night about Villagrana being "A useful idiot." Under further questioning, Lance admitted he didn't know what that term meant and didn't know why Mr. R. had used it. When asked if he thought the former mayor knew about his kidnapping, Lance looked over at the man seated at a table remarkably similar to the one he, himself, had sat at last summer.

Villagrana looked old, Lance thought, his hair graying, his cheeks sallow. And yet those eyes, gazing up at him from the table, exuded peace and hope, just as they had when the man had visited him at New Camelot.

"No," he answered finally. "I don't think he had anything to do with the kidnapping."

When prodded, he explained his own tangled relationship with Mr. R. and how the man had always wanted revenge for being disrespected. Without mentioning Justin, he told how the man had sent thugs to kill him the night he first met Arthur. The district attorney cross-examined Lance, but he stuck to the same story and admitted he didn't know anything for sure. Then he was excused.

As he stepped down from the witness box to exit the courtroom, he saw Villagrana offer him a smile of gratitude. He nodded and returned to his family in the hallway.

The trial ended two weeks later with Villagrana found guilty on corruption and bribery charges, but not guilty on conspiracy to commit murder. According to Helen, who spoke with Lance after the verdict, it was *his* testimony that had convinced the jury of the mayor's innocence. He would do prison time, she told Lance, something on the order of fourteen years, but he'd be out in less time with good behavior. Lance felt a sense of peace that this tragic part of his life was over and he could focus on the present, and the future.

The other trial upcoming in April would be for Richard Thornton on child rape charges, and Lance's testimony would be required. As Chief Murphy had previously hinted to Lance, the statute of limitations had run out on prosecuting Richard for raping him, but there had been two other victims who'd come forth to accuse the man, and Lance's testimony would be necessary to demonstrate a long-standing pattern of criminal behavior.

Lance dreaded that moment. Of all his horrific past experiences, those three years retained the greatest hold on him and remained the chief cause of his 'emo' behaviors. He wanted to put it behind him. He wanted to move on, have a full life with Ricky, without freaking out. But Richard, and what he'd done, inevitably stood in his way. Even the current threat against him didn't cause as much anxiety as facing that man in court.

Still, Lance wanted to see the monster put in prison life. And he knew he'd have Ricky and the family there supporting him. However, he also knew he needed to face Richard, stare the man down, and quash his childhood fears once and for all. That was the moment he dreaded most of all, because he didn't honestly know if he was strong enough.

Fortunately, Mr. D.'s trial did not require Lance's involvement, as the man had never paid him to have sex. There were other boys the LAPD had unearthed to testify against him, and Lance hoped he, too, would spend the rest of his days in prison.

Lance still hadn't eliminated Mr. D. as a suspect in the attacks on him, since the man clearly hated him and had tried his hardest to send him to prison. Still, when Lance gave the matter more thought, the attack on Arthur didn't fit with Mr. D.'s profile. He also didn't think Mr. D. smart enough to cover his tracks so well. In any case, that was one man Lance was happy he'd never see again.

Also, in January, all prosecution of juveniles as adults ceased, and those with cases still pending were returned to juvenile court. Lance had been in regular contact with Father Mike, who informed him that The Compound, where Lance had been held while awaiting trial, still housed the same kids, but they were no longer shackled or handcuffed, and the Sheriff's Department had no more jurisdiction over them. Likely, Father Mike said, The Compound would go back to housing those kids headed to juvenile camps or mental health facilities, depending on their needs.

Lance could see that impish grin in his mind's eye as the priest thanked him once again for giving those kids a second chance. He assured him that all who had been there when Lance was incarcerated sent their gratitude and a "What's up? Even," he said with a chuckle, "Antonio, the kid from W-1 who I understand called you some inappropriate names in school."

Lance almost laughed. He'd never even known the kid's name. "Tell them I said what's up right back and when they get out to come on over and hit me up."

"I will, *mijo*," Father Mike replied warmly. "Keep doing what you're doing out there—you're a warrior of light, remember."

Lance felt warmth engulf him. "I know. Thanks, Father Mike. Come over any time you want."

"I will. Good-bye, reverend."

After that conversation, the enormity of what the Round Table had accomplished hit home for him. No more kids in shackles. No more cages. Kids were kids again, and had to be treated as such. At least in California. The realization strengthened his resolve to get their CBOR through Congress, so all kids in the country could keep their childhood, too.

To that end, he had every available knight online as often as possible, chatting up kids in all fifty states, securing their input and support. He especially targeted the children of representatives and senators. What better way to get to the parents than through the kids? If it worked in California, it could work nationwide.

He and Ricky walked the rows of computers, commenting on this question or advising a response to that remark. Dakota and Kai were given the email addresses (uncovered by Techie) of any tribal councils across the fifty states that had Internet access. Their job was to upload the CBOR, ask for feedback, and request their support in rallying Congress people from their states to the cause (not to mention the children of those Congress people.)

February and most of March whizzed by in this fashion, with Lance and Ricky overseeing an Internet outreach of tsunami proportions, working to rally as many kids as possible. On their Facebook page, those whose parents were U.S. representatives or senators were asked to private message him, so Lance could personally contact them.

As with the proposition, both Lance and Ricky recorded videos to post on FB and YouTube explaining the need for the CBOR and how important it was for parents, as well as children, because it would protect good parents from having their children taken away, or bullied by the school system or other government entities.

Likewise, they did live chats during which kids and adults could send in questions right on the spot, and the boys would answer them. Lance always felt creeped out watching the playback later because his mouth was never in sync with the words coming out, reminding him of those old Japanese Godzilla movies he'd seen on TV.

Karen Aragon, Sir John's mother and a "second mom" to Lance and Ricky, dropped by often to work with the kids in the Computer Lab. She was working in her home community of Santa Monica to drum up adult support, and wanted to contribute as much time as she could spare for the cause. Mostly, that meant weekends. She also confessed that her main reason for coming to New Camelot was to see her "other sons," as she called Lance and Ricky.

Much as they didn't like politics, the boys immersed themselves in most of the political chat shows because the topic of debate was frequently the CBOR. As Lance had noted before, it was always "left" versus "right," with almost no one coming down in the middle. And both sides contradicted themselves, but would never admit it.

He noted that the leftists argued that humans were inherently good, but still needed big government controlling them to keep society more humane and make everyone more equal. The right argued that humans were fallen, that they were inherently self – centered and needed restraints put on them in the form of laws, but that they should have freedom of individual choice without big government trying to force everyone to be the same.

In Lance's experience, he'd side with the self-centered notion, with the good people working hard to keep the selfish part of their nature under control. So, those who argued that children were people and thus self-centered and needed parental controls, seemed to forget that parents were self-centered, too. Problem was, they were self-centered *and* had total power over their kids. The other side seemed to say that only people in government could be trusted to know what was best for kids, much more than individual parents.

It made Lance's head swim with the twisted foolishness of it all. In his young life, and Ricky concurred, he'd seen enough selfishness from both parents and government to last a lifetime. That's why the boys continued to use the argument that children, just like adults, required basic protections under the law, protections from wayward parents *and* wayward government.

Due to the death threats, the boys had to appear by live feed from New Camelot on Fox, CNN, and MSNBC, debating people from the right and the left on the merits of their amendments, and the inherent need for them. Always, no matter what argument was launched against them, each boy returned to the notion that everyone, no matter their age, was an individual who deserved basic civil rights to protect them from those who chose to abuse their power, whether the abuser be parents or government. As living survivors of both those abusive groups, Lance and Ricky could always point to themselves as proof.

Many "experts" argued that Lance and Ricky were "extreme examples," and not the norm. The boys would just smile grimly and read off some of the messages and comments they'd received from kids all over the country. Some of these kids had more horrific stories to tell than they did. The experts would huff and puff and claim "Anecdotal evidence is not evidence," but the boys knew their goal wasn't to convince these hard heads, but rather the viewers who might be watching.

They were grateful that the CBOR had stirred up such a massive debate throughout the country on what basic human rights people ought to have, and at what age. It was a start, they knew, but eventually they needed to secure real commitments from real politicians, or their CBOR would be dead on arrival.

Thus far, they'd gotten polite communications from a few Congress people that their CBOR was "An interesting idea that needed further exploration." Always, the messages were non – committal, couched in fancy, but meaningless words. Most of these people, Lance clearly understood, weren't taking him or the CBOR seriously. *That* was an attitude he determined to change.

Reyna, in her usual blustery, take-charge manner, insisted that Lance go to Washington D.C. and stump for his bill, and she would accompany him, of course. So would Este, Dakota and Kai.

"After all," she reminded him one afternoon in late March, "the president invited you to the White House for dinner, remember?"

Lance glanced at Ricky and the two burst out laughing. Kai joined in, though Dakota's deadpan expression clearly indicated he was missing the joke. It was true the president had invited him, shortly after he'd become The Boy Who Came Back, but he'd felt at the time that the invite was just political posturing for the cameras.

"Reyna, can you see us in the White House?" Lance chortled. "We got three Two-Spirits, two Indians, one rich girl and an ex-gang member. They'll be locking down the furniture."

Reyna laughed, obviously seeing the irony of it all. "I don't care," she insisted. "He invited you and I'm gonna make him live up to his word. I'm also going try to get some appointments with congress people, too, so we can drive them crazy until they agree to support you." She grinned and that sparked a new fit of laughter from the boys.

"Hey, go for it, Reyna," Lance said, clearly not believing she could pull it off. "But from what I read, the president doesn't have anything to do with amendments."

She smiled knowingly. "That's correct, baby boy, but a lot of those congress people will listen to him, so if we get him on our side, that's a big deal."

Lance stopped laughing. That was an angle he hadn't thought of. "See, Ricky, our big sister comes up with a good idea once in a while."

Reyna's smile faltered, and her expression put Dakota's glower to shame.

"Just kidding, sis," Lance said quickly and flashed that beautiful smile he knew she loved. It worked. She grinned and left to work her own in-your-face kind of magic.

Lance looked at Kai and Dakota. The Indians appeared skeptical. He shrugged. "Hey, if anyone can strong-arm the president, it's Reyna."

Kai laughed.

Dakota stared.

Since Villagrana's trial, Arthur and his family had not ventured forth from New Camelot, except to attend mass on Sundays, and even that was done under heavy guard. Lance felt he needed that weekly connection to God, and Ricky agreed. At first, the pastor and parishioners were wary of the LAPD officers standing in the back of the church, but after a few weeks, no one felt uncomfortable anymore. Many a parishioner greeted them warmly as they entered or exited the church, and Arthur's family was always welcomed. Lance got the youth group involved in his campaign, and often communicated with its members via social media about what they could do on their own.

Sergeants Ryan and Gibson remained in residence at the hotel, and Justin and Darnell kept the nightly patrols running smoothly. The two FBI agents, who always stared at Lance and Ricky like they expected them to start performing show tunes, returned a couple of times with tech experts, but none could trace the source of the broadcast that had burst into the New Camelot system and bypassed the firewalls Techie had put in place.

Even more than before, Lance and Ricky were joined at the hip. Only when they showered, slept, or used the toilet would they be out of each other's sight. Ricky's bed had been moved across his room so that it rested next to the connecting door, just as Lance's did. That way, with the connecting door always open, even at night each could hear the other's breathing in the next room, and that gave them comfort.

Dakota and Kai, per their commitment as bodyguards, traded off shifts during the night, standing guard outside in the hallway between Lance and Ricky's bedroom doors. Even with all the patrols at every window and entrance to the hotel, the Indians felt they needed to protect the hallway doors, too.

April blew in all too quickly with scattered showers, lots of blooming flowers, green trees, and Richard's trial. Thankfully, since Lance was to be a witness, he wasn't allowed to attend the proceedings until the day of his testimony, for which he was grateful. To hear the other boys, who he understood to be a few years younger than him, detail what Richard had done to them would've sent Lance into freak-out mode big time. He knew he'd have the family there with him, but his heart beat with frenetic palpitations whenever he conjured the moment he'd have to sit in the witness box and confront the man who'd stolen his childhood and nearly ruined his life.

Ricky, too, had been subpoenaed by the district attorney because he'd told the media the previous year about Richard finding him on the street and raping him. So the boys sat for hours each night discussing the fears they harbored about confronting this man.

The date finally arrived, and the family made its way downtown to the Criminal Courts Building, with Ryan, Gibson and several LAPD cruisers for protection. Because they were sworn Knights of the Round Table, Kai and Dakota were allowed to carry their bows and arrows most places, but not into the Criminal Courts Building.

Having to leave their weapons in the car irked both, but Kai laughed as always and squeezed Dakota's upper arm. "You still got these guns, Sir Cloudy Boy," he said with an admiring grin.

Watching them as they moved from the parking lot to the entrance, Lance half expected Dakota to shrug his arm away and glower at the other boy. But for once the Lakota youth did neither. He merely gazed at Kai with almost a sense of wonder, as though he'd never considered that Kai might admire him in any way.

Nerves already frayed, Lance filed that look away into the soul-whisperer part of his brain for future reference, and focused on the grim task before him.

The metal detectors seemed to unnerve the Indians, Lance noted, but not nearly as much as the tiny elevator carrying them slowly to the twentieth floor. Dakota, in particular, looked like he'd prefer to be anywhere else.

When they reached their destination, the elevator doors popped open and Dakota stepped out quickly, releasing the breath he'd been holding. The group wandered down the wide corridor to a gaggle of press corps pooled outside one of the courtrooms. Helen was there, of course, looking chic and pretty as always. When they spotted the group approaching, reporters swamped them with questions and cameras began filming.

"Sir Lance, Sir Ricky, how do you feel now that this man who raped you both is finally on trial?" Helen asked, always the most tenacious and, for such a petite woman, the loudest.

The boys looked at each other for strength.

"I hope he goes to prison for the rest of his life," Ricky announced firmly, his deep voice surprisingly calm given the butterflies in his stomach.

Lance sighed and looked at all the expectant faces. Even Yellow Hair was there, but not smirking or leering. He looked sympathetic.

"That man in there did things to me and Ricky and other boys that should never happen to any kid," he said, his voice laced with sadness and pain. "We got lucky, Ricky and me, 'cause our Dad and Mom found us and took us in and loved us the way grown-ups are supposed to love kids."

He glanced over at Arthur and Jenny, standing just to the side, arms around each other's waist, and smiled with shy gratitude. They smiled in return.

Lance turned back to Helen. "One of our amendments says kids on their own can charge adults for rape, and the justice system will have to act. Maybe if that amendment had been in place, my friend Michael Maitland would've gotten justice the right way, instead of doing what he did."

There were a few surprised gasps from the reporters at the mention of Michael. Lance glanced quickly at Ricky to see if his boy looked offended, but Ricky offered a nod of encouragement.

Lance indicated Kai and Dakota, nervously shifting their feet and eyeing the cameras and microphones with deep suspicion. "These are my Native brothers, Sir Kai and Sir Dakota," Lance announced. "On Tribal Lands, Indian children can be raped by non-Indians and the tribes can't go after the rapist. Did you all know that?"

Blank stares and wide eyes from the reporters were his answer.

"There's some stupid and evil law out there that stops it," Lance went on, his heart thumping with anger. "That's why we need our Children's Bill of Rights. Yes, I want to see Richard go to prison forever because of what he did to me and Ricky, and to those other kids in there who I don't even know. But I can't imagine being a Native kid who got raped like I did and then find out the rapist would get away with it and live free for the rest of his life. I'd probably kill myself." He paused and lowered his eyes to the floor.

Ricky squeezed his upper arm and Lance glanced up. Ricky gave him the "look," and Lance breathed once more.

At that moment, the bailiff stuck his head out the door and called for Lance. That started his heart pile driving with fear, and he met Ricky's gaze straight on. He saw love and courage and strength.

Ricky grinned. "I love you, fool. Now go send that bastard to prison."

Lance blew out his breathy nervous laugh. God, what would he do without this boy? He followed the bailiff into the courtroom.

Arthur and Jenny followed, but Ricky had to wait in the hall because he was a material witness and wasn't allowed to hear the testimony of others. Kai and Dakota stayed with Ricky, following their orders to protect him. The reporters began peppering Ricky with more questions, which he did his best to answer.

The courtroom was packed, as this was a high-profile case. The plaintiffs had charged Richard with child rape, but also charged the Department of Children and Family Services as an accessory after the fact for covering up Richard's abuses. Thankfully, this one appearance would be Lance's sole involvement.

Arthur and Jenny stood on either side of him, each with a hand on one shoulder for support. The district attorney, a tall, handsome middle-aged man named Reed, glanced back and spotted them. Then he turned to the judge. "The state calls Lance Pendragon to the stand."

Heads turned and eyes filled up with expectation as Lance nervously started forward up the center aisle toward the swinging wooden gates, one of which was held open by the bailiff.

Lance felt everyone staring at him, but he walked with as strong and upright a posture as he could muster. Dressed in his fancy tunic and freshest leather pants and boots, Lance knew he needed to project an air of both strength, and victimization, at the same time. He glanced left toward the wide-eyed jurors seated in the jury box, forcibly keeping his eyes from drifting right, to the defendant's table, to the face of the boogeyman he knew was seated there.

The judge, Lanced noted peripherally, was a white-haired guy with a neatly trimmed beard and mustache and rather sympathetic blue eyes. Lance stepped into the witness box and faced the court clerk, who had him raise his right hand and swore him in.

Once seated, Lance was asked to state and spell his name for the record. He did so, his eyes fixed on the little microphone before him. He still hadn't glanced up and over at the table. Would he see a repentant Richard, or one who'd gladly do those things to him again, if given the chance?

Once Lance had spelled his name, Reed stepped up to the witness box and smiled. It felt odd to Lance that now he was on the other side of a case and the D.A. was his friend, not his enemy. Crazy system.

"Lance, thank you for coming here today. I know this must be difficult for you."

Lance bit his lower lip nervously, but still didn't glance to his left. He didn't have to, anyway. He felt Richard's eyes boring into him, and knew the answer to his earlier question.

"You have stated on several occasions that you were raped by a foster parent at the age of six," Reed said, his tone surprisingly gentle.

Lance stiffened. "Yes."

"Do you see the man who raped you in this courtroom?"

That was it. Now he *had* to look. Expelling a breath, struggling to calm his pounding heart, Lance pictured Ricky's face, felt the touch of Ricky's hand in his, and calmness enveloped him. Even the tightness of his body began to loosen. Looking to his left, Lance beheld the man of his nightmares, his personal Freddy Krueger, the man who'd destroyed his childhood.

Richard's eyes fixed firmly on his, squinty and hard. The boogeyman was dressed in a brown suit and light burgundy tie, looking professional and innocent, until he smirked.

Lance found he wasn't tight with fear. No. Ricky made him strong. He was King Arthur's son, heir to the crown. He was a Knight of the Round Table. He was one spirit in two boys. And this man had no power over him. He raised one arm and pointed at Richard. "That's him, sitting there in the brown suit."

He gazed another long moment at Richard, and suddenly saw him for what he was—a sick, twisted little man who had made it his life's work to destroy children and render them socially and psychologically impotent. He'd seemed so huge, so toweringly evil and terrifying when Lance was a child. But he wasn't. In truth, he was nothing.

Renewed, the feel of Ricky in the palm of his no-longer-shaking hand, Lance turned back to Reed.

The district attorney asked Lance to describe, however he was able, the abuses Richard had perpetrated on him as a child. And Lance did, evenly and in detail. He described every atrocity the man had ever committed against his mind and body. One memory led to another, and one by one he purged himself of their power over him. Finally they were out in the cold light of day. Most of these, he'd never even shared with Ricky. Now the whole world knew. And suddenly Lance felt free of their ponderous weight.

He even looked Richard straight in the eye while detailing his crimes, met that haughty gaze without fear. His heart felt tranquil, his breathing steady. Tears forced their way out. Those he couldn't control. But he never broke. Ricky kept him strong. It took him nearly an hour of testimony, and more questions by Reed, to detail every horrific act Richard had committed against him, and Lance could see from the corner of his eye the appalled and disgusted faces of the jurors.

When Reed finished his questions, rather than feel exhausted and drained, Lance felt rejuvenated, strong and secure. He was almost a man and today was the day his childhood demons were sent to the scrap heap of distant memory, hopefully never to rise again. There was no word for a child's fear, he knew, but there was a way to conquer it. And this was it. This was the beginning of the end.

Richard's attorney asked a few questions, trying to suggest that Lance was exaggerating or even lying, but Lance remained rock solid and steady, a coolly restating in even more graphic detail exactly what Richard had done to his young body and spirit. Finally, the attorney must've decided he was doing his client more harm than good and said, "No further questions."

"Witness is excused," the judge intoned. His voice sounded strained, and Lance heard sadness there, too. Standing, Lance nodded to the jury and the D.A., cast one more placid look at the man who would no longer control his life, and strode briskly down the center aisle without looking back. Arthur and Jenny, both of whom had cried during Lance's heartbreaking testimony, wrapped loving arms around him and just held him a moment before the bailiff ushered them out.

As soon as Lance stepped into the hall, reporters threw questions at him from all directions. But his eyes sought out only one person—Ricky. The boy he loved sat on one of the benches with Kai on one side and Dakota on the other. Upon seeing Lance, Ricky leapt to his feet.

Lance's face broke into a smile of such joy that Ricky almost laughed. And then they were together, arms enveloping each other in a tight embrace. Lance didn't care that everyone was watching. He was finally breaking free of Richard's hold over him because this boy gave him the strength, courage, and love to break free.

"I love you, Ricky," he whispered with breathless abandon. "God, I love you so much!"

Ricky smirked. "I know."

Lance shoved him away. "Dumbass." He saw Kai grinning and Dakota scowling beside him, but nothing mattered except Ricky.

The reporters flung questions at Arthur and Lance just as the bailiff stuck his head out of the court and called Ricky inside. Lance grabbed Ricky's hand and squeezed, eliciting a smile from the keeper of his heart. "Go get 'im, fool."

Ricky, accompanied by Arthur, followed the bailiff through the double doors.

Dakota and Kai flanked Lance protectively as he answered reporters' questions, and explained how confronting Richard in this way had felt cathartic, even empowering. While they waited for Ricky to finish, Lance answered more questions about the CBOR, clarifying some of the points he'd made previously.

Wiping away tears, Jenny shared her feelings on hearing the horrific details of Lance's childhood, and expressed immense pride in her son for his courage in sharing such humiliating experiences. Lance allowed her to hold him, not caring that it might make him seem like a little boy in front of the media. From loving parents, he knew, we always need hugs no matter how old we are, and he cherished the love this woman felt for him.

Unlike Lance, Ricky was inside for about twenty minutes, since he'd only had one unsavory and painful encounter with the child rapist. When he emerged with Arthur, Ricky went straight to Lance.

"You know what, fool?" he said, eyes alight with power. "I thought I'd be sacred outta my mind facing that son of a bitch, but you made me feel like Superman in there!" He laughed. "I mad dogged that piece of garbage when I described what he did to me, and thinking of you made him into nothing. Man, Lance, you make me so strong!"

Lance laughed. "I better, 'cause your weak ass couldn't do anything without me."

Ricky grinned. "Yeah, how 'bout I body slam your dumb ass right here in front of all these nice reporters?"

"Bring it on, fool."

The boys high-fived and each threw an arm around the shoulders of a startled Dakotaand a chuckling Kai.

"C'mon, guys, let's go home," Lance said, feeling that he'd taken a major step toward shedding his past once and for all. "Ready Dad, Mom?"

Arthur and Jenny happily followed the boys toward the elevators, Ryan and Gibson in the lead, leaving the press behind to pounce on the next hapless person to exit the courtroom.

Dakota squirmed beneath Lance's arm as they road down in the elevator, but Kai seemed content resting beneath Ricky's. Lance felt so giddy he wanted to grab Dakota's face and forcibly stretch it into a smile, but the Indian stood stiffly between Lance and Ricky and kept his eyes narrowed.

As the group stepped through the glass doors leading out of the building, Ryan and Gibson stopped everyone at the top of the stairs just outside to scan the parking lot for potential danger. Dakota and Kai also sent their keen-eyed gazes roaming every which way.

Perhaps out of instinct, the Indians glanced upward. "Look out!" they shouted simultaneously and shoved Lance and Ricky forward, sending all four of them sprawling to the pavement. A second later something big slammed into the ground with a tremendous *CRASH* right where they'd been standing!

Everyone whirled at once, Ryan and Gibson whipping out their guns, Arthur and Jenny staring aghast at the fallen boys a split second before running to them in fear. Dakota had jumped atop Lance and Kai atop Ricky, but still managed to cushion their falls to the hard concrete by rolling slightly as they went down.

"Lance, Ricky!" Arthur called out as he reached for them.

Then Ryan and Gibson were there, too, and security officers, with visitors from inside the CCB lobby spilling out the doors to find out what had happened.

Lance scrambled to his feet, grasping Arthur's right hand while Ricky took his father's left. The boys were more stunned than hurt, gazing at the two Indians with admiration and gratitude.

"Thanks, man," Lance said to Dakota, who stood as impassively as ever, while Ricky gushed, "Wow, you're fast, Kai," and drawing a nervous laugh from the Navajo.

"Are you all right?" Jenny asked breathlessly, checking over all four of the boys for injuries or cuts.

"We're good, Mom. Thanks to these guys," Lance said with a nervous grin aimed at Dakota and Kai. Truth be told, that near miss spooked him more than he wanted to admit. He'd been so caught up in his feelings of liberation from Richard that he'd almost gotten Ricky killed. Himself, too.

Now they turned to see what had fallen. Ricky gasped. It was one of those oblong window-washing units, easily fifteen feet in length. It would have crushed them for sure. More people continued pouring out of the building, staring in horror at the twisted metal, and the most famous family in the world.

Lance looked up the massive side of the building and frowned. Cables dangled loosely near the top floor, but no one was visible on the roof. He turned his gaze back to Ryan. "That was close."

Ryan's gaze flew everywhere protectively. "You're telling me. Lucky these guys think smart," he said indicating the Indians with a tilt of his head. "C'mon everyone, let's roll."

"You lead, Ry, I'll take the rear," Gibson said, his own eyes up and roaming.

Ryan nodded, gun still poised and ready, and led the group down the flight of steps to their parked cars. He didn't breathe easy until pulling into the New Camelot parking lot, and even then he had his gun out until everyone was safe within the hotel.

The falling equipment had not been an accident. Everyone already knew that, so it came as no surprise when, just before dinner, Gibson received a call from LAPD explaining that the cables had been purposely severed.

Dinner was more somber than it should have been, given Lance and Ricky's purging of so many personal demons in court, but everyone's thoughts were focused on the next attack that would inevitably come. The last had been in December, and this one four months later. Would their enemy step it up or would they have to wait several more months before the next one? They couldn't get complacent. Arthur and Jenny knew it; Ryan and Gibson knew it. The adults hammered this idea home to the boys all through dinner, and once again Arthur expressed his gratitude to Dakota and Kai, and his happiness that they were among his most loyal knights.

Kai almost turned red at the compliment, and Dakota looked shocked, as though no one had ever expressed such sentiments to him before. Lance filed this observation away along with the other bits and pieces he'd noted about the boy.

Later that night, after Lance and Ricky took turns reading parts of *Treasure Island* to Chris, they gathered in Lance's room with Dakota and Kai to talk strategy. The four of them sat in a circle on Lance's bed. Lance and Ricky wore tank tops and workout shorts, and Lance noted, with some discomfort, Kai's eyes drifting to Ricky's toned arm muscles on more than one occasion.

"So," Lance began, finally getting to ask the question he'd wondered about all day, "what made you guys look up today?"

Kai shrugged, and Dakota tilted his head as though considering his answer. "Out on the rez," he finally said after a pause, "there are no tall buildings. Only Father Sky. But birds of prey roam the sky and we Indians are trained never to be surprised from any direction."

"Yeah, same for me," Kai added. He glanced shyly at Dakota, and Lance noted his eyes drop downward toward Dakota's brown, muscular forearms. He wondered if the Navajo was comparing Ricky to Dakota.

"That's smart," Lance finally said after pulling his own gaze from Dakota's arms. He looked at Ricky. "Any thoughts?"

"Just that we gotta be way more careful, Lance," he said, for once deadly serious. "We gotta start having eyes on top and in back of our heads."

Dakota squinted in confusion at Ricky's choice of words, and Kai laughed at his expression.

Lance sighed. Lance sighed. "We have to figure that whoever this guy is. Besides being a coward who has to sneak around like a little bitch, he probably knows everything we're gonna do and everywhere we're gonna be." He eyed his new friends soberly. "If we go to Washington, you guys are going with us."

The Indians exchanged a look.

"To the White House?" Kai said incredulously.

"Where we go, you go. We're a team now. The Native Knights, just like Reyna says." Lance grinned, drawing a smile from Kai, and a nod from Dakota.

Ricky shoved him playfully. "I'll native knight your fool ass, Lance," he said with a laugh.

Shortly after, Kai took up residence outside in the hall for the first watch while Dakota slept. Lance and Ricky stretched out on Lance's bed, Ricky's head resting on Lance's chest, their hair splayed out in every direction. They lay there in peace, enjoying the quiet, their hands finding each other's, as always.

"Do you think you're over Richard now, Lance?"

Lance turned inward as he recalled Richard's face and haughty eyes. "I'm not saying I won't still have nightmares, but thinking about him, like I'm doing right now, doesn't scare me anymore. He's less than a little bitch, Ricky. He's nothing."

"Does that mean you won't be emo anymore?"

Lance shook his head in feigned annoyance. "I'm *not* emo, fool. But I might still be moody sometimes. I don't know. I can't forget what he did, how he made me feel so… dirty."

Ricky lifted his eyes and fixed them on Lance's face. "Do you think, you know, eventually, you'll be able to—" He blushed then, but didn't look away. "—you know, without freaking out?"

Lance's eyes went wide with surprise, and he felt a sudden chill wash over him.

"Oh, no," Ricky said quietly. "There's your emo look again."

"I'm gonna emo your face with my fist if you keep calling me that," he said with a playful squeeze of the other boy's hand. Ricky smiled, but Lance knew he still wanted an answer to his question. "I don't know. It's just, you know, he did so many things to me that, well, anybody touching me certain ways causes a freak out. Unless I'm drunk, and I'm done with that. For now, I just love loving you. Is that okay?" He tried for a smile, and it drew one from Ricky.

"It's perfect," Ricky answered, looking relieved. "I just wanna make you happy."

"You do, fool. I've never been happier."

Ricky grinned, and that's when they kissed, long and deeply and seemingly without end. They had a killer to catch and a bill of rights to get passed, and after all of that had been accomplished, they'd take their time figuring out the rest. They had their whole lives to make everything perfect.

CHAPTER SEVEN

SIR LANCE GOES TO WASHINGTON

RICHARD'S TRIAL ENDED THE FOLLOWING week. The jury barely deliberated an hour before they came back with a verdict of "guilty" on all charges. The sentencing was scheduled for some time in May, with his punishment likely to more than one hundred years in state prison. Due to the possibility of flight risk, the convicted rapist was denied bail.

Lance and Ricky sat in stony silence when Ryan told them the news, and then both simultaneously breathed a sigh of exhausted relief. Finally, that chapter of their lives, especially for Lance, had come to a close. Richard was out of his life forever.

Later, Lance wondered if he should take Father Mike's advice and forgive Richard for what he'd done, and discussed the possibility with Ricky. Ricky wasn't so inclined, and so they decided to let it be for now.

In the meantime, Reyna had been busy with her own brand of strong-arm politicking, and proudly displayed at the gathering in late May a fancy invitation from the President of the United States inviting Lance to dinner at The White House with whichever members of his team he chose to bring.

The invite was on thick paper embossed with the presidential seal, the printing in fancy calligraphy. Lance had stared at it in awe when he'd first opened it, as the envelope had been addressed to him. He and Ricky almost giggled where it said, "The President and First Lady request the pleasure of the company of Sir Lance Pendragon and his Knights of the Round Table at a dinner to be held in their honor at the White House."

Lance shook his head in amazement. "No one ever requested the pleasure of my company before."

Ricky had laughed. "That's 'cause you're Sir Dumbass. Obviously, that part means me 'cause, I'm buffer and better looking."

Lance laughed and they bumped fists.

The gathering went wild with applause when Reyna held up the invitation and, of course, everyone wanted to go. At that point, a smirking Reyna turned the meeting over to Lance, and he grinned at her before stepping up to the microphone.

"I know you all wanna go, but unfortunately I can't take everybody," he announced to groans and drooping expressions. "If I did, they'd lock down the silverware for sure." That drew a laugh. Then Lance grew more serious. "Like you all know from the courthouse thing, Ricky and me and Dad are still under attack, and I'm sure that little bitch would be just as happy to kill us in Washington as here." He paused to glance at Ricky, felt rejuvenated and all-powerful, and then turned back to the crowd. "So, here's who I'm taking with me. I talked things over with the king, and he and the queen will remain here with all of you to continue New Camelot business. I'll take Ricky, Dakota, Kai, and Justin as protection, Reyna because she'd kill me otherwise, and Esteban because he'd kill me twice if Reyna went anywhere without him."

Reyna and Esteban, seated in the front row, grinned and clasped each other's hands, while the crowd chuckled.

"While we're gone," Lance continued, "Sir Darnell will take over security duties for Sir Justin, and Sergeant Gibson will remain behind as law enforcement. Sergeant Ryan will go with me." He paused and looked out at all the expectant faces. Most were teens already, and depending on how long it took to get the CBOR passed, many wouldn't legally be kids anymore. But they had younger brothers and sisters, and it was for those kids they were fighting.

"This is a big deal, going to the White House," Lance said with a nod to Reyna seated before him. "But our own Lady Reyna, and her parents, pulled off something even bigger." He turned to Ricky and waved him over. "Thanks to Reyna's parents, who, I guess, donated a lot of money to their local congressman, Ricky and me have been invited to speak to what's called a joint session of the congress." He saw mostly blank faces gazing up at him, and smiled. "That was my reaction, too," he said with a laugh. "It means we'll be pitching our CBOR to both houses of congress at the same time. Usually they get together for presidential speeches and important stuff like that, but this time it's just for us. Even the president and the Supreme Court will be there."

Now the crowd responded with shocked expressions and animated murmuring.

When the excitement quelled, Lance said, "Imagine a couple of street kids like us, boys with long hair and messed up childhoods talking to the whole U.S.

government at the same time. It's crazy, and 'cause it is so crazy, I decided I'm gonna let Sir Ricky do all the talking."

He threw an arm around Ricky's shoulders. Ricky looked mortified, which made everyone laugh.

"Seriously, though," Lance went on, releasing Ricky and taking on that determined, intense look that made people take notice. "This is a big chance for us to convince those guys that kids need real rights in this country, and I'm gonna need all your hopes and prayers coming my way. Do I have them?"

The room erupted with a resounding, "Yes, Sir Lance!" And then everyone burst into applause.

Lance winked at a beaming Reyna and then turned to Ricky beside him. He leaned in and whispered, "I wasn't kidding about you doing the talking, fool."

Ricky shoved him, but Lance looked at him so seriously Ricky's smile faltered. Then Lance burst out laughing and Ricky visibly relaxed.

Later that week, Reyna blew into the Computer Lab like a typhoon. As always, she looked stylish in her designer shirt and tight jeans. College classes were ending for both she and Esteban the following week, so they would be free to go to Washington. Congress typically took the month of August off, and Lance hoped to get them discussing the CBOR before that summer recess.

"I've got everything arranged, baby boy," she told Lance as she plopped heavily into one of the rolling computer chairs, guiding it with her feet so it playfully slammed into both Lance and Ricky's at the same time.

"Oh, cool," Ricky said. "Bumper chairs."

Lance elbowed Ricky, while the Indian boys sat watching, Dakota deadpan, and Kai bemused.

"So, sis, how long will it take to drive there?"

Reyna eyed him a moment, as though to see if he was kidding. "We're not gonna drive, baby boy, we're flying."

All four boys suddenly turned ghostly white with trepidation.

"What?" she asked. Then she got it. "You've never been in a plane before?"

All four heads shook soberly.

She watched carefully as Lance locked eyes with Ricky, and Kai with Dakota.

Kai found his voice first. "Is that safe?"

Reyna smiled warmly. "It's safer than driving."

Lance digested this information. He should've realized they'd have to fly, but the idea made him nervous. "What about our weapons? I know we can't take anything like that on a plane. We need our bows and arrows, at least, 'specially these guys." He pointed a thumb at Kai and Dakota.

"That's the best part. Because of the death threats against you and the open investigation by the FBI, the president is sending Air Force Two to pick us up! Isn't that just way cool?" She sounded practically giddy.

"What's Air Force Two?" Lance asked, confused. He'd heard of Air Force One, but…

She shook her head in exasperation. "That's the vice president's plane. We'll have Secret Service protection and everything."

"Wow," Lance said, taken aback, turning to Ricky. "That means you can be the Second Fool." He laughed at Ricky's scrunched face, and then Ricky shoved him hard.

"Dumbass."

Reyna shook her head in wonder. "You two are something else. I've gotta go see Arthur and Jenny and finalize our plans." She kissed air at them and then blew out of the Computer Room like a retreating tornado.

The four boys turned as one and looked at each other, wide-eyed. Then three of them burst out laughing, with only Dakota scowling.

Kai playfully shoved him. "C'mon, Sir Cloudy Boy, your name is Cloud Eagle. Flying should come easy to you."

That made Lance and Ricky chuckle, but Dakota said nothing.

His narrowed eyes did widen a bit, which was at least a reaction.

Mr. D.'s trial began the final week in May, but fortunately neither Lance nor Ricky had to testify and they did their best to *not* follow the proceedings. They were training extra hard with bows and arrows for their trip to Washington. All the boys practiced diligently with the bow, even Justin, since they would only be permitted to carry those in Washington, though not, of course, inside The White House or the Capitol. They'd have Ryan and Secret Service protection within those venues. However, they were told that swords and knives would not be permitted anywhere within the District of Columbia because those weapons somehow violated the "no concealed carry permit" laws, which were supposed to apply only to guns. Lance merely shook his head at the weirdness of adults.

The group was due in Washington the second week of June, with a busy schedule on tap: dinner at The White House their first night, Lance's address to the joint session of Congress the next, and then a senator from Maryland, who'd apparently become enamored of the CBOR, arranged for his intern to give everyone a tour of Washington and surrounding environs. And they would also meet with any representatives or senators who were willing to see them.

For Lance, the impending five-hours in a plane, even Air Force Two, caused more apprehension than anything else he'd be doing, and he wasn't sure why. Maybe it was the lack of control he'd have over his own destiny. He'd always been accustomed to keeping track of himself, and choosing what and whom to interact with, but in an airplane he was at the mercy of people he didn't know, and that scared him.

He and Ricky discussed the possibility of a terrorist-type attack on the plane, not from the usual extremists, but from their mysterious stalker. Would he want them dead that quickly? Given that they'd be heavily guarded in the vice-president's plane, the only possible means of attack would be something like a missile strike. Did their stalker have that kind of money or power?

Lance reviewed in his mind the messages the guy had sent, and finally concluded that it was unlikely he'd take them out in so boring a fashion. The mastermind behind all these attacks had promised to reveal himself before killing Lance, and had promised to "play" with him before the final death stroke.

"So," he told Ricky a couple of days prior to departure, "I don't think he'll try anything while we're on the plane."

Ricky offered something between a smile and a smirk. "You soul-whispering on that bastard now, Lance?"

"Yeah, something like that."

The following day, with everything packed and ready to go, the announcement came over the news that Mr. D. had been convicted on all counts of soliciting sex from minor children, lewd and lascivious acts with minors under the age of fourteen, and a host of other salacious charges the D.A. had brought against him. While his sentencing was set for another day, the speculation ran high that he would get upwards of fifty years to life in state prison.

Lance watched the coverage, saw the shocked and stunned look on Mr. D.'s normally smug face as he was led from the courtroom in handcuffs, and whispered, "We got him, Jack. Your brother got him. Rest in peace. Both of you."

Ricky looked over, but when Lance said nothing more, he gently took the hand of the boy he loved and pulled him quietly out of the Throne Room to finish their last minute packing.

Reyna had gone shopping, as always, picking out luggage for all of them, including an enormous canvas bag designed for their archery equipment. Once

Lance and Ricky, under Jenny's watchful eye, had packed their things, they assisted Dakota and Kai, both of whom were uneasy at the prospect of going up in a plane, even more so than Lance and Ricky.

While they were helping the Indians, Arthur and Jenny appeared at Dakota's open door. They were dressed casually, both wearing sweatpants, which they'd begun wearing after dinner on a nightly basis, with a t-shirt for Arthur and a pullover blouse for Jenny. It still tickled Lance and Ricky to see their dad wearing such clothing, but since getting married, he'd adopted many more modern ways.

Both parents entered the room, Jenny eyeing the boys' packing job appraisingly. She'd practically hovered over Lance and Ricky to make sure they had "Enough underwear and socks and, oh, don't forget your best tunics for the White House." They loved her dearly, but she almost drove them crazy with all her suggestions. Ah well, they said to each other afterwards, thank God they had a mom who *wanted* to hover.

Now her motherly instincts swept over Kai and Dakota and she scanned their open suitcases for anything they might have forgotten. She made sure the new boys also packed more underwear and socks, which made Kai blush and Dakota lower his eyes to the floor in embarrassment.

She suddenly stopped rearranging their bags as silence filled the room. She looked up to find all the men, including Arthur, eyeing her with amusement. She laughed. "Can you blame me?" she asked with a grin at her two boys before settling her gaze on Kai and Dakota. "You two have been with us for six months now, can you believe that?" She didn't wait for an answer. "You've saved my sons' lives twice already and, as far as I'm concerned, that makes you my sons, too."

Both boys, especially the excessively reticent Dakota, looked genuinely surprised by her outburst. She reached over and pulled Kai into a hug. Though startled, he gratefully accepted it. Then she pulled back and eyed Dakota. "May I hug you, Dakota?"

The taciturn boy looked touched by her offer, nodding hesitantly. She enveloped him in a loving hug. At first he seemed unsure what to do and let his arms dangle at his sides. Then he raised them and wrapped them shyly around her back and let her hold him.

When she pulled away, Dakota did something none of the group had ever seen – he smiled. "Thank you, Lady Jenny."

She beamed. "No, thank *you*. Both of you." Then her face clouded with worry. "Watch over each other," she added. "Keep each other safe."

All four boys assured her that they had each other's backs and, no matter what happened in Washington, they'd all come home safely.

Their confidence helped ease her fears.

"Our boys are strong and smart, Jenny," Arthur assured her as he slipped one arm around her. "Remember what you said to me last November? If it came down to our boys against the world?"

Jenny laughed. "I pity the world."

Lance and Ricky chuckled.

Jenny stood a moment and gazed at Lance so intently, he squirmed a little. "What, Mom?"

"I'm just thinking back to when I first met you at Mark Twain, Lance, and how far you've come, from a beautiful, shy boy to an amazing young man on his way to meet the president. Wow."

Lance turned red at the praise.

"He's not so shy any more, Mom, but he's still beautiful as hell," Ricky put in with a grin.

"Fool," Lance said, which made Jenny laugh with delight.

"That part hasn't changed," she added lovingly, and then announced like it was a headline, "Sir Lance goes to Washington."

Everyone looked at her quizzically.

"You never heard of 'Mr. Smith Goes to Washington?'" she asked. Their blank looks were her answer. She laughed again. "I guess it's too old school. I used to watch that movie on TV with my dad sometimes. This ordinary guy gets elected to congress and shakes everything up in Washington because he's so genuine. There's no one more genuine than you, Lance. I think I saw that quality the first day we met."

Lance reddened again, and a laughing Ricky shoved him. "Yeah, well, if this fool has his way, he'll be running that place by next week."

Lance shoved him back. Kai grinned, and Dakota half-smiled.

Arthur and Jenny eyed the four boys with wonder, and then turned to each other. He kissed her.

"Uh, Dad," Lance admonished playfully. "There's impressionable kids here."

Arthur pulled his lips reluctantly from his wife's and grinned at Lance. "I think you'll survive."

The boys laughed.

But then Arthur lost his smile. "I nearly forgot, Lance. Merlin asked me to send you to him."

Lance frowned. He hadn't spoken with the wizard in quite a while, at least not at any length. "Library, right?"

Arthur nodded.

As Lance left the room, Ricky said he'd check their luggage one more time, and Jenny trailed after him through the adjoining door. "Just to make sure you're not forgetting anything."

That left Arthur alone with Kai and Dakota. The king eyed them thoughtfully. "You have both been a blessing to me and to the Round Table. I have no doubt God sent you to us to protect Lance and Ricky from harm. Guard them well, my noble knights, and bring them home safely."

The boys exchanged a look, and then both bowed their heads respectfully.

"Yes, sire," Dakota answered before Kai could speak. "No harm will come to them. You have my word as a warrior."

Arthur smiled. "My wife is indeed correct. You are also my sons." Then he bowed respectfully and left the room.

The boys eyed one another uncertainly. Kai shoved Dakota playfully in much the same way Lance and Ricky shoved each other. "Look at it this way, Sir Cloudy Boy. It'll be our greatest adventure yet."

Dakota allowed the tiniest hint of a smile to split his lips. "And whatever happens, you'll laugh about it."

Kai laughed.

Lance found Merlin in the library in his usual large, comfy chair, a tome of considerable age spread open in his lap. As always, the man had ear buds stuck in both ears, but instead of his usual heavy metal t-shirt, he was attired in something so weird Lance stopped and gaped. Merlin wore a black Sons of Anarchy bathrobe!

The man didn't even look up from his book. "Your Majesty's mouth is hanging open, a clear invitation for flies to enter."

Caught off guard, Lance clamped his mouth shut and crossed the room to stare in wonder at the man seated so casually, legs crossed, eyes glued to the pages of the book. "How do you do that?"

Finally Merlin looked up. "As I've told you, Your Majesty, it's my gift, or my curse. I take it you find my attire amusing?"

Lance shook his head as though to clear cobwebs. "No, it's just, well, do you watch that show?" He, himself, had only seen bits and pieces of it. He watched almost no television, except the news to get updates on the CBOR.

The older man smiled, crinkling his face into almost troll-like contortions. "I sometimes amuse myself and have it on the television as I read and listen to my music."

"You can do all three at once?"

"Of course." The wizard's gray eyes almost twinkled. "Can't everyone?"

Befuddled, as always, by this peculiar man, Lance also knew his quirkiness belied a wise and sensible person. "My Dad said you wanted to see me."

Now Merlin lost the smile. "Yes. It's about your trip to Washington."

A chill ran up Lance's back. "You saw something? Something that's gonna happen to me?"

"Never anything so clear as that, Your Majesty. Merely bits and pieces. Hints, if you will."

Lance waited, nervously fisting his t-shirt. "And?"

The wizard looked him right in the eye. "Bring your skateboard with you. And have Sir Ricky bring his. You'll have need of them."

Lance waited, but the old man said nothing more. "That's it? Bring our skateboards?"

Merlin nodded.

"Why?"

"That I do not know, but having them may well mean the difference between life and death, Your Majesty."

Lance sucked in a startled breath. "Did you tell this to my Dad?"

"Is he traveling to Washington?" Merlin asked with raised salt and pepper eyebrows.

Lance shook his head. A sudden fear engulfed him, not from the warning, but from the wizard's salutation. "Why do you keep calling me 'your majesty'? I'm just Lance."

Merlin eyed him soberly. "Are you not the king's son and heir to the throne?"

Lance nodded.

"And does not the protocol of courtly chivalry require the king's wizard to refer to the king as 'Your Majesty'?"

"Yeah, but I'm not king yet."

"Indeed." Lance frowned, but the wizard went on before he could say anything. "Heed my warning. Bring your skateboards and carry them with you whenever possible."

Lance felt great trepidation assail him. "Okay, I will. We will. Thanks, Merlin, for the heads up."

"Merely doing my duty." The wizard's eyes lowered to his book and he resumed reading.

As Lance turned to exit the library, something occurred to him and he looked back. He'd been right. During their entire conversation, the old wizard had never removed his ear buds. Not even one of them. And yet he heard everything Lance had said, even over that obnoxious music he listened to. With a sigh, Lance hurried from the library to tell Ricky what he'd learned, feeling certain that he'd never understand this odd man.

"Our skateboards?" Ricky said with an astonished look on his face, as sat facing each other on Lance's bed.

Lance nodded. He also told Ricky about the wizard calling him 'Your Majesty' the whole time and how it creeped him out. "I mean, Dad's not going anywhere, so what's Merlin up to?"

Ricky could see how unnerved Lance was feeling, and grinned broadly. "Maybe he's just setting you up for your real title—King Dumbass."

That drew a grin to Lance's pensive face, and he yanked Ricky's hair playfully. "Yeah, and you'll be *Queen* Dumbass," he offered with a chuckle.

Ricky's exasperated expression was so comical Lance busted up. Ricky slipped into a grin, and all was perfect with the world.

The president had arranged for a limo, and Chief Murphy provided armed police escort to LAX for early the following morning. That meant Reyna and Esteban blew in at six a.m., Esteban lugging Reyna's three bags to his one up the front steps and depositing them outside the double doors.

The limo was a Lincoln stretch version, sleek and long and gleaming black. It looked magnificent as it pulled up to the curb in front of New Camelot. So as to not call even more attention to them than they had to, all the boys dressed in casual clothes, including beanies to hide their all-too-familiar long hair, and Arthur and Jenny chose not to accompany them to the airport.

Everyone gathered on the front steps and said their goodbyes, with lots of hugs, especially Chris, who refused to let go of Lance or Ricky.

"How come I can't go?" he asked for probably the hundredth time.

Jenny lovingly took one of his hands and Arthur the other. "Because then we'd have nobody here to keep us company," she said.

Chris scowled. "It's not fair."

Both Lance and Ricky squatted down before their little brother. "We'll bring you some cool souvenirs, Chris, and send lots of pix to your iPad."

"Okay," Chris said with a sigh. "I guess somebody's gotta watch mom and dad so they don't get in trouble."

That made everyone laugh.

Gibson hugged Justin and advised him to be careful. "I envy you, son. You get to meet the president."

Justin grinned. "I'll tell him you said what's up."

That made Gibson laugh. Then he turned to Ryan. "How come you get the fun jobs?"

"Must be my rugged good looks."

The two men shook hands.

As everyone piled into the limo, Lance noticed fewer picketers and Cultists loitering out front. As The Boy Who Came Back, he had engendered a massive, worldwide following, both positive and negative. Some thought him messiah, others devil. Atheists figured the whole "death and resurrection" thing was nothing but an elaborate hoax. But that had all started over a year and a half ago and, as was always the case with human nature, people had short attention spans, so the obsessive fascination for The Boy Who Came Back aspect of Lance had waned. He'd noted over the past few months that he was now more frequently referred to in the media as The Boy Who Wants To Amend The Constitution and found that appellation much more to his liking.

Upon first entering the back of the limo, Lance felt a wave of panic assail him, because the last time he'd been inside a car like this had been when he and Jack were prisoners of Mr. R. He forcibly shook that memory off as they pulled away from the curb and he joined Ricky at the window waving to his parents and Chris.

Once out in traffic, the excited young people chattered on about the trip, especially Reyna who wanted to go clubbing in Washington with Esteban. Esteban laughed and winked at Lance.

"That's me, right, Lance? Gangsta to Sir Club Rat." Lance laughed and Reyna punched Esteban in the arm.

Lance and Ricky discussed their speech to Congress for the entire journey to the airport. They'd been working on it ever since the invite had come in, with input from their parents, and both almost had their parts memorized. Lance didn't want to be one of those guys who just read off the paper, because he'd discovered from all his press conferences that making eye contact with people was the best way to keep their attention.

Air Force Two awaited them on runway 24L at LAX, and because Secret Service agents were at the airport to greet them, the group passed through a private security screening, including their baggage, before they were allowed out on the tarmac for boarding.

Everyone eyed the plane with wonder. It was a C-32 jet, they were informed later, a modified Boeing 757 airliner, not nearly as large or swanky as Air Force One, but fancier than any plane these kids had ever seen, with the exception of Reyna. Her parents never traveled in anything less than First Class and Reyna could recall trips as a child where they'd only stay in the most expensive hotels. For her part, she enjoyed experiencing opulence through the eyes of the man she loved, and her adoring brothers. It made her feel more a part of them, rather than separate.

The plane was white along its top two-thirds and bright blue along the bottom. The two engines and front of the tail were the same blue, and the tips of each wing curled upwards at an angle. In bold letters above the single row of windows was written "UNITED STATES OF AMERICA," and the tail sported an American flag.

Lance and Ricky walked alongside Dakota and Kai as they approached the moveable air-stairs leading up to an open door. The four boys eyed the plane with a mixture of awe and dread. Two Secret Service agents in dark suits and wearing the standard earpieces stood at attention at the bottom of the stairs. Despite the presence of Sergeant Ryan, as well as Reyna and Esteban who were nineteen, and Justin who was eighteen, Lance instantly understood that he was considered the leader of the group, despite being only sixteen and a half.

"On behalf of the president and vice president," the one on the right said in a deep, serious voice, "welcome aboard Air Force Two, Sir Lance."

Lance studied the man's face for any sign of mockery like he'd gotten from the FBI guys, but there was none.

"Thanks." He flashed his smile, but they remained expressionless.

Man, he thought, *these guys could give Dakota lessons in blank looks.*

He glanced at Ricky, hoping the fear churning around inside him wasn't visible on his face, and then ascended the air stairs. Ricky followed, and the rest trailed after. Last up were the two agents. The presidential seal was affixed to the inside of the open doorway, but Lance barely glanced at it as he stepped into another world. There was a lounge of some kind in front of them with its door cracked open so he could see the sectional sofa lining the walls.

A female Secret Service agent indicated that the group should follow her. They walked alongside one row of porthole-like windows on their right, with rooms for lounging or meetings on their left. The meeting rooms contained large black leather chairs surrounding wooden tables. After passing the final meeting area, Lance was shown the rows of seats at the rear of the plane.

"Make yourself comfortable in any seat, Sir Lance," the agent said with the crispness of a new dollar bill. "And the rest of your party, as well. We'll be underway in ten minutes." Then she left them to return to the front of the plane. Everyone gathered around Lance to survey the seats, all wide-eyed from their walk through the lavishness of the plane.

"And this isn't even Air Force One," Reyna said with a shake of her head. "Can you just imagine what that looks like?"

Lance nodded, reaching once more for the safety of Ricky's hand. Both boys eyed the seating arrangements. There was a row of single seats alongside the windows, and then double rows of seats in the center.

Reyna grabbed Esteban's hand and dragged him toward the window seats, but he balked.

"Hell, no." He shook his head.

She turned to him, exasperated, and was about to offer a snippy retort when she must've realized. "Oh, no, you too?"

He just stared at her, and Lance noted the fear in his eyes.

"We're ghetto boys," Lance nervously told Reyna. "We don't do planes." That brought a slight smile to Esteban's face as Lance added, "We'll sit in the middle."

He dragged Ricky by the hand to the first two seats in the middle and directed the petrified Kai and Dakota into the two directly behind them.

Esteban pointed to the third row. "That's where I'm sitting, Reyna, right behind them."

"Oh, all right." She followed him to the third row and they sat.

Justin looked at Ryan. "I been in a plane before. I'll take a window seat."

Ryan looked at the obviously nervous Lance, whose gaze kept flitting from the carpeted floor to the windows and to every exit within view. "I'll join you," he told Justin as they sat in two window seats.

Lance looked at Ricky and Ricky at Lance. Both tried to reassure the other with 'the look', but this time it didn't work. They were way too nervous. Glancing back over his shoulder, Lance saw Kai and Dakota were wide-eyed, with that deer-in-the – headlights expression on their faces. He smiled as comfortingly as he could and turned back to Ricky.

"I have a feeling this is gonna be a *long* flight," he said with a tight little grin.

Ricky shoved him. "Fool."

That, as always, made Lance smile.

The female agent returned and instructed them to fasten their seat belts. Then the two male agents joined her in finding seats behind Reyna and Esteban.

The captain's voice came over the loudspeaker instructing everyone to fasten seat belts and make sure electronic devices were powered down for takeoff. The kids had brought their phones and iPads, but these were already turned off and inside their backpacks beneath the seats.

The plane started to taxi toward the runway. Lance and Ricky looked at each other nervously. Hands clasped, they felt whole and strong, though still terrified.

Behind them, the wide-eyed Kai and Dakota gripped their armrests firmly as the massive plane rolled onto the runway in preparation for takeoff.

Reyna sat comfortable and relaxed, her eyes roving the cabin, taking in the luxury and functionality of the aircraft.

Almost in awe, she turned to Esteban and saw him clutching at his armrests, as though fearful of falling. His face looked ashen, his eyes closed. She reached out a hand and took one of his. He nodded gratefully, but refused to open his eyes.

Suddenly the engines roared and the plane picked up speed. Faster. Faster. Faster still. Lance and Ricky kept their wide, terrified eyes fixed on each other as the plane bumped and thumped and then rose into the air. The boys squeezed each other's hand tightly, green eyes locked on brown, their hearts thumping wildly with unabashed terror.

Behind them, Dakota gripped the armrests so hard his knuckles turned white. Kai had his eyes pressed shut as the sensation of suddenly leaving the ground made his stomach drop. A hand whipped out and grabbed one of his. In surprise, he opened his eyes and looked down to see Dakota's hand gripping his. The Lakota boy's head was pinned to the back of the seat, his eyes pressed tightly shut. Dakota looked pale and scared. Kai gently squeezed Dakota's hand to ease his fear.

Up, up, up the plane rose into the sky. To Lance, it seemed they would never stop climbing, and it reminded him way too much of Apocalypse, the roller coaster at Manic Mountain that had nearly killed him last summer. He saw in Ricky's eyes the same memory surfacing. Finally, after what seemed an eternity, the plane leveled off.

A loud noise and slight jolt sounded from beneath them. Esteban flung his eyes open and turned a fearful gaze on Reyna. "What happened? Did we hit something?"

She squeezed his hand. "Just the wheels pulling back into the plane. No worries, baby. We're fine."

Ghostly pale face sharply contrasting with the brown of his hand, Esteban squeezed back.

Dakota finally opened his eyes as the plane leveled off and glanced hesitantly over at Kai. "We're still alive," he whispered.

Kai nodded.

Then Dakota saw his hand in the other boy's and turned red with mortification. Slowly, he released his grip and Kai let him go, eyeing him uncertainly.

"I'm sorry, Sir Laughs A Lot," he mumbled, finding it difficult to make eye contact. "I didn't mean to embarrass you." He looked away. "Or me."

Kai reached over and touched his arm. Dakota turned his head and Kai said, "No worries. I was scared out of my mind, too." He offered a smile. Dakota returned it.

Lance and Ricky had calmed down, but kept their hands clasped because it relaxed them. They leaned in and rested their foreheads one against the other, and smiled. "We're a couple of dumbasses," Lance said softly. "You know that, right?"

Ricky grinned. "Damn straight."

"Let's not tell Dad how scared we were, okay?" Lance suggested.

Before Ricky could answer, both of them heard Reyna call from two seats back, "Don't worry, baby boy, I'll tell him. He'll love it."

Lance craned his neck to look back, and saw her leaning around into the aisle grinning. "Thanks, Reyna."

"Hey, what are big sisters for?" she riposted happily and then settled back into her seat.

After about ten minutes in the air, the captain announced that everyone could walk about the cabin and use their electronic devices. Lance and Ricky tentatively unfastened their seat belts and stood, as though expecting to be thrown down by buffeting wind. The carpeted floor of the plane felt weird beneath their skate shoes. It thrummed and vibrated, but the roaring of the outside engines was muted.

Probably has shielding, Lance surmised, *since it does usually carry the vice president.*

They stepped around their seats to Kai and Dakota. The Indians were eying each other in a way that gave Lance pause and set his soul-whispering gene into overdrive. Then they noted Lance and Ricky staring and turned their heads.

Kai laughed. "Some warriors we make, huh?"

Lance laughed with him. "C'mon, it's safe to walk around. Let's check the windows now."

As Kai and Dakota unbuckled themselves, Lance led Ricky to the nearest window. He nearly gasped at the sight of clouds… underneath them! He and Ricky looked at each other in astonishment, and then they giggled like little boys.

"This is so cool!" Ricky gushed, and Lance excitedly agreed.

Kai and Dakota took up residence at the windows beside theirs and stared out in abject wonder. It was clear from their facial expressions that they'd never expected to find themselves in such a position. Kai clapped Dakota on the back. "I told you a Cloud Eagle could fly."

Dakota turned to him with a childlike grin on his normally unresponsive face. Lance noted how handsome the boy looked when he smiled, and wished he'd do so more often.

Reyna finally dragged Esteban to his feet and they joined Ryan and Justin at the other row of windows, gazing out at the clouds below, and occasional patches of land when the cloud cover opened up a hole in the sky.

"This is amazing!" Reyna gushed excitedly, dragging Esteban down the side corridor to explore the offices and rooms.

The Native Knights wandered the plane, marveling at both the luxuriousness of its layout. Once they got used to how the plane moved and felt beneath their feet, they relaxed and enjoyed the ride.

Settling on the room up front with the sectional couches, Lance sat and Ricky kicked off his shoes to stretch out on the sofa, his head in its rightful resting place on Lance's lap. Tired from lack of sleep the previous night, due to trepidation about the flight, both boys dosed off quickly.

Kai and Dakota found them a short while later and Kai hurried to get his backpack. While Dakota watched, Kai pulled out a sketchpad and charcoal pencils and sat sketching the two sleeping boys. Dakota had never seen Kai draw before, though he'd seen many of the boy's art pieces at powwows.

Despite his derisive comments some months back about Kai not being a true warrior because "He draws," Dakota secretly loved the other boy's talent and wished he had some talent of his own, other than what Ricky called his horse-whispering. As he sat and observed Kai's deft, slender fingers grip the pencil at just such an angle and bring the sleeping boys to vivid life in shades of gray, he thought back to their days as children, to all the powwows they'd shared since they were six.

Even at that age, Kai had been the social one who wanted to dance with every girl he could find. Dakota had been cloudy and reticent from the get-go, and he usually just watched everyone else dance. Even his mother couldn't get him to participate.

He'd always known Kai was Two-Spirit even before he knew what it meant. It was just something he sensed about the other boy. Growing up as he had, wanting so much to be a warrior like the Indians of old, Dakota tried desperately to be a man at an early age. But he knew he wasn't a man. He'd always been just a boy trying to act like a man, hiding his fears and insecurities behind the welcoming bliss of alcohol, or firewater, as he'd heard it called by older Indians on the rez. And that firewater destroyed everything it touched.

Watching Kai scrunch up his face as studied the two subjects of his drawing, Dakota marveled that his Native brother had never succumbed to the temptations of drink.

Maybe cause he's okay with himself, Dakota considered, *and I don't like who I am.*

Despite his dismissal of Kai as not hard and tough because he couldn't shoot or wrestle or fight as well, Dakota sadly realized that of the two of them, Kai was the stronger. He was the greater man because he was secure within himself.

Should I tell him, Dakota asked himself? *Would he laugh like he always does? If he did, I couldn't take it.*

Allowing the fear to win out over the strength, Dakota merely sat back in this wonderfully comfortable sofa and watched his fellow knight create magic with just his hand and a charcoal pencil, wishing, not for the first time in recent months, for a drink to calm his nerves and free him from reality.

By the time Lance and Ricky awoke, they had been in the air for several hours and it was lunchtime. Some of the middle rooms had tables with thick, high-backed black leather chairs, and that was where the yawning and stretching boys found the others eating. There were bowls of fruit, platters of vegetables, plates heaping with French fries, bottles of water and cans of soda. Most of the knights were munching on thick, juicy-looking hamburgers that put the ones from In-N-Out to shame.

Justin and Esteban gave them the chin nod in between mouthfuls of food, but Reyna smirked lovingly. "So, you boys sleep well… together?"

The mortified looks on their faces drew a hearty laugh from her. "Just kidding, baby boys," she chided happily. "Get some of this food before the two garbage disposals shovel it all in." She indicated Esteban and Justin with her thumb, and they froze, each wearing a chagrined look. She shoved Esteban and he grinned around his mouthful of burger.

Lance and Ricky sat at the adjoining table with Kai and Dakota.

"We saved you seats," Kai announced proudly as the boys lowered themselves into the plush softness of the chairs. "The native knights gotta stick together, right?"

Lance raised a fist. "Right." The other three raised a fist and all bumped at the same time.

Then they settled down to eat the amazing food provided by the chefs aboard Air

Force Two. Lance marveled that this food was easily as good as what the hotel staff at New Camelot made in their enormous kitchen, and here they were aboard a plane thirty thousand feet in the air!

As they ate, Lance noted a manila folder with part of a pencil drawing sticking out of it on the edge of the table near Kai. "You been drawing again, Kai?" Since joining the Round Table, Kai would often be seen sitting here or there in the house, or out in the gardens, sketching something, and Lance loved his talent. His wedding portrait of Arthur and Jenny had gotten thousands of likes on Facebook.

Kai nodded shyly, but didn't offer to show it.

"Is it, like, a big secret? Maybe even someone you're crushing on?"

He smiled to assure Kai he was joking, but even as the words left his mouth he found his eyes drifting from Kai to Dakota. Kai's own gaze flicked involuntarily to the Lakota boy, as well, and quickly down at his food. Dakota also lowered his eyes, as though fearful Lance might see something in them.

Kai cleared his throat. "It's just a drawing of… you guys. I did it while you were sleeping."

Lance's eyes went wide. "Can we see it?" he asked, suddenly very interested in how the Navajo boy saw them.

Looking uncharacteristically shy, Kai picked up the folder and handed it across the table to Lance. He took it, wiped his hands clean on a fine cloth napkin, and then slid out the drawing. He gasped slightly, and heard Ricky do the same.

It showed Lance sleeping back against the high cushions of the couch, Ricky's head in his lap. One of Lance's hands clasped one of Ricky's and the other rested within Ricky's long dark hair. The hair splayed out beside Lance's legs onto the couch and dangled over the edge. Lance's own silky mane draped down around his face to partially spill onto Ricky's chest. The details were astonishing and so lifelike that both boys gazed upon it in amazement.

But the most striking feature was the expression on the face of each boy. Displayed was such a mix of contentment, love, peace, and almost beatific radiance that Lance couldn't bring himself to speak for a long minute. This was clearly the best work he'd ever seen Kai produce.

"Wow," Lance finally whispered, realizing he'd been holding his breath.

"Double wow," Ricky muttered, still pinning his eyes to the drawing.

Lance looked up with a mystified smile. "Do we really look like that?"

To his great surprise, both Kai and Dakota nodded simultaneously, which amused Kai and seemed to embarrass Dakota.

"You guys are beautiful together," Kai said, almost a whisper. "I hope someday to have what you have." Slightly embarrassed, he lowered his eyes, but Dakota turned his gaze on his Native brother uncertainly.

Lance smiled warmly and handed the folder back to Kai.

The Navajo shook his head. "No, I drew that for you."

Lance stopped in mid-motion, the folder suspended over the food. "You sure?"

Kai's face reddened a little. "Yeah. Look at the back. I called it 'True Love'. Lame, I know."

Lance slipped out the drawing and looked at the back. In flowing script were just those words, "True Love." He grinned happily at Kai as he slipped the drawing back into the folder and set it aside away from the food.

"Thanks, Kai," he gushed. "It's amazing, man, and we love it." He elbowed Ricky hard.

"Ow!" Ricky glowered and then laughed. "We do love it. I just never thought we looked like that. Crazy, huh?"

Kai laughed and resumed eating.

The remainder of the flight was uneventful, and soon enough they were told by the captain to turn off electronic devices and buckle themselves into their seats for landing at Reagan National. It must have been windy in the skies approaching Washington, because the plane buffeted and rolled as it made its way into the airport, sending renewed tremors of terror through all of the inner city boys, and generating amused chuckles from Reyna and Justin.

The bumpy landing also provided each of them with another white-knuckled mini-freak-out, and Lance had to confess he'd never felt so glad to be on the ground as at that moment.

The air was balmy with humidity as they debarked Air Force Two to find another enormous black limo waiting to take them to their hotel. Two Secret Service agents met them at the limo and rode with them. There were other agents in unmarked cars leading and following.

They checked into the Westin Washington Hotel, a monstrous edifice of glass and light that straddled a corner in downtown Washington six blocks from the White House. While Reyna's parents were still not one hundred percent on board with what she was doing, they were so excited that she would be meeting with the president that they footed the entire bill for hotel and food, and this was some swanky hotel, Lance noted as they entered the cavernous interior atrium that was its lobby.

It was already four-thirty, Washington time, and dinner at the White House was scheduled for six thirty. Everyone had to get checked into his or her room quickly and cleaned up for the presidential dinner. This meant no exploring for the wide-eyed boys, none of whom, Justin included, had ever been in a hotel this nice in their lives. Since Reyna's parents had made all the arrangements, they'd booked rooms with two beds for all the males except Ryan, who had a single, and Reyna who also had her own.

She laughingly told Esteban as they rode up in the elevator that her parents booked her a separate room and made her promise "No funny business." She punched him hard, and he looked embarrassed, turning to meet Lance's eye.

Lance recalled the conversation he and Este had on the roof of New Camelot a long time ago about the bigger boy wanting to marry Reyna someday, and smiled knowingly.

Lance and Ricky shared one room with two gigantic beds, while Kai and Dakota had the room next-door—identical in layout. Esteban and Justin shared the third double-bed room. Reyna and Ryan's single-bed rooms were just as elegant.

Lance knew this whole trip hinged on him more than anyone else. He was The Boy Who Came Back and The Boy Who Wants to Amend the Constitution. He needed to look and act such that the adults would take him seriously, starting with the president and his family. He and Ricky tossed their suitcases and backpacks onto the two beds and briefly scanned their room. A forty-inch flat screen hung on the wall above a large wooden dresser. There was a writing desk beside that, complete with Internet access, a large comfy chair for reading, and huge bay windows looking out at the city below. They were on the eighth floor, and the view wowed them.

They felt excited as they gazed out at the nation's capital. Arms wrapped around each other, bodies pressed together, the boys fell into a thoughtful reverie.

"We're having dinner with the president of the United States," Lance whispered in awe. "Can you believe that?"

"Because of you. Because you're the most amazing dumbass in the world."

Lance laughed. They turned and rested their foreheads one against the other. After a moment, Lance grinned wickedly. "I call shower first!"

He shoved Ricky aside and bolted for the bathroom, vaulting over one corner of the bed and beating the other boy to the open door. Both laughed and Ricky shoved him inside the lavish-looking bathroom. "Get your dirty ass in there 'fore you stink up the whole hotel."

Lance stuck out his tongue and closed the door before Ricky could retaliate.

When Lance emerged a short time later, hair blow-dried and spilling about his bare shoulders and back, wearing only a thick, luxurious bath towel around his waist, Ricky was laying out clothes for both of them on each bed. He turned, and froze.

"What?" Lance asked uncertainly.

"Don't move," Ricky whispered and then slipped his phone from his pocket and held it up. He snapped a few pictures while Lance looked at him with amusement.

"Man, if you like these towels so much, take one home."

"It's not the towel I'm looking at, fool," Ricky said breathlessly. "It's the beautiful boy wearing it. God, Lance, you are *so* perfect!"

Ricky's look and breathless declaration sent a powerful charge of excitement through Lance. "So are you, Sir Fool," he said with a grin, forcing himself to stay calm and focused. They had no time for making out. "But you'll be even more perfect after you shower, 'cause then you'll smell better."

Ricky grinned and hurried into the bathroom.

Ryan wore a suit, and Reyna the glittery white dress and tiara she'd adopted for knighting ceremonies and formal get-togethers, but the boys, as representatives of Arthur's Round Table, wore their most striking tunics, pants and boots. Lance wore his usual green and Ricky his red, while Justin chose royal blue and Esteban a dark brown. Lance also wore the small crown given him by Arthur, and Ricky sported the golden circlet Lance had given him. They had planned to take their skateboards, per Merlin's instructions, but were told no weapons of any kind were allowed in The White House, and apparently a skateboard could be used as a weapon.

The group cut a striking image spilling out of the elevator and striding through the atrium to the front door. Everyone in the lobby stopped and stared. Some snapped quick pictures with their phones.

A limo awaited them outside with the two Secret Service vehicles for escort.

Once ensconced within the luxury of the limo, Reyna kept eyeing Lance. "Nervous, baby boy?"

Lance smiled. In truth, he was. Somewhat. The old fears and insecurities seemed to flood in on him at times like these, childhood memories, feelings of unworthiness. But he knew he couldn't give in to them. He had to show no fear. Showing fear in politics, he'd been told, was no different than showing fear on the streets, or even in juvenile hall. If you show fear, the other guy wins.

"Yeah, but it's all good," Lance responded, squeezing Ricky's hand. "After all, I got my big sister as back up."

Reyna tossed off that delightful laugh of hers and squeezed Esteban's hand. "You got that right. Pity the fool who messes with my baby boy. Even the president."

Lance glanced at Ryan, who'd been especially quiet since leaving the hotel.

"You okay, *nino?*" he asked. "You haven't said much."

Ryan looked at him with such a mix of wonder and incredulity that Lance was taken aback. The man squirmed, his craggy old face scrunched with his usual emotional reticence. "I keep thinking back to where you came from, Lance, and I'm… well, I'm just so proud of you. You humble me, and I've never said that to anyone. Ask Gib, he'll tell you." Suddenly embarrassed, he lowered his gaze to the floor of the limo without awaiting Lance's response.

That was good because Lance was too stunned to respond. He knew Ryan cared about him, loved him even. But this? He had no idea he'd inspired the man in such a profound way. "Thanks, *nino*," he whispered, barely able to speak. Ricky squeezed his hand and they faced one another. Ricky gave him 'the look', and Lance became Superman once more.

The limo turned onto Pennsylvania Avenue and the White House loomed large up ahead. Everyone felt a rush of excitement, and a sense of awe. As bad as some of them had had it in life, even at the hands of the government, this was The White House they were visiting and the President of the United States they were going to meet. Badass to the core they may have been on the streets, but even Justin and Esteban looked at each other with wide-eyed wonder, suddenly little boys again— eager and childlike.

The stately guard gates stood just ahead. The Secret Service car leading the limo stopped at the northeast gate and showed credentials of some kind to the guards on duty. Lance couldn't see too much of this process, but his eye did fall on the tall, wrought iron fence surrounding the grounds. After a few moments, their driver pulled slowly forward and the guard waved them through.

They entered on a semi-circular driveway that circumnavigated a huge expanse of lawn with a circular pool and fountain set dead center. Everyone pressed forward as the towering, six-storied, colonnaded north portico of the president's house grew ever larger in his or her field of vision. The sun hadn't set yet, but the front entrance and the entire house blazed with warm, comforting light.

Lance and Ricky pulled back to lock eyes on each other as the limo eased to a stop right in front of the entrance, grinning like giddy little kids about to enter Disneyland for the first time. The driver stepped out to open their door, and suddenly two street boys from Los Angeles were honored guests of the president.

An enormous hanging light illuminated the steps of the portico as Lance and Ricky climbed them, followed in silence by the remainder of their group. The boys could not pull their eyes from the towering columns, the fancy carved window copings, and the intricate flower-like patterns carved above and around the double front doors. These doors were glass and modern, they noted, and no doubt bulletproof, Lance thought as they reached the top stair and started down a long, dark carpet.

Then he stopped, Ricky beside him. The president and the First Lady stood just in front of the door awaiting them, grinning with welcome. Their two children, one in high school and the other junior high, stood next to them. Lance stole another quick look at Ricky and then started forward.

And then they were there, the president extending his hand. "Welcome to the White House, Sir Lance," he said with a grin. "I finally get to shake the hand of The Boy Who Came Back." And shake Lance's hand he did, vigorously. So did the First Lady.

Somehow finding his voice, Lance said, "Thanks for inviting us, Mr. President." Then he introduced Ricky and all of the others. The president and his family greeted each of them graciously.

The First Lady wore a striking blue dress, while the president sported a gray suit with a dark green tie. Lance wondered if the tie was aimed at him, since everyone knew he favored that color.

The president's kids smiled at him like they were old friends, and said they wanted to hear more about his bill of rights. That drew a look from the president, but Lance couldn't interpret the look because it passed too quickly.

They followed the First Family in through the double doors onto a maroon and white checkerboard-patterned marble floor and stood beneath a gigantic crystal chandelier. The ceiling was so high Lance felt dwarfed in comparison. To his left, he saw towering red draperies with huge scallops framing the front windows, and stairs leading to somewhere unknown. Straight ahead were four towering marble columns, and the longest hallway Lance had ever seen, spreading out like the top of a "T" in both directions and covered by a scarlet red carpet outlined in gold.

Chattering away about how he hoped their flight was good and how he wanted them to enjoy their stay in Washington, the president led everyone to the top of the "T" and turned left down that seemingly endless red carpet. Lance's gaze traveled up and around and down, trying to take in all the opulence and history at once. There were portraits lining the hallway, most likely former presidents, but they passed too quickly for him to read the little plaques under each one. He saw fancy chairs covered with beautiful red upholstery, and marble busts of people's heads he did not recognize, and fancy tables carved of wood that looked like they might be centuries old.

It was too much to absorb, and with the president chatting away amiably,

Lance felt his nerves start to unravel as they continued toward double wooden doors standing open at the end of the hall. Ricky glanced at him and smiled.

That relaxed him and then they were into the state dining room and Lance stopped to gape. A long wooden table sat before them. It was rounded at each end and so shiny it looked like a mirror, partially covered with a rich green tablecloth. A huge centerpiece of roses rested elegantly in the center, and the table was surrounded by twenty high-backed wooden chairs upholstered in patterned gold. The floor was dark burnished wood, but an enormous area rug, thick and expensive-looking, stretched almost wall to wall. A golden chandelier glowed overhead with electric candles. To their right was a gold-encased mirror the size of Lance's hotel bed, and to the left tall draped windows looking out into the gardens beyond. To one side of the table was a fireplace with a carved white mantel, and above that on the wall hung a huge painting of a pensive, thoughtful Abraham Lincoln.

Ricky nudged Lance and pointed to the painting, and both boys giggled.

"A private joke?" the president asked with a grin.

Suddenly mortified, Lance said, "No, Mr. President, it just reminded us of something Mayor Soto always says."

The president cocked his head with interest. "And what might that be?"

Lance reddened, and Ricky whispered, "Fool," before looking at the president with a smile. "The mayor always calls Lance young Mr. Lincoln, 'cause of how well he handles crowds and speeches and stuff."

The president chuckled as the First Lady moved to his side. "Tell the mayor I agree with him," he said with a wink at Lance.

Then the First Lady directed everyone to sit. There would be a nameplate in front of each place setting, she told them, and the group scattered to locate their assigned seats. Lance and Ricky, it turned out, were given the two seats on either side of the president. Each place setting consisted of a magnificent china plate outlined in filigreed gold with a green folded napkin containing a replica of the invite sent to Lance at New Camelot. Flanking each plate were utensils made of gold, and long-stemmed crystal wine glasses. Both boys were speechless at the sight of so much wealth.

Since there were only twelve of them, the First Lady did not sit at the opposite end as Lance figured she usually must. Rather, she seated herself beside Reyna and Esteban, directly across from Ryan. Kai was seated beside Ricky and Dakota beside Lance, then the president's kids, and Justin. Almost immediately servers brought in the first course, some kind of salad topped with halibut, and baby kale that the First lady proudly declared had been harvested "From my own garden right here."

Lance noted that none of the First Family bowed their heads in momentary thanks for their food the way Arthur had always taught his knights to do, but Lance did so anyway, and his fellow knights followed suit. After his quick prayer of gratitude, Lance looked up to find the president eyeing him, as though wondering whether or not he was genuine.

The salad was followed by soup and then the main course. It looked like beef, but as the plates were placed in front of Lance and Ricky, the president proudly announced that it was Bison Wellington that used buffalo tenderloin from North Dakota.

"In honor of our native brothers with us tonight."

He grinned at Kai and Dakota, who stared at him aghast and then down at the food on their plates, so well laid out it looked like modern art, instead of dinner. The two boys eyed each other across the table and then each turned to the boy beside him as though for a cue how to respond. Lance saw the insult in Dakota's eyes and gently touched his arm beneath the table to calm him.

"Uh, that was thoughtful, Mr. President, but you really shouldn't have," Lance said with as much grace as he could muster.

"Especially since there aren't that many buffalo left," Kai added with a forced smile as he glanced down at his food.

Obviously hoping to salvage the moment, the First Lady piped up with, "We always try to tailor state dinners to the taste of our visitors."

Lance shrugged. "In that case, hamburgers and fries would've been perfect."

Everyone laughed, and the awkward moment faded. Lance and Ricky and the Indians, however, lost interest in their bison steak and focused on the vegetables and potatoes accompanying it.

As the meal continued, the president asked each of the kids to describe his or her life before joining the Round Table, and how associating with Arthur had helped them. Esteban talked about his absent father and hopeless years of gangbanging; Justin described his father the workaholic and how that had driven him to the streets; Reyna talked about her rich, but careless parents; Ricky shared his story of abandonment; Kai and Dakota described the poor conditions on their reservations, especially focusing on the government taking Native children from their parents; Lance shared his childhood horrors in less detail than he'd done in the past. But all essentially said the same thing about Arthur: he'd brought them together, taught them how to work as a team, taught them that the community is the solution to most problems, not the government, and that life works best when people do what's right, rather than what's easy.

The president, his wife and kids all listened attentively, asking occasional questions, but mostly absorbing each of their stories. By this time, dessert was served, some kind of steamed lemon pudding that tasted to Lance like lemon-flavored plastic. As he was eating it and trying not to make disrespectful faces, he put down his spoon and looked at the president.

"Mr. President, you haven't said anything about our bill of rights. Have you read it?"

The president looked slightly surprised that Lance would ask such a direct and pointed question. He smiled. "As a matter of fact, I have."

"And what do you think?"

The president took a moment to wipe his mouth with a napkin Lance figured cost more than all the clothes he was wearing, and eyed him appraisingly. "I found it well-written and thought out. I found myself questioning some of them."

"Such as?" Lance's gaze never wavered.

The president sat back in his chair, obviously amused and impressed by his direct approach. The rest of the table had fallen silent to observe the exchange. "For example, I'm not sure what you have against labels. After all, they help us categorize people."

Lance cocked his head, green eyes wide and fiery. "You mean labels like black or brown or white or Latino or African-American or gay or straight or fat or thin? Stuff like that?"

The president looked slightly uncomfortable. "Something like that, Lance. It's partly how government keeps track of people and trends. And labels are sometimes necessary, don't you think? To define certain people?"

"Mr. President, 'human' defines us. All of us. Every other word should just be, you know, about what we accomplish *as* human." He paused now and lowered his eyes to his plate. "That's what I think anyway."

He heard no response and looked up to find the president eyeing him, as though seeing him in a new light.

One of the president's kids blurted out, "That's so cool, isn't it, Mom?"

Lance glanced over and saw it was older child speaking. The First Lady smiled broadly. "Yeah, honey, it is." Then she turned a warm look on Lance. "You're quite the charmer, Lance. I can see why the world fell in love with you."

Ricky grinned at Lance across the table. Lance grinned right back.

The First Lady gave them a long look. "You two make a cute couple."

That caused both of them to turn almost as red as the hall carpet, and Reyna laughed. "Uh, oh, now you started them blushing. They'll never stop."

"Reyna!" Lance whispered in embarrassment.

"See?" Reyna said to the First Lady, and both women laughed.

Lance glanced over at the president and found the man still sizing him up. "I can definitely see the young Mr. Lincoln, Lance."

That made everyone laugh, but Lance wasn't done yet. "Mr. President, as young Mr. Lincoln would say, can we count on your support for our bill of rights? I know you don't vote on it, but you have lots of friends in Congress who will."

The president furrowed his brow in thought, clearly not wanting to say the wrong thing. "I'm trying to keep an open mind on the subject, Mr. Lincoln," he said with a grin. "I'm looking forward to your speech tomorrow to perhaps convince me."

Lance nodded, realizing that was the only answer he was going to get.

I guess, he thought, *I'd better kick major butt tomorrow.*

All too soon, the dinner was over. Everyone lingered at the table for a time. The conversation became light and airy and relaxed, and everyone but Kai and Dakota seemed comfortable by the time the event came to a conclusion. The president's kids asked for Lance's autograph on their invitations, which he signed with red-faced embarrassment while Ricky chortled.

The first family escorted the group from the dining room back to the north portico entrance, where their limo awaited. The First Kids caught Lance's eye and winked, which elicited a grin from Lance in return. Neither the president nor the First Lady caught the exchange. Both adults shook hands with everyone, and the First Lady paused a moment at Lance, eyeing him in that motherly way he'd come to expect from Jenny and Karen.

"Do you mind if I hug you, Lance?" she asked, and Lance looked at her in momentary surprise.

"Sure. I can always use a hug."

She enveloped him in her arms and held him a moment before releasing him. Smiling warmly, she said, "That's for all the hugs you didn't get as a child."

Lance choked up a moment, and then smiled shyly. "Thank you." He turned and followed the others toward the limo.

"Uh, Sergeant Ryan," the president said as Ryan made to follow. The detective looked back. "A private word, if I may?" the president said.

Ryan turned to Lance and Ricky, who stood together waiting for him. "I'll be right along."

They waved good-bye to the First Family and headed for the limo.

Ryan approached the president as the First Lady led the two kids back inside the house. "Yes, Mr. President?"

The president reached into his jacket pocket and slipped out something that looked like a thin wallet. He handed it to Ryan. The detective flipped it open and nearly gasped with surprise. It was a Federal Special Agent badge replete with Ryan's photo and personal stats. The man looked from the badge to the president uncertainly.

"Sergeant Ryan," the president said in a sober voice. "You are now Special Agent Ryan, answerable to no one but me. That badge grants you full access to any federal agency, including FBI and Secret Service."

Ryan knew he must look like an idiot because he sure felt like one. "Mr. President, I don't—"

"Keep that boy safe," the president said in a commanding tone. "That's my order. And I've just put all the resources of the federal government at your disposal to do so."

"Mr. President, I'm honored, for sure, but why not assign Secret Service to him if you're so worried?"

"They'll be around, but I don't want Lance feeling like he's a prisoner. And he trusts you."

Ryan eyed the man, wondering if maybe he should've voted for him last time. "May I ask why the sudden interest in Lance?"

The president looked at him with cold, serious eyes. "Sergeant, Lance is the most famous boy in the entire world, beloved by millions. I'll not have him getting killed on my watch."

Ryan sensed that the man was saying, 'Once I'm out of office it's the next guy's problem'. But he didn't articulate that thought. Instead, he thanked the president with a firm handshake.

"Keep me informed of everything, Sergeant," the president decreed, and Ryan could tell that *was* an order.

"Yes, Mr. President."

Turning, Ryan slipped the badge into his pocket and strode purposefully for the limo, wondering if he'd just sold his soul to the devil, and feeling glad after all that he *hadn't* voted for the man.

Back at the hotel, everyone was so excited, they weren't even tired, despite the three-hour time difference. Reyna, Esteban, and Justin decided to go out to an eighteen and older club the concierge told them about, which left the four Native Knights, still underage, to debrief at the hotel, which they did in Lance's room after an exhausted Ryan bid them goodnight and retired to his room next door.

The four boys sat in a circle on Lance's bed, legs crossed beneath them, replaying in their minds the events of the evening. Lance noted the more-broody-than-usual look on Dakota's face, and felt certain he knew the reason.

"Uh, I'm, like, real sorry guys," he said, feeling embarrassed just recalling the moment. "About the whole buffalo meat thing."

Ricky scowled. "Yeah, what was up with that, anyway?"

Dakota remained silent, but Kai laughed. Unlike his usual, however, this laugh was bitter. "It's just what us Indians always get from the government, Ricky."

Ricky nodded, but Lance's eyes were locked on Dakota's cloudy expression.

"You okay, Dakota?" he asked.

The boy looked up, but said nothing. Then he turned to face Kai, looking by turns ashamed and angry and sad. "You stood up to him, Laughs-A-Lot. I did not. I call myself a warrior, but I'm just a boy. You're the real man."

He leapt off the bed in a swirl of flying hair and bolted from the room before anyone could respond.

Kai looked stunned, but Lance wasn't surprised. From what he knew of Dakota's past, and his soul-whispering of the boy, he felt he understood him.

Kai gazed at Lance and Ricky in silent uncertainty. Actually, Lance noted with extreme discomfort, Kai's eyes were mainly on Ricky, as they'd often been over the past few months. That made him squirm.

"Are you gonna go talk to him?" Lance finally asked, when Kai still didn't speak.

Pulling his gaze from Ricky, Kai shook his head in consternation. "About what? I don't even know what I did."

"You spoke up against the president's insult, even though it wasn't an insult on purpose. He thinks you represented your people against the most powerful guy in the country better than he did."

"Oh. Yeah. Cloudy always has had that manly warrior thing going on in his head." He laughed. "You should've seen him when he was like seven or eight, challenging the men to arm wrestling matches. Funny as hell."

Lance pictured the boy, face deadly serious, planting his elbow on some table to take on a guy three times his weight. But that fearlessness was what had saved him and Ricky at Griffith Park and it was that fearlessness he didn't want to lose.

"Tell him you just said the first thing that came into your head, like you always do," he suggested. "Remind him how kick ass he is."

Kai turned slightly red, his eyes drifting toward Ricky. "He might think I'm hitting on him or something."

Lance caught the look in his eyes before the Navajo lowered them to the bedcovering, and it started his heart to racing. "I don't think so. You guys go way back. Challenge him to an arm wrestling match and make sure he wins."

Kai laughed. "I won't have to make sure. He's strong as hell."

Lance noted Ricky locking eyes momentarily with Kai before the Navajo looked away.

"Okay, I'll go let him kick my ass, and hopefully he'll feel better," Kai announced as he untangled his legs and clambered off the bed. "See you guys at breakfast."

He went to the door and then paused, turning back to eye them enviously. "The First Lady was right. You *are* a cute couple." Then he went through the door and closed it behind him.

Ricky offered Lance an inviting smile. "So, do *you* think I'm cute?"

"Hell, yeah. But so does he."

Ricky frowned. "I know, he just said that."

Lance eyed him. "No, he thinks *you're* cute. He's into you."

Ricky looked away.

"But you knew that, didn't you?"

"Yeah."

Lance didn't respond, merely gazed at the boy he loved.

"I love you, Lance, and only you," Ricky affirmed breathlessly. Lance soul-whispered him, and that made Ricky squirm. "I mean, yeah, it's kind of hot that he's, like, you know, into me. Everybody's usually all into you, ya know?"

"Does it bother you," Lance asked hesitantly, "that so many people are all about me and not you?"

Ricky paused for a moment. He nodded. "But only 'cause I get scared sometimes."

"Scared about what?"

"Scared you might leave me for some really hot boy."

Lance gently took one of Ricky's hands in his. "There is no hotter boy. There is no hotter body. And there is no one I will ever love but you."

Ricky grinned. "No hotter body? Really?"

Lance laughed. "Really." He paused as their eyes locked a moment. "Now is your emo-ass gonna practice our speech or what?"

"*I'm* not the emo one here, fool, but yeah, let's get to work."

And work they did, late into the night. The joint session of Congress would convene at two o'clock the following afternoon, with Lance's speech carried live on CSPAN and all the cable and broadcast networks. By the time each boy retired to his bed, it was already two a.m., and they were wiped out.

They awoke at nine in the morning and quickly rose to clean up and dress. They wore normal teen boy clothes today, looking like a couple of skaters with beanies to hide their hair. Recalling Merlin's warning, Lance and Ricky took their skateboards before heading next door to find their Native brothers. They knocked on the door, and Kai pulled it open almost at once. He was dressed in jeans and a t-shirt, too.

"Hello cute couple," he said with a laugh, and the boys joined in.

"So, who won the arm-wrestling match?" Lance asked with a grin.

Kai rolled his eyes. "Cloudy, who else. C'mon in."

They stepped into a room that was the reverse twin of theirs and found Dakota standing at the window looking out over the capitol city. He turned when they entered. As always, his hair hung loose down his back, restrained only by feathers tied at strategic points. He, too, wore jeans and a plain brown shirt.

"Ready for breakfast, guys?" Ricky asked, his stomach rumbling.

Lance chuckled. "Yeah, it's not like we ate the main course last night, right?"

Kai laughed and elbowed Dakota. To the surprise of Lance and Ricky, the boy smiled.

Lance texted Ryan that they wanted to go downstairs for breakfast. The detective messaged back that he'd meet them by the elevator in five minutes.

The breakfast area was in the atrium, tucked away in a corner, with a huge buffet of fruits and eggs and waffles and muffins and juices and everything Lance could ever imagine eating. The smells alone set his stomach to growling, and the hungry boys quickly filled their plates before spotting Reyna, Esteban, and Justin talking and laughing at one of the circular tables.

Ryan joined that group and the Native Knights took the table next to it. Everyone chatted about their White House dinner, and even Esteban was appalled by the president's boneheaded move serving buffalo meat to Indians, thinking it would make him seem "cool" or "hip" or something.

"Don't sweat it, guys," Reyna offered around a bite of toast. "These politicians are out of touch with reality." Then she grinned at Lance. "At least until my baby boy here gives 'em a real dose of it today."

"Yeah, lay it on 'em, Lance," Justin said with a grin of his own.

"Hey, don't forget, we need these people on our side," Lance reminded them. "Wouldn't do me much good to piss 'em off."

"At least not till we get the CBOR passed," Ricky added, and everybody laughed.

Lance noted Ryan fingering a wallet-like object, flipping it open and closed. "What's that, *nino?*"

Ryan handed it over. Lance's eyes bulged as he gazed upon the Special Agent badge and tossed it to Ricky, who looked equally surprised. They turned to Ryan with raised eyebrows.

The detective grunted and took back the badge. "The president wants me to make sure nothing happens to you, Lance, at least while he's in office."

Lance pulled a stunned face. "He said that?"

"Implied it. Anyway, I have full access to any federal muscle I need. Can't hurt." He pocketed the ID and dug into his plate of scrambled eggs and hash browns.

Reyna reminded Lance that Senator Cairns' intern would be arriving at noon to take them over to the Capitol Building for a tour prior to the joint session.

"This senator seems really interested in the CBOR, baby boy, so be nice to his intern," Reyna admonished with a twinkle in her eye. "Flash those baby greens of yours and turn on that smile. He'll melt like butter."

Lance blushed right down into his orange juice glass, setting it down and gazing aghast at her amused expression. "Reyna!"

She shrugged. "Never know. Can't hurt."

Esteban shook his head and mouthed, "She's crazy," but Reyna whirled on him. "I saw that!"

They all cracked up.

Because of the imminent danger, Ryan confined the boys to the hotel until the intern and his security team arrived to fetch them.

Lance grumbled, but Ryan glowered, and he knew there was nothing more to be said.

The remainder of the morning, the four Native Knights spent wandering the hotel and checking out the fitness facility, wherein Lance saw for himself that Dakota was much stronger than his wiry frame suggested. After a good, hard work out, they returned to their rooms to dress up for their congressional appearance.

Lance always wore a green tunic, at Reyna's urging, to "Set off your amazing eyes," and this one was a pale forest green with small, gold-trimmed ruffles around the cuffs and open collar. Ricky brushed Lance's hair so thoroughly, gushing, "It has to look perfect," that Lance thought he'd scream with frustration until the small crown settled around his brow and he finally slipped into his light brown, soft leather boots to complete his princely appearance.

Not to be outdone, he tortured Ricky with just as much hair brushing and then fastened a golden circlet around the head of his boy.

As nervous as he'd been going to the White House, Lance felt terrified at the prospect of facing the entire U.S. government and pitching his bill of rights. These were the most powerful people in the country and he needed them to take him seriously. But would they? Never in the history of this nation had a juvenile addressed a joint session of Congress on his own. The fact that it was being allowed gave him some hope. But he already knew how cavalierly Congress had been taking his bill of rights, so perhaps they were acting like adults always did with kids—humoring him so he'd do his thing and then go away. Stressed and anxious as he was, Lance knew for certain that was one thing he would never do—give up and go away.

With Ricky sporting a pale maroon tunic, they joined everyone else at the elevator at eleven forty-five. Reyna wore her fanciest tunic with lots of fringes and folds along the front and sides, while Esteban looked especially badass, Lance thought, in his almost shimmery black, while Justin wore a muted blue and had his 'fro sticking out so much the others had to duck to avoid hitting it. Dakota and Kai wore shades of brown and burnt orange, but in keeping with their tribal traditions, wore their colorful headpieces, and had attached feathers to their sleeves and the fronts of their tunics. Dakota's hair trailed behind like a million skinny snakes, while Kai had again turned his long tresses into two perfect braids that dangled down his chest almost to his waist.

Reyna stopped to gaze a moment at Lance and Ricky with an appraising once-over. "I approve. You are the two most beautiful boys in the world."

That made them redden, and she engulfed them in a tight, loving hug. Pulling back she locked eyes with Lance. "Kick ass today, baby boy."

Lance grinned, and Esteban piped up with, "Give 'em a day they'll never forget, *carnal*." He extended a fist, and Lance bumped it.

"I'll do my best." Then he glanced over at Ryan, pensively watching them. "How's the special agent doing?"

Ryan grimaced a moment at the title, and then offered a stony grin. "He's about to ground the prince for being a smart-ass."

Lance laughed, and then the elevator arrived.

They hovered around in the atrium awaiting Senator Cairns' intern, drawing a lot of stares and finger-pointing, and more than a few autograph seekers. Ryan and the others tensed any time someone approached Lance, and hovered protectively, eyeing each newcomer suspiciously. But none behaved in a rude or threatening manner. And then the man they'd been awaiting arrived.

For some reason, Lance had assumed a man working for a U.S. senator would be older, but when he saw the guy approaching, he was startled to find him not much older than Reyna, young and Latino-looking, though even in his mind Lance didn't want to use that label. The man had light skin, in any case, a shock of black hair that looked like it would be unruly if not for gobs of gel to keep it at bay, and a small nose. He had smooth, unblemished skin and dark eyes surrounded by big glasses, and faintly reminded Lance of someone, maybe an actor he'd seen on TV.

The young man was dressed in a simple, unassuming light brown suit with a grayish tie and practically bounced on his heels as he approached the group. He beamed with an enormous smile that made Lance instantly like him.

"Wow," he gushed as he breathlessly reached them. "This is such an honor!" He thrust out his hand to Lance. "Edwin Romo, Sir Lance."

Lance shook his hand, amazed at the reaction he'd engendered.

The young man grinned at him almost shyly. "I've been following your crusade all through college. I think it's fantastic."

"Thanks, man," Lance said to the newcomer. "And thanks for helping us. Oh, and just call me Lance, okay?"

He flashed his smile and the young man grinned more broadly. "You got it, Lance. Man, I'm so stoked. I've been the senator's intern every summer since I started college and he's way cool. I turned him on to your crusade, and he's really excited about your bill of rights. Me too. I have a younger sister." He paused because everyone was looking at him with bemusement. "Sorry, I get carried away sometimes."

Lance laughed and introduced the group. Everyone shook hands, and the excited young intern led them outside to yet another limo.

Once inside the elegant car, Edwin made it a point to seat himself next to Lance, and off they went. Lance commented that Edwin seemed young to work for a senator, and the man laughed.

He had an infectious kind of laugh, Lance noted, one that made you want to laugh along with him.

"I go to Brown University and I'm majoring in Poly Sci," Edwin explained.

"Where's Brown?" Ricky asked.

"It's in Rhode Island," Edwin explained. "As you can probably guess, I wanna go into politics someday." He laughed again, and Lance decided Kai now had some direct competition.

"How old are you?" Lance asked. The guy was small, after all, not much bigger than him.

Edwin grinned. "Twenty this month. This internship has been great experience for me. I really get to see how Washington works."

Lance glanced at Ricky and noted the jealous look he'd seen on a few occasions. Smiling at the boy he loved, he said to Edwin, "That's cool, man."

As they drove through traffic toward the Capitol, Reyna chatted with Edwin about life in Washington, and the intern prattled on about everything from the Fourth of July fireworks shows to long sessions of Congress he'd slept through because they were so boring. Lance and Ricky vaguely listened, mostly focusing on the speech Lance held in his hands, with Ricky mouthing the parts he needed to talk about.

By the time the immensity of the Capitol dome and its side extensions loomed into view, Lance felt his hands sweating.

Ricky's were too. Both boys knew this was the biggest challenge they'd likely ever face—politically, that is. They still needed to figure out how to defeat their unseen enemy, but for now this one was panic-city.

The limo drove past the front, so everyone in the car could see the vast expanse of lawn leading up to the most important building in the country other than The White House. Everyone was silent but Edwin, who chattered on about this aspect of the building or that little-known fact. Lance wasn't even listening anymore. His eyes were wide with awe as the limo drove around the side and then pulled into the East underground garage through a gated entrance.

The underground garage was pretty ordinary and Lance barely gave it a look-see as he gently pulled Ricky from the car the second they were parked. More nervous than he'd been before any public speaking engagement, he dragged Ricky behind the limo and kissed him, drawing on the strength he always got from the other boy. Reyna's cleared throat drew both of them out like turtles peeking from their shells.

"Ahem," she said with a grin as she approached. "I promised your parents that neither of you would get pregnant this trip, so break it up."

The boys gaped at her in horror before she busted up, and so did everyone else. Even Edwin laughed, which caused the appalled, embarrassed boys to mad-dog Reyna good-naturedly. But Lance suddenly felt more relaxed thanks to her well-timed, if rather inappropriate, joke.

"I'll remember that, sis," Lance said as they followed Edwin to the elevators.

"Me, too," Ricky affirmed, his face still flushed with embarrassment.

But Reyna just laughed with delight and pretended nothing at all had happened.

Edwin effusively showed them the Capitol rotunda area, currently teaming with summer tourists. The tourists were more fascinated seeing Lance and the other knights than they were the historical artifacts, and many a child asked Lance or Ricky or Reyna for an autograph. Even Esteban and Justin got requests, something unusual for them.

As the hour approached for the joint session to begin, Edwin led them all into the enormous House of Representatives chamber through a side door. At the moment it was empty, and the enormity of the place took Lance's breath away. Curved row upon curved row of bench seats extended outward from a raised podium that in itself was three levels high, with a giant American flag hanging on the wall dead center. All around the walls above were curved benches that Edwin called the Gallery, used for invited guests and the public to sit in on sessions of Congress. The ceiling was an enormous sunken area with a skylight and hundreds of embedded lights shining down. Everything seemed to be made of burnished, shining wood with carved and fancy copings and other decorative elements. And it was eerily quiet after all the voices that had filled the rotunda.

Lance had never seen anything like it, and he squeezed Ricky's hand with momentary dread. Every one of these seats would soon be occupied, he knew. He felt his brow break out with sweat.

Edwin explained that the rest of the group would have prime locations down on the floor in the front row to the right of the podium. The Supreme Court justices always occupied the first row to the left. The Speaker of the House and the vice president would introduce the Round Table members, Edwin went on, and all would file in and take their seats.

"Then the speaker will introduce you and Ricky," he said to Lance with a grin. "That's when you enter. Walk straight up the center aisle and around to the steps alongside the dais. Then step to the podium and do your thing."

He laughed at Lance's look of mortification.

"I've seen you speak to tougher crowds than this, Lance," he offered with a slap on the shoulder. "You'll do great."

Lance nodded, but Reyna beamed. "You'll knock 'em dead, baby boy. And so will baby boy number two."

Lance and Ricky reddened, glancing at Edwin nervously. "Reyna, you're embarrassing us *again*," Lance mumbled.

She shrugged. "Hey, that's my job."

Edwin laughed at their antics. "You guys are fun. I'm dying to hear your speech." Then he checked his wristwatch. "Okay, time for me to get you all to the waiting room. When it's time, I'll show you where to enter."

He led the group down the center aisle to exit the house chamber. There were closed doors to either side when they stepped out into a hallway, and Edwin led them to one and opened it.

"You guys hang out here until I come back. The senators and representatives should start arriving in about ten minutes. Help yourself to water from the cooler." Then with a wide-eyed grin he stepped out of the room and closed the door.

The room was small, but like everything else about this building, lavishly appointed, at least by the standards of a bunch of street kids from L.A. Lance and Ricky sat together on a comfortable sofa and held each other's hand with desperate abandon. They lay back against the sofa and Ricky rested his head against Lance's shoulder.

Reyna snapped some pictures of them with her phone, and Justin had Esteban take some of him beside portraits of famous people.

"For my Dad," he explained with a grin.

They waited about forty minutes before Edwin re-entered the room and told everyone except Lance and Ricky to follow him. The boys stood as the others wished them good luck. Reyna gave each a hug and a kiss, and Esteban and Justin offered the chin raise. Kai gave them a laugh, and Dakota the fist bump. Then Ryan shook both their hands and said, "Just don't make any cracks about buffalo meat."

Lance's mouth dropped open, and Ryan cracked a lopsided smile. He'd never once heard the man make a joke since he'd known him, except the one about grounding the prince, and it brought a huge grin to his face. Ricky's, too.

Ryan winked and followed the others out, and suddenly the boys were alone. They gazed at one another soberly.

"You're making history today, Lance," Ricky intoned almost breathlessly.

"*We're* making history."

Ricky shook his head. "You're the one, Lance. If it was up to me to talk to these people, we'd lose for sure. I'm nobody."

Lance grabbed his shoulders and forced their eyes to meet. "You'll never be nobody," he assured Ricky with passion. "Without you I couldn't do this, don't you see? Ever since I came back, it's been you that's gotten me through everything. You make me strong. Without you, *I'm* nothing."

Ricky smiled now, his self-doubt dissipating.

Then the door opened and Edwin stepped into the room, grinning broadly. "You're on, guys."

Lance and Ricky took a deep breath and exhaled, then followed the young intern from the room. Two Secret Service agents flanked the double doors into the House chamber, which meant the president had already arrived. Edwin motioned to one agent and he cracked open a door. Edwin glanced into the opening a moment and then waved Lance and Ricky forward. The two agents swung wide both doors and suddenly Lance was gazing upon a terrifyingly large group of people, most with their backs to him. The chamber and the gallery were full to bursting.

At the far end of the chamber, standing at the podium, the Speaker of the House stood at the microphone wearing a gray suit and dark tie. From this distance, Lance couldn't tell what color the tie was. Then he heard the man's voice echoing off the walls and ceiling.

"And now, Mr. President, Mr. Vice President, Honorable Justices of the Supreme Court, and respected members of Congress, for the first time in our history we are gathered here as one body to be addressed by juveniles, albeit two rather extraordinary juveniles. Please rise and welcome Sir Lance and Sir Ricky of New Camelot."

He stepped back from the microphone and began to applaud. Lance nearly lost his breath as the entire assemblage, all five hundred thirty five senators and representatives, the justices, the president, and everyone up in the gallery stood as one and began applauding. He froze, then met Ricky's eyes. Ricky gave him 'the look', and fear vanished. Grinning like little kids, the two most famous boys in the world stepped into history and made their way up the aisle.

They smiled at the faces swimming past. Some of those faces smiled back, others scowled. Some, Lance noted, eyed them with dismay.

As they made their way to the front dais, the president stepped forward and shook their hands with a big grin on his face. Suddenly Ryan's joke about the buffalo meat flashed through Lance's mind and he laughed as he shook the man's hand. The president laughed, too, obviously thinking Lance was happy to see him again. Then the boys stepped up to the podium, acknowledged the vice president seated behind it, and shook the Speaker's hand.

"Welcome, boys," the man said with a warm smile as he shook each of their hands vigorously. Lance and Ricky thanked him and then turned to the microphone, and the massive crowd before them. Everyone ceased their clapping and resumed their seats, and Lance stood gazing out at the most powerful body of people on earth. His heart pulled into his throat, and he swallowed nervously. He stepped closer to the mic, lifting one sweaty hand to pull the notes from his pants pocket. The notes were rumpled, and some in the front rows chuckled as he laid the messy pages onto the podium. Ricky stood just to his right and slightly behind, awaiting his part of the proceedings.

Lance saw his fellow knights seated in the front row. Reyna blew an air kiss, and Lance smiled broadly. Then he leaned into the microphone and gazed out at the lawmakers. "I bet you all never expected to see this, huh?"

That drew some laughter, and Lance relaxed a bit.

"Mr. Speaker, Mr. President, Mr. Vice President, Honorable Justices of the Court, and respected members of the House and Senate, we thank you for inviting us here today to make our case for the children of this amazing country."

He scanned the faces below him, noting some attentively paying attention, while others were looking away.

"I'm pretty sure some of you were against Ricky and me speaking today," he went on. "You probably said to yourselves, what's a couple of kids from the streets of L.A. gotta say to us, the most important people in the world?" He offered a smile. "Don't worry, I won't ask you to raise your hands on that one."

More laughter rose from the chamber, and from the gallery above.

"But we are gonna play a game, right, Ricky?"

Ricky stepped up shoulder to shoulder with Lance. "Yup. Truth or dare, right?"

Lance nodded. "You call it. Shall we ask them for truth or give them a dare?"

Ricky tilted his head, giving an exaggerated performance for the assembled lawmakers. "How about truth?"

"You got it," Lance said with a grin and they high-fived. Then he turned to the vast assemblage, feeling more relaxed by the second. Just brushing up against Ricky calmed him. "So, you all know how to play, right? Ricky called truth, so whatever I ask, you have to give a truthful answer. Got it?"

He noted bewildered looks and heads glancing this way and that. Obviously, he decided, this wasn't how these joint sessions usually went. Oh, well, this was his show and he'd run it his way.

"Okay, first question," Lance went on with an inviting smile. "Show of hands. How many of you have read all or part of our children's bill of rights?"

The lawmakers turned to one another uncertainly, as though waiting for someone to instruct them on proper protocol.

"C'mon, class, don't be shy," Ricky said into the microphone, and that drew a large laugh.

Hands slowly rose into the air throughout the chamber. Once all movement ceased, maybe half of the lawmakers had their hands raised. Lance was pleased to note that all nine justices of the Supreme Court had their hands up.

Lance shook his head in exaggerated dismay. "Boy, in my mom's English class, this would be a big fat fail."

More laughs followed, and the lawmakers awkwardly lowered their hands.

Lance didn't look at all upset—he'd already known what to expect and continued to play out his hand. "Okay, this one is, like, super easy. How many of you feel you're in touch with the needs of kids in your own districts?"

Now every hand rose into the air, and both Lance and Ricky looked impressed.

"Wow," they both said simultaneously, drawing another laugh as they playfully shoved each other.

"That's awesome," Lance added with sincerity.

Ricky leaned in to the mic and asked, "So how many of you talk to your own kids, like, you know, regularly?"

Most hands rose into the air since some of the representatives did not have children.

Ricky flashed a big grin, sharing a look with Lance before continuing. "And of that group, how many of you listen to your kids when they talk? Not just hear, but really listen?"

All the same hands from the last question shot up into the air. The lawmakers were obviously confused by what the boys were doing, but played along anyway, maybe just to look good for the television cameras carrying the session live.

Lance looked soberly out at the entire assemblage. They all sat and waited. Not a sound could be heard.

"I'm glad to hear that because it means you already know that every one of your children who isn't, you know, like a toddler, has been in regular contact with Ricky and me since our bill of rights went live. Isn't that cool? It's like we're all one big, happy family here."

Rustling uncertainty rippled throughout the chamber, and heads turned confusedly toward one another. There were shrugs and headshakes, but not a single hand rose into the air.

Lance's grin couldn't get any broader if it broke out of his cheeks. "So, seeing as how you know this, you must also know that all your kids support our bill of rights. Isn't that amazing?"

Now murmuring conversation erupted throughout the chamber and the House Speaker had to gavel for silence.

Lance feigned shock at their stunned reactions. "Oh, wait. You mean you didn't know those things? Oh, I'm sorry. I thought you said you listen to your kids. My bad."

In the front row, Reyna burst into applause, and the other knights joined her. Glancing up, she noticed the president smiling in admiration.

As though on cue, Lance turned to look down at the man. "Oh, and that includes your kids, too, Mr. President."

Suddenly the president lost his pasted-on smile and frowned with shock.

Lance turned back to the stunned and silent chamber, gazing down at them with a shake of his head.

"At least your children know how to do their homework, huh?" He sighed heavily. "Now maybe you see why us kids need our own bill of rights, because you adults don't take us seriously. I know some of you are on the right and some on the left, but most of us live life in the middle, because that's where problems get solved." He looked out over the sea of faces. "Why can't adults just accept kids as we are? And listen to us when we talk? You all just admitted you don't even know your own kids, so how can you know all the other kids you represent? You can't, and that's not your fault. It's just the way it is. And you all are probably pretty good parents. Maybe great parents. But if even *you* don't make time to listen to *your* kids, how can you expect careless or bad parents to do that?"

He paused a moment to scan the lawmakers below.

"How many of you want your kids to think like you do?"

This time, a lot of hands went up.

"If you're on the right you want them on the right, if on the left, you want them there. Because, for some reason, you think all life's answers can be found in only one direction. But they can't. And your kids aren't mini-me's. We're real people, different from you, with likes and wants and opinions of our own. We don't need to be brainwashed to be successful. All we need is for you to show us how to think, and how to make good choices, so we can grow into good adults. How hard is that for grown-ups? Based on my life and Ricky's and hundreds of thousands who have emailed us from around the country, I guess it's pretty hard. Because to you, the adult world, we're nothing but property. Actually, we're less than property because property is worth money, and *we're* not, at least not 'less a parent can sell their kid like my mama sold me as a baby. Did you all know that? Yeah, I got sold to a stranger, so she could have money for drugs. Some parents sell their kids to modeling agencies or movie studios so they can make money off of them. See what I mean? Property, not human. It kills me that some of you think kids are safe in this country, that parents will *always* take good care of them. Think again."

He paused a moment as every eye fixed on him with wide, stunned expressions. No one was fidgeting now, or even glancing down at their laps. They were riveted.

"Some of you," Lance went on soberly, "think government is the answer, that government will step in and take care of kids like me, to, you know, protect us from bad parents. 'Cept you guys don't even know what your own kids are doing, so how can you protect me? I already know what government can do. It put me in homes where I got raped and abused, locked in closets, and forced to wear old clothes. Yeah, that's what government can do for kids. Government won't even let Native children who get raped and kidnapped legally fight back against that stuff. If people are selfish and careless, then so is government because government *is* people, right?"

His eyes passed across the dumbfounded faces of America's lawmakers seated before him.

"A lot of us kids don't have it so good in this country, and that's why my father, King Arthur, came along, to make things better for us. Because of him, L.A. isn't the hellhole it was when I was growing up. It's better. It's cleaner, there's less drugs and not so much crime. And you know what? He did it by bringing us together, instead of pushing us apart. A lot of these kids were in gangs, like Este and Justin with me today. They used to be enemies. They even tried to hurt me. Now they'd take a bullet for me. You all think kids join gangs for fun or because they wanna be criminals? Get real. They join because there's no other choices. All you give them is school and the school system is out of touch with reality. We have no choices there, either. At least with our bill of rights, kids will know that when the adult world fails them, they still have rights under the law. All those gang kids we have in the Round Table left the hood behind because my dad gave them a real way out, a way to make a difference and be part of life, not separate from it."

He swept his eyes over them.

"My Dad did all that without your help, or even the help of the local mayor. In fact, the mayor tried to stop us, because we made him look bad. He didn't care that life sucked for us kids. He just wanted to get re-elected. I've even heard a rumor there are other politicians like that."

A few scattered laughs followed his joke, but Lance didn't smile.

"Our children's bill of rights is not a joke or a ploy for attention. Trust me, I've had more than enough attention over the past couple of years to last forever." He earned a few chuckles and even some scattered applause. "You know a lot more about me than I know about you. And my life experience in this country isn't that unusual, sadly. We've heard from kids in every state talking about how they have no rights and adults have all the power. Things were different, I'm sure, when the Founding Fathers wrote the Constitution. Maybe most parents took good care of their kids. I don't know. I wasn't there."

That engendered another nervous laugh.

"We're property in this country," Lance reiterated somberly, "and... I know a lot of you are gonna be insulted by this, but here goes. I think you want to keep the option of aborting us right up until the moment we turn eighteen and finally become human beings and have real civil rights under the law."

There were gasps and shakes of the head and glowering faces throughout the chamber.

"The lives of children don't matter when they interfere with what grown-ups want. That's just how it is. There are many of you who want to say we're adults if we commit a crime, but we're not adult enough to have any other rights. What kind of society says its kids only have the right to go to prison? If that's not aborting us, what is it?" That remark drew more scowls and a lot of squirming, but Lance didn't care. "And that's only the tip of the iceberg. Ricky."

Ricky stepped nervously forward and leaned in to the mic. Lance placed a comforting hand on his arm as Ricky described some of the crimes against children that had been sent to them from all across the fifty states. Some were seemingly small, like parents forcing their son to participate in a girl's *quincienera* against his will, even though that commitment required him to give up all of his free time for two straight months. Others were downright preposterous, like a school suspending a first grader because he bit his Pop Tart into the shape of a gun, or the middle school boy who'd been suspended for dying his hair green and the school ordered him to go back to his natural color or he would remain on suspension.

Other episodes would be clear violations of the First Amendment if the accused had been an adult, like the case of some American kids in a California school who got suspended for wearing American flag shirts because the principal was afraid the shirts would offend immigrant students. There were stories from kids who'd been beaten or abused in foster homes or group homes, kids who were bullied nonstop at school for being gay and the school would only "talk" to the bullies; there were kids who got punished by their parents for listening to "the wrong music," and even kids in high school who got suspended for bringing their own lunch from home, because they were required to eat the school food.

And of course, he explained about the Native children having no rights against rape and removal from their families. Ricky told story after story for fifteen solid minutes and never wavered once. Lance was proud of him for his aplomb, since he knew how much Ricky hated public speaking. Then Ricky turned to Lance with a nod and stepped back from the microphone.

Lance stepped forward. "Whether you all take us seriously or not, your *children* do, and so do millions of kids across this country. We're willing to work with you if you have problems with our amendments, but how can we work with you when you don't even bother to read them? Isn't that proof alone how seriously adults take children? Here you are, the most powerful people in the world and you couldn't even take ten minutes to read a document Ricky and me poured our hearts and souls into drafting." He looked forlornly out at them. "Do yourselves a favor, please. Talk to your kids. No, I take that back. *Listen* to them. Your kids aren't stupid, and we aren't either. Even your kids who come from good homes know life is not fair for most children in this country." Lance offered that angelic smile everyone in the world seemed to love. "That's your homework assignment, class," he said with a chuckle, and many in the chamber nervously joined him. "To listen to your kids about our bill. When we contact you for your support, or your reasons for not supporting, we wanna know how those talks went, and why you agree or don't agree with your own children."

Ricky joined him at the microphone and together, they said, "We, the young people of the United States of America, in order to form a more perfect union, hereby seek under the Constitution the same rights and privileges you and every other adult have had since that document was drafted. We wish to become real human beings under the law, with civil rights no one can ever take away. We wish to finally, more than two hundred years later, become real citizens of this greatest country in the world. Thank you for your time and your attention."

The boys stepped from behind the podium, and, as Arthur had always modeled, bowed respectfully to the assembled lawmakers. Suddenly the vice president leapt up behind them clapping.

"Aren't they great!" he gushed excitedly. "C'mon, kids, stand up and take a bow!" The two boys turned to the man agape, and he seemed to realize his error. "Oh, of course, you're already standing. Well, take another bow, boys!"

Lance and Ricky turned back to the crowd. But the vice president seemed to have broken the spell of silence and, like the wave at a baseball game, the lawmakers began standing and applauding, some lightly, others with great enthusiasm.

Lance glanced down at the front row and saw the knights and Ryan on their feet, clapping louder than anyone else. The Supreme Court justices were also on their feet, applauding with gusto.

Lance turned to eye the president, who grinned at him with respect as he clapped. The chief executive gestured for the boys to step down off the dais and into the aisle, where suddenly they were engulfed by men and women extending their hands and congratulating them. The justices seemed especially impressed by the boys' speech and told them so. As they made their way slowly down the aisle to the back exit, lawmakers from both parties extended their hands and praised their impassioned words. Some congratulated them on catching everyone off guard with their truth or dare questions.

They felt so overcome by mixed emotions—elation, nervousness, pride, and terror—that Lance and Ricky could later recall little of that long, protracted exit from the House chamber, which seemed to take forever as they were stopped along the way by this senator or that representative.

Finally they were at the rear door and Edwin was there, beaming with a goofy grin on his face. "Wow, you guys knocked 'em dead! I've never seen those people so rattled before. Usually everybody's all PC and nicey nicey, but you nailed 'em."

He laughed and shook both their hands. The boys grinned in response to his gushing reaction, and suddenly felt overcome with exhaustion. The crushing weight of what they'd just done almost sent them to the floor in a dead faint.

Noting their nervous fatigue, Edwin led them back to the waiting room where they plopped down on the sofa and sat in a daze. Edwin left to bring the others back. Absorbing the monumental nature of what they'd done, Lance and Ricky simply sank into the softness of the couch and allowed their fingers to intertwine.

The door flew open and Reyna burst in, followed by Esteban and the others. They swamped the boys with backslapping and congratulations and running commentary about how everyone was still talking and arguing with each other after the boys left the chamber.

Kai laughingly told them some of the senators promised to "Look into that Native American problem."

Lance shook his head in amazement. "Did they offer you buffalo meat too?"

Kai laughed again and shoved the scowling Dakota. But then Lance jumped up and threw his arm around Dakota's shoulders, grinning. "C'mon, Dakota, at least a smile for what we did today."

Dakota met Lance's wide-eyed expression, and a shy smile crept across his lips. "My people are grateful."

Lance pulled him in and yanked Ricky up from the couch. Then Ricky pulled Kai into the mix.

"Our people," Lance affirmed. "The Native Knights." Then all four gave a loud *whoop* that set everyone to laughing.

At this point, Edwin stepped forward and said, "Senator Cairns would like to meet with you all in his office, if that's okay."

The four boys released one another, and Lance grinned. "That'd be great."

And so they followed Edwin out and down to the underground tunnel leading from the house side to the senate side, which took about ten minutes to traverse. But

Lance and Ricky needed the exercise after such an intense afternoon, and welcomed the lengthy walk.

They found Senator Cairns waiting in his office when they arrived. He stood and stepped from behind a large, ornate wooden desk that put the one in Mayor Soto's office to shame. There were fine art prints adorning the walls and several large, comfortable – looking chairs for people to sit and chat.

The senator was of average height, maybe forty, Lance surmised, with short dark hair, well-groomed, and small brown eyes that squinted happily as he smiled.

"Well, well, here's the boy who came back *and* the boy who wants to change the Constitution," he said with a grin as he extended his hand.

With a laugh, Lance reached out to shake it. "Not change, Senator, just amend, like it's s'posed to be done."

The senator shook hands with Ricky, who playfully nudged Lance with his shoulder and said, "Just call him what the mayor of L.A. does—young Mr. Lincoln."

Cairns released Ricky's hand and grinned approvingly. "Young Mr. Lincoln it is."

Looking embarrassed, Lance shoved Ricky. Then Edwin introduced the rest of the group and brought in chairs from the outer office so everyone could sit.

When all were seated, Lance looked at Cairns, now seated behind his desk, and tried his soul whispering. The man's eyes seemed to hide nothing, but Lance knew these politicians became experts at shining people on.

"So, senator, what did you think of our speech?"

"It was masterful. Especially that truth or dare bit." He laughed. "I think I was the only one who knew my kids were in contact with you. The looks on everyone else's face will be Internet fodder for months, especially since your speech ran live. Oh, I can't wait to watch the replay."

Lance and Ricky grinned.

Cairns went on to explain that he was the junior senator from Maryland and had only been in office for three years, "So a lot of the old-timers don't take me seriously. But, having said that, I believe in your CBOR, as you call it, and I'll do my best to push it through some committees for consideration."

The boys thanked him, and then the senator asked questions of the entire group, about their lives before and after joining the Round Table, and said he'd like to meet Arthur some day and thank him personally. Cairns seemed genuine enough to Lance, who decided to reserve final judgment on the senator's character until he'd spent more time around him.

Cairns did say he would keep in regular contact with Lance and Ricky via email, and would send them names of senators and representatives he felt were more centrist and might get the ball rolling for the CBOR. He reminded them that they really had Edwin to thank for "Dragging me into all this." He laughed. "Edwin is an outstanding intern and will make a great senator himself one day."

Edwin made a goofy face and chuckled, and Lance detected a trace of hero worship in the young man for the senator.

Everyone thanked Cairns for arranging their tour of Washington the following day, and for lending them Edwin.

Edwin eyed Lance in particular. "He's not lending anything. I told him I'd quit if he didn't let me hang out with you tomorrow."

"He did," Cairns confirmed. "See how indispensable he is? He can even blackmail me." He laughed again, and Edwin shrugged.

With that, they said their goodbyes and made the long trek back through the tunnel to the underground garage, and then battled late afternoon traffic returning to their hotel. Edwin bade them good-bye and told them he'd bring the limo around at nine the next morning, promising them a fun day they'd never forget.

The group went to Buca de Beppo Italian restaurant that night for dinner because it was a funky, loud place with tons of food and a freewheeling atmosphere. Everyone sat around a huge table, and the food was served in gigantic bowls, or plates, big enough to feed four people. There were laughs and excited talk from everybody but Justin. Lance kept noting the boy glancing up from his food and eyeing him in a peculiar way throughout the meal. He didn't join in the fun, nor could Esteban or Reyna get a laugh out of him.

Finally, halfway through the meal, Justin rose from the table and made his way around to the opposite side where Lance and Ricky were goofing around tasting each other's pasta.

"Uh, hey, Lance," Justin stammered, his eyes downcast. "Can I, uh, talk to you outside a minute? It's important."

All conversation ceased to observe Justin's odd behavior. The brawny boy had almost shrunk into himself, barely able to meet Lance's eyes as he spoke.

Lance eyed Ricky a moment and then turned back to Justin. "Sure, man."

He stood and followed Justin between tables toward the door, looking back once with a shrug before exiting the noisy restaurant and stepping off to one side of the entrance, where Justin stood shuffling his feet and looking down at the sidewalk.

"Uh, so, what's up, big guy?" Lance asked uncertainly. He'd never seen the supremely confident Justin look so small and weak. Then it occurred to him. "Is Bridget okay?"

Justin looked up at that. "Bridget's awesome. No, it's you, somethin' you said today during your speech."

He stopped and looked down again, causing Lance to shift uncomfortably. He didn't like seeing the other boy so distressed. It unnerved him.

"Yeah, about what?"

Still gazing intently at the sidewalk like it held all of life's secrets, Justin said, "When you said how I almost hurt you, but now I'd take a bullet for you?"

Still mystified, Lance tried for jest. "You mean you wouldn't take a bullet for me?"

Now Justin looked up, his eyes wide, his mop of hair wafting in the warm summer breeze. "Hell, yeah, I would."

Lance frowned. "I was joking, man. What's up?"

Justin's face, so hard and unfeeling when Lance had first met him, now dissolved into an expression of intense guilt. "I almost killed you, Lance, that night in the ally with Dwayne," he said, his voice low and whispery and sad. "I almost let him cut your throat. Only reason you're still here is 'cause Arthur showed up."

Lance remembered that night all too well. Man, that seemed like forever ago, but it was only what, three years back? So much had happened… He looked soberly at the guilt-ridden Justin. "It's all good, man. We're brothers now, right?"

Justin nodded. "'Cept I never said I was sorry, man. Hell, Lance, I was such a puffed up fool back then, thinking I was all big and hard, working for R, rolling in all that cash. I thought I could do anything, even kill people. Do ya think ya could, like, forgive a screwup like me?"

Lance gazed into the young man's face, and noted how much he'd begun to resemble his dad as he'd gotten older. Justin looked so stricken, so pathetic and sorrowful that Lance felt bad for him. He flashed his smile, and put a hand on Justin's shoulder. "I already have, man. That's why you're my brother."

Justin grinned. It lit up his face, and Lance for the first time realized how handsome he was.

No wonder Bridget likes him, he thought, *if he gives her that smile.*

"Bridget's lucky to have you."

Justin almost blushed, and looked away in embarrassment. "Thanks, man. She's pretty cool."

Lance eyed him searchingly. "Are we falling for her, methinks?"

Justin raised his eyes and looked at Lance. "Methinks so, yeah."

"That's awesome," Lance said with conviction, and he meant it. Bridget was an amazing girl and she deserved someone who could love her the way she needed. "Now let's get back 'fore our food gets cold."

Justin grinned again, and they returned to their family to finish out a fun, joyful evening.

Later, in their room, lying atop their beds, Lance and Ricky thought back on the day, and considered its ramifications. They'd likely pissed off some of the members of Congress, but they'd known there were a certain number who would never support them no matter what. Their hope was that maybe they'd at least gotten most of those people thinking about the CBOR. At the very least, they expected all the men and women with children to read it, so they wouldn't look so bad in front of their own kids, especially since their kids had probably seen them admit on TV just how out of touch they were. It was a beginning, they knew, the first major salvo in a much larger and more complicated war.

As a rule, neither boy wore a shirt to bed, only workout shorts, and this trip was no exception.

"Don't let your fool ass faint while checking out my abs," Lance said with a chuckle as he slipped beneath the covers of his soft, cool bed, while Ricky slid into his own. The night was warm so they kept the air-conditioner on low.

"Yeah, right, you just don't wanna admit my chest is bigger than yours."

"In your dreams, dumbass," Lance shot back.

"You're always in my dreams, fool. Didn't you know that?"

Lance felt warmth fill him. "And you're in mine. Fool."

They laughed and reached up to turn out their night-table lamps. In the dark there was silence a moment, punctuated by the steady hum of the air whizzing out of the wall unit.

"Hey, dumbass," Lance mumbled after a moment. "Don't let me forget our skateboards tomorrow."

"Don't worry, dumber ass," came Ricky's voice floating through the darkness. "I'll remember."

Both of them settled into their pillows. Exhaustion soon pulled them under, and they fell into a sound asleep.

CHAPTER EIGHT

YOU GO, I GO

THE BOYS WOKE TO THEIR phone alarms chirping and rose to get showered and ready for their tour of Washington. Unlike the day before, they felt relaxed and calm, since nothing was expected of them. Today they would be regular kids on vacation, and it felt liberating not having the weight of the world on their shoulders.

Lance insisted Ricky shower first so he could examine the map of Washington he'd gotten from the concierge. Of course, seeing Ricky step from the bathroom clad only in a towel was an added bonus that Lance didn't mind. As always, the sight of Ricky's beautiful face and body nearly took his breath away, and sent his heart fluttering into overdrive.

Ricky chuckled at Lance's open-mouthed expression. "What? Too much hotness this early in the morning?"

"Yeah." Lance grinned. "At least till I come out wearing a towel."

They laughed, and Lance pushed past him to enter the bathroom.

They met everyone else by the elevators and descended to the atrium for breakfast. They had all watched portions of the news the night before to gauge reaction to the boys' congressional appearance, and the debate raged on. Many callers to chat shows were initially against the CBOR, but expressed a favorable impression of Lance and Ricky from their speech, and promised to give the amendments another look-see.

Edwin bounded into the lobby precisely at nine o'clock, and ebulliently escorted them to the waiting limo. Lance found the guy a funny combination of nerd and goofball, and yet he seemed to be extremely efficient at his job. He could see why Cairns liked the intern, but there was still something about the way he'd be eyeing him and Ricky when he thought neither was looking, something disconcertingly familiar.

Maybe, Lance decided, *he just doesn't care much for boys who love boys. Oh, well...*

Ryan expressed surprise that no Secret Service agents would be accompanying them, but Edwin shrugged. "The senator called them off. Thought they might call more attention to you than you want."

Ryan thought that was probably true, but wondered if the senator had cleared it with the president first. He considered calling The White House, but decided he was perhaps being overcautious. They'd be in public all day, surrounded by tourists, and the kids carried their bows and quivers of arrows if the need should arise to use them. And, of course, he was armed.

For their part, Lance and Ricky preferred not having the creepy, robotic guys in black sunglasses shadowing them everywhere they went. The boys brought their skateboards as promised, though so far the trip had been uneventful and Lance considered the possibility that Merlin might have been wrong. His visionary skills were still not back to where they should be, and all he'd seen were skateboards.

They slipped into the cool luxury of the limo and set off on their tour. Everyone was dressed casual, as it was going to be hot and humid, according to the weather report. Lance and Ricky wore shorts and skater tank tops, with beanies and big sunglasses to hide a large portion of their faces. They laughed and joked about the other having chicken legs, but Esteban commented that they both looked bigger and more buff.

"You're growing up, little *carnales*," he joked as they settled in for the ride, and the boys shoved each other around as usual.

They cruised by Ford's Theatre and the Peterson House where President Lincoln had been shot, and where he'd died. It was a somber moment for Lance. He had a sudden irrational premonition of his own death and quickly shrugged it off.

Edwin took them to the National Archives where they got to see the actual Declaration of Independence and Constitution. Both were housed in airtight, heat and cold-regulated glass enclosures to preserve the integrity of the documents. Other tourists gathered around, as well, but for Lance and Ricky it was a seminal moment in their lives to view the original document they now sought to amend.

They stopped briefly for lunch at a hamburger place Edwin favored, and all the boys, the younger and the older, ate enough food to make Reyna shake her head.

Lance gave her a mock scowl and flexed his right arm. "Hey, sis, we're growing boys, right Este?"

"You got it, *carnal*," he replied and they bumped fists.

After lunch, the limo driver parked not far from the Lincoln Memorial and everyone headed in that direction since, as Edwin joked to Lance, "You're the young Mr. Lincoln, after all."

That shiver of fear ran up Lance's back once again, and Ricky, walking beside him, noticed the change immediately.

"You okay, Lance?"

Lance looked over, the premonition fading. "Yeah. Just a weird feeling."

Ricky grinned. "You mean just a dumbass feeling, don't you?"

Lance mimed a punch, and they kept walking. The temperature was already in the eighties and humid. The boys had bought bottles of water and swigged them as they walked. The skateboards became cumbersome with their bows and quivers, and made taking pictures with their phones that much more of a hassle. Edwin had informed them that skateboard riding was forbidden anywhere near the reflecting pool or national monuments, and expressed curiosity about why the boys were carrying them. Lance simply said they completed the disguise and left it at that. Their bows and quivers, as well as the two obvious Indian boys, did draw the attention of a number of tourists, but thus far no one had recognized the group for who they were.

The Lincoln Memorial was immense, and looked to Lance like a massive Greek temple with towering stone columns surrounding it and a steep rise of stairs into the inner sanctum. Within sat the titan-sized statue of a pensive Lincoln, arms laid out along the stone armrests, eyes gazing outward at the city beyond as though guarding the Union, like he'd done during the Civil War.

After ascending the numerous steps and entering the shadowy interior, Lance simply stopped, Ricky beside him, and stared up at the gargantuan statue in awe.

"Wow," they both heard Reyna utter as she moved to Ricky's side and tilted her head up at the solemn, bearded stone face. Surrounding Lincoln, carved into the walls, was the text of his Gettysburg Address, and passages from other speeches. Tourists milled around, gazing at the words and staring up at the statue, but the overall effect of the monument was one of reverence, and almost no one spoke.

Reyna pulled out her camera and asked Ryan to get some pictures of all of them standing in front of the statue, which he gladly did. Then she smiled mischievously. "And now I need a few with just the young Mr. Lincoln and the old Mr. Lincoln together."

Moved by the statue, and still feeling that odd premonition about his ultimate fate matching that of the sixteenth president, Lance hesitated.

"Please?" Reyna begged. "We have to send one to Mayor Soto."

Lance nodded, and Ricky gave him 'the look', so he stepped beneath the stone chair and Reyna crouched down so she could shoot up and capture both faces. Lance didn't smile and ended up looking almost as solemn as Lincoln.

When she was done, Lance hurried back to Ricky, fighting to shake off the chill that kept rippling up and down his back. As hot as the temperature was, he felt cold inside.

From here, they made their way past hordes of tourists along the Vietnam Veterans Memorial, a shiny black wall inscribed with the name of every man who had died in that conflict. Some people, Lance noted, were asking a park worker to trace over the name of a loved one onto a piece of paper, so they could take it home, he supposed.

After that, they skirted the Lincoln Memorial once more and passed though the Korean War Memorial, a creepy scene of metallic, realistic-looking soldiers trudging through rice paddies and fields. All of these memorials, amazing though they were, sent more chills down Lance's back, for they were all devoted to wars and young people who'd died before their time.

From here they passed through the World War II Memorial circle with its fountain in the center. The circular wall was made up of fifty stone pillars representing each of the fifty states that had sent soldiers to war.

From there the group followed a large number of tourists along the curving pathways to the five hundred fifty-five foot tall Washington Monument, at the top of which, Edwin told them, "You can see thirty miles in any direction. It's so cool."

Because Edwin had connections through the senator, he'd already gotten tickets for the group to ascend to the top viewing windows, and finally Lance began to shake off the melancholy sense of dread that had been plaguing him since Ford's Theater.

The boys wanted to walk up all eight hundred ninety-seven steps to the top, but Ryan nixed that plan. "Not going to happen, boys."

Even Reyna sided with him, so they all gathered into the elevator for the seventy second ride to the top. Dakota looked nervous being in the small space, and Kai offered him a grin of support.

Lance and Ricky stood silently together at one of the small openings around the top, in awe of the breathtaking view. Spread out below was the World War II Memorial, the vast reflecting pool, and in the distance the Lincoln Memorial. Beyond that sprawled the Potomac River, with two bridges spanning it, and the city of Washington laid out for miles on either side. Without thinking, their hands found each other and squeezed. So enraptured were they by the view, that neither noticed a couple and their teenaged son eyeing their handholding with disgust.

Reyna and Esteban mad-dogged the family something fierce until they chose another viewpoint and left the boys alone. Once everyone had looked out each of the four sides, it was time for the elevator ride back down.

The afternoon sun beat down on them mercilessly. Rather than walk all the way back, Edwin called the limo driver and told him to bring the car down Constitution Avenue to pick them up. They'd take the pathways across a large expanse of grass and meet the limo in a small parking area just off Constitution.

Thus far, only a few of the tourists had recognized Lance, and even then had only hesitantly asked if it was him. Kai and Dakota continued to warrant many stares for their obvious Indian hair and bows and arrows, but for the most part, people were so engrossed in sightseeing that the most famous boys in the world hid in plain sight all afternoon.

Now, as they trudged along the winding paths toward the parking lot, Lance and Ricky settled into a chattering conversation with Kai and Dakota about what they'd seen. Both Indians agreed that George Washington had been pretty fair to Indian tribes and mostly kept his end of a treaty. But as a whole, they felt strange seeing all this history and knowing that it had come about by trampling over their ancestors.

Lance digested their assessment, and realized that history, like everything else, was in the eye of the beholder, and there were always two sides to every story.

All in all, everyone had enjoyed their day, and seeing these impressive monuments helped solidify the reality of the country in their young minds, a reality that was, at least on paper, a great idea, but which needed constant vigilance to make certain it didn't spiral out of control.

As they arrived at the small, paved parking lot connecting the monument area to Constitution Avenue, the limo had not yet arrived, so they stood around chatting. Lance kept eyeing his skateboard anxiously, that premonition wafting over him again. Feeling anxious and uncertain, he met Ricky's eyes. "Let's skate around right here so you can practice more."

"Why? You don't think I'm as good as you?"

Lance laughed nervously. "C'mon, fool."

So they set their sunglasses on the hood of a car, dropped their boards and began skating around the mostly empty lot. Edwin was about to say something when Ryan flashed his Special Agent badge and said it was fine. Edwin fell silent and watched the two boys like everyone else.

Lance and Ricky skated lazily along the roadway in the direction of Constitution Avenue, and Lance joked, "Wanna see me ollie over those cars out there?" He pointed to the busy, six-lane thoroughfare just ahead.

Ricky laughed. "Sure. And then you can watch me ollie over one of the painted white lines."

Lance laughed. Something whizzed past his arm and he heard a *thump* behind him. Startled, he whirled around on his board to look at the parked car, stunned to see a large nail embedded in the soft metal of the driver's door.

Ricky rolled over and squinted at the nail. "The hell?"

Another whizzing sound whipped past Ricky's head and both boys heard a thump from the wooden fence separating the monument area from the street.

They spun around to where Ryan and the others stood, apparently unawares. Then Lance saw them. Men on motorcycles, clad in black with visored helmets covering their heads and faces. There were five, all heading their way across the expanse of grass from the direction of 15th Street NW, and coming on fast. All of them held long barreled guns.

"Ricky," Lance exclaimed, "they're shooting nails!"

"Oh, hell," Ricky whispered.

Lance turned to his family. "*Nino*, behind you! Take cover!"

And then four of the motorcycle men took aim at Ryan and the others and fired. The group scattered, ducking behind parked cars for cover. The fifth cyclist headed straight for Lance and Ricky.

Lance grabbed Ricky and pulled. "C'mon, now's the time to ollie over them cars!" They bolted forward on their boards, Lance deftly weaving from side to side. "Weave, in case he shoots!"

Ricky did his best to copy Lance's movements, but he was nowhere near as proficient. Another nail sailed past his head and out into the traffic just ahead. Then the boys were at the sidewalk, facing a wall of oncoming cars on their side and a steady flow going the opposite way. Lance turned. The cyclist was gaining, arm up and ready to fire. He glanced at the oncoming traffic. A UPS truck was almost on them.

"C'mon!" He grabbed Ricky, pushed him out onto Constitution Avenue, and followed. Ricky kicked and pushed his board out into the street, Lance pounding along right beside him. They only just cleared the UPS truck as it sped past behind them, but even over the traffic noise Lance could hear the *thunk, thunk, thunk* as three nails embedded themselves into the side of the truck.

Suddenly, cars going the opposite way started honking and swerving as the boys weaved their way through them. Two mounted D.C. police officers happened to be trotting down the sidewalk and spotted the boys disrupting traffic. One of them called out, "Hey, you kids, get the hell outta the street!"

Lance glanced over, but ignored the command as he twisted his body to navigate between two cars, and Ricky followed suit. He glanced back. The motorcyclist was stopped by traffic going the other way, clearly awaiting an opening to pursue. Suddenly a bus loomed in the far right lane, bearing down on them. Lance noted that it said Arlington Metro Express above the windshield and prayed that meant it wouldn't stop at every corner.

He grabbed Ricky's arm and they slammed into the sidewalk hard. Ricky knew he'd have gone sprawling if not for Lance's firm grip on him.

Lance spotted the two mounted officers trotting angrily toward them, and then looked back at the bus. "When the bus passes, grab on to the back."

Ricky's face was etched with terror. "What? That's crazy. I can't do that, Lance!"

Lance looked at him with determination. "Don't worry, Ricky. I got you." He patted his heart. By then the bus and the cops were almost on them. The bus got there first. "Now!" Lance screamed as he pushed Ricky forward and skated after him. Ricky fumbled to grab the back right corner, while Lance grabbed for the left. Lance found his grip, but Ricky didn't.

"Lance!" Ricky called as the bus began pulling ahead without him.

Clinging to the side of it, Lance shouted, "C'mon, you can do this!"

Ricky pounded along, his right leg kicking hard against the asphalt. The bus slowed, and Ricky was there, flailing outward with his hands, his fingers just finding purchase before the bus continued forward.

The mounted police started after them, but then Lance spotted Ryan and the others running up to them. At that point, there must have been a break in the traffic because the bus picked up speed.

Lance's wheels rattled along the pavement and he looked across at Ricky's terrified expression. He tried for a smile. "Just like the X Games, huh?"

Ricky didn't smile back. "Screw the X Games!" He clung desperately to the accelerating bus and fought to stay atop his wobbling board.

That's when Lance saw the motorcycle speed across the traffic to their side of the road in pursuit.

Ryan flashed his badge at the two cops. "Federal agent. Call for back up. Sir Lance and Sir Ricky are under attack. And we need to commandeer your horses."

The two officers, clad in standard police attire, sat atop their brown horses looking bewildered. "No way. We can pursue."

Ryan shook his head and pointed at Kai and Dakota, barely winded from their frantic run across six lanes of traffic. "These two are better. Now off!"

The officers did not comply.

"Do I need to call the president direct?" Ryan asked angrily, flashing his badge once more.

The two officers looked at one another, and then reluctantly dropped down from their mounts.

Ryan turned to Dakota and Kai. "Go!"

Without hesitation, each boy grabbed a horse by the reins and leapt deftly up into the saddle. The other four motorcycles had now whipped into traffic and were pursuing Lance and Ricky. Dakota and Kai spurred the animals into a gallop after them.

Ryan spotted the limo finally pulling up near the entrance to the monuments on the opposite side of the street. He whipped his head around to the officers. "That back up, now! And block this traffic so we can make a U-turn." Then he turned to the others. "C'mon!"

Edwin looked totally flustered, but the others didn't hesitate. As one officer got on his radio, the other stepped out into traffic waving his arms, gradually slowing the cars in both directions. Ryan and his group pelted across the street and jumped into the waiting limo. This time Ryan sat up front with the driver. "U-turn, now! Follow those horses!"

The driver didn't wait to be told twice. He peeled away from the curb and spun the wheel sharply, tossing everyone in back onto each other, and almost onto the floor. Then the massive car swung around the uniformed cop and headed in the same direction as Lance and Ricky.

"Reyna," Ryan said, whipping his head around to her. "Get Techie on the line. Have him activate the trackers in Lance and Ricky's phones. And have him tell Arthur."

Everyone had gone to lunch but Techie. He sat alone in the Computer Lab coordinating when and how Arthur would visit a number of neighborhoods throughout Los Angeles, where his knights, in conjunction with Mayor Soto, had been putting interventions in place. With Reyna gone, that job seemed to have fallen into his already cluttered lap. And he wanted to finish early so he could meet Ariel and go to the movies. But that was before his phone rang and he saw Reyna's picture pop up.

"Hey, Reyna, how's—"

"Quick, Techie, activate Lance and Ricky's trackers," her voice bellowed over the phone, cutting him off. "And tell Arthur."

"On it!" he said instantly, tapping keys on his computer and activating the satellite tracking feature in the boys' phones. Almost simultaneously, he put Reyna on hold and speed dialed Arthur. As the satellite map of Washington came up on his screen, he heard Arthur's voice over the phone speaker.

"Yes, Sir Techie."

"Arthur, get down to the lab. The guys are in trouble."

There came a sharp intake of breath. "On my way."

Techie took Reyna off hold. Leaving the phone beside his keyboard, his fingers raced over the keys, attempting to triangulate on the boys' location. "They're on 23rd Street NW, Reyna, heading toward the Arlington Memorial Bridge."

In the limo, Reyna leaned forward toward the open window separating her from the driver. "Did you hear that?"

"Yes, ma'am, I got it," the man replied and focused on weaving through the traffic on Constitution Avenue.

"Are we close?" Ryan asked the driver, gun out his window.

The motorcycles were just ahead in traffic, cutting between the cars, but Dakota and Kai galloped in between the cars in pursuit of the attackers, and blocked any shot Ryan might have had.

"Yes, sir," the driver informed Ryan in a surprisingly calm voice. "It's the next street over."

As though confirming the man's words, the motorcyclists turned left at the light, the two horses galloping desperately after them. Traffic was paralyzed by the sight of the cyclists and the horses, and people simply stopped their cars to gawk. The limo driver honked steadily, and Ryan leaned out the window screaming, "Out of the way! Police business!"

Cars attempted to pull to the side, but slowly.

Esteban handed over his phone. "I got me a siren app, Sergeant. You want?"

"Hell yeah! Can you sync it to the car stereo?"

"Can I, driver?"

The driver punched a couple of buttons on the dashboard. "Now you can."

Esteban synced his phone, opened the siren app, and cranked the volume. The driver turned up the stereo system full blast, and a strident imitation of a police siren ripped through the car and almost deafened everyone.

"Windows down!" Ryan commanded, and all windows quickly lowered.

Edwin had turned white with fear and looked like he might vomit.

Justin eyed him. "You okay, man?"

Edwin nodded, but clutched at his seat belt with white-knuckled intensity.

With their windows down and the blasting siren audible to surrounding motorists, the cars began to scurry out of the way with greater speed. Still, Ryan noted, the bus carrying his boys had long since turned out of sight, and the enemy, as well.

Lance and Ricky had their knees bent as they clung to the sides of the bus and fought to keep their boards level beneath their feet. As the bus swung on to Lincoln Memorial Circle and curved around behind the monument, Lance kept his head pressed against the rear corner of the bus to keep at least half of Ricky's terrified face in his line of sight. Ricky's hair flew every which way as the wind yanked the beanie right off his head. It sailed lazily back into traffic and he gazed wide-eyed at Lance.

"I got you, Ricky!" Lance called over the wind and road noise. His long hair whipped around in his face frenetically—he'd lost his own beanie when the bus had taken the sharp left off Constitution.

It hadn't seemed windy before, but then they hadn't been going thirty miles per hour before.

Lance spotted the cycles, and the men in black riding them. They were five or six car lengths back, weaving in and out of traffic. The closest one raised his right arm, and fired the nail gun.

Lance nearly lost his grip as a nail tore through the rear of the bus near the taillight. And then he saw Dakota and Kai, galloping fiercely between the cars, holding the reins and simultaneously reaching for their bows.

Dakota had pulled ahead of Kai as they galloped headlong through the traffic in pursuit of the attacking cyclists. He knew he could fire an arrow effectively from horseback, but wasn't certain about Kai. His Native brother had honed his skills at New Camelot these past few months, but other than that one frantic ride through Griffith Park, had not been on a horse since. Thus, Dakota knew it would likely be up to him to take these guys out at this stage of the pursuit.

As they turned left at the green light, oncoming cars screeched to a halt or swerved violently to avoid colliding with the motorcycles and the pursuing horses. Just the sight of two Indians, hair streaming, feathers flying, caused mass confusion amongst the motorists. Tourists along the sidewalks, however, seemed awed by the display, holding out their phones and filming the chase. All of this Dakota became of aware of peripherally while gazing intently ahead at the closest motorcycle to him. Further beyond, heading toward a bridge, he saw the massive Metro bus dragging his two brothers along with it.

Spurring his horse forward, Dakota flung back his arm and snatched his bow from around his back. The other hand flew back and plucked an arrow from his quiver. Holding the reins in his clenched teeth, Dakota raised his bow arm and pulled back on the arrow. He saw one cyclist fire at Lance, and miss. Just as the bus started out over the six-lane bridge, Dakota saw the second motorcyclist raise his nail gun. Dakota squinted, took careful aim, and let his arrow fly.

The arrow sailed out and over the intervening cars, past the other cyclists and struck the one with the gun square in the back. The arrow bounced off without piercing the man's heavy jacket, but the rider did flinch and it threw off his aim. The gun fired, a nail sailing over the railing into the Potomac.

Now the cyclist furthest back turned on his bike and fired randomly. The nail missed Dakota by a wide margin, but must've struck an oncoming car behind him because he heard the screech of brakes, and then a crunch of metal against metal. He hunched down his head against the horse's neck and glanced over at Kai, who eyed him right back, also crouching low. Kai dodged a light post and galloped onto the sidewalk, scattering the gawking tourists as he did. Dakota kept straight up the middle of the bridge, straddling traffic in either direction as he zeroed in on the guy who'd shot at him.

He figured they must be wearing some kind of armor under their jackets, so arrows wouldn't penetrate. He raised his arms again and took careful aim at the back tire of the closest cyclist. It was mostly covered with a metal frame, but there was a small area of exposure where the rubber could be seen spinning. He let loose the arrow and it sailed forward between two cars to plunge deep into the exposed portion of tire.

The cycle went wildly out of control, spun and swerved. The driver tried to keep it straight, but the loss of his back tire caused the bike to career up onto the sidewalk, almost ramming Kai who was fast approaching. But the Navajo jerked his reins to the left and the bike sailed past him to slam into the stone fence designed to keep pedestrians from falling into the river. The impact pitched the rider forward over the wall into the Potomac below.

Lance desperately clung to the bus, his arm muscles already tiring from holding on to the uneven rear corners, which were slippery and didn't provide much area to grip. In addition, his legs trembled with fatigue from holding the board taut beneath them. He saw that Ricky was having even more trouble staying on his board. Glancing back, he spotted Dakota taking out the first guy's aim, and sending the second into the river. But horses were no match for motorcycles, and neither was this clunky-ass bus! They had to find a place to hide!

Once over the bridge, the bus approached a large stone structure. Lance was able to crane his head around and catch a glimpse of the massive circular stone wall that looked like part of a castle. The bus swung onto a road that would circumnavigate this structure, motorcycles and Indians in hot pursuit. He turned back and spotted one of the cyclists taking aim at Ricky. "Ricky, duck!"

Ricky did, without hesitation, squatting down as far he could. A *thunk* struck the metal right where his head had just been, and a ghastly looking nail protruded from the silver siding of the bus. Face etched with terror, he peeked around the corner of the bus at Lance, who grinned with intense relief.

Lance looked back at the pursuing cyclist as Dakota let loose another arrow. This one struck the rider in the leg, but it bounced harmlessly off. It did distract him, however, and he lowered the nail gun to steady the wobbling bike.

"Lance!" Ricky shouted in desperation. "What're we gonna do?"

Lance flicked a look back toward the front of the bus as a sign came into view: Arlington National Cemetery. Two massive wrought iron gates stood open before them, but everyone was walking through them. Another bus had stopped, and there was some kind of station ahead with a train disgorging passengers.

Lance looked back across at Ricky. "We'll lose 'em in the cemetery! Get ready to let go on my signal."

Ricky's face collapsed into a look of horror. "Let go?"

Lance locked eyes on those of his other half. "I got you, Ricky!" As the bus began slowing to a stop, Lance shouted, "Now!" He let go.

The forward momentum kept him speeding forward, but he couldn't see Ricky on the other side of the Metro bus. Frantically, he kicked and pushed until he was around the front, startling the driver who gawked out the window at him. And suddenly there was Ricky, kicking and pushing, not so steady as him, but alive and safe.

Lance's pounding heart almost missed a beat. "C'mon, Ricky, follow me!"

Dodging tourists right and left, the two boys pressed their way forward, hearing the revving of the motorcycle engines closing in from behind. They bounded through the gates as a guard shouted, "Hey, you can't skate in there!"

And then the four remaining cyclists plowed their way through the scattering, screaming crowd and barreled through the gates. "Hey!" the guard shouted again.

Before the guard even lifted his radio to call for help, Dakota and Kai were past him, pounding hooves causing the man to ape in astonishment. He stared a moment in bewildered surprise, and then raised the radio to his mouth.

The siren helped the limo driver scare off some of the cars blocking his path, but it was a bright summer day and tourists abounded, especially those trying to visit Arlington, and the going was hit and miss. The driver must've been former military, Ryan decided, because he deftly twisted the wheel and weaved the enormous vehicle in and around other cars, even swerving into the oncoming traffic lanes when an opening presented itself.

In the backseat, Reyna, Esteban and Justin were all crouched like panthers at every open window, bows and arrows at the ready, while Edwin looked like he might be sick at any moment.

Ryan had his gun out the passenger window as the limo started over the bridge. He saw Dakota send the one attacker over into the drink with his arrow, but the boys on their horses were blocking any shot he might have had. Frustrated, he bided his time as he watched the bus head into Arlington.

"Reyna," he barked, "anything from Techie?"

Now Reyna lowered her bow and snatched up the phone. "Techie? You have 'em?"

In the Computer Lab, a tense Arthur, and a terrified Jenny, stood behind Techie gazing intently at his screen. A map of Arlington National Cemetery filled his screen, and two moving dots sped along one of the pathways. He whipped his phone up to make sure he was heard.

"They're in the cemetery, on one of the pathways," he said breathlessly.

Arthur placed a comforting hand on his shoulder and Techie sighed fearfully.

Reyna looked up at Ryan. "Did you hear that?"

Ryan turned to the driver.

"No can do, sir," the driver responded regretfully. "No cars allowed in Arlington."

Ryan cursed. "Get us right up to the gate, even if you have to plow through the tourists to do it."

"Yes, sir." The man kept his eyes focused on the road ahead, executing a neck-snapping move into the oncoming traffic lane. Ryan held his breath as an SUV bore down on them. Then, just as it looked like they'd all be killed, the driver swung the wheel sharply to the right and moved them back into the proper lane, having passed two cars in the process.

If I survive, Ryan thought, *I'll have to ask the president to give this guy a medal.*

They were off the bridge and onto the road leading into the cemetery. Just ahead stood the wrought iron gates, a wildly agitated crowd of tourists, and the flustered security guard. The limo screeched to a halt and Ryan was out before it even stopped. He ran to the guard, the knights close on his heels. Ryan flashed his badge.

"Did you see—"

He didn't get any further because the exasperated guard pointed. "They went that way."

"Call for backup," Ryan barked at the man, and then he pelted forward into the cemetery, the others following.

They bypassed the Visitor's Center, a colonnaded, colonial – style building with an enormous glass dome on top, and raced down the nearest pathway.

"Reyna," Ryan breathlessly called as they ran, "do you have them on your phone?"

Sprinting beside Esteban and Justin, Reyna slipped her bow over her shoulder and opened the home screen on her phone. A map of Arlington appeared, exactly the same as the one on Techie's computer. The two dots could be seen moving away from them, weaving back and forth along Roosevelt Drive heading east.

"I got 'em," she shouted. "Follow me!"

Lance and Ricky were winded and tired and, though neither would admit it, terrified. They pelted and kicked their way along the concrete path, drawing angry glares from tourists who had to leap out of their way. But that was nothing to the screams they heard punctuating the normally reverent silence of the cemetery as the cyclists bore down on the same tourists waving their nail guns threateningly.

Plunk!

A nail struck the grass just past Ricky's feet.

Pling!

Another struck a gravestone and chipped off a small chunk of the masonry.

Lance began to panic. That one almost got Ricky in the back! They had to get to cover, some place they could turn and fight. But where? There was a path just to their right and Lance swerved onto it. "This way, Ricky!" he shouted.

But in his obvious panic, Ricky missed the turnoff and continued along the other pathway.

Lance stopped. "Ricky!"

But Ricky couldn't stop now. The cyclists bypassed Lance and roared after him. Lance's breath nearly stopped. Frantically, he looked ahead and saw another path not far from this one, running parallel to his. "Ricky, take the path to your right! Hurry!"

And then he unslung his bow and whipped out an arrow faster than most cops could pull their guns. He raised his arms and fired at the cyclist closest to Ricky. The arrow bounced harmlessly off and clattered to the roadway, only to be crunched beneath the wheels of the next cycle.

They must be armored up, he realized, desperately thinking of how he might stop them. Then, for some reason, he thought of Achilles, the unstoppable guy in *The Iliad* whose only weak spot was his heel. He eyed the cyclists moving away from him only a moment before taking aim and firing at the first guy's heel. The arrow pierced his boot and the man screamed in pain. His cycle spun out from beneath him and the cyclist directly behind crashed right into him, sending both riders sprawling onto the grass to strike hard against a gravestone.

That was when Lance heard the approaching horse hooves pounding along the path and glanced up with relief to see Dakota and Kai bearing down on the other two cyclists.

"Go for their heels!" he shouted as the boys galloped past. Then Lance spotted Ricky on the parallel uphill path. "C'mon, Ricky, I'll meet you at the top. I got you right here!"

He punched a fist against his heart and saw Ricky grin with gratitude. Then he turned and kicked his board forward as fast as he could. His mind flashed back to the last frantic run he'd made on a skateboard, the one that had saved his dad, but had gotten him shot in the process. This time he had to save Ricky. He had to!

Panting and heaving, he made his way to the top and found himself at the gravesite of President John F. Kennedy, with its eternal flame burning, and a gaggle of tourists ogling him with a mix of fear and wonder.

He was higher than Ricky, and looked out over a gigantic sloped plaque engraved with words from Kennedy's most famous speech. The cyclists continued firing nail after nail at Ricky, who'd abandoned his board and sprinted across the grass in between the gravestones. Nails struck the masonry of these stones and sent chips flying. Lance held his breath, praying and hoping.

"Run, Ricky, here!" he shouted desperately. "You got this!"

Just then the galloping Dakota let loose an arrow. Lance leaned over the small promontory and saw the arrow strike the heel of one cyclist. Almost simultaneously, Kai took out the last one in the same manner. Both cycles careened off amongst the gravestones, sending their riders sprawling.

The Indian boys raised their bows and war whooped with abandon, and Lance was about to join them when suddenly, from around the trees, came a helicopter with a long rope-like grapple device dangling beneath. It bore down on the sprinting Ricky.

"Ricky, run faster!" Lance shrieked. But he knew it was too late.

Ryan and the others sprinted down the walkway and split up. Ryan took off after Kai and Dakota and the others pelted up the shorter path to Lance.

Reyna, Justin, and Esteban joined Lance beside Kennedy's grave and watched in horror as the copter closed in on the running and weaving Ricky.

His breath on hold, Lance realized that they planned to capture Ricky, not kill him. And that could be worse. They'd torture him and…

His heart hammered as the plastic grapple unit, which resembled something he'd seen on construction sites, swooped down on Ricky, clamped itself around his torso, and snatched him off the ground. His legs still ran, but his feet no longer touched the grass.

The unit held him firmly by the waist and around his upper body as the copter rose and made its way to where Lance and the others stood.

Reyna turned to the tourists. "Get out of here, now!"

They scattered.

Ricky struggled and fought, but could not loosen the restraint. He cast a desperate look down in Lance's direction. "Lance, I can't get loose!"

Reyna raised her bow to fire, but Lance pushed her arrow down. "No way. You might hit him."

He surveyed the copter *whup whup whupping* its way in their direction, and then the angle of the plague proclaiming the slain president's famous words.

Yes, he could do it.

"Get ready to take down the copter after I get Ricky," he ordered and ran back a ways from the sloping plaque.

The others looked at him aghast.

"What are you gonna do?" Reyna asked, her eyes wide with fear.

Lance tossed his bow to the ground, his eyes blazing. "I'm saving my boy. Now be ready. You'll know when."

And then he launched himself forward along the concrete surrounding the president's grave. He kicked and pounded harder than even that night a few years back when he'd saved Arthur.

The copter rose higher and higher, but the dangling weight of Ricky slowed its assent, and the struggling boy was only a few feet out, and nearly over the president's speech.

Lance leapt onto the plaque and sailed upward, launching out over empty space. The board dropped from his feet, but he didn't care. The momentum had been enough. He slammed into Ricky and grabbed onto his waist. Ricky looked down at him with breathless abandon, but Lance wasn't done yet. He clambered up, using the claw-like pincher device for leverage, until his face was right up against Ricky's. Their eyes locked a moment.

"I got you," Lance whispered, "and I'm never letting you go."

Ricky grinned, and then both turned their heads as the copter rose above the heads of Reyna and the others and continued to rise higher and higher in an attempt to clear the roof of the three-story Arlington House further up the sloping hillside. Once the home of General Robert E. Lee, the stone house with its six-column portico loomed huge in Lance's vision as the copter dipped and then rose, and dipped again. It was not a large chopper, and apparently hadn't planned on two boys as captives.

Lance looked up into the cockpit of the helicopter and saw two men, one struggling with the controls to keep the machine steady. Lance lowered his eyes as the house rose grand and spectacular before his eyes. The copter began rising higher and cleared the roof. Now was his chance. Lance knew once they got out over the river, they'd be lost. And his arms were already tiring as they dangled and spun in the wind.

"Grab an arrow from my quiver," he hissed at Ricky, his eyes flicking downward at the steep pitched roof of the house just below them. Ricky instantly snaked one arm around and snatched out an arrow, handing it silently to Lance. Eyeing the approaching roof, Lance said, "Get ready. On three. One, two, three!"

They were right over the pitch where the two sides of the roof came together in a point when Lance used the arrow tip to slice through the rope holding them up.

They plummeted downward at an alarming rate, and the sharp pitch of roof rose up to strike at them like a spire from hell.

The moment the boys dropped, Reyna yelled to Esteban and Justin, "Now!"

Three arrows launched simultaneously, and then they whipped out a second and fired even as the first ones struck the copter. The distance was too great to do any real damage, and the chopper swung back around toward the house.

Lance and Ricky plowed into the pitch of the roof with bone-crunching intensity, nearly knocking the wind out of them both. But they landed together and managed to turn on their sides to soften the impact. Unfortunately, that set them to rolling… right toward the edge! The claw arm had disengaged itself once they landed and Lance snatched it from around Ricky as they rolled, throwing it in the direction he thought a chimney to be. The device swung around the chimney and Lance held fast the rope, his other hand scrabbling for Ricky.

But Ricky was pitching headlong toward the edge, and Lance wasn't close enough. With a cry of fear, Ricky slid over. He flung out a hand and just managed to grab the rain gutter as he fell, and dangled helplessly by one arm, his shoulder nearly wrenched from its socket, groaning in pain.

As the chopper arced back toward the boys, the D.C. Metro police arrived on foot. The officers began firing. Between the arrows and the bullets, the pilot must have had enough, for the copter banked sharply back over the Arlington House and *whupped* its way out over the Potomac. The cops spotted the boys on the roof and ran in that direction.

Lance's fall had been slowed by the rope around the chimney, but not enough. He whipped around and yanked an arrow from his quiver and shoved it as hard as he could into the roof shingles. The sharp point dug in and held, and his precipitous slide halted with a jerk to his shoulder. Terrified for Ricky, Lance swallowed his fear and carefully eased his legs up and behind him, rolling onto his stomach and wrapping his feet around the arrow. Then he inched closer to the edge, gasping in horror at the sight of Ricky dangling from one hand, three stories off the ground.

Lance flung his hand over the side. "Give me your hand!"

Ricky swung slightly, and threw his free hand upward, but Lance swiped at it and missed.

"Again!"

Frozen with fear, Ricky hesitated.

"Ricky!" Lance shouted desperately. "Give me your hand!"

Ricky swung again and this time Lance was able to clasp his hand around Ricky's.

"Now… ugh… pull… up!" Lance grunted, the pain in his shoulder hot and stabbing as Ricky struggled for some kind of traction. But he couldn't do it. His wide, brown eyes gazed up at Lance hopelessly.

Lance began sliding ever closer to the edge.

"Let me… go, Lance," Ricky begged, almost without breath. "If you… don't—" He gasped for breath, his voice straining as he fought to hang on. "—we're both… gonna fall!"

Lance shook his head emphatically, as his feet kept slipping from around the arrow under Ricky's extra weight. He locked his eyes on those of his other half. "You go… I go," he croaked, his voice barely able to function from the pressure against his chest and lungs.

Just then he heard, "Lance!" and looked to his right to see Kai scrambling up onto the roof from the adjoining wing beneath the twin chimneys. Kai grabbed the claw device from around the chimney and tossed it up and over the pitch of the roof, holding on to the rope as he did. Once he felt the rope grow taut, he ran across the steep sloping roof to Lance's feet and tied the rope around them.

Lance had never been so happy to see anyone in his entire life. With the rope around him, his sliding motion ceased. Lance glanced gratefully at Kai easing himself carefully down onto the slope behind him. But then Ricky suddenly lost his grip on the rain gutter and swung wildly out over the drop, with only Lance's hand holding him.

And Lance's sweaty grip was slipping.

"Kai!" he shouted.

The Navajo boy scooted as fast as he could down the steep sloping roof and peered over the edge. "Oh, hell!" he muttered, and then carefully stretched himself out onto his stomach so he could reach over the edge for Ricky's flailing hand.

"Lance!" Ricky screamed. "I'm gonna fall!"

The pain in Lance's shoulder was excruciating, but he fought it back. "Like… hell… you… are!" he asserted breathlessly and squeezed Ricky's hand with all his waning strength.

"Give me your other hand!" Kai shouted, his head over the edge and his right arm swinging about for Ricky's free hand.

Ricky twisted his body and made a grab for Kai's hand. He nearly missed, but the Indian seemed to sense where the hand would be and snatched it from the air and clamped onto the wrist.

"Pull!" Lance called to him, and the two boys struggled to pull the flailing Ricky up and over the edge. But the slope was too steep and even with Lance's feet secured, Kai's weren't, and there wasn't enough purchase.

Lance heard galloping horse hooves and glanced down in shock to see Dakota pelting toward them on his horse. Only he wasn't sitting on the horse—he was *standing* on it! The saddle was gone and so were Dakota's boots. Lance's mouth dropped open, and he heard a gasp of surprise from Kai beside him. Still holding the reins, the bare-footed Dakota stood atop the horse like some kind of circus performer and brought the mare to a halt directly below the dangling Ricky. He whipped his head around to Esteban.

"Este!"

Esteban didn't hesitate. He pelted forward across the grass to gape in awe at Dakota standing atop the horse.

"Climb up and get on my shoulders," Dakota said calmly.

Esteban's face registered momentary shock, and a trace of fear at the prospect of clambering up onto the enormous animal. But as he realized what Dakota was suggesting, he held out one hand. Dakota grabbed it while Esteban awkwardly swung a foot into the stirrup. With a forceful pull by Dakota, Esteban was up and onto the back of the horse. Eyes wide with fear, Esteban glanced back at the terrified face of Reyna. She blew him a kiss and that strengthened his resolve.

He marveled at Dakota's strength as the smaller youth practically yanked him to his wobbly feet atop the horse. Then Dakota squatted down for Esteban to clamber up onto his back. The Indian boy's footing never wavered, as though standing on horses was a daily ritual.

With obvious nervousness, Esteban climbed up Dakota's back to his shoulders. The Indian remained rock solid beneath him. Holding Dakota's head, Esteban placed first one foot and then the other on each shoulder. Dakota's hands flew up and gripped Esteban's ankles. Then Dakota rose to his full height, and a quaking Esteban rose to his.

"We'll push and you pull!" Dakota shouted up at Lance and Kai, who'd watched in stunned amazement the prodigious strength and courage of their two brothers.

Before either boy on the roof could react, Esteban reached upward for Ricky's dangling feet and, still standing atop Dakota's rock-steady shoulders, grabbed one of Ricky's shoes in each hand and pressed the boy upward, lifting almost all of Ricky's weight above his head. Lance was so flabbergasted that he momentarily forgot to pull, but as Ricky's weight went from dead to supported, and his head got closer to the roof edge, he and Kai pulled with all their might.

Below, Reyna, Justin, Ryan and the cops stared in open-mouthed astonishment as Esteban lifted Ricky all the way up to his arms' length, like a cheerleader at a football game. For his part, Dakota's feet never wavered, and the horse beneath them seemed to sense the need for stillness, and didn't move a muscle.

Lance and Kai hauled upward, sweat pouring forth and soaking their tank tops like they'd been swimming. But with Esteban pushing from below, Ricky was able to fling his elbows and arms up onto the roof. With his free hand, Lance snaked back to snatch another arrow from his quiver, thrusting it into the shingles near the edge for Ricky to grab onto. Ricky did, and pulled himself up. He threw one leg up onto the roof, and then the two boys pulled him the rest of the way.

The three terrified, sweaty boys flopped exhaustedly back against the sloping roof, their heads aimed at the peak, panting and heaving as their hearts pounded frenetically.

Every muscle in his body ached, but Lance had never felt so exhilarated. He reached out one hand and found Ricky's. They locked eyes and smiled tiredly. Then Lance swung out his other arm and found Kai's hand, taking it gratefully in his. He mouthed a wearied, "Thank you." The panting Kai grinned right back.

The boys lay there for a time while the police and security personnel found a ladder high enough to get them down. Lance didn't mind, actually, just lying there with Ricky, holding hands, allowing his heart and breathing to draw down, savoring the life they'd both nearly lost. He even held onto Kai's hand the entire time and the Navajo boy didn't seem to mind at all.

With the ease and strength he'd used to heft Esteban onto his shoulders, Dakota carefully lowered himself to a squat so Esteban could clamber off his back, and then both were off the horse. Esteban gazed at the stoic Indian with openmouthed awe, but Dakota did not respond to the obvious admiration. His eyes flew up to the roof in search of his brothers, and remained so fixed until they'd been brought back to earth.

When they were finally able to clamber down the ladder to safety, Lance, Ricky, and Kai were met by Dakota, Esteban, Ryan, Justin, and a wildly grinning Reyna. A crowd of tourists had gathered, and they burst into applause when the boys touched ground again, and camera phones and video worked over time. The boys grinned self-consciously at the crowd, knowing they'd seriously disrupted the hallowed atmosphere of this place, and bowed hesitantly. That made the crowd clap even more forcefully.

Once everyone was back on the ground, Ryan flashed his badge and said, "I need to get these kids outta here." The cops agreed and escorted them all back to the limo. The driver sat patiently waiting, and Edwin paced anxiously back and forth outside the car.

"What happened?" the intern asked as the kids and Ryan appeared through the wrought iron gates.

Lance shrugged and threw his aching arm around Ricky. They both had scraps and cuts, and would likely be sore as hell the next day, but they were alive.

"Typical day for the Round Table." He grinned at Ricky, his heart beating with joy.

Ricky rolled his eyes, while Kai stared at the silent Dakota as though he'd never met him before, and shook his head in wonder as they slid back into the luxurious comfort of the limo and wearily headed back to their hotel.

Lance and Ricky spoke with Arthur and Jenny on the ride back, and both parents were relieved beyond measure. By the time they arrived at the Westin, the story had already hit local and national news, and the kids got another round of applause from everyone in the hotel atrium as they entered. Lance and Ricky bowed foolishly, grinning and nudging the Indians and Este to bow, as well, which they reluctantly did.

Edwin thanked them with a grin. "This is a day I'll never forget, and neither will my heart," he added, holding a hand dramatically over his heart. He promised to be in touch with them about the CBOR and then left with the limo driver, who thanked them for "The most exciting day I've had in years."

Ryan also found a contingent of five Secret Service agents awaiting them in the lobby. The one in charge informed him that the president wanted him to call immediately. As everyone retired to his or her room to get cleaned up, the agents stationed themselves outside of each door and told the occupants they would be there the entire night.

Ryan settled into the easy chair in his room and dialed the president. The chief executive was furious, demanding to know where his agents had been during the melee.

Ryan informed him about Senator Cairns' decision to call off the agents.

"Special Agent Ryan," the president said, his voice testy and annoyed, "Senator Cairns would not be held accountable if harm came to those boys in this city. I would. Now those agents I sent *will* accompany you back to L.A. on Air Force Two tomorrow and *will* remain housed at New Camelot until this maniac is apprehended. Arthur will just have to accept that. Are we clear?"

Ryan sighed heavily. "Yes, Mr. President. Crystal."

"Good. Keep me in the loop on everything that happens."

"Yes, sir."

The phone went dead, and Ryan slumped back in his chair. He'd blown it today, and those boys almost suffered on account of his laxness.

Maybe I'm just too old for this kind of work, he told himself. *Maybe it's time I did retire.*

Feeling dejected and more like a failure than he ever had, Ryan pushed his way stiffly from the chair and entered his bathroom to shower.

Lance and Ricky had invited Kai and Dakota into their room, and the four tired, battered boys sat in their usual circle atop Lance's bed.

They watched the coverage for a while on the flat-screen, not surprised to see most of what happened captured on video from numerous cell phones. The news stations pieced together bits from different phones and pretty much showed the entire escapade. The boys held their breath as they watched the frenetic chase through the streets of Washington, and clapped when Dakota took out the cyclist on the bridge. Then they all watched in breathless silence as Lance sailed over JFK's speech to grab Ricky in mid-air, and then nearly gasped at the sequence on the roof.

As Dakota and Esteban muscled Ricky up and onto the roof, Kai whistled in admiration. "I never knew you were that strong, Cloudy."

"Me, either," Lance agreed. "That was like something Jack could've done." His face darkened and Ricky smiled supportively.

Kai eyed Dakota shyly. Of them all, Dakota was the only one who'd chosen to wear a baggy t-shirt, despite the heat of the day. "C'mon, Cloudy Boy, off with the shirt, man. Let's see how buff you are."

Dakota snorted, but Lance and Ricky jumped into the fun. "Oh, c'mon, Dakota," Lance admonished. "It's only us guys. And Kai's right—you always wear those big ass shirts."

Dakota shook his head defiantly, and the other guys started chanting, "Take it off, take it off!"

Sighing with distaste, Dakota reached up and slipped the shirt over his head. Kai gasped, and even Lance and Ricky gaped. The Lakota boy was corded with muscle, across his chest and shoulders and arms; not bodybuilder thick, but wiry and ripped and solid.

"Damn, Cloudy Boy," Kai mumbled. "How'd you get so buff on the rez?"

Dakota shrugged and slipped his shirt back on. "Wrestling foals and calves, splitting wood with an ax, hunting. Stuff like that."

Kai nodded, lowering his gaze and falling silent.

Lance noted the moment of tension between them and cleared his throat. "Don't know about you guys, but I stink like a barnyard and need a shower. So does this fool." He gently shoved Ricky and toppled him back onto the pillow.

"Speak for yourself, fool," Ricky shot back with a grin as he sat up.

Kai and Dakota excused themselves to get cleaned up before dinner.

Lance killed the volume on the TV and looked solemnly at this boy he loved more than life itself. "Don't ever do that again, Ricky," he whispered.

Ricky pulled a face. "Do what, get shot at by nail guns?"

Lance shook his head. "Tell me to let you go."

Ricky bowed his head sadly. "I'm sorry. I just didn't want you to die for me."

Lance took Ricky's hands in his. "Don't you get it, Ricky?" he said, his voice barely a whisper. "I'd die *without* you."

Ricky expelled a throaty laugh. "That's 'cause you're a dumbass."

"No, that's 'cause I'm crazy in love with a dumbass."

They rested their foreheads together, savoring the touch and presence of the other. Then they reluctantly separated to get ready for dinner.

Dinner was uneventful except for the hotel guests wandering past and asking for pictures or autographs. Knowing they needed as many people on their side as possible, Lance and Ricky were gracious to all. Some people even wanted pictures with the "other heroes" and Lance shoved the other three boys out in front.

The heat and exertions and stress of the day got to everyone early and, despite it being their last night in Washington, they all retired early and fell asleep almost instantly. Lance had barely whispered, "I love you" across the room to Ricky before he drifted into a dreamless slumber.

The trip home on Air Force Two was, thankfully, unexciting. Lance half expected their mysterious stalker to send him a gloating text message, but none was forthcoming. Unfortunately, all of the cyclists had gotten away in the confusion of rescuing the boys, and the helicopter cleared Washington airspace before the Metro Police could get their chopper airborne. Once again, they were left with nothing in the way of clues except the motorcycles, and those were ordinary Hondas outfitted with protective plating to withstand arrowheads.

Lance had been right about the aftermath of their adventure – his body hurt everywhere it was possible to hurt, and he knew Ricky felt the same. Plowing into that roof was like what he imagined being hit by a truck would feel like and his whole body suffered painfully the next day from that bone-crunching impact.

As he napped on and off during the flight home, with Ricky's head in his lap where it belonged, he considered how Merlin's simple warning had saved their lives. He knew the wizard couldn't zero in on details, but he decided to make a point of spending more time with the old guy when they got home. Perhaps Merlin knew something he didn't realize he knew, something that would make sense to Lance, something about the identity of this psycho who sought revenge on him.

He knew they had a long way to go with their bill of rights, and he couldn't be too frightened to go out and campaign for it. That might be his stalker's intent, but Lance swore it would never happen. He only wished he could leave Ricky at home when he ventured forth, but the other boy's pride would be too badly hurt. He also understood that the progression from falling objects to rubber bullets to nails meant the stalker was upping the ante. What would be next, he wondered? Another time bomb like San Francisco? He shuddered at the thought and drifted off once more, the droning of the plane engines lulling him to sleep.

TO TASTE THAT TREE

CHAPTER NINE

YOU HAVE LESS THAN A YEAR TO LIVE

DUE TO THE PUBLICITY SURROUNDING the boys' speech to Congress and their near-death experience at Arlington, a huge crowd of well-wishers, nay-sayers, and media awaited them at LAX. The Secret Service agents deplaned first, scouting the area for potential threat assessment, and finding nothing suspicious, allowed the party to descend the air stairs to the hot tarmac. The sun was shining and the temperature in the upper seventies, but Lance relished the lack of intense humidity they'd experienced in D.C.

The public lined the fences around the tarmac, many waving signs, and media personnel shouted questions their way. Lance spotted Helen and waved, shooting a grin her way. She waved in return, but did not shout out questions like many of her colleagues.

Lance felt Ricky squeeze his arm, and when he turned Ricky pointed at some signs being waved around by protestors. Lance scowled as he read them: 'God hates Fags!'; 'Parents Should Control Children'; 'Children Should Be Seen, Not Heard'. There were more of a similar nature, but Lance ignored them. Instead, he pointed out to Ricky the bigger part of the crowd waving signs of support: 'Way to Sock It To Congress, Lance!' and 'The CBOR Rocks!' Many in this section were children and teens.

He shrugged, and Ricky shrugged right back as they made their way toward the media personnel.

Lance turned to Ryan. "I'm gonna answer some questions, *nino*."

Ryan frowned. "Not too many. This place is too open for my taste."

Lance agreed, and led Ricky out the gate to where a limo awaited them. Arthur and Jenny practically leapt from the vehicle and ran toward them, grabbing each boy in a crushing hug, all caught on camera as the media swarmed around like bees to a hive, held at bay by the Secret Services agents. After the greeting, Lance told his parents he wanted to answer a few questions. The agents scanned the crowd intently, eyes roaming everywhere at once.

Lance smiled for the cameras, and that drew an equally photogenic smile from Ricky. The questions came at them like machine gunfire, but Lance held up his hand for quiet, and waited until everyone settled down.

"Thank you for welcoming us home," he began, and then grinned. "I suspect you all have some idea what went down in Washington."

There were laughs and cheers. The naysayers tried a few boos, but were shouted down by the majority.

"First off, I wanna apologize to everyone watching who was at Arlington yesterday. I mean, we spoiled what's supposed to be a quiet place that's meant to honor people who died for this country. And I'm, like, really sorry for skating over President Kennedy's speech and all."

That drew a few laughs from people, but Lance didn't join them.

"No, seriously, it was disrespectful, but I just want everyone to understand that I did it to save Ricky. I hope I didn't wreck anything, but if I did, I'll figure out some way to pay for it."

That drew some gasps of surprise from members of the crowd, and Lance waited for them to quiet down before he continued.

"Besides all that drama yesterday, I think we got off to a good start on our campaign to get the CBOR through Congress. Our plan from here on out is to keep hitting up every single rep and every senator until they either agree with us, or get so tired of us they vote our way just to shut us up." He grinned, glancing at Ricky. "You wanna say anything, fool?"

Ricky shook his head. "No."

Lance looked out at Helen and the other reporters. "So, I can take a few questions and then we gotta bounce. Anyone?"

Of course, every hand shot into the air, including Helen's, and naturally Lance chose her first. "Lady Helen."

"Do you honestly think adults want to abort kids up until they turn eighteen?" Her tone wasn't challenging, and Lance had expected the question, so he was happy it came from her.

He looked straight into the cameras. "Yes, I do."

That started a furor of follow-up questions, which Lance ignored until everyone settled back down.

"What other reason is there for not giving us real rights as human beings?" he asked, not expecting an answer. "Right now we're property, and property can be thrown away because property has no rights. And children are thrown away every day in this country, in so many ways. Isn't that basically aborting us after the fact?"

More hands flew wildly into the air and Lance called on a reporter from CBS.

"Sir Lance, do you have any idea who might have perpetrated this latest attack on you, and the other attacks? Or what the motive could be?"

"No, I still have no idea who's doing these things," Lance answered truthfully. "In the threats, he says it's about revenge, but for what, I don't know, and my dad doesn't know, either. We haven't done anything to hurt anybody, unless this is about politics and stuff." He paused a moment to collect his thoughts. "If it's about politics, then maybe there is no hope for this country, you know? If somebody or some group is so extreme they wanna kill kids like me and Ricky just 'cause we're trying to make things better, well, then I guess we're all doomed."

He pointed to another hand in front, and the CNN reporter asked, "Do you and your family intend to go into hiding until this alleged terrorist, or whatever he is, is apprehended?"

Lance stood straight and tall. He turned to his fellow knights gathered around him. He eyed his parents behind him. On every face was the same answer to that question. He turned back to the reporter. "Hell, no!"

The crowd burst into applause and cheers and whoops, and Lance heard his family behind him clapping, too. He waited until everyone settled back down.

"I been running my whole life and I'm not gonna run any more. I got outta that dark place I was in. I'm happy with who I am and nobody, including these people here with their nasty-ass signs, are gonna bring me down."

The people waving the rude signs booed, but were drowned out by the cheers of the others.

"Ricky and me have work to do," Lance went on, his intense gaze sweeping over the expectant faces in the crowd. "Important work that'll help all kids in this country, especially kids like me and Ricky and Este and Dakota and Kai and Justin. We're gonna be out there with the people in their neighborhoods, meeting with grown-ups and kids, selling our bill of rights. Later, we're gonna travel the country and do the same. We're gonna win this thing, and if some little bitch with a fleet of helicopters thinks he can stop me, he doesn't know me. I grew up on the streets and I'm a survivor."

More cheers followed his passionate statement, but Lance wasn't done yet. When they quieted down, he glared fiercely into the camera.

"If you're watching, and I'm sure you are, yeah you who can't fight like a man so he's gotta send other guys to do his dirty work, you don't scare me. You don't scare Ricky. You don't scare any of us. We're gonna get our bill of rights passed and then we're gonna find you. And when we do, we're gonna kick your little bitch ass from here to China!"

Reyna whooped loudly behind him and more cheers erupted. Lance grinned as Ricky playfully nudged him.

Then Ryan was at his side, announcing, "That's all the questions for now."

Lance waved. "Follow our campaign online. Thanks, everybody!"

There were more cheers and waves as the boys were led quickly to the limo and everyone piled into the back. There was room for only Ryan and one Secret Service agent, so the others rode in a car driven by a local FBI agent. After a tumultuous week, the kids were finally on their way home, and Lance, for one, couldn't wait to get there.

A joyous homecoming met the group as they re-entered New Camelot. Chris threw himself at Lance and Ricky and hugged them desperately for several minutes, gushing with love at their safe return. Lance suddenly realized how it must have felt being the eight-year-old, watching on TV as his older brothers nearly died on the other side of the country. He and Ricky assured Chris that no one was going to hurt them, but Lance knew their words were just words. He remembered that age all too well, and he knew how easily children could be hurt, and hurt badly.

"Don't ever leave me again," Chris begged when he finally released the stranglehold he had on them. His big blue eyes swam with fear and desperate need, and Lance's heart flew right into his throat.

He looks more like Mark every day, he realized, as he studied the young boy's face and mop of unruly blond hair. *And I failed Mark.*

"Don't worry, Chris," he said, reaching out a hand to stroke Chris's cheek. "We're never gonna leave you again." Then he grinned. "We need our badass little bro protecting us, right?"

That brought a smile to Chris's round face. "Damn straight."

Jenny told the Secret Service agents to select any empty rooms they thought best for their purposes, and then Darnell, Justin, and Gibson would give them the lay of the land for security weaknesses.

For his part, Gibson, not known for being overly emotional, almost choked on his greeting when he saw Justin enter through the front door. The attack in Washington, while aimed primarily at Lance and Ricky, could easily have taken out

Justin, too, and he silently engulfed the boy in a tight hug. Justin hugged him back. Neither was adept at words, so they just let the hug say everything.

Dinner was filled with a recounting by the knights of their trip to Washington, details and feelings not available to Arthur and Jenny through the news. Arthur eyed his sons with intense pride, couching the fear deep within him that, despite Lance's strong words at the airport, this enemy was implacable and determined. That shadow of doom that had portended Lance's near death several years ago returned in force, and the king had to fight to keep it at bay.

Jenny laughed and gasped as the boys told of their adventures, but she, too, masked an extreme dread deep within her.

All of the adults praised the boys' speech and their handling of the appearance before Congress. They shook their heads in dismay when Ricky recounted the buffalo meat story. Arthur knew full well how out of touch leaders can become, and how that always led to bigger and less effective government, whether it be a monarchy or a republic like this one.

Arthur heaped voluminous praise on Dakota and Kai for their heroics in saving Lance and Ricky. "How blessed we are to have you amongst us."

Kai grinned and laughed, while Dakota looked embarrassed and simply said, "Thank you."

Arthur raised his goblet to Esteban. "And thank you, Sir Este, for your strength and courage."

The young man looked self-conscious, and Reyna laughingly punched him on the arm.

After all the excitement in Washington, they were happy to be back home safe and sound.

The following day plans were set in motion for Lance and Ricky, accompanied by ever-present bodyguards Kai and Dakota and their phalanx of Secret Service, not to mention the officers Chief Murphy insisted on providing, to travel with Arthur into neighborhoods around Los Angeles to gauge the progress made by Mayor Soto, the knights, and local community leaders towards bettering the lives of children in the city.

In addition, Lance and Ricky would make daily outreach to senators and representatives in Washington, angling for their support. And, of course, they would keep in regular contact with the children of those elected officials. Many of those senators and representatives had emailed Lance expressing their happiness that the boys had not come to harm when they were attacked, and promised to review the CBOR. Lance joked that maybe they should get themselves attacked more often to wake these guys up.

There was also the matter of the midterm elections approaching in November. Edwin had clued them in that some senators, and many representatives, were up for reelection and it would be smart to target their supporters in those states to challenge them about the CBOR.

"These guys'll do anything to get reelected," Edwin laughingly told Lance. He emailed a list of everyone up for reelection, and the boys could see they had their work cut out for them.

"I hate politics," Lance said to Ricky for the umpteenth time.

"You and me both," Ricky agreed with a sigh.

At the insistence of the Secret Service, who didn't want either Lance or Ricky alone in their rooms at night, Dakota's bed was moved into Lance's room and Kai's into Ricky's. Lance thought the move something like overkill, since it was unlikely anyone could breach New Camelot security, and if they did, they could just as easily kill Dakota as him. However, when the agents had "strongly suggested" the move, Lance volunteered to house Dakota in his room because he wanted to get to know the other boy better.

Knowing how Kai felt about him, Ricky assured Lance there was nothing to worry about. "You're the only one I love. 'Sides, I'm the jealous one, remember? You're Mr. Emo-Ass."

"I promise not to be jealous anymore," Lance assured Ricky that first night. Which was about eighty-percent true. Kai may have been skinny and sort of ordinary looking, but his sunny personality kicked ass, and Lance knew Ricky enjoyed it.

It took a few nights to get into a routine, especially since Lance and Dakota typically slept with no shirt on. For Lance, it was hard not to stare at the other boy's physique, even though Dakota was about the same size as him. Lance's childhood and, he knew, childish body-consciousness, always tugged at the corners of his omnipresent self-doubt. Having been so skinny growing up, he couldn't get used to the idea that all his training had packed on real muscle. Inside, he still felt like that skinny little boy.

He attempted to engage Dakota in conversation as they drifted off to sleep, but most of the boy's responses to questions were vague and short.

Ah well, Lance thought, *I'll keep trying.*

And then on top of all these other activities and changes, Lance and Ricky still had junior year final exams to take within the next couple of weeks that would move them on to the next grade. For Lance, who'd so disdained school before meeting Arthur, the thought of being a senior excited him, even though he wasn't part of a traditional high school environment.

I'm growing up, he realized with a mix of exhilaration and wistful abandon. His childhood had been miserable, and he knew adulthood would be fraught with responsibility, and yet he welcomed it, despite the knowledge that he'd eventually be running New Camelot in Arthur's stead.

Your Majesty.

His mind kept repeating Merlin's salutation. It unnerved him each time he recalled it. He'd entered the library the day after returning from Washington to thank the wizard for saving his life, and Merlin had continued addressing him as such.

As always, Merlin was sitting alone, reading and listening to his music. The man had not joined the family for dinner the previous night, and, as Lance stepped into the brightly lit solitude of the book-filled room, he felt shame that he hadn't realized it until just then.

The wizard looked up when Lance entered. As usual, he closed his book without marking the page and pulled an ear bud from one ear. He smiled, his gray eyes dancing with mirth.

"Your Majesty looks rested after such a dramatic week," he remarked. "Perhaps I shall adapt your tale into one of the epic poems I have so enjoyed reading."

Lance had to smile at that. Him? An epic hero? Yeah, right. "I just wanna thank you, Merlin," he said, his voice quiet and filled with emotion, his mind replaying the image of Ricky dangling from the copter, completely out of his reach had he not had his skateboard. "You saved Ricky's life."

"I do what I can. I trust the other young prince is well?"

"Yeah. He's still showering. I just wanted to, well, thank you."

Merlin bowed his head respectfully. "My pleasure, Your Majesty. I trust the rest of your visit proved fruitful?"

Lance tilted his head in surprise. "You didn't watch my speech?"

Those eyes looked amused. "Of course I did. I thought you were masterful. I merely sought your own assessment of the experience."

Lance considered a moment. What had he accomplished anyway? Sure, he'd let those people in Congress know just how out of touch they were, and the president too. But would his speech win any support for his cause?

"I think I got their attention," he told the old wizard. "But now I need to get them on my side."

"A wise assessment, Your Majesty. You are indeed your father's son."

Lance beamed at that, despite the repeated salutation that creeped him out. More than anything he wanted to be a man in the mold of his father.

"Thanks, Merlin. Catch ya later."

Merlin smiled. Then he returned the bud to his ear and reopened his book, presumably, Lance thought as he exited the library, to the same place he left off. But with Merlin, who knew?

While Reyna worked with Esteban and Arthur to plan out their neighborhood visiting schedule, Lance and Ricky split their time between studying for junior year exams, networking with kids and adults, encouraging members of Congress to read and comment on the CBOR, and physical training for two hours per day. The episode in Washington hammered home yet again the need to both boys that they had to stay in top physical shape. Their lives might depend on it.

Being a year older, Kai and Dakota had already completed their senior year coursework, and would earn their diplomas that summer once the state mailed them to New Camelot. Seeing their Native brothers finishing high school further inspired the two younger boys to achieve that particular milestone.

As they sat alone, under Jenny's watchful eye, in one of the classrooms of to complete their junior year tests, Lance considered once again how much the CBOR was needed to give kids more say over what the schools should, and shouldn't, be doing. The exams took several hours, but both boys were confident they were now officially seniors and high-fived each other on their way to the Training Centre.

Techie had told them that both Kai and Dakota had birthdays in July, with Dakota's falling on July fourth. To Lance, anyway, it seemed ironic that his birth coincided with the birth of the nation that, while, on the whole, was good for the world, hadn't been so good for Dakota's people. Yeah, Lance thought, he'd been seeing much irony of late. Maybe that was a symptom of growing up, he mused. There was always a monthly birthday party for any knights whose dates fell that month, but he felt that Dakota and Kai deserved special recognition at the event for their courage and bravery, for graduating high school, and for the attainment of their eighteenth year.

He and Ricky had Jenny order lots of gifts for the boys, as well as clothes they thought the two would like. Lance had noticed in the days following their return that the Indians seemed distant from each other. Kai still laughed and joked around, but there was a sense of sadness beneath it all.

"More soul whispering?" Ricky asked one night when Lance mentioned it. He'd nodded, but said nothing more.

Dakota seemed more withdrawn and taciturn than ever, and Lance's attempts to draw him out failed. His aloofness had always made his soul harder to read, but Lance sensed something besides guilt over his brother's condition, something similar to his own childhood fears. But try as he might to engage the other boy, Dakota remained stubbornly silent.

In addition, on more than one occasion, he was certain Dakota had been drinking. While not smelling alcohol on the boy's breath, Lance knew the signs well enough. During weapons training, Dakota would miss the bull's-eye when firing an arrow, causing Kai to gasp and Lance to eye him with surprise. On those occasions when he missed a shot, Dakota would lay down his bow and leave the Training Centre without a word. Lance and the others followed him with their eyes, and Lance noted a slight, almost indecipherable lurch to the other boy's step. The lurch that came with drinking.

Sharing a room with Dakota at night, which was when he mostly noticed the signs, gave Lance plenty of opportunity for suspicion. Dakota's responses were occasionally garbled, or mumbled. But not in his normal grunting, noncommittal tone. No, these were mumbles of someone whose tongue was not quite working alongside his brain. Lance recalled trying to talk to Ricky on the phone that night he'd left Bridget's and was drunk on vodka. He could barely get his tongue around the simplest of words. Dakota didn't sound that bad, but there were traces of it, enough to make Lance suspicious.

He knew the hotel kept alcohol somewhere, but he'd never asked where, because he wasn't interested. Dakota was clearly depressed, and that bewildered Lance given all the stunning success he'd had within the Round Table. Not wanting to get the boy in trouble with Arthur, Lance chose to watch him more closely, and if it appeared the drinking was getting out of hand, he'd confront him about it.

The end of June also marked the high school graduation of Bridget and Ariel. They invited Lance and Ricky, but the boys felt it might be awkward, and Ryan nixed the idea anyway as being "Too risky." Of course, Justin and Techie attended and gave everyone a full report afterwards, and took lots of pictures with their phones. Bridget, never the most conscientious of students, would be attending community college in the fall, while Ariel had been accepted to UC Santa Barbara.

Lance insisted they invite the girls to the July 4th birthday gathering, and both boys readily agreed. He was happy that the two couples had gotten together and honestly wished them well. He and Ricky agreed that neither felt the least bit uncomfortable around them anymore, which was about ninety percent true.

The boys kept in regular contact with Senator Cairns, mostly through Edwin, who frequently reiterated that "I thought I was going to die" when referring to the attack on them. He assured them the senator was "massaging" other senators toward supporting the CBOR and that, for now, the boys should concentrate on the House of Representatives. With four hundred thirty-five members, getting the needed two-thirds would prove daunting.

The July birthday party was a grand success. Congratulations were given to all the high school graduates, and Reyna did a fantastic job of party planning. Kai laughed a lot as always and seemed to have shaken off his recent somber mood. Dakota appeared uncomfortable with all the adulation, especially with knights praising his heroics in Washington, gushing over his abilities on a horse, with the bow and arrow, and "How freakin' strong you are!"

Lance and Ricky had given Dakota a fancy, powerful new bow as a gift, which the eighteen-year-old humbly accepted. Kai was presented with an enormous collection of art pencils and paints, as well as canvases for his work. He was speechless, something of a first for the usually loquacious Navajo.

After the cake had been cut and distributed, Kai presented Dakota with a wrapped package, which surprised the other boy. As always, both wore a mix of knightly tunics and pants, with added Native headbands, feathers in their hair, and sewn into their tunics. Over his colorful shirt, Dakota wore his breastplate that replicated strung-together bones.

Dakota hesitantly took the flat package that looked like a framed picture.

Kai grinned nervously. "Go on, Cloudy, open it."

Lance and Ricky watched as Dakota fumbled with the wrapping. Somehow, Kai had found paper decorated with horses of various breeds, which Lance thought was perfect. But Dakota looked uncomfortable as he tore open the paper and let it flutter to the floor by his moccasined feet. He held out a picture frame, easily 11 x 17 in size, but looked only at the back. He hesitated, obviously reluctant to turn it over.

"Flip it over, Cloudy," Kai said with exasperation, and Dakota slowly turned the picture front side up.

Lance gasped, and he heard Ricky suck in a breath beside him. But Dakota remained obdurate and stony faced as they all gazed at the most exquisite drawing Lance had ever seen. This one was even better and more detailed than the one Kai had drawn of him and Ricky.

It showed Dakota, sitting astride Llamrei, wearing no shirt, but sporting the breastplate he now wore, his hair streaming past his shoulders, feathers dangling at strategic points. The boy looked majestic and powerful, like the Indian warriors of old. Kai had captured Dakota's bearing in stunning detail, including his inscrutable expression, and his eyes, alive, but guarded. It was a stunning piece of art.

"That's amazing," Lance finally whispered, his eyes riveted to the drawing.

"It's fantastic," Ricky agreed. "But Dakota was never on Llamrei wearing only that breastplate thing."

Kai smiled shyly. "I have a great memory for detail. Seeing Cloudy with his shirt off in Washington was all I needed."

Lance shook his head admiringly. "Man, do you have talent! I can't even draw a circle."

He laughed, and Kai joined him. But so far Dakota had said nothing. He just stared at the drawing with that same guarded look in his eyes.

Kai frowned. "You don't like it?"

Dakota seemed unable to speak a moment. Then, in a quiet, breathy voice he asked, "Is that how you see me?"

Kai lowered his gaze to the floor. "Well, yeah." Then he looked back up and met Dakota's uncertain eyes with his own. "Is that okay?"

"You see what's not there, Laughs A Lot, but I accept the gift with gratitude."

Kai smiled with relief.

Then Dakota did something that surprised all of them. He handed Lance the framed drawing, and reached around to untie the breastplate. He slipped it over his head and placed it around the neck of the astonished Kai.

"Wait, Cloudy Boy—"

But Dakota had already moved around behind Kai, gently shoved his braids out of the way, and tied the leather thong securely. Then he stepped back around. Lance handed him the framed drawing, and observed as the two young men looked solemnly at one another.

"I made that with my own hands," Dakota said quietly. "It is the symbol of a warrior. I was wrong, Sir Laughs A Lot. You *are* a warrior, and a better man than I will ever be." He turned, passed through the crowd without another word, and exited the Throne Room.

Lance, Ricky and Kai exchanged bewildered looks as they watched him retreat.

"What did I say?" Kai asked helplessly, suddenly looking lost and bereft.

Lance eyed him knowingly. "It's not you, Kai, it's him."

"Do you know what the problem is, soul whisperer?" Ricky asked with a raise of his eyebrows.

"Not yet, but I will."

Ricky fell silent.

"Maybe I should go talk to him," Kai suggested.

Lance shook his head. "Let it go for now, Kai."

Kai looked reluctant. "Okay."

"Let's get more cake 'fore Este eats it all," Ricky suggested, and the other two followed him through the crowd to the refreshments table.

The following week Lance and Ricky accompanied Arthur back to Boyle Heights. At the insistence of the president, Secret Service agents outfitted Arthur, Lance, and Ricky with full upper body bulletproof vests to wear under their tunics. The boys protested, but Jenny insisted, and so did Arthur. The vests were uncomfortable and Lance worried they would restrict his movements if he needed to fight, or even fire an arrow at a moment's notice. Ricky complained about the same, but Ryan insisted the word came down from the president himself and there could be no argument.

Once again, Lance found himself wondering what happened to freedom in this country, even for adults. Yeah, he knew the aim was good—to protect him and Ricky and their Dad from harm— but shouldn't the choice be left up to them? Why should the government have that much power?

Rather than make a big deal out of it, he insisted that his mother and Chris also be outfitted, since they would be making the neighborhood tours. Chris thought the big vest was "Super cool," and Jenny grimaced as she squirmed within her own.

Because Esteban was usually at New Camelot conducting business, Jaime had overseen the mayor's programs within Boyle Heights, a vast area east of downtown Los Angeles. Accompanying the family were Reyna and Esteban, but also Justin and Bridget, which surprised Lance. Since school had let out, she'd been to New Camelot almost daily, shadowing Justin on his various security duties. Ariel, he knew, was back at New Camelot with Techie in the Computer Lab. It cracked Lance up that Ariel, never known to be a computer nerd until she met Techie, now wanted to major in computer studies in college.

Yeah, he realized as he glanced over at Ricky beside him, *love will make you do almost anything.*

The Secret Service insisted on driving the boys and Arthur in one car, Jenny and Chris in another. The rest followed in Reyna's black, stylish Escalade, now hers by ownership—a gift from her parents. They found Jaime, Sonia and Little Arturo awaiting them at Esteban's house, along with Esteban's mother and sister.

As they exited the car, baby Arturo, eighteen months old, waddled up to Lance for a hug. Beaming with delight, Lance bent and scooped the toddler into his arms and kissed him on the cheek. "Hi Lanie," the boy said excitedly, still unable to pronounce the "ce."

Lance laughed. For reasons only Ricky seemed to understand, Arturo had taken a shine to Lance immediately, and every time Jaime brought him to New Camelot, the little one wanted Lance to hold him.

"*Come estas*, Arturo?" Lance asked with a grin.

Arturo's round, cherubic face broke into a huge smile. "*Bien*," he answered with an emphatic nod of his small head.

This was the first time Arthur and Lance had been in the neighborhood since it had kicked off their internationally famous Clean-up Tour, and they were major celebrities. Everyone spilled from homes and nearby storefronts to welcome the king and his son, and the other visiting knights. They eyed the black-clad, sunglasses-wearing Secret Service agents with suspicion, but otherwise there was a festive party atmosphere felt by all. The elderly *abuelita* hugged Lance and Arthur, and the proprietor of what was now the most famous Round Table Pizza in the world presented Arthur with a ceremonial meatball pizza on which all the meatballs were in the shape of little crowns.

Esteban's mom hugged him and Reyna warmly. Little Rosa had grown so much, Lance barely recognized her. She looked healthy and happy as she threw her arms around Reyna and looked like she'd never let go. It seemed Reyna had indeed gotten the little sister she'd always wanted, Lance happily thought, as he nudged Ricky with a grin.

And Mayor Soto joined them, as well. He was anxious for the king to witness all the success that his people, in conjunction with the locals and Arthur's knights, had brought to this and other communities throughout the city. The short, rotund politician beamed as he stepped from his car and approached with one of his aides in tow.

Lance had already handed Arturo back to Sonia, and now greeted the mayor. He grinned, noting with surprise that he was even taller than the last he'd stood beside Soto at the wedding. The mayor noticed, too, as he looked up at Lance's grinning face and shook his head in wonder. They hugged warmly, and then the mayor eyed him with admiration.

"Another Lincolnesque performance in Washington, Lance," he said, and then added with a laugh, "I mean your handling of Congress, *not* skating over President Kennedy's speech."

Lance laughed, knowing the man was only jesting. Thus began a day of celebratory reunions and glowing pride from Jaime and the others in Boyle Heights. The homes and buildings remained mostly graffiti-free. If gang members sought to claim a street or a building, the locals, usually led by one of Arthur's young adult knights, instantly painted over it and reclaimed the area for freedom. Jaime, now almost nineteen and still working for Homeboy Industries—in addition to overseeing the makeover of Boyle Heights—took Arthur and the others on a tour of the various Children's Centers that had been set up in every neighborhood.

They'd gotten a lot of help from community leaders associated with Dolores Mission Catholic Parish, as well as local citizens who, now that so many youth were openly rejecting gang affiliation in favor of community rebuilding, saw results that were staggeringly successful. Kids in crisis could be referred by their schools or even parents to these Children's Centers, which were connected to mental health and other services on an immediate basis, so the problems weren't allowed to fester into drug use or suicide attempts, as had so often been the case prior to Arthur and Prop 51.

Jaime and the mayor displayed a relaxed, easy rapport, often joking with each other as they recounted funny stories about this neighborhood or that one, and Arthur was thrilled to see the long – term effects of what he'd begun taking root so strongly. Lance and Ricky continually marveled at the happy, positive demeanor of the people they met. No, these neighborhoods weren't suddenly rich, and neither were the people. But now there was real hope of a better future for themselves and their children, a future they were actively helping to bring about. And that excited them immensely.

Kai and Dakota flanked Lance and Ricky protectively, marveling at what could be done when the government worked with the people, and the kids, toward a unified goal. Both lamented the pathetic state of their own, and other reservations across the country, and longed for this kind of renewal.

Lance promised that when they traveled the country, they would visit Kai and Dakota's reservations, and hammer home the poverty issue to every federal official they encountered. They encouraged the Indians to send pictures back home, and to every Indian publication or website, to spread the word about what could be done. They could inspire the Indian youth across the country to stand up and take charge, as had the youth of L.A.

Kai thought it a great idea, but Dakota was taciturn and remote as always, and shrugged noncommittally. Ever since his birthday, Dakota had been more withdrawn than ever, though Lance had noted he'd hung the framed drawing Kai had given him in a place of honor above his bed back at New Camelot. Lance observed his friend whenever possible for signs Dakota might be drinking again, but hadn't seen any recently. There was just so much to do every day, he feared he'd lose touch with the knights he was supposed to lead and inspire, like Arthur had inadvertently done back in the beginning. That, he knew, had almost led to the downfall of everything. It had almost killed him. And it *had* killed Mark and Jack.

I can't get like that, he swore to himself that day as he eyed Dakota when the other wasn't aware. *I can't lose touch or I've failed, and then everything will come crashing down like it did before.*

All in all, it was a grand day of reunions and successes and well-deserved kudos for a job well done. Arthur expressed his immense pride in Jaime for spearheading the operation, especially in neighborhoods that used to consider him a dangerous thug. Jaime, who always wore a tunic in public, turned red around the ears when Arthur threw an arm over his shoulders and told the crowd of onlookers, "This is an outstanding man right here and I could not be more proud of him if I tried." The crowd agreed with loud applause.

By the time Arthur and the family returned to New Camelot, it was almost time for dinner, so everyone retired to his or her room to get ready.

Thus began a hectic few months. Mornings were spent in school and the Computer Lab, as Lance and Ricky communicated with this representative or that senator, while also maintaining a strong relationship with the children of these elected officials. Reyna and Esteban—when they didn't have college classes—helped coordinate the schedule of neighborhood visits.

Dakota and Kai, with Techie's invaluable assistance, made contact with every online Native site and Indian publication they could find, sharing the success Arthur's knights had achieved in the poorest neighborhoods of L.A. They encouraged the young people of the various tribes to step up and take charge of their own destiny. Most didn't have Internet access, so viewing Arthur's website and Facebook page was a problem, but those who could get online promised to spread the word locally amongst the youth and start a "tribal revolution," as Kai called it.

Lance and Ricky became so busy every day with senior coursework and CBOR business in the mornings, afternoon visits to various neighborhoods, and then evening homework, that they seldom had time for any personal drama, or even much for just being together, which bothered them immensely when they had the energy to give it some thought.

Lance vowed one night, "Once the CBOR is passed, I'm quitting politics for good."

Ricky, head in Lance's lap, with *Macbeth* in his hands, grinned slyly. "Does that mean you changed your mind about running for president?"

"Does that mean you changed *your* mind about being First Fool?"

"Good point."

They shared a laugh.

Arthur and his family continued to suit up in their bulletproof body vests every weekday afternoon to tour the city. Most of the time Mayor Soto came along, but always the tours were led by his knights, like Darnell, Tai, Duc, and every other knight who'd agreed to organize the operation in his or her neighborhood. Lance got a big hug from the older African-American man who had stood up to the drug-addled Dwayne when Arthur and his knights sought to enter Watts for the first time, and he was happy to see the neighborhood vastly improved.

Lance was especially heartened to see how much improved Hawthorne had become since his last visit. Enrique and Luis had taken charge of the effort. Both graduated that summer and had been spending every afternoon since December working with the mayor of Hawthorne to implement changes that would help the kids in the city. They'd taken it upon themselves to contact the man and offer New Camelot's services, which the mayor was only too happy to accept.

Lance showed Ricky the mural of him and Arthur that Enrique had painted so long ago in Eucalyptus Park. He noticed that someone, fortunately, had painted over the graffitied "Youth Sucks" that he'd scrawled there the night of Mark's death. He felt wistful and sad as those memories flooded back in, and Ricky wrapped a comforting arm around his shoulders.

Unable to leave the area without at least one turn on the swings, Lance got Arthur and Ricky to join him, while Jenny snapped pictures with her phone. As it had the first night he'd shared this experience with Arthur, the moment filled Lance with joy.

Mark Twain High School welcomed them with open arms. The construction had mostly been completed in front, and new classroom buildings now rose in back near the swimming pool. Enrique proudly displayed a large mural he and Luis had spearheaded on the side of the cafeteria. A large group of MTS students had worked tirelessly on the project. It depicted their most famous student—Lance—wielding his sword and slashing his way through the words "ignorance", "discrimination", "conformity," and "apathy" with the school's Cougar mascot in the background.

But Lance's biggest surprise came when the president of Student Council, a pretty, effervescent senior named Ana, invited he and Ricky to attend the Senior Prom next May, despite the boys being home schooled.

"You're, like, the most famous kid we ever had here," the girl gushed, "and you guys are *so* cool. We'd be, like, *so* stoked if you came."

Lance and Ricky looked at each other in shock, and then smiled broadly.

"Thanks," Lance told her happily. He'd never considered the idea of going to prom, but as he pictured himself going on a real date, he felt almost giddy. "That'd be awesome!"

The girl practically jumped for joy. "Oh, that is *so* cool! We'll message you on Facebook the date and everything. Wow, I can't wait to tell everyone!" Then she was off and running back to the student council room. Arthur and Jenny joined the principal in a laugh.

During their many neighborhood visits that summer, Mayor Soto explained to the boys how the law of unintended consequences had kicked in big time for Los Angeles. After so many weeks of seeing very little gang graffiti, Lance finally thought to ask the mayor and the local knights what happened to the older gang members who used to roam those areas recruiting kids. Soto informed them that, apparently frustrated by the lower number of kids currently interested in gang membership, the leadership seemed to have moved their recruiting efforts out of the city, to places like Covina and Pomona, where gangs were now on the rise. Since he had no jurisdiction in those areas, it would have to be up to any local youth, in solidarity with Arthur's Round Table, to spearhead changes for anything positive to occur. He'd offered the mayors of surrounding cities access to the programs L.A. had put in place. Other than that, he could do nothing.

As the summer wore on, weekends were the only down time for Lance and Ricky, and even for Arthur and Jenny. Since it was in the nineties most days, and often over one hundred during the infamous dog days of August, roughhousing in the pool became a weekend ritual for the family. Almost always, Kai and Dakota joined the boys, and it was funny to see them, especially Dakota, acting like little kids. They wrestled, learned to do cannonballs from Ricky so they could splash the adults lounging poolside, and played chicken against each other. Lance continually marveled at how strong Dakota was, especially since he wasn't terribly large. He was just wiry as hell and amazingly powerful when put to the test, and he knew Ricky was impressed, as well.

But Kai was the one who seemed unable to resist peeking whenever he thought Dakota wasn't looking. Unlike Dakota, Kai did not sport much in the way of muscle. He'd been into art growing up and looked somewhat skinny in his swim trunks.

Unfortunately, Kai also snuck frequent looks at Ricky's body, and that sent Lance's jealousy meter into overdrive, even though he'd promised Ricky he'd control it. If either boy noticed his wandering eyes, Kai quickly glanced away.

Of course, Lance never tired of seeing Ricky in board shorts, and he couldn't blame Kai for his attraction, but he wished the boy could find someone to love the way *he'd* found Ricky. Mainly, he wished Kai wouldn't keep looking at Ricky *that* way, period. Especially since he knew Ricky was flattered by the attention. But, he supposed with a sigh as he watched Ricky execute another cannonball, he'd have to get used to that. Ricky was gorgeous, inside and out, and both girls and guys would always be interested in him.

Lance had to force the jealousy from his mind before he "emo'd-out" again. He fixed his eyes on Dakota once more. The Indian still puzzled him. He knew they shared a lot in common at an elemental level, and not just their inability to handle alcohol. Lance watched the other boy as often as he could without seeming to spy, and had to admit Dakota was the most difficult person besides Michael he'd ever tried to soul-whisper. As with Michael, however, he knew he'd figure out the truth eventually. He just hoped it wouldn't be too late for him to be of help.

Reyna and Esteban spent most of their weekends at New Camelot, as well, but had also taken to spending more time with Reyna's parents or Esteban's mom and sister. For their part,

Reyna's parents had come a long way toward accepting Esteban as their daughter's boyfriend. As a consequence of that, and of attending several of Arthur's gatherings, they came to be far more accepting of "those people" they used to disdain. In fact, they stunned Reyna one day in early September by asking to travel with their daughter to Boyle Heights and eat dinner with Esteban's family.

Reyna had been floored, but delighted, and though the high society couple initially seemed on edge as they exited their Mercedes and entered Esteban's small, unassuming house, they quickly warmed to seven-year-old Rosa's delightful yammering's, and her obvious love for Reyna. And Esteban's mom was all smiles and graciousness. It was, Reyna knew, a major step forward for all of them.

The other development of note that summer was the appearance of Hector at New Camelot to join the Round Table. He'd been Lance's friend in The Compound at juvenile hall, and at that time was being tried as an adult, but those adult charges had been dropped. He'd just gotten out of a juvenile camp program and returned home to East L.A., astonished to see the changes in his neighborhood thanks to Arthur's knights and Mayor Soto's Community Partnership Program. No longer feeling shackled to the gang life, Hector was thrilled to participate in the Round Table, and wanted to help make his neighborhood even better.

Father Mike had already told Lance that Angel and Joey had been returned to juvenile court and then sentenced to the California Youth Authority, now known as the Department of Juvenile Justice. It was a state-run system for juveniles charged with serious offenses, but unlike the prison system, its aim was to rehabilitate, not warehouse. Joey had been given two years, and Angel four. But at least they'd be treated as juveniles, rather than adults, and that's what Lance wanted.

Because he was so busy juggling all of his responsibilities, Lance couldn't spend a lot of time with Hector. He gave the boy their schedule of weekly gatherings and invited him to attend school at New Camelot if his local school wasn't working for him, and assigned him to the knights who were in charge over in East L.A. so he could become an active participant in the movement.

As October rolled around, Lance finally realized there had not been a single attack on them since June, and no gloating text messages from "the little bitch," as he'd taken to calling his stalker, relative to the Washington incident. Of course, their 24/7 protections continued, and Lance knew the tactic could be to throw them off guard, let them become complacent, and then *wham,* the next attack would blindside them.

In addition, Lance, Ricky and their youthful constituents across the country were getting fed up with the inability, or lack of desire on the part of Congress, to act on the CBOR. Senator Cairns, Edwin regularly informed them by email, was pushing it hard in the senate, and several California and New York representatives were working on convincing the House membership, but so far little had been achieved. The CBOR hadn't even been taken up in any committees of either branch. Not surprisingly, the children of many representatives and senators had been forbidden from maintaining contact with Lance and Ricky, which only made the kids more determined than ever to make the CBOR law.

"So much for listening to their own kids," Lance commented to Ricky after a bunch of these messages had come through.

Ricky shrugged. "You didn't expect them to, did you? They *are* grown-ups, after all."

Lance chuckled at that. Many of the millions of kids who messaged or tweeted or emailed them said they were willing to engage in the "Operation Silent Treatment" that had worked so well in California for Prop 51. Lance considered that, and decided to keep it as a backup plan. He figured the adults would be expecting it, and thus might not let it bother them. No, he had something bigger in mind, something that would damage the reputation of the United States worldwide, maybe even make other countries look at America with disdain. But that plan couldn't go into effect until April or May, and the effects of it wouldn't even be felt right away. Still, he and Ricky began plotting all the same. If nothing substantial had occurred within the Congress by that time, they'd go for it.

In the meantime, the boys and their fellow knights and supporters around the country targeted local representatives, because amending the Constitution also required approval of three – fourths of the states. Lance figured if the Congress in Washington wouldn't take them seriously, maybe they'd listen to state legislatures that called for an up or down vote on the CBOR.

The boys were happy to see that Internet buzz regarding the CBOR did not let up, but kept increasing. Almost daily, the radio talk shows and all the TV political chat shows held debates on the merits or foibles of the ten amendments. As it had from the moment he'd spoken it, Lance's line about adults wanting to keep alive the option of aborting kids up until they turned eighteen continued to be the most controversial, and the most oft-repeated. Many pundits remained appalled, while others agreed that, yes, the remark was youthfully hyperbolic, but not without merit, especially considering the country's penchant for putting juveniles in prison for the rest of their lives. Capitol Hill might have been hoping the whole thing would just "go away," but the people had other ideas.

Kai and Dakota signed up to take two online courses from Diné College in Arizona, an accredited university founded and operated by the Navajo Nation. They decided to take American Government and Politics, and English 101, since those were basic requirements. Both felt, and Lance agreed, that by interacting with the professors in these classes, and their fellow students, they could outreach to the young Navajos about what Arthur had achieved in L.A., while also lobbying for support of the CBOR.

Because of the attack in Washington, Ryan had managed, after much cajoling, to convince Arthur and Jenny that the Native Knights should learn how to fire a handgun in case of emergency. At first, both parents said no. Arthur, in particular, hated guns and considered them a cowardly weapon. But when Gibson joined his partner in assuring both parents that the boys' lives might depend on this knowledge, the adults reluctantly agreed. So, in addition to their other duties and activities that summer, the four boys were taught how to grip, aim, and fire several types of handguns with ease, enough to become proficient. Kai and Dakota had fired guns on the reservation, but mostly rifles, and took to the training quickly. Lance and Ricky took a bit longer, but eventually became confident in their ability to fend off an attacker if the need arose. All four boys preferred the bow and arrow, but they were grateful for this new knowledge.

Chris turned nine that October and had grown two inches since the year before. He'd also gotten a lot stronger, and could wield many of the larger swords from the armory. He was part of the monthly birthday party, but the family also threw him his own private celebration. It touched Lance deeply to the heart when Chris raised his glass of sparkling cider and toasted the memory of Jack.

"When I'm in high school, I'm gonna wear his number and play quarterback just like him. And I'm gonna tell everybody about him, so nobody will ever forget."

Lance felt tears burning his eyes as he clinked glasses with his brother and smiled with gratitude. Sometimes he felt guilty because he didn't think of Jack every day like he used to. But Jack had told him to go on with his life, to make the world better for boys like him, and that's exactly what he was trying to do.

By the time Lance and Ricky's birthdays rolled around in November, Arthur and the family had visited almost every community in Los Angeles, and had seen nothing but progress and positive results. He and the mayor had discussed the ever-present issues of homelessness and drug addiction, since there still seemed to be an inordinate number of these people. But, as the mayor explained, many of the homeless and drug addicts were mentally ill, and mental illness remained an area politicians refused to deal with in the country as a whole, probably because it would take hard work to make real progress.

"Just look how those guys in Washington are stalling on your CBOR?" he'd told Arthur one afternoon while they visited a homeless shelter in downtown LA. "They can't even agree to vote on the thing!"

All things being equal, the king and his sons were pleased by what they had helped bring about, and Arthur reminded Lance that "Someday you shall be in command, and must make certain the powers that be continue in this manner."

Lance nodded, but, as always when his father made reference to him taking over, a chill slithered up his back.

That wouldn't be for many years, right?

But then Merlin's salutation of "Your Majesty" would ring in his ears and he'd shiver anew.

What if there's something they're not telling me?

As with Chris, the boys had two birthday celebrations, one during a gathering for every knight with a November birthday, and a separate one with the family. Everyone seemed to make a huge deal over Lance and Ricky turning seventeen because it was their last legal year as kids. A lot of their fellow knights ribbed them about getting old and being almost grown up, and it scared the boys a little, knowing what would be expected of them the moment they turned eighteen. Even though they'd still be teenagers, to society they would be adults and expected to act accordingly.

Lance had come to understand this more clearly the previous year during their Proposition 51 battle when he'd fought for kids to have adult rights. He'd finally realized how disastrous that would've been if he, as a teen, was any example. He knew then, and now, that he wasn't ready to be an adult yet, and if Prop 51 had passed, the law of unintended consequences would likely have been catastrophic. His birthday only reinforced his resolve that the CBOR was the way to go in this country to ensure that kids had rights and protections, but not the responsibilities of adults.

The midterm election happened, as always, the week of their birthday and Lance had been happy to see the CBOR a heated topic of debate throughout the election cycle. According to Edwin, a larger number of moderates were elected to both houses of Congress and that boded well for the eventual passage of their amendments.

The birthday party was loud and fun with food and music and dancing. As at every celebration, Reyna insisted on "The Cha Cha Slide," but Lance didn't mind because he and Ricky had finally gotten the hang of it. Since they were Arthur's sons, they were given the choice of first song to dance to, and they chose "Little Things." Its message about the little things in the person we love being the most important, touched them deeply, and since Arthur and Jenny's first wedding anniversary was around the corner, they also wished to honor their parents.

So Lance and Ricky, Arthur and Jenny, and Reyna and Esteban slow danced to the soulful ballad just as they had at the wedding. When they could pull their eyes from each other, Lance and Ricky noted Bridget and Justin clinging tightly to each other as they moved to the music, and Ariel and Techie doing the same. Lance spotted Kai and Dakota standing awkwardly side-by-side, but neither made any move to ask someone to dance, despite Kai's assertion that he loved dancing. Everyone looked happy and content. Love filled the air. It was perfect.

Of course, Lance knew it couldn't last.

The night of their birthday, after the family dinner, presents and cake, Lance and Ricky sat cross-legged on Lance's bed, holding each other's hands, gazing into each other's eyes, and feeling wistful.

"We're seventeen, Ricky," Lance said quietly as he looked into the eyes of this boy he loved, his voice tight with emotion. "After I turned six and Richard, you know… I just wanted to die. I wanted to die every time he hurt me. I never even thought I'd get to be this old, you know?"

Ricky nodded, knowing instinctively that Lance needed this moment to get his feelings out in the open.

"But now that I have you, I wanna live forever. Crazy, huh?"

Ricky squeezed Lance's hands gently. "I guess we could become vampires. We're already Team Lance and Team Ricky, so why not?"

Lance laughed. Then their eyes locked, and Lance forgot how to breathe. "Happy Birthday, dumbass boy of my dreams," he whispered so softly it was barely a breath of air.

Ricky smiled. "Happy birthday to you, dumber ass boy of *my* dreams."

They kissed, and all the troubles of the world melted away as their lips made contact and their souls converged into a single entity. It was perfect, the most perfect moment of the entire celebration of their shared birthday.

And then Lance's phone vibrated with an incoming text.

The boys pulled apart, dread welling up in them simultaneously. Lance reached for the phone on the bedcover beside him, and felt his breath freeze. The number read: 000-000-0000.

He exchanged a look of trepidation with Ricky before thumbing in his password and opening the message.

'Happy birthday, fag boys! Did you like my early present back in Washington? Fun, wasn't it? Don't think I couldn't have had your boyfriend killed, Lancey. It just wasn't his time. As for your Indian bodyguards, they can't stop me, either. If they know what's good for them, they'll go back to the hellholes they came from. Anyway, you dumbass boys of each other's dreams enjoy your seventeenth year on this planet, because it will be your last. By this time next year, you'll be dead. And so will your old man. So go on back to your repulsive lip locking, but remember – you have less than a year to live.'

Lance held his breath while reading the two connected text messages, locking his gaze on Ricky's wide, anxious brown eyes. Then it suddenly hit him and he focused once again on the words that seemed so wrong: 'you dumbass boys of each other's dreams'. Of course! How could they have been so stupid?

"Lance," Ricky began, reaching out a hand to his arm, but Lance quickly shushed him and opened the memo app on his phone. He typed in a message and showed it to Ricky.

'The room is bugged. Probably the whole house'.

Lance cursed himself for not figuring it out sooner. No way could their stalker know they'd just called each other the dumbass boy of the other's dreams unless he'd just heard it.

Lance placed a finger to his lips, and then said loudly, "I guess we better show this message to the Secret Service guys, for all the good that'll do."

"Yeah," Ricky said as both boys untangled their legs and clambered off the bed. Lance pulled open the door to his bedroom to find the expected agent standing guard just outside. The man, tall and broad-shouldered, turned his impassive gaze on the boys and pulled a face when Lance put a finger to his lips and held out his phone.

First, he displayed the text message, and then he flipped to the note he'd typed. The agent's eyebrows shot up in surprise, and Lance and Ricky's quiet birthday evening turned to pandemonium. The man alerted his fellow agents and they rounded up everyone in the family, and all other knights in residence, gathering them together in the lobby. Everyone had to wait in silence for hours while the Secret Service called in their bug-detecting equipment and swept the entire hotel from top to bottom.

Even the president was notified, per his orders, and he was not happy his agents hadn't been doing regular sweeps for listening devices. Ryan and Gibson stood watch over everyone in the lobby during the search.

Lance and Ricky sat together in the same enormous chair, hands clasped, Ricky resting his head against Lance's chest. For both boys it was a long, pensive night as the words of the text flitted in and out of their minds: 'You have less than a year to live'. Could their vengeful stalker carry out his plan, Lance wondered over and over again? Thus far, he seemed to be one step ahead of them. Of course, bugging the hotel had obviously clued him in to everything the boys and Arthur had been planning.

He and Ricky exchanged several looks throughout the night as agents passed by them heading to one part of the hotel or another, and the same question was in the eyes of both: who could've planted the bugs and when?

Kai sat cross-legged on the floor beside Lance's chair, and Dakota sat cross-legged a short distance away. Lance noted him eyeing Kai when the Navajo boy was looking away or dozing, but Dakota said nothing to anyone. Occasionally he'd glance over at Lance and Ricky cuddled together in the chair, but Lance couldn't read the look in his flinty eyes. Finally, exhausted from the birthday activities of the past few days, Lance and Ricky drifted off to sleep.

When they woke the following morning, they were still nestled together in the big lobby chair, but everyone else had departed, except one Secret Service agent who'd clearly been left to stand guard over them.

As Lance awoke and found Ricky's head on his chest and his own arms wrapped around the boy, he momentarily forgot why they were there and just relished the moment of perfect peace. But then he remembered, and gently nudged Ricky to wake him.

"Morning, dumbass."

Ricky sat up and stretched. "Morning to you too, dumber-ass."

Lance waved his hand in front of his face dramatically. "Ooh, morning breath."

Ricky punched him. "Keep talking like that and I'll tell mom we slept together."

Lance rolled his eyes. "I think she already knows that." Then he shoved Ricky off the chair and stood to stretch out his achy limbs. His legs felt almost numb and he walked to get the circulation going. So did Ricky. They stretched and walked off their stiffness before Lance finally noticed the agent watching them. The man's lips were curled into a look of disdain.

Oh, great, Lance thought, *another hater.* He sighed and stepped over to the man. "Where is everyone?"

"Throne Room, I believe," the man answered crisply, without inflection.

"Thanks."

The boys strode down the hall to the Throne Room and entered. Everyone was there, milling and talking. Arthur and Jenny turned to greet them with big smiles.

"You boys were so tired, we wanted to let you sleep," Jenny said as she kissed each of them on the cheek.

Arthur engulfed them in a hug with his strong arms, and Lance suddenly felt like a little boy again, but in a good way – a little boy whose father loved and nurtured him and would always keep him safe. But as Arthur pulled back, Lance felt that chill ride up his back with a fury, because he knew deep down that his dad wouldn't always be there to keep him safe. And that realization scared him more than the guy stalking him.

Ryan approached looking more rumpled than usual, with Gibson at his side. It was obvious both men hadn't slept at all and Ryan, in particular, bore the brunt of that lack because of his age.

"Morning boys," the older man grunted, swigging from a mug of steaming fresh coffee that filled the air with its enticing aroma. Lance loved the smell, but hated the taste. More irony, he knew. "Let's get everybody together and I'll let you know what we found."

Arthur called everyone to order. Reyna and Esteban had arrived early, at Arthur's request, and sat with Darnell and Justin and the family in the front row. The numerous patrol knights sat behind them.

Looking uncomfortable up on the stage, Ryan gazed down at them and took another swig from his mug. "Okay, here's the deal. Secret Service and FBI have combed the entire hotel. They found bugs in this room, the computer lab, the boys' rooms, Arthur and Jenny's room, the training center, the Renaissance dining room, and the kitchen. Those have all been neutralized and no others were found. How they got there and for how long remains a mystery." He gestured to one of the Secret Service agents, a guy whose name Lance remembered to be Clancy. He was the agent in charge.

Clancy stepped forward, his crisp black suit almost shimmering beneath the chandelier lights, his little coiled earpiece glinting ominously. "Bottom line, everyone, you trust no one. I know the Kabbalogy folks don't like it, but this place is a non-profit and from now on, all traffic in and out is strictly curtailed. Anyone even setting foot on the premises must be vetted by me or my men. We can run their names through our national database. We still don't know if these attacks might be related to terrorism, foreign or domestic, or if it's just a personal vendetta like the perp keeps indicating. However, our job per the president of the United States is to keep all of you alive, and that's what we intend to do. Your wireless access code will be changed daily and you'll need to update your phones and computers. I know that sounds excessive, but we're dealing with smart people here, and we can't take any chances. We will do our best to backtrack the latest text sent to Sir Lance, but thus far the perp has proven cleverer than our IT guys. As for venturing out in public, same protocol as before. Vests, full upper body, for everyone, and you travel only in our cars, which have bulletproof glass installed. The listening devices we discovered will be sent to our labs for analysis. Any questions?"

Chris raised his hand. "Do *I* still get to wear one of your bulletproof vests?"

The man didn't smile, but Lance thought he detected the beginnings of one. "As before, whenever you venture out of this place, young man, yes, you will be vested."

"Cool," Chris said with a grin, turning to Lance. "I like those vests."

Lance threw his arm around his little brother and pulled him in close. God, how he loved this boy!

By the time the meeting broke up, Lance felt once again like he was on house arrest and hiding from his enemy, which he hated. While he'd always hidden from himself growing up, he'd seldom shied away from anyone who wanted to hurt him. Richard had made him almost feral when he'd first run from the man's house, and he lashed out at anyone just for looking at him the wrong way.

But this time, he realized, as he accompanied Ricky and the others to the Computer Lab, he had nowhere to take the fight building within him. He desperately wanted to protect Ricky and Chris and the whole family, but he didn't know how, since he didn't know who. And that was more frustrating than anything.

CHAPTER TEN

IT'S OVER NOW, ISN'T IT?

NEW CAMELOT SETTLED INTO A routine whereby everyone, even visiting knights who'd sworn allegiance to Arthur and the Round Table, were searched and vetted by the Secret Service each time they entered and exited. These kids, all of whom had grown up experiencing police harassment, didn't take well to that kind of scrutiny, and the gatherings often turned into complaint sessions.

Arthur assured them that the extra security was for their protection, and that of himself and his family. They grumbled every time, but grudgingly agreed. Most just wanted to find the stalker and "Kick his ass."

"Alas," Arthur reminded them after the first such complaints, his face deadly serious, "we do not know where to find him. I can assure you if I knew, his ass would have already been kicked by me."

That drew a relaxed laugh from the assembled kids, and the meeting went on as planned.

Reyna pleaded with Arthur to take Jenny out on the town for their anniversary, but the king demurred, reminding her that Jenny would be too nervous leaving the boys behind. Knowing that New Camelot security had been breached, she hovered around the kids more than she knew she ought, but her protective instincts wouldn't let her do otherwise. Arthur assured Reyna that he and Jenny would have a quiet, romantic dinner in one of the smaller dining rooms to celebrate their first year together.

November moved along quietly without any more drama until it was Thanksgiving again. This would be their third one at New Camelot and, despite all that had happened, and the apathy directed toward his CBOR from Capitol Hill, Lance had much to be thankful for.

Everyone sat at the longest table in the Renaissance Dining Room. Of course Arthur and Jenny, both dressed elegantly, as for a formal gathering, held court at one end of the massive, cheerfully decorated table. Lance and Ricky and Chris flanked them to one side, with Kai and Dakota flanking them on the other. Ryan and Gibson were there, and Justin. To everyone's delight, Justin's mother, Sandra, had joined them. Lance could tell Justin was almost giddy with joy to have his parents back together. Darnell was present, as was Techie, who said his parents didn't celebrate Thanksgiving, since they were from Vietnam. Reyna and Esteban were also in attendance, but joining them this year were Esteban's mom, Claudia, and his little sister, Rosa, and Reyna's parents—Jessica and Oscar.

Arthur spoke first. "I am always thankful for my beautiful wife and my amazing sons for whom I feel great pride." He squeezed Jenny's hand and grinned at his three sons. "However, this year in particular, I am especially thankful for the presence of Sir Dakota and Sir Kai."

He turned to gaze with admiration at the two young men, dressed in their finest regalia, who gaped at him. "These two fine young men have been with us a year now, and I have come to think of them as more than mere knights of the Table. I have come to think of them as a part of my family for as long as they wish to remain." He raised his glass of wine to the two Indians, who sat open-mouthed with shock. For once Kai wasn't laughing. "To Sir Dakota and Sir Kai, my sons by love and devotion."

Everyone raised a glass, even little Rosa, and said, "Here, here." And they drank.

The Indians were speechless, but clearly touched by the king's words and the show of support from everyone around them. Lance could even see Dakota's flinty face shimmer with emotion, and suspected he'd never been complimented like that in his life.

As everyone went around the table and offered their thanks for something, Lance was amazed to hear Reyna's parents express their gratitude to Arthur and Jenny for being better parents to Reyna than they had ever been. There was a moment of silence after that, and Reyna leaned in to hug her mom. The lady, so elegantly attired and coiffed, seemed awkward hugging her daughter, but Reyna held on all the same.

When the ritual finally got around to Kai and Dakota, they seemed at a loss for words.

Kai began haltingly, "You know, we don't celebrate this day in Native cultures 'cause, well, we told you last year." He glanced at Dakota, as though afraid he might offend him. "But I like this tradition of thanking God, or the Great Spirit, and I'm thankful for my Native brother Dakota being here with me, and for the chance to be part of something so great." He bowed his head nervously and didn't even laugh.

Lance studied Dakota, nervously fidgeting, and recognized the signs—the boy wanted a drink, and he wanted it badly. Wondering what could be so troubling, he asked gently, "What about you, Dakota? Anything you're thankful for?"

Dakota met his gaze across the table. "I am grateful and humbled to be part of this family. I do not deserve such respect."

There was a moment of stunned silence following his words.

Hoping to bypass the awkward moment, Lance turned to Ricky, nudging him to say something.

"I'm grateful for this boy beside me," Ricky began, throwing his arm around Lance. "My soul mate, the keeper of my heart, the boy who'll do anything for me, even skateboard over a president's speech." Everyone laughed. "And I'm grateful to God for sending me a mom and dad to love me when my birth parents could not."

Arthur and Jenny beamed at him, and Ricky smiled warmly over at them.

Lance cleared his throat. "I am thankful for so many things, I don't even know where to begin," he gushed, his voice choked with emotion. "God has been so good to me, bettern' I deserve. I'm beyond thankful for my parents, who chose to love me because they wanted to, especially my dad who's made me the man-in-training I am." Everybody chuckled at that. "Of course, I'm grateful to have Ricky by my side, holding my heart and soul in his hands and making sure I never stumble. He's my rock and my better half. But I'm also grateful to these guys across from me, Kai and Dakota."

The two Indians looked startled anew to hear themselves once more singled out for praise.

"Since they joined us last year, they've risked their lives for me, they've worked their butts off for me, they've educated me and watched over me and saved my life. I consider you guys my brothers, not just Native brothers, but blood brothers. *Carnales*, in Spanish. I love you both and I thank you both."

He raised his glass of sparkling cider and everyone followed suit. Kai and Dakota looked fearfully embarrassed, but raised their own glasses to acknowledge the tribute. Then dinner was served and the entire group dug in with gusto.

Lance, however, kept noting the sad, faraway look in Dakota's eyes, even as Kai would laughingly try to draw him into a joke or conversation. Dakota grunted his responses and listlessly picked at his food. Lance desperately wanted to find out what was wrong, because he saw that need in the other boy's eyes.

He was still certain Dakota had been drinking on and off for several months, but since it seemed to have stopped, he'd let the matter drop without saying anything. Now he vowed to seek his friend out after dinner and speak with him privately, hoping his soul whispering skills could read between the lines of Dakota's unspoken words and tightly wound body language.

Given the abundance of rooms, everyone elected to stay overnight so they wouldn't have to drive home. Of course, Reyna's parents made sure she and Esteban had separate rooms, which made Esteban's mom laugh. Once Jenny had assigned everyone a room, she kissed Lance and Ricky goodnight, hugged Kai, who stood with them, and then went to put Chris to bed.

Lance followed Ricky and Kai into Ricky's room and they all plopped down on the enormous bed, stuffed and sluggishly tired. It had probably been the best Thanksgiving ever for Lance, even better than his last two. He reached out and entwined his fingers with Ricky's, and grinning happily at this boy he would die to protect. Ricky smiled back and they lay side by side in silence.

Kai, who was sitting on the corner of the bed, cleared his throat and stood up. "Uh, I'll let you guys be alone."

Lance sat up, still holding onto Ricky's hand. "No, that's okay, Kai, we're not gonna make out or anything."

Ricky sat up and mock glowered. "We're not?"

Lance laughed, and Kai joined him. Then Lance frowned. "Anybody seen Dakota since dinner?"

Ricky shook his head.

"I'll go find him," Kai said with a sigh.

But Lance stopped him. A bad feeling crept up his spine as he recalled that look on Dakota's face during dinner. "No, I'll go. He's my roomie, right?" He laughed, but knew it probably sounded forced.

Ricky eyed him uncertainly. "Want me to come?"

Lance shook his head. "Naw. I wanna talk with him about something anyway." He smirked. "I'll come by later to tuck your dumb ass in before I go to bed."

That made Ricky grin and then Lance was out the door and into the hall before the other boy could tell something was wrong. Lance knew there had to be alcohol somewhere in the pantry, or maybe there was a wine cellar in this place. He'd never thought to ask.

Making his way down the front staircase, Lance ducked past the empty check-in desk and headed down the hall past the Renaissance Dining Room and into the expansive kitchen. It was empty, the household cooks having gone home after preparing dinner for the family. He snooped around, opening this pantry or that one, searching for the wine storage or an entrance to a wine cellar. Finally, in one corner at the back of the kitchen, behind tall rolling food carts, Lance spotted a door cracked open. He navigated his way between the carts and pulled open the door. Wooden steps led down, but these didn't look like they led to the basement where old furniture was stored. The light was already on, and Lance suspected he knew what he'd find down there. Heart filled with anxiety, he began his descent.

The steps creaked and groaned beneath his sneakered feet, but there were no other sounds to be heard. As he stepped onto the hard concrete floor, Lance glanced around at rack after rack of wine bottles reaching from floor to ceiling.

Then he heard what sounded like muffled crying, maybe groaning, coming from the back of the cellar. Wending his way between the towering wine racks, Lance rounded the last one and saw him.

Dakota sat spread eagle on the floor, leaning up against a hard brick wall, a full bottle in hand. Two empty ones lay on the stone floor beside him. The boy's magnificent black hair dangled in front of his face and splayed outward over his lap, his head was bent, and he was crying softly, achingly.

Lance's heart pounded with empathy. It sounded like him a few years back when he'd been lonely or depressed, and he desperately wanted to help this lost soul who had done so much for him and Ricky.

Dakota lifted his head. With one hand, he pushed aside his hair and gasped when he saw Lance looking sadly down at him.

Flashing back to that morning when Jack found him in the alley where Mark died, Lance stepped forward. "May I?" he asked, mimicking Jack's words to him and indicating the spot beside Dakota.

Dakota nodded and looked away, clearly embarrassed.

Lance sat beside him, leaning up against the cold brick wall, the coolness of the cellar seeping into his tunic and further dampening his mood. "What's wrong, Dakota? Tell me."

Dakota did not look up, but Lance saw him grip the neck of the bottle with intensity. "I have dishonored you and your father. But mostly you."

"How did you dishonor me? You saved my life, like three times already."

Dakota turned his head away, hair creating a wall between them, a trick Lance knew all too well. "I called you *winkte* and mocked you for it."

Lance was still confused. "Yeah, well, you only did that once. I forgot all about it."

"I didn't."

Lance wasn't sure just how drunk he was, so he waited patiently.

"Did Laughs A Lot tell you about him and me at the powwows?"

"Not too much. He said they were fun. He said you guys danced with a lot of different people from other tribes, but that's about all."

Dakota blew out a raspy breath. "*He* danced a lot, Lance." His voice was laced with sadness and regret. "*He* danced with every girl that was there. *He* was popular. Everybody loved him. Me, I didn't like dancing much and I sucked at all that social stuff. So I only danced with one person at every powwow. The only person I ever *wanted* to dance with."

He brushed the hair from around his face, and Lance saw the truth in his destitute brown eyes, a truth he'd suspected, but had never seen confirmed until now. "Kai."

Dakota nodded. "You see how dishonorable I am? I'm no warrior. I made fun of Two-Spirits my whole life. I... I made fun of Kai when we were kids, Lance, with my friends." His voice trembled with remorse. He laughed a bitter laugh. "I think my mother knew about me since I was little. She'd give me this look when all I'd ever talk about was Laughs A Lot and would he be at the next powwow and how I didn't wanna go if he wasn't there. I didn't know what it meant till later, and then I tried to hide it."

"You sound like me," Lance said, his voice a whisper, painful memories welling up within him. "I thought I couldn't be a real man if I, you know, liked boys like that."

"My whole life I wanted to be a warrior like my ancestors, and fight the white man for crimes against my people. I... I just wanted everyone to see me as tough and manly, you know?"

Lance felt his past fears flooding in on him, the ones he'd finally, for the most part, conquered when he admitted his love for Ricky. "You're as badass as they come, Dakota. So's Kai."

Dakota didn't respond, his cheeks streaked with dampness.

"He doesn't know how you feel?"

Dakota shook his head. "I thought he'd figure it out. I never been good with words, Lance. Like you didn't know that, huh?" He tossed off another bitter laugh. "But, I mean, what thirteen-year-old boy dances with another thirteen-year-old boy, right? He *should* know. Maybe he does, but I just don't, you know, *do it* for him. 'Sides, he's into Ricky. Can't you tell?"

Lance reacted with surprise, though he knew he shouldn't have. Kai's long-standing interest in Ricky was pretty transparent. He forced calm into his voice and said, with a bit of tightness, "Yeah, well Ricky's taken."

Dakota bowed his head in shame.

Once Lance quelled the terrifying possibility of losing Ricky to someone else, he thought back on all of his time with the two Indians. He'd soul whispered Kai and found conflicting emotions running through him. Yeah, there was the obvious attraction to Ricky. Lance could readily understand that. But there was something else. He recalled that incredible drawing Kai had made for Dakota's birthday. He remembered furtive looks and uncertain gestures, especially over the summer when they'd been messing around in the pool. He recalled the hidden fear in the other's eyes during those furtive moments.

"I learned something a while back," he finally said, and Dakota turned to face him. "But I learned it too late to help Mark. It's the things we don't say to each other that make the biggest difference."

Dakota's eyes widened with surprise.

"I think you should tell Kai the truth."

"Tell Kai what truth?"

Lance turned to find Kai standing between towering racks of wine, squinting suspiciously at their closeness.

"I came looking for you guys and saw the lights on in the kitchen," Kai said by way of explanation, his brown eyes scrutinizing Lance and then shifting to Dakota, who'd lowered his head again and refused to look up.

"I, uh, I'll let you guys talk," Lance said as he stood and nudged Dakota with his foot. The young Indian tilted his eyes upward and the imploring, almost helpless, look on his face touched Lance deeply. "It'll be okay, Dakota. Trust me." Then he turned and swept past Kai, disappearing among the wine racks.

In the pervasive silence that followed Lance's retreating footfalls, Kai cautiously approached Dakota, who looked back down at the floor, shamefaced.

"You guys were sitting kinda close," he said, an edge creeping into his voice despite his best efforts not to let it. "What's going on?"

Dakota looked up at him and Kai saw the remnants of tears, the blurry red eyes, and he looked at the bottles, the two empty and the full one Dakota clutched tightly in his hands. Dakota lowered his head and let his hair hide him.

Kai sat beside his friend, but not as close as Lance had been. He'd seen Dakota drunk once before, at the last powwow when both of them were thirteen. Alcohol was strictly forbidden and to this day he didn't know how Dakota managed to smuggle it in.

"What are you supposed to tell me?" He could only just imagine. "That you can't work with me anymore 'cause I'm Two-Spirit? That I'm not man enough to be a real Indian? What? Tell me, I can take it." Kai knew he sounded bitter and petulant, but he couldn't help it.

Dakota glanced up quickly, his eyes swimming with guilt. "Nothing like that. I told you before. You're the real warrior, not me."

Now Kai was confused. "Then what?"

Dakota couldn't face him, so he focused on his own hands clasped tightly around the bottle in his lap. "Didn't you ever wonder why I only danced with you?" His voice came out like a breath of wind, wispy and uncertain, and his fingers gripped the bottle more intensely.

Those words threw Kai for a loop. His mind raced to retrieve the memories. "We danced with everybody," he said to fill the silence.

Did we?

Dakota shook his head, but still didn't raise his eyes. "You did. I only danced once. Always the last dance. Always with—"

"Me," Kai blurted in sudden realization. He'd been such a social butterfly, chatting up everyone, dancing with every girl who asked him, that he'd somehow thought Dakota had done the same. But now the memories flooded his mind, going all the way back to when he was six. He'd be dancing around the fire and feel eyes on him. Whenever he'd look up, there would be Dakota sitting off by himself, not talking with anyone, just watching him. Until the tribal leader called for the final dance of the powwow. Only then would Dakota rise and come to him. And only then did the event feel complete.

Dakota looked up now, his angular features pinched with remorse. "I volunteered to come to New Camelot 'cause I knew you'd be here. Yeah, they wanted me off the rez, and yeah I thought being a knight would be cool. But only if I could be a knight with… you."

Kai's breath seemed to catch in his throat. "But you always made fun of me."

Dakota looked away. "Cause I'm a jerk. I always been a jerk."

Kai wanted to reach out, wanted to touch the other boy, desperately feeling the need for that basic human contact Lance always talked about. But he was too afraid. "You're not a jerk."

Dakota did not lift his eyes. His hands gripped the neck of the bottle, the fingers squeezing and un-squeezing. "Yeah, I am. I made fun of you and other Two-Spirits on the rez and all the time I was… I thought the alcohol would help me forget what I was. But all it did was kill my brother."

Kai sucked in a shocked breath.

Still staring at his twisting and untwisting hands, Dakota haltingly told of his drunken crime against his younger brother.

A deep poignant silence fell between them when he finished, and Kai honestly didn't know what to say. All that guilt, the heavy burden Dakota had been carrying around these past four years; he couldn't imagine how that felt.

"I'm sorry, Dakota," Kai murmured softly, his heart thumping with anguish. "I never knew."

"Because it wasn't spoken of by my people. Did you ever ask about me when I didn't show up anymore?"

Kai vividly remembered the emptiness in the pit of his stomach that first powwow without Dakota, when he'd been fourteen. "They just said you and your mother and brother weren't able to come and my mom said not to ask more questions, 'cause that wasn't the Indian way."

"I destroyed my family and now I don't have one," Dakota whispered, his voice laced with sadness, and such an intense loneliness that Kai almost wanted to cry.

"That's not true," he insisted. "You have me and Arthur and Jenny and Lance and Ricky. We're your family now."

Dakota didn't respond, and Kai could tell his thoughts were on the younger brother whose life he'd recklessly stolen.

"You're the only one, Laughs A Lot."

"Only one what?"

Dakota looked up, his damp brown eyes agonizingly sad, and very afraid. "The only one who ever did it for me." He laughed, another sad and bitter laugh that touched Kai to the heart. "I think I loved you from the start, before I even knew what it was. Can a six-year-old be in love? I guess so, 'cause that's when I fell for you. Crazy, huh? And then I spent the rest of my life pushing you away." In a sudden burst of fury he flung the bottle of wine against the opposite wall, where it shattered and splashed outward like a purple fireworks display. "Screw it, Laughs A Lot, screw all of it! I disgraced my people and I have no honor. These people are too good for me. You're too good for me. It's time I leave." He stood on shaky legs, and began to stumble in the direction of the stairs.

Kai threw out a hand, grasped one of Dakota's in his, and gripped it tightly, halting the boy's forward lurch. Dakota staggered, and then turned in surprise to gaze at his hand held tightly within Kai's.

"Your tribal council told my tribal council you were coming here," Kai said, gulping nervously. "That's why I volunteered. I mean, yeah, I thought Lance and Arthur were cool, and I already knew about Lance and Ricky being, you know, Two-Spirit." Then he locked eyes with the stunned boy whose hand he held. "But mostly, I wanted to see you again. Every powwow without you, well, sucked. I always thought I was having fun before, but now I know it was only 'cause you were there. I might have danced with everyone, Dakota, but you're the only one I ever wanted."

Dakota stared in silence at their clasped hands. "Kai, are you telling me...?"

Kai stood and shyly faced his childhood friend. "Have you ever kissed anyone, Cloudy Boy?"

Dakota nervously shook his head. "But you like Ricky... I seen you...."

Kai smiled sadly. "I mostly checked him out so you wouldn't catch me looking at you."

Dakota looked stunned.

"Can I kiss you?" Kai asked, a hesitant smile gracing his thin lips.

Dakota nodded. They gently pressed their lips together. The touch was like a jolt of energy to Kai and, he could tell, for Dakota, too. Their lips felt so perfect together that both said later they couldn't understand how they'd stayed apart for so long.

When finally they separated to catch their breath, Dakota staggered slightly, and Kai had to support him in his arms.

Dakota smiled as Kai's arms held him upright. "You're stronger than you look, Laughs A Lot," he said with a shy grin. "And you kiss good too."

Kai grinned right back. "So do you, Cloudy Boy."

Dakota began to sag even more. "I'm pretty messed up right now."

Kai merely shushed him. "I'll help you upstairs. You'll be fine tomorrow."

Slowly and with great deliberation, Kai supported his friend as they made their way between the racks of wine to the stairs. He gently helped Dakota navigate those stairs. Dakota seemed on the verge of passing out as they steered their way haltingly through the lobby, and Kai had to strain and heave to get Dakota up to the second floor.

When they got to Lance's door, a sweating Kai half-dragged, half-pulled the now swooning Dakota into the room. Lance and Ricky were sitting on the bed talking when the Indians entered, and leapt up quickly to help.

"Let's get him onto his bed," Lance said, grabbing one side of Dakota while Kai held onto the other. Ricky sprinted a few feet ahead to the bed and yanked back the coverings. Lance and Kai gently sat Dakota down and then laid him onto his back. Ricky pulled off the boy's moccasins and set them on the floor while Lance reached for Dakota's shirt.

"You're gonna undress him?" Kai asked, appalled, his voice tinged with jealousy. Even Ricky looked over sharply at that.

Lance reddened at the implication. "Just his shirt. Otherwise he'll sweat something crazy during the night. Trust me, I know."

That seemed to mollify Kai, and the three boys slipped the tunic up and over Dakota's head, revealing his sweat-drenched torso.

"Wow, he's sweating a lot already," Kai said, his voice tight with emotion. "Is there anything I can do for him, Lance?"

Lance looked down at the half-awake, half-asleep young man, and shook his head. "Let him sleep it off."

Lance looked over at Ricky and offered a sad smile. "Look familiar?"

Ricky nodded.

Dakota's eyes opened and he focused on the three boys standing above him. The bleary red orbs fixed a moment on Lance and he smiled. "Thank you, Lance. You're a wise chief."

"I guess that means you told him, huh?"

Dakota nodded, and then shifted his gaze to Kai, who stood eyeing him with concern. Dakota reached out a hand and Kai's met it half way. They stared deeply at one another.

Lance turned to Ricky and grinned.

Ricky grinned right back. "Us Two-Spirits are gonna outnumber the single spirits around here pretty soon."

Lance shoved him. "Dumbass."

Ricky shoved him back. "Dumber ass."

Kai laughed, and this time Dakota joined him.

Lance and Ricky hung out in Ricky's room to give the guys some time alone. Kai wanted to stay with Dakota until the other fell asleep. After about fifteen minutes, he stepped through the connecting door into Ricky's room and approached the boys, who lounged lazily on the bed. Kai looked happier than Lance had ever seen him.

"I don't know what you said to him, Lance, but thank you, thank you, thank you!" He bowed respectfully, and couldn't stop grinning.

Ricky piped up with, "Yep, that's the boy I love – Soul Whisperer to the Stars."

Lance shoved Ricky away from him. "Go to bed, fool, 'fore any more of your brain leaks out."

Ricky and Kai laughed.

When Lance awoke the following morning, he crawled out of bed to see if Dakota was awake. The Indian must've dreamt of his brother, because several times during the night he'd called out in his native language, sounding achingly sad and guilt-ridden. Lance had risen each time to sit on the edge of the bed and hold his clammy hand. Dakota's sweat-sheened face and torso glistened, even in the shadowy darkness, and he tossed and turned restlessly. Gradually, as Lance spoke soothing words to him, Dakota drifted back into sleep.

Just as Lance went to check on him that morning, the connecting door flew open and Kai padded in, wearing a pair of shorts he'd been given for his birthday. He hurried to the bed to gaze down with concern at his friend. "How is he?"

Lance stretched to pull the sleepiness from his muscles. "He had bad dreams, but I sat with him and he settled down."

"Probably about his brother."

"He told you?"

"Yeah. No wonder he hates himself so much." Kai sighed heavily. "We gotta keep him sober, Lance, at least till he accepts how much we care about him."

"I know. But he has you now and he knows it. Ricky saved me just by being Ricky. Hopefully, you can do the same for him."

Kai smiled wanly. "I'll do my best."

Later, after Dakota had arisen and showered, he suffered from a raging hangover, which both Lance and Ricky could relate to, but Dakota never complained. Lance offered to let him skip weapons practice for the day, and he smiled at that.

He did join the others in the Computer Lab to continue networking with people about the CBOR. He and Kai sat close together and continued their outreach to Native tribes.

While Lance and Ricky were fielding questions about specific amendments, Dakota rose from his own station and came to them, standing self-consciously beside Lance, his young features drawn.

Lance studied his pensive expression. "Everything okay?"

Dakota shuffled his feet. "I just wanted to thank you guys, 'specially you, Lance. I'm... proud... to be your *carnal*."

Clearly overcome by emotion, he turned away and returned to Kai, who eyed him with obvious concern. Lance stared openmouthed as Kai took Dakota's hand and held it securely while Dakota sat quietly and regained control.

Lance turned to Ricky and grinned.

The remainder of the year passed in a similar fashion. Arthur and the family ceased their neighborhood visits, since progress was evident throughout L.A. Alcohol addiction remained an enormous problem, but more for adults than kids. It appeared that fewer teens seemed to be experimenting with heavy drinking or drugs, perhaps as a result of becoming more fully and productively engaged within their neighborhoods, but Lance felt certain it was a further testament to what his dad had initiated.

Over the ensuing weeks, it became more obvious to other knights that Kai and Dakota had become a couple, though the Indians were not the least bit demonstrative in public. But the looks they directed at one another spoke the truth for all to see, and Lance was proud that no one paid it any attention. Those who knew the boys congratulated them, especially Esteban and Reyna. She kept saying they were almost as cute a couple as Lance and Ricky, embarrassing all four boys each time she did.

With the Congress in Washington off for Christmas break, Lance and his team focused on their supporters in key states that had freshman senators or representatives beginning their terms in January. And the boys began setting up their back-up plan that would begin in April, if Congress displayed further unwillingness to cooperate. Thus far, the response from kids country-wide was very enthusiastic. By April, they should have more than enough participation to rock the vote big time, and show this country where the real power lay.

Christmas was just the family, and they liked it that way. Justin and his parents had been invited by Bridget to her house for Christmas dinner, and Ryan insisted Gibson go with his family. New Camelot had more than enough protection to spare them for one day. Darnell and Techie, who more often than not remained at New Camelot now that they were eighteen, had gone home to their moms for the holiday, and would return in a couple of days. Reyna was shocked when her parents had called Esteban's mom and invited her, Rosa and Este to their home for Christmas dinner, so they were absent too.

Other than the omnipresent Secret Service agents, it was only Arthur, Jenny, Lance, Ricky, Chris, Kai, Dakota, Merlin, and Ryan for Christmas, and, despite loving all the others dearly, Lance found it to be his best Christmas ever. Midnight mass filled his heart with peace and hope, while the day itself was quiet and relaxed. There were lots of presents to open in the morning, and a wrapping paper fight between Lance and Ricky that Chris happily joined into, setting everyone to laughing.

The family gathered in the Throne Room before dinner to watch Jenny's favorite movie, "It's A Wonderful Life." None of the kids, and needless to say Arthur or Merlin, had ever seen it, and despite the fact that it was "In black and white," as Ricky had exclaimed, like it was the worst crime in the world, the whole family loved it.

The heartfelt message about everyone's life having meaning and purpose struck a cord with Lance, and with Dakota. Both boys realized that, despite their past failures and perceived weaknesses, much good would not be in existence had they never been born.

Dinner was filled with laughter and love. Dakota smiled, and even laughed at Kai's lame jokes. He seemed so much more relaxed as to be almost a new person.

The day came to a joyous close, despite the tiny fear creeping up Lance's back that this might, in fact, be his final Christmas on earth.

During this period of time, from Thanksgiving into the New Year, Lance and Ricky put a lot of extra time into their senior year schoolwork. The plan was to begin traveling the country in June when the climate would be more hospitable in the northern and eastern states, so the boys wanted to have their diplomas by then.

While completing their spring course load, Reyna, Esteban, Justin and Darnell already set in motion plans to take online college courses for the fall semester, in anticipation of their traveling with Arthur.

Justin was taking prerequisites in criminology. Despite feeling disdain for his father's profession as a boy, he had decided that he, too, wanted to be a police officer, but a good one like his dad and Ryan, not like the ones who'd beat up Lance and harassed kids.

Darnell, on the other hand, had his sights set on being a general contractor and owning his own business someday. He'd learned so much during the Clean-up Tour throughout the city about repair work and construction, that he'd fallen in love with it.

Reyna, who insisted on organizing the entire tour, sat with Lance and Ricky and plotted their zigzagging route across the country, south to north to south to north until they hit New England. After that, it would be straight back to Washington, D.C.

They would use the bus Arthur had taken around California during the prop campaign, and be accompanied by several Secret Service vehicles.

Reyna then set about finagling deals with hotel chains in every state they'd visit. Most were ecstatic to welcome Arthur and his knights, especially the world-famous Boy Who Came Back. Every venue offered substantial discounts on both rooms and amenities just for the bragging rights and publicity they'd generate from hosting such high profile guests. However, to maintain a closer relationship to middle-class America, Arthur decided not to stay in high-end hotels, but those considered more affordable to regular citizens. As plotted, they'd be on the road from June till the end of October, and Reyna was stoked with excitement.

The "Once Upon a Time in America" tour, as she'd dubbed it, would consist of herself, Arthur, Jenny, Lance, Ricky, Chris, Dakota, Kai, Esteban, Justin, Darnell, Techie, Sylvia, Merlin, Ryan and Gibson. Sylvia insisted her mother would allow her to go as long as she kept up with her schoolwork, and Reyna agreed. Ryan, as a deputized federal agent directly accountable to the president had to go, but Gibson needed special permission, and handily got it from Mayor Soto and Chief Murphy.

The biggest development around this time was Helen's promotion – she'd been hired by ABC network news as a national correspondent, and would be the sole embedded journalist recording every facet of Arthur's tour. She would have her own truck, and managed to talk ABC into hiring Charlie, her favorite cameraman, for the journey. As the journalist most prominently associated with New Camelot, Helen had been covering the crusade since day one, and Lance was stunned she hadn't gone national long before. When she told Arthur and the others the good news, she especially grinned at Lance.

"I owe it all to you," she said warmly, reaching out to hug him. Having always loved this lady and her integrity, Lance hugged her back. When she released him and stepped back, she stood a moment in awed silence, giving his face and height and size a searching look. "You're not a boy anymore, Lance." Her tone sounded wistful, yet she smiled anyway. "But you're still beautiful."

Lance groaned, and then grinned his thanks at her compliment.

Over the next few weeks, Lance and Ricky noted the skittish devotion Dakota and Kai showed toward one another. Despite them being a year older, Lance knew neither boy had ever been in a serious relationship before, so the experience was new, exciting, and uncertain.

One night in late January, the two entered Lance's room holding hands as they usually did when no one but the other two boys were looking. Lance and Ricky were reading *Paradise Lost* on Lance's bed, Lance sitting back as usual with Ricky's head in his lap. They looked up when the other two entered.

"Hey, guys, what's up?" Lance asked absently, his mind still caught up with the ambiguous characterization of Satan, the hero/anti-hero of the epic poem, and with the idea that eating from the Tree of Knowledge had been mankind's downfall. He was in Book IV and the line swimming around in his head when the two boys entered was, "God pronounc't it death to taste that Tree."

The Indians crossed the room hesitantly and stood at the foot of the bed. Dakota looked positively tongue-tied, and even Kai wasn't smiling or laughing as usual.

Their odd demeanor caused Ricky to sit up and pull his legs under him, and Lance to set down his book and.

"You guys have a fight or something?" Lance asked.

Kai shook his head, but Dakota still wouldn't look up. Their hands remained clasped together, as though they were afraid of losing each other if they let go.

"We, uh, we don't talk about stuff like this on the rez 'cause, well, it's like, personal and private and… oh, crap." Kai turned to Dakota and nudged him. "C'mon, Cloudy Boy, help me here."

Dakota turned a mortified look on Lance and Ricky.

Lance couldn't imagine what would be so hard to say after all they'd been through together.

"We don't know what to do, Lance," Dakota murmured as though afraid of being overheard. "We, you know, kiss a lot and make out like that, but we don't know what *else* to do, like who should do what and…" He clearly couldn't go on, and simply trailed off, looking humiliated.

Lance blushed as he realized just what the boys were asking about. He looked at Ricky, who reddened, too.

Great, Lance thought, *we're a big help.*

"You guys've been together longer," Kai began haltingly, "and we wondered if…" He obviously couldn't finish the thought.

Lance understood. "If Ricky and me are having sex?"

Kai and Dakota looked like embarrassed little boys instead of the eighteen-year-olds they were. But Lance understood their ignorance. They'd grown up on reservations without much Internet or other outside world influences to educate, or poison, their minds and hearts. They were, in many ways, touchingly pure and almost innocent.

The way I wish I still was, he thought wistfully.

"No, we're not." Lance noted that Kai looked slightly surprised. "We can tell you how to hurt each other with sex, but that's about all. That's been our only experience. We're waiting till we're ready to, you know, figure out how to *love* each other with sex."

He reached out and Ricky's hand instantly found his. Then he offered his warmest smile to these two boys who could be so badass in a combat situation, but now stood trembling like leaves in a summer breeze. "Like my friend Mark once told me, just let it be and it'll all work out the way it's supposed to."

Dakota eyed him quizzically, but Kai seemed to understand. "You mean we'll figure it out on our own?"

"Yup. You'll decide to do what you think is right and not something someone else told you about."

Kai smiled, looking relieved. Dakota, too, appeared more relaxed.

"There's no hurry, guys," Ricky said reassuringly. "Nobody's keeping score."

That drew a laugh from Kai, and a smile from Dakota. Once again, Lance noted what a handsome smile the Lakota youth had.

And so the four of them sat and chatted about the road trip to come, and Lance noted how tranquil the Indians became, compared to when they'd entered the room. He wasn't sure why they'd felt so pressured to have sex, since neither one seemed to be in a big hurry, and decided it was probably the media influence they'd been exposed to while surfing the net.

They may not have had much stuff growing up on the rez, he mused, but at least they had a certain innocence big city kids didn't.

City kids were exposed to *way* too much these days, but he supposed there wasn't anything that could be done about it. Maybe that's why that line from *Paradise Lost* haunted him, because knowledge, once acquired, could never be un-acquired, and Satan knew this when he tempted Eve to eat from the Tree of Knowledge. Once she did, all bets were off. Lance knew all too well that once a child's innocence was stolen by the wrong knowledge, there was no going back, and that was a tragedy of epic proportions.

The beginning of February brought Lance the stunning and unexpected news that Richard Thornton wanted to see him. Ryan found Lance and Ricky up in Lance's room one afternoon. The boys were in their usual positions on the bed discussing the themes and messages in *Paradise Lost* when the sergeant knocked at their open door. When Lance looked over and saw Ryan, Gibson, Arthur and Jenny all spilling into the room, he knew it had to be serious.

Ricky lifted his head from Lance's lap and sat up at once.

"What's wrong?" Lance asked, his heart already beginning to pound.

All four adults looked wary and cautious, as though afraid to broach whatever subject had brought them all here.

"Is everybody okay?" Ricky asked, his voice tinged with dread.

Arthur shifted uncomfortably. "Yes, son, everyone is fine."

Ryan squinted at Lance. "We got a call from the CDCR."

"The what?"

"California Department of Corrections and Rehabilitation," Gibson explained soberly, but then he fell silent.

Lance looked from one face to the next. "So? C'mon guys, you're scaring the crap outta me here."

Ryan shook his head. "Sorry, Lance, it's nothing like that. It's just, well, Thornton has asked to meet with you, face to face."

Lance's eyes widened with stunned shock. "Richard?" It was almost a breathless utterance.

Ryan nodded, and Lance saw Arthur slip his arm around Jenny and pull her in.

"Why?" He'd put Richard behind him. He hadn't even thought of the vile little man since the trial. Why now?

"He claims to know something about who's been attacking you and Ricky," Ryan went on, "but he won't tell anyone but you."

Lance glanced at Ricky and saw the same dubious look in his eyes. "Isn't he in prison by now?"

"Yeah, up at Corcoran. But if you agree to see him, we can arrange for the state to bring him down. Parker Center. A secure interview room where we would watch everything through two-way glass."

Lance sat in silence a moment, digesting this shocking news. "Do you believe him, *nino*?" he finally asked, his heart thumping with a fear he thought he'd buried forever. "As a cop, what does your gut tell you? Does he know something or is he just trying to mess with me again?"

Ryan exchanged a look with Gibson, but both men seemed reticent.

"I couldn't say, Lance," Ryan admitted with a sigh. "I didn't talk to him. One of the CO's up there relayed the message."

"You do not have to do this, son," Arthur said, his voice laced with compassion.

Lance looked at his father, at the man who had taken him off the streets and given him a new life, the man who meant everything to him.

"But what if he does know something, Dad? What if he does, and I didn't see him and you got hurt or Ricky got...." He trailed off, flicking his gaze over at the boy who made his heart flutter and his soul sing.

"I think he's lying, Lance," Ricky said quietly. "Don't forget I know him too. He's a liar."

Lance nodded. Richard's lies and evil deeds against him spun wildly through his memory like a cyclone. "I know. But I can't take any chances with you or Dad." He turned to Ryan. "I'll see him."

Ryan eyed him with a look of deep admiration on his jaded face. "Okay. Gib and me'll make the arrangements."

The two men left the room, leaving the family together in silence.

"Are you sure, Lance?" Jenny asked, coming to him and placing her hands gently around his face.

Lance's heart pounded with apprehension, but he knew he had to do this. "Yeah, Mom. I got this. No worries."

She pulled him into a hug, before allowing Arthur step forward.

"I'm proud of you, Lance, each and every day, and I love you more than life itself. I shall never *not* tell you these things every opportunity that I have." Arthur smiled warmly, and Lance grabbed him in an intense hug.

Yes, Jack's simple words about the things we don't say to each other had become a mantra for both of them, and a life lesson neither would ever forget.

Once their parents left them alone, Ricky wrapped his arms around Lance, holding him in silence and solidarity. Grateful, Lance rested his head against Ricky's solid shoulder, his pounding heart gradually easing down into a muted beat. He could do this. Ricky would be with him. With Ricky, anything was possible.

Over the next few days, while arrangements were made for the CDCR to transport the convicted rapist from Corcoran Prison to LADP's Parker Center lockup, Lance and Ricky focused on shoring up the states that had already agreed to support the CBOR, and networked feverishly to get more. They figured the more states that put pressure on Congress to vote on the amendments, the more likely Congress would act.

Mark's dad up in Washington had been in regular contact with Lance, assuring them that state was squarely behind the CBOR, by a wide margin. Idaho, where Jack's mom led the adult supporters, was proving to be more obstinate, but she assured the boys she would not give up. She owed it to her son.

According to their supporters in Oregon, that state was behind the CBOR, as were New York, Pennsylvania, all of the New England states, Minnesota, Iowa, Wisconsin, Michigan, Illinois, New Mexico, Delaware, Hawaii, and California. That made twenty states pretty solidly in their corner, but they needed a lot more than that. They needed three-fourths of the states for ratification, which meant thirty-eight total. Thus, they focused heavily on the others, especially those considered swing states during elections. Florida, which had even tougher laws against minors than California, would be hard to convince. Lance and Ricky were appalled that

Florida put kids as young as ten into adult court for the purpose of giving them long prison terms. That revelation sickened them.

Ohio was leaning in their direction, as was Indiana, Colorado, Nevada, North Dakota and South Dakota. The heavy Indian presence in the two Dakotas was having a strong influence, as more and more residents of those states learned of the injustices perpetrated against Native children. Oddly enough, Arizona was not so rapidly swinging in their direction, despite the heavy Native population, but the boys had been told through Navajo contacts that many people in Arizona apparently didn't like the idea of giving children those kinds of rights, especially Native children.

It was the middle of February when Ryan came to Lance and told him the face-to-face with Richard Thornton would be the following day.

"He'll be transported today and housed at Parker Center," his godfather told him in a voice clearly indicating he thought it was a bad idea. "We'll bring you over in the morning. That okay, Lance? You sure you still wanna do this?"

Lance and Ricky were in the Computer Lab with Kai and Dakota, Reyna and Esteban, networking with children and adults around the country, when Ryan brought him the news. Lance sat a second in dazed silence now that the reality of stepping into a room alone with the monster had arrived. But everyone would be right outside watching, and Ricky would be there. He'd be fine.

"Yeah, *nino*. I gotta find out if he really knows something or if it's just more of his sick BS."

Ryan left the lab. Reyna swept over and threw her arms around Lance. "Don't worry, baby boy. If he touches you, I'll punch his lights out."

That made him smile with gratitude and he hugged her back. When she returned to her station, he found Kai and Dakota watching him with concern. He'd told them what was planned, and they insisted on being present. Now Dakota offered a look of encouragement.

"We'll help her," he said, and Kai nodded.

Ricky placed a hand over his heart. "I got you, Lance. I always got you."

"And I always got you."

The ride to Parker Center with the Secret Service was made in silence. What was there to say anyway? It had all been said many times. All except the words Father Mike had suggested so long ago that Lance employ, words of forgiveness. He'd pretty much erased Richard from his life that day in the courtroom, but still the man's name gave him the shivers.

Richard Thornton had taken a young boy and persecuted him, humiliated him, and sexualized him, while simultaneously equating sex with pain and torment. Would forgiving Richard finally set him free, fully and completely and totally free? These were his thoughts and fears as he clutched tightly to Ricky's strong hand on the ride downtown.

He felt unsettled as he entered the crowded Parker Center with its cacophony of sound, people milling about, police officers eyeing him suspiciously. Many, he knew, had not forgotten his harsh indictment of their treatment of him when he'd been arrested. And, of course, none had ever snitched on their brethren who had done the abuse, here or in the Sheriff's Department.

Some officers glowered from their desks, while others were clearly entranced by the sight of Arthur's entourage parading through the squad room, flanked by Ryan, Gibson and four Secret Service agents. All conversation ceased as the group's presence became known throughout the very heart of the Los Angeles Police Department.

Ryan and Gibson led the way past the gawkers and down a long hallway lined with closed doors. Ryan grabbed one of the knobs and turned it, pushing the door inward. He ushered everyone inside. The room was small, and empty of furniture. One wall to the left of the door was an enormous window that looked into the next room over. And sitting at a small wooden table, dressed in an orange jumpsuit, cuffed hands resting on the table, was Richard Thornton.

Lance gazed through the glass in silence at the man who'd terrorized his life, the man who'd stolen his childhood and left a frightened, empty shell behind. Richard looked thinner than Lance remembered from that last time in court. Thinner and smaller. The man sat staring intently at the window, right at Lance, as though he could see him.

As he looked into those empty blue eyes, Lance suddenly realized that his heart wasn't thumping. His breathing hadn't become ragged. He was calm. There was no fear.

Arthur looked at him and made eye contact. Lance nodded, and Arthur gestured to Ryan. The sergeant led Lance out into the hall to the next door over. His hand on the knob, he paused. "You're sure?"

"I'm sure, *nino*."

Ryan reluctantly pushed open the door. Lance stepped through it, and closed the door behind him.

Richard turned those penetrating blue eyes onto him as Lance stood tall before him. They simply stared at each other a moment, and Lance remained almost preternaturally calm. No sign of a freak-out, not even sweaty palms. He saw this man of his nightmares in a new light, the light of adulthood. And he wasn't afraid anymore.

"Well, Richard, what do you have to tell me?"

Richard stood, and Lance almost laughed at the fact that he was now taller. Richard's eyes devoured him, just like Mr. D's had done. But Lance felt rock solid and strong.

"Still the most beautiful boy in the world, Lance," the man whispered breathlessly.

Lance looked at him calmly. "You brought me here to tell me that? You said you knew something about the attacks on me. So spill, Richard, or I'm outta here."

Richard suddenly looked panicked. "No, don't leave. Yes, I do have something to say. Come closer, Lance."

Without hesitation, Lance stepped right up to the table and looked into his wide, imploring eyes.

In the room next door, Ryan stood closest to the door in case of emergency, Arthur beside him. Ricky and Jenny were next, while the others stood behind them. Ryan and Ricky flinched when Lance stepped forward, but Arthur kept his eyes fixed on his son.

Lance looked at Richard with a mix of contempt and dismissal. Then Richard reached out with his cuffed hands to gently brush his fingers against Lance's cheek.

Ryan made a move for the door, and Ricky started to follow, but Arthur grabbed the sergeant's arm.

"No, James," he said, never taking his eyes from Lance. "Wait."

So Ryan and Ricky anxiously returned their eyes to the scene unfolding before them.

Lance didn't flinch at Richard's touch. He didn't even blink. He merely stood and allowed the man to caress his cheek.

"Still soft and smooth," Richard purred absently, like his mind had drifted back to the past. "Still my beautiful, smooth little boy."

Lance glared until Richard lowered his hands.

"I'm not little anymore, Richard, and I was *never* your boy." He laughed, a genuine laugh of release. "It's not gonna work," he went on easily and calmly. "There's no fear like a child's fear, except I'm not a child now. And I'm not afraid of you anymore, Richard."

Richard smirked, looking like the evil snake Lance so vividly remembered. "You know, I always knew you for a fag boy, Lance, even when you were six."

Lance recoiled involuntarily at that word, but remained composed and impassive.

"I used to watch you at the playground with other children," Richard went on like he was revealing national secrets. "You ignored girls even then. But the boys, oh, how you liked them. Tried to hold their hands, even kiss some of 'em. That's how I knew. That's why I came to your bed, so you would love only me and not them."

Lance almost gagged with disgust, and couldn't decide if he should feel pity or just laugh. "Love you?"

Richard nodded solemnly, his face looking almost desperate with longing. "Of course, didn't you know? I've been in love with you from the start."

In the adjoining room, Ryan blew out a breath of disgust. "I'm getting him outta there."

Again, without taking his eyes from his son, Arthur once more stayed his friend's move to the door. "Not yet."

In the interrogation room, Lance stared aghast at Richard, truly seeing this man for the first time and realizing how pathetic he was.

"You're a sick little man, Richard. I know for sure I can forgive you, 'cause you're not worth my time or energy to hate."

Richard grinned. "So, Lance, you and your little boyfriend screwing yet?"

Lance flinched, but didn't respond.

"Cause I can tell you from personal experience that boy has a great ass."

A momentary rage swept over Lance. He hauled off and slugged Richard hard to the face, knocking the grinning man to the floor in a heap of flailing orange.

Ricky blushed furiously with embarrassment, Jenny gasped, and Ryan pulled open the door to enter the hall. "That's enough."

Arthur grabbed him again and forced their eyes to meet. "Trust me, James. Let him finish."

Ryan reluctantly left the door open and turned back to the glass as Thornton used the table to haul himself to his feet.

Lance stood calmly as Richard rose, blood trickling from a cut to his mouth, no longer grinning, but looking surprised.

"Don't ever talk about Ricky," Lance hissed, his voice steady, his anger under control. "You're not worthy to say his name."

Richard lifted his hands and wiped the blood from his lips, gazing at his red-stained fingertips in wonder, as though he couldn't believe this was happening.

"You don't know who's after me, Richard. You just brought me here to try and scare me."

"No, I want you to love me, Lance, the way I always loved you!"

Lance shook his head in amazement at this sick, twisted little man who had for so long been his childhood boogeyman. "I'm leaving now, and I'll never think of you again." He stepped toward the closed door and reached for the knob.

"You should thank me, Lance."

Lance whirled around, not in fury, but in astonishment. "*Thank* you?"

Richard's coy smile crept back onto his face. "If it wasn't for me, you wouldn't be who you are today. I did you a favor."

Lance gaped at the man a long moment. "Good-bye, Richard." As he stepped out into the hall, Lance heard, "Will you write to me, Lance?" And then he closed the door forever on the man, on his past, on his greatest childhood fear.

And I thought I could turn into that.

Arthur stood before him in the hall, the others spilling out of the adjacent room behind him. "It's over now, isn't it, son?"

Lance smiled, his heart and soul free. "Yeah, Dad, it's over."

Arthur's arms enfolded him, and Lance felt more secure than ever.

Arthur released him, and Ricky took his place, his face etched with shame. Lance pulled him in.

"Lance," Ricky began falteringly, "about what he said, about me—"

Lance's lips on his cut off the rest of Ricky's words, and the kiss was thrilling and liberating, desperate with love, in a way none of their previous ones had ever been. Lance pulled back, oblivious to the group of people surrounding him. He had eyes only for Ricky.

"He's nothing, Ricky," Lance whispered breathlessly, his heart hammering from that brief touch of their lips. "You're everything."

Ricky's body seemed to sag with relief.

Lance threw his arms around the boy he loved, pulling him in tightly and hanging on.

After a moment, he felt Ryan's gentle hand on his shoulder. "C'mon, godson, let's get outta here."

Lance pulled back from Ricky. "Yeah, let's go home."

By order of the Secret Service, each driver took a different route, so as to not draw attention to a group of cars convoying through the city. Lance and Ricky were in one car with two agents, while the others were spread out in several identical vehicles.

At an intersection in Downtown L.A., just as Lance's driver was about to start forward on a green light, another car whipped around on their right to pull out in front, causing Lance's driver to hit the brakes. At that moment, an enormous city trash truck blew through the opposite red light, slammed into the car that had cut off theirs, and sent it spinning into oncoming traffic. It was struck by several others cars, and the trash truck passed right through the intersection to continue on out of sight.

Stunned into shocked silence, Lance and Ricky stared open – mouthed at each other. Lance clearly recalled the first threat he'd gotten, the one that had mentioned a trash truck.

"My God, Ricky," Lance whispered. "That driver just saved our lives!"

Speechless, Ricky could only nod as the second Secret Service agent calmly used his phone to call 911. Then he called his superiors to report the incident as the driver navigated their car through the chaos of the intersection and continued on their way. Lance and Ricky sat in stunned silence for the rest of the journey.

How had their stalker even known where they'd be? The meeting with Richard had been top secret—even the media hadn't been informed. The Secret Service, Lance knew, now regularly swept New Camelot for bugs, so it couldn't be that. Which meant, Lance concluded, something even more sinister. Someone within the Round Table must be a spy. There was a real enemy among them. The thought nearly took his breath away, but he didn't articulate this realization to Ricky, because he didn't want the agents to hear. He needed to talk with Arthur first. But the thought of a fellow knight betraying them filled him with dread almost worse than Richard ever had.

CHAPTER ELEVEN

WE'RE TIRED OF WAITING

ONCE EVERYONE WAS BACK SAFELY within the guarded walls of New Camelot, the two agents who'd accompanied Lance and Ricky informed Ryan, Gibson, and Arthur about the trash truck incident. They all understood at once that it wasn't accidental, and had it not been for the other driver who was in such a hurry, both Lance and Ricky could be dead, or in the critical condition that careless driver was now.

When they were all gathered in the Throne Room, after the agents had left to send a report to their superiors, Lance told everyone his suspicions.

"A spy?" Ricky said, aghast. "No way."

"It's the only answer," Lance said, his voice breathy and anxious.

Reyna exchanged an appalled look with Esteban, but Arthur stroked his beard thoughtfully as he strode up the platform steps and settled into his throne. Jenny followed silently to sit beside him. Arthur looked out at Lance standing before him, Ricky at his side, Kai and Dakota, as always, flanking them.

"I believe Lance is correct," he finally said, his usually sonorous voice quiet and soft. "We did inform everyone at the gathering on Saturday of Lance's meeting with Richard."

Reyna piped up, her face alight with a revelation. "Yeah, but Lance only found out yesterday that the meeting was today."

"That's true," Ryan added, "because that's when I found out."

Arthur looked to his sons and the others. "How many knights would you estimate remained behind after school yesterday to work on the computers?"

Lance cast his mind back to when Ryan entered the Computer Lab to tell him about today's meeting with Richard. "Maybe fifty?" He glanced at Ricky for confirmation, and the other boy nodded.

Arthur soberly eyed Jenny. Her hand reached out and took his, and she offered a small smile of encouragement.

"Fifty," the king said with a sigh. "I don't suppose we know which fifty?"

"Techie might," Esteban suggested. "He might be able to figure it out from who logged in."

"Ask him, if you would, Sir Este. And tell him I wish a new system instituted within the lab. Everyone entering and leaving must sign in and out. Let him know the Secret Service demands such a record. Perhaps we shall note a pattern of behavior that will narrow down our suspects."

"You got it, Arthur," Esteban said with a nod.

"Sir Dakota and Sir Kai," Arthur said, his voice in command mode, "continue your vigilant watch over Lance and Ricky. Be cautious with whom they interact."

"Yes, Arthur," both young men answered at once, no longer embarrassed that they spoke at the same time.

"Henceforth," Arthur went on, "only those in our immediate leadership team shall be privy to our plans and information. At the gatherings, we shall only disseminate that which pertains to city projects and the general role of everyone in selling the CBOR. Is that acceptable to you all?"

Everyone solemnly agreed. It would feel strange, Lance knew, to keep secrets from his fellow knights, but their numbers were now so large, and so many came and went daily and weekly, that the traitor could be almost anyone.

And thus impossible to find.

Merlin, Lance thought. Yes, he'd ask the old wizard for advice. Perhaps Merlin had "seen" something that could help.

After Arthur adjourned the meeting, he asked Lance to remain a moment. Lance told Ricky, Kai and Dakota to wait for him in the lobby, and everyone left the Throne Room.

Lance looked expectant as Arthur rose from his throne and stepped down off the stage, Jenny by his side. The king eyed him with deep admiration and love.

"You handled today better than I ever could have, son, were I in your place."

Lance felt himself redden. Would he ever be able to accept praise from this man without feeling embarrassed?

"Thanks, Dad." Then he turned to Jenny apologetically. "I'm sorry, Mom, for hitting him. I know how you feel—"

Her hands on his shoulders cut him off. "You hit him less times than I would've," she said with a grin, drawing a huge smile to his face. Then she pulled him in and held him. "I love you, Lance."

Lance suddenly felt choked up, and his voice struggled with emotion. "I love you, too, Mom."

She released him and both adults gazed at him in wonder. He was easily five inches taller than Jenny now and could almost look Arthur in the eye. He squirmed under their scrutiny.

"I shall forever thank God for leading me to you," Arthur said quietly, his voice raw with emotion. "You have made my life extraordinary."

Lance grinned so broadly that both adults laughed. He leaned in and hugged them, the three holding on to each other with deep and steadfast love.

Once back in the lobby, Lance waved for the others to follow and then headed straight for the main library. On the way, he told them what the adults had wanted, and Ricky gaped.

"Mom actually said that?" he asked, astonished.

Lance nodded.

They found Merlin lounging in his favorite stuffed chair wearing an actual New Camelot tunic and standard leather pants, instead of his usual heavy metal attire. He had a large volume in hand and ear buds jammed into both ears listening, no doubt, to some hideous metal band. The small, thin man looked up as they entered, his pale gray eyes alight with pleasure.

"Ah, the Native Knights, I presume," he said with a grin and a slight bow of his head.

"Hi, Merlin," Lance said with a smile as he waved his arms at the oh-so-ordinary clothing. "What's up? Ran out of metal bands to wear?"

Merlin did not remove either bud from his ears. "I wearied of that genre, Your Majesty. Alas, it all sounds the same."

Lance's face dropped in shock, and he looked at Ricky. They both cracked up, though Kai and Dakota clearly had no idea why. Lance turned back to Merlin astonished. "It took you *this* long to figure that out?"

Merlin smiled and shrugged.

"I'll probably be sorry I asked, but what are you into these days?" Lance tapped his ear to indicate he meant the music.

"Country and Western," Merlin answered with a smile of delight.

Lance's mouth dropped open again. "Oh, that is so wrong."

Ricky laughed, and Lance found himself joining in. There was just no figuring Merlin, so why bother trying?

Merlin's eyes seemed to twinkle as he observed the two laughing boys. "I trust Your Majesty and Sir Ricky are recovered from your near catastrophe this afternoon?"

All four boys exchanged a look.

Seeing their obvious confusion, Merlin smiled enigmatically. "My gift, remember?"

Lance nodded.

"Now, Your Majesty, how may I be of service?"

"You could just call me Lance instead of Your Majesty, Merlin. I'm not the king."

"As you command, Sir Lance."

Lance exchanged another look with Ricky, a 'See, what did I tell you?' look that Ricky clearly understood. Rather than pursue it, Lance explained his suspicions about a spy being in their midst, and the almost impossible task before them of trying to figure out who it could be.

Merlin considered a moment. "It would seem your meeting with the man of your nightmares proved fruitful after all."

Lance frowned. "Yeah, well, now I know he doesn't scare me anymore. But what does that have to do with the spy?"

"Had Richard not requested to see you, the incident that occurred on your route home would not have transpired. Thus, you would still be in the dark, so to speak, about your hidden enemy."

Lance's face lit up with understanding. "You're right, Merlin. But now how do we find him?"

Merlin paused a moment, and then held up the volume in his hands. It was *The Complete Sherlock Holmes*. "I've found this detective, Mr. Holmes, quite fascinating, Sir Lance. Have you ever read any of his stories?"

"Yeah, when I's a kid hangin' out at the library. But he's not real, Merlin."

Merlin's thin mouth curled with amusement. "Of course, he isn't, but his methods of deduction are quite ingenious. For example, consider this remark right here. 'Once you eliminate the impossible, whatever remains, no matter how improbable, must be the truth'."

Lance exchanged looks with the others. The blank expressions on their faces told them they didn't get it either. "So. What does that mean?"

Merlin tilted his head slightly and fixed his gaze on Lance alone. "Eliminate everyone who is impossible and thus, whoever remains, however improbable he or she may seem, must be the one."

Lance eyed him discerningly, considering his words. "I suppose that makes sense," he admitted thoughtfully. "But that means going through a *lot* of impossibles first."

Merlin's eyes seemed to dance beneath the glittery chandelier lights overhead.

"Ah, but consider, Sir Lance, that these attacks began some time back and were once attributed to your friend Michael, if you recall."

Lance's eyes widened with sudden realization. "Crap, Ricky, he's right!" he blurted, and then clapped a hand over his mouth. "Sorry, Merlin. Didn't mean to cuss."

"No offense taken."

Ricky was looking at Lance intently, as were Kai and Dakota. Lance rubbed his fingers over his chin as Arthur often did when contemplating a dilemma. "That means the newer knights who joined after those early attacks on me *could* be considered 'impossibles'."

"My thoughts, precisely, Your Ma—Sir Lance," Merlin said, correcting himself.

Lance smiled. "Thanks, Merlin. As always, you rock."

"Except your taste in music," Ricky threw out, with a grimace of distaste.

He and Lance chuckled as Merlin returned to his reading. As the four boys left the library, Lance realized that once again Merlin could hear their every word without removing an ear bud, for which he was grateful since he disliked country music even *more* than heavy metal.

The Native Knights headed for the Computer Lab to consult with Techie. As always, they found the young man seated at his workstation as though it were his throne, with Ariel propped into another chair leaning up against him, her head on his shoulder as his fingers flew almost magically over the keys like he was a concert pianist.

The Vietnamese knight didn't even glance up from his screen as Lance and the others approached. "Hey, guys, another close one today, huh?"

That surprised Lance and he stopped up short, his suspicions instantly flying into overdrive. "How did you know about that?" He tried for calm, but his voice came out tight and guarded.

The tone was not lost on Techie, who stopped typing and looked up at Lance, his eyes wide with uncertainty. "Reyna told me."

Lance spotted Reyna and Esteban seated several stations down, eyeing him curiously.

Damn, Lance thought angrily, now I'm suspecting Techie? Is this what that guy is turning me into?

He looked abashed at the computer whiz. "Sorry, Techie. I'm a little spooked." Then he acknowledged Ariel with a half-smile. "Hi, Ariel."

"Lance," she said, but her look was directed at Ricky. "Hi, Ricky."

Ricky lowered his eyes. "Hey, Ariel."

Lance shifted with uncharacteristic discomfort. "Um, Ariel, we need to talk to Techie. Alone."

Her smile faltered, and she looked embarrassed. "Oh. Okay." She kissed Techie on the cheek and then rose to move past Reyna and Esteban to a station at the end of the row.

Lance watched her go, feeling like crap for his paranoia and hating anew what he was becoming because of this stalker. Reyna met his eyes and he gestured for them to join him.

Techie eyed Lance with annoyance.

Lance shook off his shame. No time for that. "Everybody gather round," he told the group, and all rolled chairs over and clustered around Techie. Only Lance remained standing.

He filled them in on his conversation with Merlin, while Techie sulked in an uncharacteristic way. "I'm sorry, Techie, I'm sure Ariel and Bridget are fine, but we promised Dad no one outside the leadership team would know anything, except what we make public."

"It's true, Techie," Reyna chimed in. "I heard him."

Techie nodded, but was clearly unhappy with the arrangement. "So what do you need me to do?"

"Can you keep track of any knights who use these computers and go on the Internet?"

Techie considered a moment. "I guess I could use programs like the big companies have to monitor their employees' use of email and Internet."

Lance leaned in closer, his voice hushed and cautious. "Can you focus on knights who joined right when Michael did?"

"I'd have to filter names through the program, but Lance, there are so many kids, I don't even know 'em all or when they joined."

"But you can try, right?"

Techie suddenly looked exhausted and world-weary, older than his eighteen years, as though, like Lance, he felt the weight of the world on his shoulders. Shoving his sliding glasses back up the bridge of his nose, he sighed. "Yeah, I'll do what I can."

Lance smiled gratefully and then disbanded the meeting with the order to all of them to "Keep your eyes and ears open for any suspicious behavior from anyone."

"Even you?" Reyna replied with a grin, arms folded across her chest.

Ricky laughed. "Especially this fool."

That seemed to evaporate the tension and everyone went to work on the CBOR.

As Lance and Ricky started toward their stations, Techie said, "Lance, can I talk to you a minute?"

Lance turned to Ricky in surprise, but the other boy smiled, patted him on the shoulder, and moved a few seats down to sit at his computer.

Lance took a seat beside Techie and gazed long and hard at this young Asian who was the lifeblood of New Camelot. Had he ever told the boy how grateful he was?

"What is it, Techie?" He dreaded the answer.

Techie lowered his eyes shamefully. "You know how I put off college, Lance, to help you with the CBOR, and 'cause I wanted to travel the country with you?"

Lance nodded. They'd talked about this last summer after Techie graduated. "I know, and I love you for it, Techie," he gushed. "I don't know what I'd do without you. You're amazing."

Techie smiled shyly. He paused a moment, as though afraid to continue. "I'm, uh, well, I'm enrolling in UC Santa Barbara for next spring, Lance," he blurted before he could chicken out. "I want to be close to Ariel and I want to major in computer science."

Lance felt the weight of advancing time press down on his thumping heart and fearful soul. They were *all* growing up, not just him. And they wanted lives of their own. He didn't trust himself to speak for a moment. "I understand. You gotta do what's best for you."

"I have a replacement in mind, though," Techie offered with a half-smile.

Lance eyed him in surprise, and then realized he shouldn't have. With Techie nothing was unplanned. "Who?"

Techie pointed down the row of computers to a small, skinny Caucasian kid with jet-black hair, short and curly, wearing a pale blue tunic, wire-rimmed glasses and hunched over his keyboard. Lance struggled for the boy's name, but it frustratingly eluded him. The boy was a regular, he knew, now that he took the time to look.

So why don't I know his name?

He knew he couldn't ever let himself get so busy that he neglected the needs of his knights.

Sir Phillip! That's his name!

"Sir Phillip is as techie as you?" Lance asked, relieved that he didn't have to ask the boy's name.

"Just about. And he's only fifteen, so he has at least a couple more years of high school to go."

Lance watched the younger boy type.

Small for his age, he noted, *like I used to be.*

"What's his story?"

Techie frowned. "He got caught up in some Aryan brotherhood group out in Lancaster and wanted to get out."

"How come his parents didn't just move away?"

Techie looked disgusted. "They were the ones who got him into the group in the first place."

Now Lance recalled the boy joining them the previous summer when they'd passed through Lancaster checking out the neighborhoods. Phillip had begged Arthur for the opportunity to join, and rode back with one of the Secret Service guys. Ryan had checked out the kid's story and found out it was legit. When he'd sent officers to the boy's home in Lancaster, it had been empty, cleaned out. Everyone had split in a hurry and took their racism elsewhere.

As an interesting twist of fate, since Justin and Gibson spent most of their time at New Camelot, Gibson's ex—and soon to be current—wife, Sandra, had agreed to foster Phillip, despite the swastika his parents had tattooed onto his shoulder. It seemed to be working out well for everyone. Phillip went to school near Sandra's house, and then hopped a bus for New Camelot, where Techie had discovered his skills and taken him under his wing.

Lance smiled at Techie warmly. "No one could ever replace you, Techie, but thanks for training him."

"No prob. I figure we can leave him in charge of the lab when we travel."

"Great idea." Then he looked past Techie and saw Ariel watching them closely, clearly wondering what was going on. "I think Ariel is getting impatient. Can you start gathering your data as soon as possible. Just don't tell her you're doing it."

Techie looked appalled. "You mean I need to watch her, too?"

Lance blanched. That wasn't exactly what he meant, but… "Well, I meant don't tell her about any of it, but, well…." He paused with embarrassment, and then quickly shook it off.

I have to lead, and that means making the hard choices.

"Techie, she was there that night… the night someone tried to poison me."

Techie looked horrified, and anger flashed across his narrowed brown eyes. "You don't think Ariel—"

Lance put a hand on his arm. "No, I don't. But someone could use her to get information on us and she's so sweet, she wouldn't know it. We just have to cover all the bases. Okay?"

Techie visibly relaxed. "Okay."

Lance flashed his most disarming smile. "Thanks, man." Then he rose and moved down the stations to sit beside Ricky. The other boy looked over questioningly, but Lance just reached for his hand, which Ricky gladly offered up. They sat in silence, Ricky waiting for Lance to speak, and Lance contemplating the realities of getting older, and not being able to trust your friends anymore.

In the days and weeks that followed, Lance found himself eyeing every knight differently, whether at gatherings, in the Training Centre, classrooms, or the Computer Lab.

Could he or she be the one was his most frequent thought, and he hated himself each time it passed through his mind. *I'm becoming paranoid*, he realized, and had to fight the urge to question everyone before those urges destroyed him.

He'd even asked Techie a few days after requesting computer monitoring of his brothers and sisters if the tech genius could get access to everyone's phone records. Techie nearly gasped aloud in dismay.

"You want us to turn into the government now?"

That's when it hit Lance like a slap to the face.

My God, is that what I've become?

"You're right, Techie, forget I said that." He tried for a small smile. "Can't let the bastard get to me, right?"

Techie nodded solemnly, but Lance knew the young man was troubled by him even considering such an invasion of privacy.

Lance had walked away determined not to do this anymore, not to be so suspicious of everyone and everything.

I'm doing this for Ricky, he told himself, *to keep him safe.*

But how safe would either of them be if they trusted no one, and had no friends or family watching their backs because he had alienated them all with his paranoid snooping?

And then he realized he was going against his own bill of rights! Most of the knights "under surveillance" were also under eighteen years old. Wasn't he acting just like the grown-up world, just like the government? Kids are dangerous! Kids are property! Kids should have no rights because they can't be trusted! He sadly understood during those ensuing weeks that he'd fallen into the same mistrustful trap. Due to the actions of one, he'd condemned the many. Exactly what the adult world had done throughout the country with its "anti-kid" laws.

No, I can't become them! If I do, then everything I've fought so hard for is meaningless. There are just some risks we have to live with for the good of friendship and trust.

Having made this decision, he continued to consult with Techie on a daily basis, as did Arthur, for any suspicious computer activity, but steadfastly refused to expand the surveillance any further. Especially after his Internet snooping uncovered some of the knights trolling "adult" sites, including Dakota and Kai. Recalling the relationship questions that his Native brothers had asked of him and Ricky, Lance suspected they were looking for information, and maybe visuals. There was a filter on the system that supposedly blocked such sites, but Lance knew from his time at Mark Twain that such filters were never one hundred percent effective. In order to not embarrass the boys, Lance asked Techie to delete those sites from the list he'd show Arthur and Techie readily agreed.

Ultimately, nothing anomalous turned up from the daily computer logs, and his stalker didn't bother texting Lance to gloat over the trash truck incident.

The date to begin their Once Upon A Time in America Tour was fast approaching. The plan was to leave in early June right after Lance and Ricky earned their diplomas with the rest of New Camelot's first graduating class. The boys were anxious to get on the road, but it made sense to get high school out of the way, so they could focus on securing the support of states they really needed. And they had to be part of that first graduation, since they were figureheads for the entire crusade. Jenny was planning the graduation, while Reyna and Esteban plotted out the road trip, and the excitement for both events began to build throughout that spring.

There was also the matter of the Mark Twain Prom in May. Kai and Dakota refused to allow Lance and Ricky to attend such a big event without their protective presence, so when the president of the MTS Student Council Facebook-messaged Lance the prom time and location, he messaged her back and asked if his two friends could also attend.

"Yes," he'd said in response to her query, "they would attend as a couple."

The girl expressed great excitement that another "boy couple" would be there, which should've raised a red flag in his mind, but he just laughed and thanked her. Would society ever stop making such a big deal over two boys in love? He promised Jack he'd do his best to make it so, and hoped this prom would be another positive step in that direction.

Lance also made it a point to spend more time with Chris. He felt that he was neglecting his little brother. Sure, Sylvia had been great with him. When she wasn't shadowing Reyna to glean every one of her planning skills, Sylvia spent much of her time helping Chris with homework or teaching him new tricks with the bow and arrow.

She was now fourteen and a high school freshman, Lance knew, and had become a beautiful teenage girl with silky black hair, those big doe eyes he used to see on baby animal drawings, and an ingratiating smile.

Like Chris and the rest of us, Lance sighed inwardly, *she's growing up too fast. Probably have a boyfriend soon, if she doesn't already.*

He suddenly felt older than his seventeen years, and wistful. That was the problem with too much knowledge at too young an age. Life had nothing new to offer, so kids became jaded and indifferent. Along with the paranoia, he determined that *would not* happen to him. He simply wouldn't let it.

March flew quickly past for everyone, with no new attacks or threats of any kind. Unfortunately, Techie's surveillance of the Computer Lab continued to turn up nothing. Bridget and Ariel came over whenever they didn't have college classes, which for Ariel was weekends only, since she lived out in Santa Barbara and had a good two-hour drive each time she visited. Once in a while, she'd take Techie out to the school for a weekend so he could hang out with her college friends and get a feel for the campus. Every time he returned, Lance saw the desire written all over his happy face to be part of that life on a permanent basis.

Dakota continued to sleep in Lance's room and Kai in Ricky's, with Secret Service agents outside each door throughout the night. Lance knew the Indians wanted more "alone time," but there wasn't much he could do about the situation.

Ryan continued to keep the president informed, and the commander-in-chief had also spoken personally with Lance on several occasions, assuring him these protections were necessary and "That was that."

Edwin and Senator Cairns Skyped regularly with Lance and Ricky. The two always looked happy to speak with the boys. However, as much as the senator pushed, and as much as some of the freshmen representatives tried to keep the CBOR alive in the House, not much was happening. Edwin encouraged the boys not to give up. "Keep hitting up the kids some more. Get them to tighten the thumb screws."

As April approached with no end to the deadlock in Congress over the CBOR, Lance contacted both the Senate Majority Leader and the Speaker of the House and put them up on the large Throne Room flat-screen simultaneously. Both men lamely—in Lance's estimation—threw up their hands and said they just couldn't get enough elected officials to take the CBOR seriously.

Lance and Ricky stood side-by-side, Kai and Dakota flanking them. Lance had his arms folded across his chest.

"So even though your kids and everyone else's kids want this to happen, you're just gonna sit on your hands and claim you can't do anything?"

Both men affected looks of offense, but Lance saw it was yet another case of bad acting. He was getting sick of these two.

"You guys have no idea, do you," Lance went on, his tone sinking into cold callousness, "what the kids of this country can do to screw you over, and you don't know because you think we're powerless pieces of property. Think again. We're going to make the United States the laughingstock of the world, and there's nothing you can do to stop us. We're tired of waiting. Good-bye, gentlemen."

He used the remote to cut the signal, and the two astonished faces vanished into cyberspace. Lance eyed Ricky, and the other boy grinned.

"We're gonna do it, aren't we?"

"We have no choice." Then Lance turned to Kai and Dakota. "All the tribes on board, too?"

They nodded. The four of them left the Throne Room and retreated to the Computer Lab to unleash the children of the country *against* the country. Lance knew all of them would relish the opportunity to stick it to the government and the so-called elected representatives who spent all of their time fighting, instead of dealing with important issues, like the humanity of their own children.

Both the Speaker and Majority Leader called back, insisting they were doing their best and wanting to know what Lance was up to, but Lance only said, "You'll see." Then he hung up on them again.

They'd had their chance. He knew, of course, that no one in Washington, or in any of the state governments, for that matter, would realize what the children had done to the country until August, but somehow that made it all the sweeter. He'd see those smug looks vanish from every elected official who disdained them and their efforts. He'd have the last laugh.

April passed with Lance furiously messaging back and forth with his representatives in public schools across the nation, letting them know to put their previously arranged plan into effect. Kids in every state were more than happy to comply—gleefully so.

Also, in preparation for their U.S. tour in June, Lance and Ricky chatted often with Father Mike and Pastor Tom about what to expect from the more evangelical Christian states they'd pass through. They wanted to be prepared with counter arguments to whatever those people might say. Alas, both men of the cloth held little hope that even though Lance was The Boy Who Came Back and had inspired Christians throughout the world, the fact that he'd publicly acknowledged his love for Ricky would likely trump his return from the dead. Being gay in many states and communities was probably worse than being a murderer, and the boys had better be prepared for reactions ranging from indifference to outright hostility.

Sadly, the boys weren't surprised, and Lance ran a few of his thoughts by both men. They agreed his ideas were logical and sound, but reminded them that hate and intolerance were not logical.

For Mother's Day, Lance, Ricky, Kai, Dakota, and Chris rose early and descended to the kitchen. Being a Sunday morning, the kitchen staff didn't arrive until later, when a kind of brunch was usually offered to whomever wished to partake. Amid laughs and clanging of pots and pans and skillets, the boys managed to create something resembling food. There were eggs, supposedly scrambled, but some looking rather black and burnt.

They'd also attempted blueberry pancakes, since it was one of Jenny's favorites, but none of the pancakes came out round. Mathematically inclined Chris decided they would look better as parallelograms, and cut them so. The end results looked diseased more than anything else, but smelled good, so the boys high-fived with satisfaction. They put everything onto a tray along with some juice and a card Kai had created, and headed up to Arthur and Jenny's room to surprise her.

They stopped outside the door to their parents' bedroom and listened carefully for any sounds inside, giggling like little boys, even though only one of them was.

Lance smirked at the older ones. "Don't want to interrupt anything," he said and that set off another round of giggles, even from Chris, who must've figured out what the older boys found so amusing. Lance took a moment to look aghast at him.

Chris gave him that knowing, all-too-adult expression. "I'm almost ten, Lance," he said as though that explained everything.

Lance shook his head and had to force the wistful sadness back down into his heart. No emo today, he decided, and they knocked on the door.

The door opened and Arthur's smiling, bearded face greeted them. He'd been forewarned, and happily pulled the door back with a grin, revealing the five boys to Jenny, who lounged on the king-sized bed wearing a nightgown and robe, her blonde hair loose about her shoulders. Her face lit up with joy at seeing the smiling, grinning boys sweep past Arthur into the room. Lance held the bed tray in his hands, the other boys surrounding him. Chris bounded forward and threw himself onto the bed to engulf Jenny in a bone-crushing hug.

"Happy Mother's Day, Mom!" he gushed as he squeezed her neck.

Lance and the others stopped before the bed, grinning broadly. "Happy Mother's Day, Mom," he and Ricky said at the same moment, drawing a delighted laugh from her.

Arthur stepped up behind the boys and grinned.

Chris scooted over next to her as Lance set the tray down before Jenny and she quizzically eyed the unusual breakfast.

"Blueberry pancakes, Mom," Lance told her proudly. "Your favorite."

"And I made 'em into parallelograms, 'cause that's cooler," Chris added with a huge grin of pride.

Jenny looked them all over, her heart in her throat with emotion. She'd gone from a teacher who'd lost her way to a mother who'd found it, all because of these remarkable boys and the man she'd married.

Lance and Ricky saw her beginning to tear up and each reached out a hand to take one of hers, clutching it like a lifeline they never wanted to let go of.

"Don't cry, Mom," Lance said softly. "We love you, that's all."

"Even if we can't cook," Ricky added with a smile.

That broke the emotion clogging Jenny's throat and she laughed, reaching out to pull both into a hug, while Chris pressed himself against her joyfully. When the boys had stepped back, Jenny eyed Kai and Dakota with a warm smile. The two Indians shyly gazed at her.

"I don't get a hug from my other sons?"

They smiled and leaned in to hug her together, and she held them close for a moment.

Arthur used Jenny's camera to take pictures. She'd taught him how to use it and he looked proud to have finally mastered some 21st Century technology.

The boys, and Arthur, sat around on the bed and chatted with Jenny and each other while she ate the food they'd so lovingly and ineptly prepared. Never once did she indicate it wasn't the best meal she'd ever eaten. In truth, it *was* the best meal she'd ever eaten because of who'd made it for her.

That joyful and relaxed breakfast was a moment she would never forget.

With the MTS prom looming, Lance, Ricky, Kai, and Dakota needed tuxedos. Under heavy guard, Arthur and Jenny accompanied the boys as they visited several tuxedo rental shops. Since Arthur knew little of such matters, he deferred to Jenny's expertise. She'd had enough experience with high school proms during her years at MTS to know good quality tuxedoes when she saw them.

Of course, the boys were instantly recognized in every store they entered, and the manager of each insisted on helping them personally. It was an honor, they told Lance, to have the boys consider their business, and offered to merely charge a cleaning fee in exchange for the publicity they would garner from having the most famous boys in the world rent from them.

After settling on one such establishment that had a wide selection, Jenny set about shopping. None of the four boys knew a thing about fashion, and all hated shopping for clothes. So they let her fly from this style to that one, standing each boy up against this brand or that one until finally everyone agreed on what to select.

Lance and Ricky favored white over black and a long coat over the standard, while Kai and Dakota chose black and the standard jacket length. Lance and Ricky ended up in white outfits with an old-world feel to the long jackets that trailed past their pants pockets, and the open, no-button style. Lance chose green for his tie and vest and Ricky red, the usual colors they wore on their tunics.

Dakota and Kai decided on black tuxes, with Dakota sporting a dark blue vest, tie, and handkerchief for the front jacket pocket and Kai selecting sky blue for his accoutrements. The boys laughingly decided each color reflected the individual's personality.

Ricky gave Lance a shove. "In that case, your emo ass should have black everything. Ha!"

Lance shoved him back. "Fool."

The boys were measured and fitted out with shoes, and suddenly everything was arranged. Again, in the interest of the prestige the store would garner, the manager promised to personally deliver the tuxes to New Camelot the day before prom, and make certain the fit was perfect.

Arthur, Jenny and the boys thanked the man and left to return home. Though the adults didn't say it, both felt melancholy at this moment, knowing that Lance and Ricky, who not so long ago had been fourteen, were suddenly going to prom and about to graduate high school. The time went too fast, they silently told each other with a look. There was still Chris, but neither spoke it aloud, for they both knew that considering the younger boy's future would only engender a deeper sadness. And they didn't have the courage to think about that.

The prom was to be held at Santa Anita Race Track in Arcadia and, at least online, the venue looked appealing with lots of areas to roam and talk and eat dinner. The four boys nervously discussed how they might be received by the other prom-goers. Sure, the Student Council president was "thrilled" they were coming, but Lance was savvy enough to know it would, as with the tuxedo shop, grant MTS a lot of positive buzz by having the most famous boys in the world attend their prom.

When he thought about it in that light, Lance would instantly regret his decision to attend. His emo side would erupt with fears and uncertainties. But then Ricky would take his hand and whisper words of comfort and love.

"We're seniors, Lance," he kept saying in the days leading up to the event. "And this is our senior prom. And I wanna share that moment with you, the boy I love. If anybody there has a problem with us, screw 'em."

Lance would always laugh, they would kiss long and deeply, and then Lance would be fine until the next wave of jitters overcame him.

Ricky also assured him that there would be Secret Service agents hovering about and their presence would likely "Scare the crap out of any jerkbags that mess with us. Especially with Brooks there."

Lance laughed, and loved Ricky all the more for his rock-solid strength and unflagging optimism.

Finally, the day arrived. The tuxedo store manager had been as good as his word, and delivered the tuxes the day before. Jenny and Reyna both insisted the boys try them on, but Lance and Ricky were not to see each other so attired until the next evening, and neither could Kai and Dakota. So each boy changed in his own room, and then Jenny, Reyna, and the manager inspected each in turn, proclaiming them "perfect."

On prom night, Jenny insisted on Ricky and Kai dressing first and waiting in the lobby at the base of the main staircase. She wanted pictures of their reactions, and those of Lance and Dakota as the other two descended to join their dates. She wanted to photograph every second of this seminal event, and Arthur continually laughed at her nervous hovering as they awaited the boys in the lobby. They were joined by an equally excited Reyna, Esteban, Chris, and Ryan who, as usual, shuffled his feet nervously, like he always did when anything emotional was pending.

As Ricky and Kai appeared at the top of the stairs, they grinned at each other in wonder. Ricky wore the gold circlet around his thick, flowing hair that now dropped to his waist. The white, Old London-style jacket and matching pleated pants, capped with the bright red vest and tie made him look, to Jenny's wide and love-filled yes, incredibly beautiful.

Kai had restrained his hair into a single long braid adorned with feathers, and he looked strikingly handsome with his black jacket and sky-blue accents.

The boys descended the stairs side by side to near constant clicking of Jenny's camera. Reyna engulfed each in turn in a hug, and then stood back to check them over with her always-appraising eye for detail.

"Not bad," she said with a wink that made Ricky laugh.

Then Jenny gasped, and everyone turned to look up toward the second floor. Lance and Dakota stood on the landing gazing down at them. When Reyna turned, her mouth fell open comically. Both she and Jenny would later agree that Lance had never looked more stunning, more beautiful, and more perfect than he did that night.

His luxurious, remarkable hair trailed around his shoulders and down past his buttocks, almost aglow with shimmering luster, held back from his face by the small crown circling his brow. The green jewels in that simple crown set off Lance's eyes, and while on some, such a headpiece might have looked ostentatious, on him it looked right and proper. His green vest and tie also complemented his eyes, which had locked onto Ricky and saw no one else.

Dakota looked almost as stunning with his own fantastic hair that seemed to have a life of its own restrained by a tribal headband and adorned with scattered feathers. The dark blue of the vest accented the nervous, tenuous look on his face. Like Lance, his eyes found only one person—Kai.

As he descended the stairs, Lance found his heart thumping wildly, almost as wildly as that first time he'd confessed his love for Ricky and they'd kissed in front of the whole world. He drank in every magnificent detail of the stunning boy who had captured his heart long before he'd even known it.

He stepped up to Ricky. "You look amazing." His voice trembled with emotion.

Ricky grinned, his brown eyes drinking in every inch of him. "And you look beautiful, Lance, the most beautiful boy in the world."

Lance laughed giddily. "No, the luckiest boy in the world."

"Damn straight."

Lance grinned. "Fool."

Kai and Dakota stood beside them, eyes locked on each other. Then Reyna planted herself before Lance and Ricky, her moist eyes wide with love, mixed with a kind of shock.

"My baby boys…" she began with a shake of her head, "aren't baby boys anymore."

That drew a laugh from everyone. Then she hugged both boys and kissed each on the cheek. Esteban shook their hands and winked.

"You both look every inch the sons of a king," Arthur said with a grin.

And then Chris grabbed them both in a hug of joy. The little one stood back and threw his hands to his hips. "You guys are gonna steal the show unless Lance gets all emo again."

Lance's face fell in shock, but Ricky dissolved into hysterics. He and Chris high-fived and the little boy grinned at Lance. "So have fun, Lance, or else."

His comically threatening tone amused everyone, and another round of laughs ensued. After Arthur had Brooks, the largest and most outgoing of the Secret Service agents, snap some pictures of the whole family, it was time to head out. There was another round of hugs and goodbyes, and then suddenly the boys were inside a limo surrounded by four agents heading off to Arcadia.

As the limo swung out into traffic, Lance lovingly held Ricky's hand and vowed to take Chris's advice to heart. He would dance the slow dances, eat the food, bask beneath the romantic lighting and just love the boy whose hand he held. 'No emo no more' would be his mantra. Especially tonight.

The Santa Anita Racetrack was located on Huntington Drive, behind the Westfield Santa Anita Mall. The four boys remained very self-conscious with the agents present just across from them in the limo, and did nothing but hold hands for the entire journey, engaging in idle chit chat about how Kai was the only one who could dance and which of the other three would embarrass himself most on the dance floor.

When the limo pulled up in front, it was just before eight o'clock. There were betting windows to their right and a table near the entrance at which stood several male and female security personnel. A short line of boys stood to one side of the table and girls to the other, and Lance watched in amazement as the security guards checked inside each kid's mouth, and then patted them down more invasively than anything he'd heard airport screeners accused of.

In a moment of blind panic he thought maybe the extra scrutiny was because of him, but the boy in front of him said it was standard at every prom these days. The boy obviously recognized Lance and Ricky, giving them the once over even though they weren't holding hands, and then turned silently back around to get frisked.

When it was their turn, the Secret Service agents stepped forward and flashed their IDs, indicating the four boys. "They've already been cleared."

Prom-goers milling about the entrance stopped to stare at the agents and the boys, every eye widening with recognition. The security guard examined the IDs and then glanced at the boys. His own eyes expanded as he obviously recognized Lance and Ricky. He waved them through.

Once past the checkpoint, there was a canopied walkway leading into the building where the boys and their four bodyguards waited with a small crowd for the elevator to take them up to the venue. The other students, male and female, were decked out in stunning clothes, with the girls sporting fantastically elaborate hairstyles. They looked nervously at the agents, but stared at Lance, in particular. He tried to smile but, as always when surrounded by peers rather than adults, he felt out of place. He was still The Boy Who Came Back, he knew, and he'd never gotten to know any of these kids when he attended MTS.

Finally, after ten excruciatingly long minutes, their turn came for the elevator. Despite his earlier confidence with Ricky, Lance feared even taking the boy's hand in his while they waited, dreading some backlash from the other waiting seniors. As the elevator stopped at the third floor, the agents stepped out first and scanned the area before waving the boys out. Straight ahead was the area for paid photographs, and to their right the main venue and dance floor.

There was a table set just outside of the elevator at which sat several MTS teachers, including Jenny's friend, Karla. The boys stepped forward and Karla broke into an enormous grin.

"Lance, you made it after all," she squealed with delight. "And you brought the handsome boyfriend, of course." She smiled again, all teeth and dimply cheeks.

Lance felt his face grow hot. "Uh, yeah. Hi, Karla. Mom says hi."

The other teachers frowned at Lance's use of Karla's first name, but she'd insisted he address her as such at the wedding.

"You tell your mom hello for me and let her know you boys were the most handsome ones here."

Lance laughed nervously, and so did Ricky.

Then Karla's eyes fell on Kai and Dakota. "Except for your cute friends, that is." She winked and took their prom bids, checking their names off a list and waving them on in. "Have fun, boys."

Feeling every eye on them, from the principal and the other teachers, to every kid standing around with his or her date, Lance momentarily regretted coming. But then he flashed back to his first day in juvenile hall when he'd asked Father Mike if there would come a day when everybody wouldn't stare at him. The priest had slipped into his impish grin and said, "As soon as they realize you can't walk on water."

So he determined to ignore the staring and concentrate on the boy beside him, the boy for whom he wanted this to be the most romantic night they'd ever shared. Since Jenny had insisted on pictures, Lance led the group over to the camera set-up first, figuring the line would increase as the night wore on. They selected a background that looked like an ornate, filigreed arch and struck several poses for the photographer. Fame did have its perks and Lance didn't have to establish that he and Ricky were a couple, and not just two friends posing together.

Kai and Dakota posed next. Their cultural reticence about public displays of affection exasperated the photographer and Lance had to step in and place Kai's hand into Dakota's so the pictures could be snapped. Afterwards, Lance gave the photographer the New Camelot address and asked that the photos be sent directly there and not to the school. The man happily agreed, shaking their hands with gusto and assuring them, "I'm all in favor of your bill of rights."

Lance and Ricky thanked him, and then led the other two around the corner into the main space. There were numerous alcoves with couches and wood-paneled walls, tables spread throughout the dining area, a separate buffet section set up near the kitchen to dispense the food, and a beautiful hardwood floor for dancing. At each end of the dance floor was an ornate staircase ascending upward and ending at glass double doors. The floor was burnished, the doorways arched and fancy, and the entire area lit by numerous chandeliers dangling overhead. It reminded the boys of New Camelot as they nervously looked for a table so they could sit.

Feeling too much on display with everyone stopping their conversations to gawk and stare, Lance pulled Ricky by the hand to the wide double doors leading outside. The racetrack sprawled out below them in all its glory, its empty circular path looking sad and forlorn in the fading sunlight. Thankfully there were many tables set up along the various levels where people normally sat to watch the races, and Lance quickly led Ricky and the others to one table set for four. The last thing he wanted was to be sitting at one of the big tables with kids he didn't even know.

The four sat at the rectangular table with a plain white tablecloth and vase of red carnations as adornment, and just took a moment to breathe. They all looked at each other in silence, and then burst out laughing.

"I guess we're more nervous than we thought," Lance offered with an uneasy exhalation.

Kai elbowed Dakota. "Not us warriors, right, Cloudy?"

Dakota just looked at him and grinned, reaching out to take the other's hand.

Kai sighed contentedly. "See?"

The four agents sat at the table next to theirs and scanned the area professionally.

When Lance announced that maybe they should go in and get food, two of the agents rose to accompany them, Brooks and a guy named Andrews. The other two remained behind to guard the area.

By now, the DJ was in full swing with music and colored lights, though no one was dancing yet. The boys passed a number of occupied tables and felt every eye follow them as they made their way to the buffet area. Splendidly attired kids held plates of food and checked out the delicacies on display.

The four boys got into the line. That's where the student council president found them. She practically screamed when she saw them from across the room, and came running in their direction. She was dressed in a royal blue strapless gown with what looked like a pearl necklace, and her hair was styled like a movie star at the Oscars. She stopped before them, breathless with excitement.

"Oh, Sir Lance and Sir Ricky, I'm *so* happy you guys made it tonight. And you both look fantastic!"

The boys reddened at the same time, and she laughed with delight. Lance indicated the others. "This is Sir Kai and Sir Dakota."

She squealed as she shook hands with them. "This is just so cool! Two gay couples at our prom. Isn't that progressive?"

Lance knew he must have looked stunned because he could feel the blood drain from his face, and Ricky anxiously squeezed his arm to calm him. Kai and Dakota lowered their eyes to the floor in embarrassment, but the girl seemed not to even understand what she'd done.

"You okay, Sir Lance?" she asked with obvious concern. "You look so pale."

Lance fought the immediate rise in temper, and he carefully controlled his breathing. He forced a smile. "It's Ana, right?"

The girl nodded.

"Well, Ana," Lance went on in a calm, steady voice that Ricky knew full well held back a rising tide of anger, "we thought you invited us to enjoy the prom, not to be poster boys for some agenda. We'll leave now."

Ricky sucked in a startled breath, and both Kai and Dakota raised their heads.

Ana's perfect makeup almost cracked when her expression dissolved into something resembling an astonished cat caught in the headlights of a car. "Oh, no, please don't go," she begged. "I didn't mean it that way. I just...."

Lance watched her squirm, knowing *she* knew that *he* knew that was *exactly* what she'd meant. "Ana, when you invited us, we were so excited 'cause otherwise we wouldn't have a prom, being home schooled and all. But, we didn't come here to be put on display any more than we already are."

Ana looked abashed. "I'm so sorry, you're right. I guess 'cause MTS is so backwards about stuff like gay kids, I just got carried away. Please don't leave. I want you guys to have fun. All of you."

Lance hesitated. "No surprises waiting for us, like pig's blood dropped on our heads while we dance or anything?"

Her mouth fell open in shock, but his nervous smile made her realize he was joking. "No wonder the whole world loves you, Lance." Then she startled everyone by kissing him on the lips before turning to scurry away to her friends.

His face must have been incredibly comical because even Ricky busted up instead of feeling jealous, as Lance would've expected.

"Well, that was random," said Ricky, chuckling as they arrived at the table.

"Beyond random," Lance confirmed, with a shake of his head.

The boys filled up their plates amid ogling looks from other kids, including one guy mad dogging them from the other side of the food table, a beefy guy with slick-backed hair and a haughty look in his squinting brown eyes. Lance thought he recalled the kid from freshman year. The guy always called him "Pretty Boy" in the most derisive tone possible. The guy's date stood beside him gathering up some of the veggies.

She was shorter than him, attractive, big fluffy yellow dress to go with her big fluffy hair.

The guy locked eyes with Lance. "Faggots," he said loudly enough for his girl and everyone around the food table to hear. All talking ceased instantly.

Lance's breath caught in his throat and his blood began to pound. Ricky quickly grabbed his arm as Lance started forward. But before anything could escalate further, the hulking, six-foot seven Agent Brooks, the coolest of the agents assigned to guard them, loomed behind the mad dogging boy. The onlookers rippled with surprise, but the boy remained oblivious. His disgust-filled eyes never left Lance's face, though Lance obviously noticed the enormous bodyguard. The boys had taken to calling the monstrous African-American The Rock, after the famous actor, due to his size and strength. He loved to spar with them in the Training Centre and, man, could he wield a broadsword!

Brooks tapped the kid on one shoulder. The boy whirled around and then lurched back at the sight of the huge man in the black suit towering over him and glaring fiercely.

Everybody laughed as the boy nearly landed on the food table in his haste to back up. Without so much as a smile, Brooks stuck a finger into the boy's chest.

"I just overheard you insult my boys, and that's not only rude, but disrespectful to this lovely young lady who sadly made the mistake of dating you. Be that as it may, you will refrain from using such profane language or I shall personally escort you from the premises. Are we clear?" His voice remained low, but gained in intensity until his face was right in front of the now-terrified boy's when he finished.

The boy's head bobbed up and down frantically. "Uh, yeah, I mean yes, sir, I mean, I got it," he stammered as his girlfriend and everyone around him laughed. Then he grabbed the girl's hand and they vanished into the dining area. Brooks looked across the table at Lance and winked.

Lance's momentary flare of anger dissipated, and he grinned back at the big man. After that, no one so much as looked sideways at them, especially with Brooks always hovering somewhere in the vicinity.

The four boys sat under the stars and ate and laughed, and each held the hand of his beloved, and the night was perfect. Until Kai suggested it was time to dance. Always awkward and self – conscious about their dancing abilities, Lance and Ricky tentatively agreed to check out the action and see what was playing. Dakota looked like he might faint as Kai took his hand and laughingly pulled him from his chair, and they all made their way inside to the sound of raucous, blasting hip hop music.

The dance floor was packed with gyrating, writhing bodies in formal attire, the music pounding forth from gigantic speakers set up around the perimeter. The four boys stood at the fringe of the crowd looking in, with only Kai wanting to wade into the mass of youthful energy.

"C'mon, guys, it's a dance," he urged, but the other three balked.

At times like these Lance realized what a failure he was as a teenager, since he had never even tried to learn these kinds of dances, and he didn't even like this kind of music. Ricky, he knew, felt the same way. Both preferred oldies to this stuff.

Dakota looked ready to faint as Kai grabbed his hand and dragged him to the edge of the jumping, hand waving teens.

To the astonishment of both Lance and Ricky, Kai could dance to this music. Coming, as he had, from a small reservation, Lance figured he only knew Indian dances. But he moved so fluidly, it was like watching water flow. Poor Dakota could barely get in one or two moves before Kai completed six. Lance gaped in amazement. and knew for sure he didn't even want to try competing with that.

But then the song ended and a familiar beat replaced it—"The Cha Cha Slide".

Lance grinned at Ricky. "Thank you, Reyna," they both said at the same time and laughingly got into line next to Kai and Dakota.

Now on familiar ground, Lance and Ricky laughed their way through the number like they always did. Amidst flashing, colored lights, the boys slid and stooped and jumped with abandon, melting into the familiar rhythms, and thoroughly enjoyed themselves.

After the song ended, there were several more big party numbers that everybody danced to with synchronous movements. Though all four boys were inexperienced with them, the lyrics were directions, of sorts, and they laughed and shoved and goofed their way through each and every one. Not once did any of them even wonder if people were staring or laughing. They were lost in the moment of pure fun and togetherness, and the sensation was both exhilarating and freeing.

After nearly thirty minutes of these crazy group dances, the boys were hot, sweaty, and giddy with pleasure. It was then that they heard Ana's voice come over the sound system and everyone turned to one of the two staircases that rose upward behind the DJ and his equipment. Ana stood five steps up on a carpeted landing that opened out onto the racetrack via large double doors.

"It's now time to introduce the prom court, and reveal your choice for king and queen!" she announced with a huge grin. There was applause, but Lance noted many scowls directed toward him and Ricky.

What did we do now, he wondered?

Then Ana's eyes found him and locked on a moment before she continued. "Before we do that, I have an apology to make. Lance and Ricky, can you please come up here?"

The boys exchanged a startled look, and even glanced toward Kai and Dakota. Both shrugged with uncertainty, and Lance looked apprehensively at Ricky, wondering what new humiliation awaited them.

Those on the dance floor opened up a path and the two boys walked across it to ascend the five stairs to where Ana stood. Silence filled the room, and Lance felt every eye on his back as they crossed. When he turned around on the landing, he saw all their faces gazing up at them. Some looked annoyed, some were smiling, but many just looked confused.

Ana stepped to them and stood beside Lance before once again addressing the seniors milling about on the dance floor. "I'm the one who invited Lance and Ricky to the prom tonight, and their friends Kai and Dakota too," she began, her voice strong and loud. Then she lowered her eyes, and her voice lowered with them. "I mean, Lance is for sure the most famous kid ever to go to MTS and I think these guys are, like, an incredibly cute couple, but I also thought it would make us look good, the kids of Hawthorne, to show how we support gay rights by having two same-sex couples here tonight. And I was hoping they might even win prom king and king."

She stopped as Lance whipped his head around to gape at her. His crack about the pig's blood was supposed to have been a joke!

Ana shifted uncomfortably. "I think some of you have been rude to them tonight 'cause you thought they wanted to run for those titles and they don't even go to this school. But they had no idea. I put their names in and campaigned for them. It was me trying to be all progressive and stuff and...." She trailed off. "I'm sorry, Lance and Ricky, for being such an idiot, and I told the teachers who counted the votes not to count any for you guys. I'm so sorry."

She almost looked like she was going to cry and stuck the microphone into Lance's hand before he could even respond. Then she lowered her head and stared at the carpet.

Lance and Ricky looked long and hard at each other, and then Lance gazed out at the crowd of kids below. He knew he should be mad at Ana, but he wasn't. She was just copying the president with his buffalo meat and so many other so-called progressive adults who pandered to kids and "causes" to show how "with-it" they were and to make themselves feel good. Sadly, all they usually accomplished, like Ana, was to embarrass themselves and hurt the people they supposedly wanted to help. He sighed and raised the mic to his lips.

"Thanks, Ana for clearing that up, 'cause all you out there been giving us such weird looks, I figured maybe you were thinking there might be another attack on us like in Washington." He smiled and many of them tittered nervously. "Well don't worry, I got The Rock with me this time," he added, pointing to the hulking Brooks loitering just at the edge of the crowd. That drew an even bigger laugh. "We're here tonight because home schooled kids like us don't get a prom, so when Ana invited us we jumped at it." But then his smile turned to a frown. "But we sure as hell never wanted to be prom king and whatever."

He collected his thoughts before continuing. "I know Ana meant well, but so do most of the people screwing up this country, especially for us kids. They think if they mean well, that gives them permission to do whatever they want or use whoever they want *how*ever they want, but it doesn't. And I know some of you out there hate boys like me and Ricky and Kai and Dakota. Somebody called us faggots earlier."

He paused as some who hadn't overheard the earlier slur reacted with "Oohs" or head shakes.

Lance reached out to Ricky, and Ricky placed his hand where it belonged. They stood facing the crowd, Lance having no clue how many were hostile to boys like them.

"I love this boy and he loves me, maybe more than some of you guys love your girls. If you saw what happened in Washington, you know we'd die for each other. How many of you guys would die for your girl, or you girls for your boy?"

He paused again to glance over at Ricky. The 'look' was there, in his eyes, and in the slight smile revealing his dimples to the world.

"Ricky and me've been in love for, like, three years now, and together for almost two," Lance went on, his voice becoming breathy with emotion. "But tonight is our first date."

There were gasps of surprise, especially from the girls.

"That's why tonight is so cool. Our first real romantic night out, and I'm *so* thankful you let us share it with you. It's been amazing. So thank you, Ana, and thanks to all of you for letting us be part of your senior prom."

He flashed his smile and handed the microphone back to Ana, who stood speechless.

The crowd below remained silent, and then a male voice called up to them, "Hey Lance, c'mon, man, kiss your boo!"

That ignited a rousing cheer of approval, and Lance burned with embarrassment. He turned to Ricky, who looked equally caught off guard.

"Do you want me to kiss you?" Lance asked timidly.

Ricky grinned. "Fool, that is the dumbest question you ever asked me."

That generated a huge laugh and more applause.

Then Ricky was there, in Lance's arms, their lips one with each other, and the world fell away. Vaguely, Lance was aware of cheering and hooting and clapping, but none of it registered as his whole body melted into the kiss and he trembled with love and desire. Flushed and breathless, he pulled back, his eyes locked on those of his soul mate. "I love you so much, Ricky."

Ricky's smile nearly made Lance weak in the knees. "And I love you, Lance, even more than so much."

Lance grinned, and suddenly became aware of the thunderous hooting and clapping and cheering from the kids. The boys stepped away from each other, embarrassed at getting so carried away in front of their peers.

Ana grinned broadly and lifted the mic to her lips. "Now *that's* what I call a prom kiss," she said happily, and the applauding crowd vociferously agreed.

Lance and Ricky bowed theatrically and descended the steps to the floor, making their way to where Kai and Dakota stood with Brooks. They got slaps on the back and "Way to go" and other salutations of support from kids. Kai and Dakota grinned as they approached, and even Brooks nodded his approval.

The prom court was then introduced and each candidate for king and queen descended the stairs to cheers and applause. The winners were announced, but Lance didn't know any of them and just clapped along with everyone else. The newly crowned king and queen shared the first dance, a slow number, and gradually the others kids folded into it. This was the part of prom Lance and Ricky had been waiting for—the slow dances.

They watched Dakota slip into Kai's arms and lean in to the other. Then Lance stepped toward Ricky. Just as he did, Lance felt a finger tap his shoulder. He turned, and scowled. It was beefy boy, the one who'd called them faggots. Over beefy's shoulder, Lance spotted Brooks starting their way, but he shook his head to wave him off. He locked eyes on those of the boy, who stared at him with a noncommittal expression. The guy's date hung by his side looking uneasy.

Lance sighed. "Look man, you wanna try and kick my ass, fine. But this isn't the place or the time."

Beefy shook his head. "No ass kicking. You're *firmé*, Lance." He raised a fist.

Surprised, Lance raised his and they bumped. Then the guy led his girl out among the dancers.

Lance and Ricky gaped at each other a moment, and then burst out laughing. There was no figuring people, so why bother trying?

From that moment until the night ended, for every slow dance they held each other close, pressed in tightly, their eyes brimming with love. Sometimes Lance laid his head on Ricky's shoulder, and sometimes Ricky did the same for Lance. Sometimes they danced with arms around each other's necks, foreheads gently resting against the other's. It was perfect. No politics and no attempt on their lives. Just the two of them basking beneath a halo of love, and Lance wished the night would never end. Sadly, however, it did.

At midnight the announcement came that prom had concluded and it was time for everyone to head out. Ana found Lance and Ricky with Kai and Dakota, and all four boys gushingly thanked her for inviting them.

"Sorry for almost screwing it all up," she apologized again with a shy smile. Then her face lit up excitedly. "You guys wanna come to an after party?"

Lance and Ricky exchanged a look, and Dakota's eyes went wide. 'After party' usually meant alcohol. Lance gave his nervous breathy laugh. "You probably already know we don't party so good, Ana."

Ricky guffawed. "That's another way of saying we get drunk and act stupid."

Lance laughed. "Yup. So thanks anyway, but we're just gonna head home. Thanks again for an amazing night."

"Thanks for coming." Then she kissed each of them—on the cheek this time—and stood back to observe the four boys. "You guys are two of the cutest couples I've ever seen. Good luck with your bill of rights. MTS kids are participating next week." She winked, and Lance realized she meant the underclassmen were participating in the August surprise to Washington.

"Cool," he said, and then Brooks and the three other agents stood with them in line for the mass exodus to the parking lot.

The ride home was made in relative silence. Ricky rested his head against Lance's shoulder, while Kai's head rested against Dakota's. For all of them it had been a night that lived up to its theme: Once Upon A Time.

As had been the case throughout April, Lance continued to receive messages from his "representatives" from public schools during the month of May that Operation August Surprise was going off without a hitch, without the teachers or administrators even suspecting anything amiss. He received over a hundred thousand of these messages during those two months, covering all levels of public education, except post-secondary. Combined with the Once Upon a Time in America Tour, if this didn't get the focused attention of those people in Washington, nothing would.

The final event that month was the first formal high school graduation of the Round Table Educational Center – the official name given the school portion of New Camelot. Some of the older kids, like Esteban, Justin, Darnell, Techie and others had already earned their diplomas the previous couple of years, but this was the first actual ceremony to confer diplomas on one hundred thirty-six graduating seniors, all kids who'd been deemed "at-risk" of dropping out by their home schools.

The state had printed the diplomas and mailed them to Jenny at New Camelot, and Mayor Soto had volunteered to hand them out. The ceremony had been set for the last Saturday in May in the expansive gardens where Arthur and Jenny had gotten married, and they expected a huge gathering of parents and supporters of the graduates. Helen was invited, of course, given her new status as a network correspondent and embedded journalist. As with all things Round Table, virtually every major media outlet confirmed their attendance.

To his utter astonishment, Lance learned he'd earned the highest overall GPA of the graduates, and been selected valedictorian. He knew his grades had been good, but as a rule he was so focused on the crusade for children's rights he hadn't realized he'd gotten an "A" in every class, including those he'd had to make up from freshman year, and had a 4.0 grade point average. There were no AP or honors classes at the home school level, but he felt Jenny had challenged them heavily with her curriculum, and achieving those "As" hadn't been a cakewalk.

Graduation day dawned bright and sunny, and Reyna had made sure to order festive balloons and colorful streamers to adorn the gardens and outdoor stage. At Lance's urging, the caps and gowns were royal purple to represent King Arthur and the Round Table's allegiance to liege lord and chivalry. Ricky thought some of the guys might object, but when Lance explained it to the graduates in the weeks prior, they all agreed that royal purple was appropriate.

The gardens filled up with family, friends and media a full hour before the ceremony was to begin. As Master of Ceremonies, Mayor Soto had taken a cue from Lance and wore a shimmering grey suit with a royal purple tie. Beside him sat Arthur and Jenny, both resplendent in formal royal attire, with Jenny now sporting a golden, jeweled tiara befitting her status as the wife of a king. Chris, looking leaner and more athletic than ever, sat beside them decked out in a formal tunic with a golden headband encircling his flowing blond hair.

Seated to one side of the stage were Kai, Dakota, Reyna, Esteban, Justin, Darnell, and Techie. Bridget and Ariel were seated in the row behind them and the rest of the crowd fanned out in all directions around the stage. There was a center aisle laid out with a red carpet that the graduates would traverse as they entered and exited.

Those knights who'd provided musical accompaniment during their neighborhood clean-ups had gathered with their instruments at the back of the stage. Some were graduates themselves and wore their purple robes. At Reyna's cue, they raised their instruments and began the traditional march, "Pomp and Circumstance."

The graduates, led by a grinning Lance and Ricky, marched out of the hotel and up the center aisle. On every young face was a look of pride and achievement, and many a mother in the crowd had to brush away tears at witnessing this moment they obviously never expected to see.

Lance and Ricky peeled off to the right when they reached the front row and their line followed, while the other line turned left. Lance caught Arthur's eye as he stopped at his chair, and the man grinned so broadly, Lance laughed. Both boys stood at attention until everyone was in position.

At this point, the music ceased and Ricky peeled himself away from the row to step up on stage. He crossed to the microphone. "Welcome graduates, family and friends. Will everyone please rise for the flag salute?"

Sir Charley, the knight who'd once believed Arthur would favor his son over any of the others, marched forward carrying the American flag. It flapped lazily in the warm spring breeze, and Sir Charley looked very military in his tunic, chain mail, and metal armbands. He stood straight and tall as he climbed the steps onto the stage. He stopped beside Ricky and tilted the flag forward so it rested at an angle.

"Place your right hand over your heart," Ricky told the crowd. "Ready, begin."

And so the entire crowd, parents and kids alike, regular working people, former gang members and drug users, did something most had probably scorned while in regular school: they actually recited the pledge, at least as best as they could remember it. Ricky's voice sailed out loud and clear so those who stumbled over the words could quickly correct themselves. When the pledge concluded, Sir Charley continued to hold the flag while the band struck up "The Star Spangled Banner." Ricky remained standing, hand to his heart. Lance and all of the graduates followed suit. When the anthem ended, there was clapping and hooting. Sir Charley raised the flag and placed it into a stand set back behind the podium. Then he and Ricky bowed to one another and retreated from the stage.

Now Mayor Soto rose and stepped up to the microphone, grinning broadly. "Welcome family and friends to the first graduating class of New Camelot!"

The crowd went raucous with applause. Many knights were still in high school or junior high, and had showed up to cheer on their graduating brothers and sisters.

"As you all know, I've been working side by side with most of these graduates in their neighborhoods to better our city and make life stronger and safer for children and teens, and I have to say I've never met a finer group of young people in my life, hands down!" The graduates, and crowd, went wild again, and the mayor waited for them to settle. "It is my pleasure to hand out one hundred thirty-six diplomas to these splendid young adults and it will be my distinct honor to do so."

The crowd cheered once more.

"Before I do, however," the mayor went on, "I want to pay homage to the man to whom we all owe so much, a man who came to us like a miracle and transformed all of our lives for the better. Let's give it up for King Arthur!"

Now the response was thunderous as everyone leapt to his or her feet clapping and cheering and whooping and whistling.

Soto turned with a grin and waved Arthur forward. The king stood reluctantly, having instructed Soto and Jenny to let this day be about the kids, not about him. But the response of the assembled knights and their families nearly brought him to tears.

"Arthur! Arthur! Arthur!" they chanted over and over again.

The king walked to the microphone and shook Soto's outstretched hand. The shorter man stepped back and allowed Arthur to survey the results of his handiwork. Amid the chanting and cheering, he was rendered momentarily speechless.

When the crowd gradually resumed their seats, the king grinned out at the kids below decked out in their purple gowns and mortarboard caps. "I thank you all for your fealty, for your astonishing hard work and dedication, and for sharing your lives with me. You may feel you owe something to me, but you're wrong. It is I who have been blessed from the moment I awoke here in your city, and I am forever blessed that you have shared yourselves with me. Stand proud, my young knights, for this is but the beginning. All that we have achieved in this city and state, yea, across the country, is but the beginning. The greatness of New Camelot will continue to grow through you and those youngsters who come after you, and your achievements shall be boundless, your legacy one for the ages. I have such pride in thee, I cannot even put it into words. You humble me."

He stepped back and bowed to the graduates, which led to another deafening standing ovation. Arthur smiled warmly down at them. He glanced over at Lance and Ricky, and gave them a thumbs up sign.

He resumed his seat and Soto returned to the mic. "And now we will hear from one among you who is without question the most extraordinary boy I have ever had the pleasure of knowing. Your valedictorian, our very own young Mr. Lincoln, the remarkable Sir Lance."

Another rowdy cheer arose as Lance stood and stepped up onto the stage. Soto's ebullient face and outstretched hand elicited a big smile from him. They shook, then Soto clapped him on the back and resumed his seat.

Lance stepped to the microphone and looked down at his fellow graduates, his fellow knights and their families, and momentarily choked up with emotion. Less than four years, he realized, had elapsed since Arthur had saved him in that alley. It astonished him and filled him with pride that they had accomplished so much in so short a time. Even this event, one he'd never deemed of much importance growing up, was a *huge* deal.

"Fellow graduates, fellow knights, brothers and sisters of the Round Table, family and friends, I'm honored to be up here today with all of you. How I managed to get the highest GPA still blows me away, and I told my mom everyone would think she'd fudged the grades. She just laughed and taught me a new word, like she always does. Nepotism. That means you do things for your family or friends at the expense of others. She promised me that wasn't what happened. Actually, I hoped to see Ricky up here, 'cause I love hearing him twist his tongue into knots talking to crowds."

He pointed to the boy he loved. Ricky grinned and made a swinging motion with his fist, drawing laughs from the other graduates.

"Growing up like I did, I never even thought about graduating high school. I just wanted to survive each day and make it to the next. I know most of you grew up that way too. We know most of the schools out there suck. They still try to make everybody the same instead of helping us achieve greatness in the areas we want and are good at. But here things have been different. All of you used to be in gangs or grew up like me or did drugs, and didn't care about stuff like this. But look at you today, sitting out there wearing purple."

He chuckled, and many of the boys joined in. The female graduates nudged the males beside them, obviously not uncomfortable wearing purple.

"You're all going to graduate high school today," Lance went on, his voice deep and strong and tinged with sentiment. "But unlike most kids who graduate, thanks to my dad and all he's taught us, you're ready to take on life as adults who've learned the most important lesson of all, one that's sadly absent from the regular school system—that we must do what's right, not what's easy."

There was more boisterous applause from the graduates and the crowd, so Lance paused to let it die down.

"You've already done more for your neighborhoods and communities in the last four years than many adults have done their whole lives. And you'll continue to give hope to your friends and neighbors, to your younger brothers and sisters, to all the children of this city. The times they are a changing, thanks to you, changing for the better!"

The graduates cheered and applauded once more, and Lance beamed out at them, tossing a special grin to Ricky, whose love practically screamed at him from the first row.

"As you know, we're heading out across the country next week to convince the American people our bill of rights is not only needed, but right and proper and long overdue. You all here will be running New Camelot while we're gone. You'll be working with Mayor Soto to keep this city on track, and to encourage our supporters throughout the country that the Round Table is alive and well. You'll be reminding people that New Camelot will continue to thrive and that this graduation today is only a small step in a much larger journey." He paused, choked up again, and fought for control. "You have all made my life so amazing, I couldn't thank you enough if I lived a thousand years. You are my brothers and sisters, and I love you." He lifted his sword from behind the podium and held it aloft. "Long live the Table Round!"

The graduates rose to their feet and raised their fists in solidarity.

"Long live the Table Round!" they shouted as one, causing Lance to grin with a mix of pride and joy and wistful abandon. Would he see any of them again? The threats against him and Ricky clung tenaciously to the back of his mind.

You'll never see your eighteenth birthday.

He shoved those thoughts aside and replaced his sword as Soto returned to the podium. Lance shook hands with the man and resumed his seat.

At this point came the distribution of the diplomas. The official photographer rose and stood just to the side of the podium. Jenny crossed to the microphone. Grinning with joy, she waited to announce the first name. One row at a time would stand and the graduates would march around the stage and up the side steps. Each would meet Soto, who would hand him or her a diploma in a purple cover. The graduate would then shake hands with Soto and then with Arthur and Jenny, posing for a picture with all three, and then march back to his or her seat. That was how they had practiced, and that was how it proceeded.

As the first two in their row, Lance and Ricky stepped forward to receive their diplomas with huge smiles on their faces. As Lance handed Jenny his card, she grinned so broadly, he laughed. Then she leaned into the microphone. "Lance Pendragon," she intoned, her voice loud and clear across the vastness of the gardens. Ricky immediately followed, eliciting another joyful smile from Jenny as she announced, "Ricky Pendragon."

The boys took individual shots with Arthur and Jenny and Soto, clinging to the three adults with heartfelt strength, and then got a group shot with their arms around each other flanked by the adults. Lance would never forget the look in Arthur's eyes as they shook hands. It was more than filled with love and pride. It was a look of sheer elation, as though nothing in the world could be more perfect, as though the king wished this moment in time could stretch into eternity.

For Lance, that look was one he would cherish for as long as he lived, even if that time turned out to be shorter than he wanted.

He stood across the street and watched as the multicolored school bus pulled out of the New Camelot parking lot onto Franklin Street, flanked front and back by black, unmarked cars carrying Secret Service agents. He pressed a button on his phone and put the device to his ear.

"Bus is just pulling away now, sir," he said, as crowds of people, supporters and naysayers, milled around the sidewalks waving their signs while the bus pulled out into traffic.

"Excellent, Mr. G," he heard in his ear.

"I take it you have surprises waiting for them along the way?" He knew the boss, but he didn't know the plan. The boss was slick – didn't trust anyone.

"Naturally, Mr. G," came the excited voice in his ear. "The beginning of the end is at hand."

He squinted against the bright sunlight as police on motorcycles pulled out into traffic to escort the bus to the freeway, and then cleared his throat. "So, anything else you want me to do here?"

"No. Bring it in," he heard, and he could almost see the boss smiling. "If all goes according to plan, none of them will ever return to Los Angeles." He heard a chuckle. "Alive, anyway."

"Yes, sir."

He ended the call and watched as the bus carrying Arthur and his kids trailed the police escort to the corner of Highland Avenue. The procession waited for the light to turn green, and then the entire line of vehicles turned the corner and passed from his sight.

Once upon a time in the City of Angels, a boy took charge, and an enemy closed in.

The Lance Chronicles Conclude in Book V:

ONCE UPON A TIME IN AMERICA

THE LANCE CHRONICLES

Book I:

CHILDREN OF THE KNIGHT

Book II:

RUNNING THROUGH A DARK PLACE

Book III:

THERE IS NO FEAR

Book IV:

AND THE CHILDREN SHALL LEAD

Book V:

ONCE UPON A TIME IN AMERICA

Michael J. Bowler is an award-winning author of nine novels—*A Boy and His Dragon, A Matter of Time, Children of the Knight, Running Through A Dark Place, There Is No Fear, And The Children Shall Lead, Once Upon A Time In America, Spinner,* and *Warrior Kids: A Tale of New Camelot.*

His screenplay, "THE GOD MACHINE," won First Place in the 2017 Scriptapalooza competition.

He grew up in San Rafael, California, and majored in English and Theatre at Santa Clara University. He went on to earn a master's in film production from Loyola Marymount University, a teaching credential in English from LMU, and another master's in Special Education from Cal State University Dominguez Hills.

He worked producer, writer, and/or director on several ultra-low-budget horror films, including "Hell Spa," "Fatal Images," "Club Dead," and "Things II."

He taught high school in Hawthorne, California—both in general education and to students with learning disabilities—in subjects ranging from English and Strength Training to Algebra, Biology, and Yearbook.

He has been a volunteer Big Brother to eight different boys with the Catholic Big Brothers Big Sisters program, and a decades-long volunteer within the juvenile justice system in Los Angeles.

He has been honored as Probation Volunteer of the Year, YMCA Volunteer of the Year, California Big Brother of the Year, and 2000 National Big Brother of the Year. The "National" honor allowed him and three of his Little Brothers to visit the White House and meet the president in the Oval Office.

He has completed three new novels aimed at the teen market, and one for middle grade.

His goal as an author is for teens and middle schoolers to experience empowerment and hope; to see themselves in his diverse characters; to read about kids who face real-life challenges; and to see how kids like them can remain decent people in an indecent world. The most prevalent theme in his writing is this: as a society, and as individuals, we're better off when we do what's right, not what's easy.

Website: www.michaeljbowler.com

FB: michaeljbowlerauthor

Twitter: https://twitter.com/MichaelJBowler

tumblr: http://michaeljbowler.tumblr.com/

Pinterest: http://www.pinterest.com/michaelbowler/pins/

Amazon: http://www.amazon.com/Michael-J.-Bowler/e/B0075ML4M4

YouTube: https://www.youtube.com/channel/UC2NXCPry4DDgJZOVDUxVtMw

Google+: https://plus.google.com/u/0/+MichaelJBowler

Instagram: michaeljbowler